DARK
DIVINITY

Her breath was shaky, and when her eyes finally did meet mine, they were filled with sheer terror.

"Night... wretches," she shuddered. "They have wretches with the night!"

I had no idea what the hell she was talking about. My sister might not be human, but she wasn't crazy. She was trying to explain something to me, but she was afraid of it. Max didn't seem to know what she was talking about either. He closed his eyes the way he often did when he was trying to use his psychic gift. I looked at Sephiel. He had gone completely rigid, and seemed paler than before.

He knew what she was talking about. And it terrified him.

Beside him, Warrick looked just as uneasy. He walked over to us. Warrick gently put his hand on my sister's shoulder.

"Dro, are you absolutely sure that's what you sensed?"

She straightened and looked at him with the same scared expression. She held her breath and nodded quickly. He dropped his hand and stepped back.

"*Fuck,*" he breathed.

"Can someone give me a fucking clue here?" I demanded.

Warrick was moving to the front of the alley, looking more serious than I had ever seen him. Sephiel was still frozen in a panic-stricken state that worried me. Finally, he answered my question.

"She is not indicating it as you may assume, as in 'the dark of night.' She indicates the word *knight,* as in a demon Knight." His eyes were grim. "They are the most elite of Lucifer's soldiers. The assassins for Hell."

I didn't need any further explanation. I knew earth-shattering bad news when I heard it.

DARK DIVINITY

A *Cursed* Novel

Amy Braun

For my friends, family, and Connie and Dro's fans.

More From Amy Braun

DEMON'S DAUGHTER

PATH OF THE HORSEMAN

NEEDFIRE

ANTHOLOGIES AND COLLECTIONS

THE MAKER OF MONSTERS in SPAWN OF THE RIPPER.

HELL TO PAY in LEGENDS OF SLEEPY HOLLOW: ORIGINAL TALES OF TERROR FROM AMERICA'S SPOOKIEST VILLAGE.

SURVIVALISM in THE DEAD WALK: VOLUME 2 .

DISMANTLE in THE STEAM CHRONICLES.

LOST SKY in AVAST, YE AIRSHIPS!

SECRET SUICIDE in THAT HOODOO, VOODOO, THAT YOU DO.

BRING BACK THE HOUND in STOMPING GROUNDS.

HOTEL HELL in DEATH'S CAFÉ.

CALL FROM THE GRAVE in TOIL, TROUBLE, AND TEMPTATION.

CHARLATAN CHARADE in LOST IN THE WITCHING HOUR.

DARK INTENTIONS AND BLOOD in AMOK!

Hell is empty and all the devils are here. – William Shakespeare, "The Tempest"

[Vestras spes uritis.] You burn your hopes. – Virgil

Chapter 1

"Something's wrong," I said. *Story of my life.*

Warrick used the sleeve of his brown leather jacket to rub away the dust from the warehouse window. "You're right. It shouldn't be taking him this long." He looked over at me, bright green eyes illuminated from the moonlight shining outside.

"Do you think something happened to him?" he asked.

I stared through the murky glass and put my hands on my hips. My thumb ran up and down the hilt of the hatchet attached to my waist.

"Maybe," I answered truthfully. "Seph knows the risks better than us. He also knows we can't find him if he's in trouble."

Warrick hesitated, then said, "Dro could."

I shot him a dark glance. Yes, my adopted sister could find our resident Seraphim warrior by using supernatural skills that continued to confuse, amaze, and terrify me. But I wasn't going to ask her to do that. Not even for Sephiel. It was too dangerous, especially now.

"We can't keep waiting for him," I said, turning away from the window.

I walked deeper into the crumbling warehouse, my scuffed combat boots splashing in thin puddles of God knew what. Steel support beams were scattered through the metal building. The large windows on the rusted walls were cracked and grimy. There was a dirty, multi-paned skylight over our heads and decaying concrete under our feet. It wasn't the best place to hide, but we assumed it would be temporary since Sephiel said he was coming back soon.

So much for that plan.

I made my way to the four door truck Sephiel stole for us before he left. I looked in the truck bed, where my little sister was asleep with her boyfriend.

Max and Dro were snuggled close together underneath a sleeping bag. Max looked younger than most eighteen year olds with a mop of curly black hair and a sweet, boyish face. A stubbly, black goatee was growing around his mouth. It was the only thing that kept him from looking like he belonged in a teen-pop band.

The contrast of Dro lying next to Max was jarring. His skin was a dull gold like my own, but Dro was as pale as a person could be without being called a ghost. Her skin was milk-white and smooth, stretched over a shapely body and an angelic face. Snow-white hair spilled around the top of her head, her ice-blue eyes closed in sleep.

I looked at Max's arm as it was draped over my sister's ribs, keeping her close to him. Even though his arm, the sleeping bag, and her clothes were blocking it, I knew exactly where her scar was. The raw, gaping wound that had poured blood when her rib was torn from her body, making my little sister scream with more pain than any living person should have.

My heart felt heavy even as I shook off the memory. It had been two months since that night. Two months since the Gates of Heaven and Hell were opened. Two months since Lucifer had risen and found his child.

My brain taunted me with the phrase "time flies," and I told that bitch to go fuck herself.

Dro shifted, moaning softly. I tensed, waiting to see what she would do. She always got nervous about sleeping beside Max. It was impossible to predict when Dro would have a nightmare. They were horrendous for her, and deadly for us. The only consolation we had was that Max was gifted too. He was a psychic whose foresight increased by touch. If he sensed a nightmare coming, he would warn us. After that... Well, our survival would depend on how fast we could run.

I watched her pinch her pale eyebrows together, as if she was in pain. I didn't know what my sister was dreaming, wasn't sure if I would ever know. She didn't like to talk about the things she saw in her sleep, not even to me. It couldn't be anything good, and there was no way for me to take her nightmares away.

"Constance?" Warrick's gentle, deep voice came from behind me.

I turned sharply, facing the tall, incredibly handsome demon slayer. His thick brown hair was a tired, wavy mess on his head. His goatee was now becoming a beard. Sincere green eyes fixed on my dark brown ones. Just looking at him made my heart rate speed up. He seemed to know I was off my game, something that didn't happen often. The readiness to help me burned in his eyes. He was waiting for me to tell him what to do.

The gesture was kind, but pointless. There was nothing Warrick could do to help me with Dro. I was beginning to think there was nothing any of us could do.

I could have lied and said I was fine, or that I wanted to be alone, but there was no point to that, either. I hadn't slept in almost two days. I was too damn exhausted to try faking otherwise.

"We should get moving," I muttered. "Seph will have to find us on his own."

I turned and slapped my hand against the edge of the truck bed to wake up the kids. My sister shifted and started stretching, blinking her icy blue eyes open. Max groaned and turned his head closer to Dro, burying his golden face in her shoulder and pulling her closer.

"Good dream," he mumbled. "Go away."

I hit the side of the truck bed again. "Too bad. I can't drive the truck with you sleeping in the back."

Dro's eyes found mine. She pushed herself up onto her elbows, white hair falling down her back. She was sixteen, but looked older every day since her injury. I tried not to notice, but I couldn't fool my little sister. She could read me like a book and knew when something was bothering me.

"Con? What's wrong?"

She also knew I wouldn't tell her what was on my

mind until we were alone.

"Seph isn't back yet. We need to leave."

My sister's eyes widened. "He said he was just going on a scouting mission," she said worriedly, sitting up.

"I know. But something must have delayed him."

I didn't tell her that Sephiel might have been tracked down, maybe even killed. Dro wasn't a naive girl. She was smart enough to understand the possibility that he was dead. Sephiel was a soldier of the Heavenly Host, but he was in a human vessel, and humans could be destroyed all too easily.

"He'll find us, Dro," I offered to make her feel better. "If we don't hear from him soon, you can connect to him."

She looked at me nervously and bit her lower lip. Dro's powers had been growing ever since Lucifer used her as a conduit to open the Gates of Heaven and Hell. The strength of her powers had nearly doubled, and it was easier for her to sense any demons or angels nearby.

After all, Dro was a mix of both.

But the catch was that while she could sense them, they could sense her. We hadn't had any problems with angels yet, but the threat of Lucifer turning up out of the blue was a constant terror we were forced to live with. It was part of the reason I hadn't slept in nearly two days.

"Come on," I pressed. "We need to go."

The kids started sliding out of the truck. Max played the gentleman and offered Dro his hand to help her down. She smiled at him, but as soon as her feet touched the cement, she gasped and clutched the truck bed.

"Dro? What is it?" I asked, stepping forward.

She was breathing heavily, placing one hand over her heart. Max gripped her other hand. She couldn't focus, so he used his gifts to read her. Dro lifted her head to meet my eyes. She looked terrified. Max turned his head to mine and his expression matched hers.

"Demons," he breathed.

Shit.

My hand went to the hatchet on my hip. Warrick took his sawed-off shotgun from the inner lining of his jacket. "How many?" I asked.

"Four."

"What kind?"

"Two Reds and two Shredders."

"Shit," Warrick cursed under his breath, voicing my thoughts.

"Get the truck started. We'll hold them off."

Max darted from Dro's side, running for the truck cab. Dro took a step closer to me.

"I can help," she offered.

I looked at my little sister. A half angel, half demon girl who had heightened senses, could heal almost any injury, use telepathy, and create hellfire blasts as hot as the sun.

Dro had more power than I could comprehend. But she couldn't control it.

"No," I told her. "Warrick and I have this. You stay safe."

Dro narrowed her eyes to show her irritation. "Seph isn't here, Con. You need as much help as you can get. I know how to fight."

Of course she did. I taught her myself. But being a big sister came before her desire to play hero.

"Look, if we get pinned down, you get our backs. But I'm not having you directly in the fight, Dro. Not since you're the exact thing they want."

That gave my sister pause. A flash of terror went through her eyes. Demons had been chasing her for years. They wouldn't give up until she was in their clutches, and there had been some damn close calls. Not that I was going to give the bastards any more chances.

A high-pitch screech sounded just outside the warehouse and made me spin around. I tightened my grip on the hatchet. Warrick finished loading his sawed-off shotgun and snapped it closed. His expression was completely calm and blank of fear. He wouldn't be a very good demon slayer if he were afraid of demons.

"They're almost here," he stated, casually walking to the middle of the empty building.

I glanced at him, then turned back to Dro and gave her a final, pleading look. "Please, little sister. Stay safe for me."

She frowned. She never liked standing back and watching me fight. I was a plain, simple human. Dro had seen me bleed and nearly die more times than she could count. She told me that she hated herself for being weak, and not being strong like me.

I told her that she shouldn't have to be.

Dro backed away to the truck where Max was standing. He wasn't a fighter, and he had the smarts to keep very far away when the demons made their unwelcome entrances. I turned away from them and walked to Warrick. The demon slayer was rigid, his eyes hard and trying to be everywhere at once.

"There's not a lot of cover out here," he said without looking at me.

I unhooked the hatchet from my belt and spun it in my hands, slipping a silver knife out from my lucky jacket. "Yeah, well, it's not like we have a lot of–"

Glass shattered on our left. The first demon had jumped through the window.

It was a Red, a hybrid *eurynomos* and *oni* demon if you wanted to be technical with your demonology. I called them Reds because their bodies were the color of blood. They were six-foot tall, humanoid monsters with smooth, poreless skin, hooked black claws, and oily chunks of hair. Their ears were pointed like a bat's, their fangs were razor sharp, and their almond shaped eyes were completely black from lid to lid.

The Red twisted its head in our direction, hissing once before it charged toward me with inhuman speed. I hefted my knife and threw it at the demon. It slammed into the speedy creature's shoulder. The Red shrieked as the angel-blessed silver weapon sank into its flesh. But it didn't stop running. More glass shattered on my right, followed by a loud *boom* from Warrick's shotgun. I didn't have to worry about him. This was his job. He knew how to take care of himself.

The Red swiped its claws at my face. I leaped to the side, tucking and rolling. The Red reached around its stomach to grab my hair. I spun on my knee and sliced at the monster's arm. Black blood sprayed out of the wound and onto my face. It burned against my skin, but I'd been covered in demon gore so many times that I could almost numb the pain.

Screeching in fury, the Red lunged for me. I rolled away and shot to my feet. I jumped and spun a kick to its head, knocking it onto the ground. Even before it was finished landing, I was driving my hatchet into the monster's face.

It bucked and howled as the blade split its cheek in half. More demon blood coated my hand and arm as I hammered the blade down. This new hatchet was more powerful than my last one. It was blessed by Sephiel, coated in silver, and cleaned in salted holy water. It didn't take nearly as many hits to kill a demon now. It wasn't my father's hatchet, but it got the job done.

After one more strike, the demon's skin began to blacken and crumble inward as it turned to ash. I grimaced at the acidic smell of sulfur from the dead demon's remains. *One down, three to go—*

Instinct tugged at my brain and said there was movement behind me. I kicked back and felt my foot connect with something. For a second, I thought I'd kicked a pale concrete wall. Then I looked up, and up, into the snarling face of a Shredder demon.

Oh, shit.

It raised its claws over my leg. I yanked my foot back before the gigantic creature could slice it off. I stepped back to look at the beast taking up every inch of my vision. The monster was triple my weight and almost two feet taller than me. Its skin was pale and covered in long, bumpy scars. Greasy, shoulder-length hair hung from its head in thick, black strings. The Shredder had a blocky face and milk-white eyes that made it look blind.

Its teeth were nasty and sharp behind its thick lips, but that wasn't going to be what it tried to kill me with. The foot long, solid bone claws at the end of its fingers were made for that.

The demon didn't hesitate to slash at me again. I weaved from side to side, only barely escaping the Shredder's claws. It pressed on, determined to cut me in half. I was quick, but I was human. I was already feeling weary from the fight with Red and all the sleep I denied myself.

And there were still at least two more demons to kill.

The Shredder shoved its claws toward my gut. I twisted away at the last second, but I didn't get as far as I wanted. My stomach brushed across the demon's thick, mutilated arm. The smell of sulfur and sour rot almost choked me. I tried to cut it with my hatchet, but the Shredder yanked its arm away. Before I could react, its elbow slammed into the side of my head.

Stars exploded behind my eyes. I felt like I'd been hit with a brick. I landed hard on the ground, rolling to catch my fall. The Shredder stabbed down with its claws, forcing me to wrench my body to the side so I didn't get skewered. I swung around in a crouch, drawing another silver knife from inside my jacket so I was doubly armed. I got to my feet and backed up, my head still pounding from the hit. My sight was semi-blurred, which made dodging and ducking the Shredder's claws much more of a challenge.

Then I backed up too far. My spine hit a metal beam. I panicked for half a second, giving the Shredder a chance to swing its claws at my face. I ducked and twisted behind the post. Metal screeched as the bony claws sliced across it. I took cover behind the post and hurled my silver throwing knife into the Shredder's eye.

Its head rocked back and it roared in fury. One of its hands went for the weapon. It curled its hand around the blessed weapon, bellowing its rage as the silver burned it. I could hear flesh sizzling, but at least it was distracted. I kept away from its good eye, hoping it wouldn't be able to sense me before I found a way to kill it. I'd faced this kind of demon before, but the fight hadn't gone well for me that time.

Holding my hatchet tightly, I crept behind the Shredder and slashed the blade along its heavily scarred back. The Shredder cringed and stumbled forward a step, still gripping my knife. It screamed when it ripped my knife from its eye, then swung its arms back at me. The claws narrowly missed my chest, but I still kept away from its good eye. I darted around its back and lashed out again, the hatchet blade catching it in the back of the knee.

Thick, oily blood splattered onto my jeans and combat boots. The demon didn't buckle like I hoped. Instead, it twisted sharply, and finally saw me with its uninjured eye. Its lips peeled back in a nasty snarl, and I knew I was in trouble.

The Shredder charged at me with more speed than something its size should have. I barely had time to dive out of the way, and even then I felt the tip of its claw scratch along my leg. I winced and bit back a cry as I collapsed onto my side. It felt like being lacerated by a rake, and this was a damn *graze*. I twisted as the Shredder swiped for my head. I laid flat on my back, watching the claws sweep inches from my face.

I tried to roll out from under the demon, but it grabbed my shoulder and pinned me in place with its hand. Sharp bones poked up into my cheek, blood oozing out of the wounds. All I could smell was rotten eggs and sour body odor. It raised its other clawed hand, ready to tear off my face. It kneeled down and completely trapped me under its weight. The air whooshed out of my stomach, making it impossible to worm free. The monster was panting over my head, suffocating me with breath that smelled like a corpse. I tried to think, but I knew I wouldn't be able to figure out a counter attack before it killed me.

The Shredder suddenly jerked and reared back, turning its head away from me and roaring at whatever had struck it.

That was the only opening I needed.

I sliced my hatchet across its throat, black blood pouring onto my chest and burning me. The sharp, putrid smell of sulfur from the monster made me gag. Holding my breath so I wouldn't puke, I raised the hatchet again and slammed it into the Shredder's face. I hacked at the monster a couple more times until it finally started crumbling into dark ash.

I squeezed my eyes shut and covered my face with the sleeve of my lucky jacket, hoping I wouldn't breathe in a dead-demon-dust. The ash coated the entire front of its body. Once it finished dissolving, I risked opening my eyes.

Dro was standing a couple feet away from me, the silver knife in her hand slicked with demon blood. I wasn't surprised she saved my life—again—but she'd taken a risk when I told her not to. Sometimes I worried that she was taking after me a bit too much.

I wiped away some more of the demon ash, then pushed myself up and looked at her with sharp eyes. "Didn't I say something about staying out of the fight?"

"You did," Dro said, handing my knife back. Wickedness crossed through her eyes. "But you're not the only one who can kill a demon."

I gave her an exasperated look as I dusted myself down, then turned my head to where Warrick had finished fighting the second Red.

Demon blood stained his leather jacket and jeans, but he was in one piece. He didn't even have a mark on him. He shouldered his sawed-off shotgun, eyeing me up and down. He looked mischievous and dangerously attractive.

"Did you have fun?"

I shrugged, the last of the demon ash flying off me like dirty snow. "I don't know about you, but that seemed a little too easy and too quick."

Warrick raised his eyebrows at me, thinking I was insane. Maybe I was. Who the hell knew anymore?

Realization suddenly hit me. "Max said there were four. Where's the other Shredder?"

Just as I said it, something exploded out from the skylight in the ceiling and dropped heavily onto the truck's hood. Max, who had been waiting outside the truck's cab, jerked back as fast as he could. The Shredder's weight had the back end of the truck rearing up once before slamming onto the ground again. The demon turned its head to the right, seeing my friend. It jumped off the hood, landing only feet from him. He backed up because there was nothing else for him to do. He didn't have any weapons. He couldn't fight. He was the perfect target.

"*Max!*" Dro screamed.

She raced for him, Warrick and me racing behind her. Even though my leg howled in pain every time I put pressure on it, I was faster than my sister. I flipped my knife in the air and hurled it at the Shredder.

My aim was off because I was running, but the blade still sank into its shoulder. Not that it stopped the demon from raising its claws and slashing into Max.

My heart skipped a beat when I saw blood spraying out from his chest. He screamed as he fell to the ground. The Shredder raised its claws again, ready to drive them into Max's back. We were almost in front of him. I stopped to find my aim, arched my arm, and threw my hatchet at the demon.

This time, I found my mark. The hatchet went straight into the Shredder's chest. It howled and stepped back, forgetting about Max. Dro and I grabbed his arms and started pulling him out of range. I looked up to see that the Shredder was still alive. It yanked both my knife and hatchet from its torso, roaring against the smoke coming from its burning hands. The demon dropped the weapons and swung its claws at us. Dro wasn't paying attention, so I threw an arm over her back and pushed her down with me. The claws sailed over our heads by about an inch, moving our hair with it. There was a loud *boom* from my left followed by another thunderous howl.

Warrick had shot the demon full of rock salt.

Dro and I continued to dragging Max to safety. He was still breathing, but it was raspy and shallow. Three heavy slashes were cut along his chest to his ribs. The whiteness of his shirt made the appearance of the dark red blood on him even more terrifying. It stuck to the wounds, which were much worse than mine. Dro was on the brink of tears.

I left her with Max, unable to focus on the severity of his wounds right now. Dro would heal him, and he would live. Hopefully.

Drawing the last two knives from inside my black jacket, I gritted my teeth and took off for the Shredder. Warrick had its complete attention. It hacked and slashed its claws wildly, forcing the demon slayer to move back. One swipe knocked the shotgun from Warrick's hands, but he never missed a stride. He reached into his leather jacket and brought out a combat knife. The demon swung for him, making Warrick duck as low as he could. In one fluid movement, he stabbed the Shredder in the arm. Its sharp, coughing bark echoed off the walls.

Warrick went right to his next move. He lunged forward, stabbing the Shredder in the ribs. The knife was stuck deep in the monster's thick side, and Warrick had to grip the knife hilt with both hands to yank it down against the Shredder's ribs. His moves were perfect, but he had gotten too close to an angry monster. The Shredder growled sharply and kicked Warrick in the chest. The force of the hit sent the demon slayer was back five feet, slamming him into one of the support beams. His head cracked sharply against the metal. He crumpled and landed face first on the hard concrete, then was still.

The Shredder took a step toward him, at the same time I made my move. I jumped up, my good foot hitting the side of the truck. The angle was a bit awkward, but I had more leverage to push off and land on the Shredder's back. I buried my knives deep into the demon's shoulder blades, trying to make the cuts as damaging as possible.

Black blood squirted out of the wounds as I dragged

them through the Shredder's tough skin. My hands were covered in the burning, sickly smelling blood. I was hanging onto them so tightly I could feel the plastic hilts biting my palms. My face was pressed against the demon's back so it couldn't grab me, and my cheek was rubbing against the coarse Shredder hide. The smell was so bad my eyes started watering. I tugged on the blades. I squeezed my eyes shut and turned my head away as more blood splashed onto me.

Needless to say, the Shredder wasn't appreciating my piggyback ride. It stabbed its claws over its shoulders, nearly embedding them in my skull even when I ducked. It twisted back and forth violently, not caring that my legs flopped around and smashed into its side, thighs, and back. I hung on as tightly as I could, but my blood-slick hands were starting to slip from the knives.

One sharp twist finally hurled me off the demon's back. I slammed into the truck's windshield, glass cracking against my spine. I shook off the dizziness in my head as the Shredder turned around, stabbing at me with both of its claws. I rolled just as its bony talons punched through the glass next to me. I felt the windshield sink behind me, and rotated my body until I fell off the hood of the truck.

I landed hard on my side and I turned onto my back. I was about to get up when the Shredder pounced onto the truck's hood. Metal squealed as it bent under the huge monster. Its lips peeled back in a snarl as it stared at me with enraged, pale eyes. It held its claws out on either side of its massive body, ready to pounce for the final kill.

My heart bounced in my ribcage as I scrambled for an idea. I was out of weapons. No one was around to help me. When that demon jumped on me, it was going to slice me to ribbons.

Just as I was thinking about how quickly I could move before the Shredder caught me, a blast of white light filled my vision. I threw my arm over my eyes while the temperature in the room ratcheted up fifteen degrees in a single second. The heat was like standing in front of a furnace. I scrambled to my feet. Once my head cleared, I turned around, and saw that the truck was on fire.

Blinding white flames wrapped around the vehicle like they were coming from a flamethrower. There were four shotgun-like pops as the tires exploded. The demon was consumed by the blaze. I couldn't see the shape of the Shredder any more, but I could still smell rotting, burning demon flesh. I could hear it screaming.

I followed the direction of the flames, and saw Dro standing with her hands outstretched in front of her. Her pale, angelic face was pinched in concentration. Two streams of hellfire blazed out from her palms.

I stared, trying to understand what I was seeing. Dro had never been able to use hellfire like this. It only happened when she was dreaming. She would scream in her sleep and burst into flames that wouldn't hurt her, but would destroy anything around her. She had never been able to control it before.

But now she was.

Max was standing behind Dro. His shirt was still torn and bloody, and he looked a little pale, but I couldn't see any wounds on his chest. He was staring at my little sister with the same emotions I was feeling. Shock, wonder, and fear.

Ear-shattering explosions made me duck and cover my head. I whirled around, seeing the enflamed truck lift five feet off the ground before dropping with a loud crash. I dragged my eyes more to the left, and I saw a smaller, burning white heap. *At least the Shredder's taken care of,* I thought grimly.

The sudden explosion broke Dro's concentration. She exhaled in a tight gasp, abruptly ending the hellfire. Her eyes fluttered closed and she swayed. Max rushed to catch her, wincing as he lowered her onto the ground. I ran over and dropped by their side.

"Dro! Dro!" I called, gripping her shoulders.

Her skin was scorching, but Max and I didn't care. I shook her gently, but urgently.

"Come on, little sister, wake up!"

Dro sucked in a deep breath and blinked at the ceiling. Her eyes unfocused as she turned her head in the direction of my voice. She looked at me with concern.

"Are you okay?" she asked in a rushed breath.

I sat back on my heels, relaxing my sore muscles and trying to smile. "Yeah, Dro. I'm fine. Covered in dirt and demon blood, as usual."

My sister didn't smile back. Max helped her sit up, brushing some snow-white hair off her forehead. "Pretty girl, you're crazy."

She leaned against him, letting him pull her into a hug. Max kissed the side of her head and held her close. Then he looked at me with confused eyes. I shook my head at him. If anyone was going to ask Dro about what she'd done, it was going to be me. Dro pushed away from Max and looked at me again.

"You're hurt," she said, seeing my face and my leg.

"It's okay," I said. It was almost the truth. "It's not as bad as it—"

Dro was already kneeling in front of me, placing one hand on my face and the other on my leg. Her hands filled with a golden light as she used her magic to heal my wounds. I bit the inside my cheek to keep from wincing as my injuries were surrounded by an uncomfortable pins and needles feeling. I should have been used to it since Dro had healed me a thousand and one times, but my brain refused to shake the *wrongness* of it all. I looked over her shoulder at Max.

"Go check on Warrick," I told him. "He took a bad hit to the head."

Max nodded, got to his feet, and jogged over to the demon slayer. He still hadn't moved from the floor, so I could only hope that he was unconscious. He'd thrown himself in the line of fire to save Dro, Max, and me. Warrick had been in our group for about three months now, and it was hard for me to imagine him not being with us. It made my life a million times easier knowing I didn't have to be the only fighter in the group, that someone else could take watches, and he was an expert at killing demons.

"I'll heal him too, Con," Dro said. A small smile grew on her lips when I looked at her. "I'll have him looking gorgeous again in no time."

I frowned, having forgotten that she could read my thoughts and sense my emotions if she wanted to. She very rarely did, though. Dro knew me better than anyone else, and respected that I wanted to keep my thoughts and feelings to myself. If I had something to say, I was going to say it. I didn't keep secrets from her.

But like all younger siblings, Dro loved to drive me crazy.

"You do that, little sister. I don't care how he looks."

She laughed, a sweet, gentle sound that always managed to cheer me up no matter how black my mood was.

"Liar. I've seen you sneaking glances at him."

"Because I don't want him reaching for his phone to call the cops on me."

"Uh huh." The glow left Dro's hands when she pulled them away from my freshly healed body. "So if I said he was giving you the same kind of looks, you'd say it's just because he's thinking about collecting that Marshal's bounty?"

"Yup."

Dro smiled and shook her head. "It's your loss if that's all you're thinking about, big sister. Warrick is the perfect man for you."

I groaned. Our friend was missing, we narrowly survived a demonic attack, there was a burning truck in the background, and my sister was trying to play matchmaker. I didn't have time or patience for romantic fantasies, no matter how easily Warrick would fit into them. I had serious trust issues in that department, and for good reason. The last relationship I was in ended about as well as a gang war, since my then boyfriend and I had tried to kill each other.

Pushing away bitter memories, I looked at the

flaming truck. "We're gonna need new supplies."

"I'm sorry."

I glanced over my shoulder at Dro again. She was holding her upper arm and staring at the ground. She was blaming herself for what happened.

"It's okay, Dro," I said. "It was time we got another vehicle anyway. The new one will help us stay under the radar. We can always find more supplies."

She nodded, but I knew she would sulk for a while. Everything in the tuck was replaceable. A couple small bags of food, some clothes, and sleeping bags. All our weapons were on us or scattered around the warehouse. Walking around was going to be difficult with the world beginning to spin off its top, but if we didn't have a choice, then we didn't have a choice. I wasn't going to blame Dro for anything. The girl had been through enough in her life. She didn't need unnecessary guilt thrown on her shoulders.

I touched her arm so she would lift her head. I smiled at her. "I know how you like to shop."

Dro stifled a laugh, then put her arms around my torso and hugged me.

"I'm sorry, Connie. I saw the Shredder hurt Max and Warrick, and then it was going after you, and I just... I had to stop it. I don't know how it happened."

I stroked the back of her snowy head. "We'll figure it out. We'll meet up with Seph and he'll tell us."

If we're very, very, very lucky.

Even if Sephiel was alive and he made his way back to us, he might not be able to answer our questions about Dro. There was nothing in the world like her, the first successful hybrid of an angel and a demon.

A child directly from Lucifer's blood.

Our knowledge of her was still so limited. Since Hell and Heaven had been set loose, it had only become harder to protect her. I glanced at the burning truck again, and knew it was only going to get worse.

Chapter 2

It was hard to believe that two months ago, things were normal. Maybe not normal for our group– a Seraphim warrior, a psychic, a demon slayer, a fugitive, a demon/angel hybrid– but it was normal for the rest of the world.

People woke up in their warm beds, ate breakfast, went to school or work, came home, had dinner, and went to sleep in the same warm bed. They bought groceries, treated themselves, fell in love, and got married. They got into arguments and broke hearts. Babies were born and seniors died. Some people saved lives, while others destroyed them. Life had been unpredictable, but easy.

Not one of those people was living on the run from demons from Hell and angels from Heaven. Not one of them literally checked every dark corner for monsters. Not one of them slept with a hatchet and silver knives close by, worrying about how far away they could get if their sister had a nightmare and spontaneously combusted.

Now that the Gates of Heaven and Hell were open, cracks were showing in their blissfully ignorant lives. They were seeing things, hearing things, being tempted into doing things they wouldn't normally do. Churches were preaching more than usual, half of them saying we were going to be saved, the other half saying it was too late and we were all damned. Very few knew what was really going on.

A lot had changed since the Gates were opened. Before he'd taken off on his latest scouting mission, our lone angel ally, Sephiel, said the angels were looking for us. As the days since Lucifer's rising went on, Dro began to mention that angels were trying to get into her mind and track her down. They considered Dro an abomination with too much power, a threat that needed to be eliminated.

The only way to stop them was to close the Gates of Heaven and Hell again, something I wasn't sure would be possible given how many enemies we'd gotten over the last few years.

Before we started worrying about angels and demons, my sister and I lived under the thumb of a psychotic drug lord. Things had quickly gone downhill when we left, and they weren't the 'forgive and forget' type of group. Naturally, I became a fugitive, and naturally, every law enforcement agency wanted to lock me up in a three by three cell.

But I would stand in front of them all to protect Dro. It would kill me if that's what it came down to, but I would die smiling as long as I knew she was safe.

"Constance," a deep voice rumbled.

I jumped out of my thoughts, my hand going to my hip. I *hate* when people sneak up on me. I took a deep breath and forced myself to relax as Warrick came around me. The circles growing under his eyes were even more prominent now, making his green eyes seem even brighter than usual.

"We have what we need," he said.

I peeked over his shoulder to where Dro and Max were idly browsing the shelves of the convenience store. They were holding a small grocery basket filled with new backpacks, pre-packaged shirts, water, and dried food. Warrick had gone to an ATM machine at the back of the store and withdrawn some money so we wouldn't leave a paper trail. In the past, I would have just stolen it all. But I was a wanted woman, and with all the chaos the demons were causing, the law was out in full force. I wasn't about to risk being separated from my sister by being stupid and getting arrested for stealing beef jerky.

I made sure my hoodie was hiding my face as I moved away from the shelf and tried to look composed. I didn't like being in shops. They were cramped, there were cameras that may or may not work, the street was close by, robberies were common, and the shopkeepers were usually scowling at me. I wouldn't be surprised if the overweight clerk staring daggers at me now had a double barrel under the counter pointed right at my ass.

"Then let's go," I said.

He looked like he wanted to say something else, but I brushed past him before he could. Warrick had seen me collapse before, the night Dro was captured by demons. I'd fallen apart and he literally held me together, taking me into his arms so I could scream and cry against his chest.

I didn't want to be that damaged twenty year old woman on a hotel balcony again. Emotion had nearly broken me that night. I refused to let it happen twice. I was colder now than I was before, and being cold meant pushing Warrick away.

Dro and Max saw me coming, and left their conversation. I felt a little depressed about that. It seemed like I could only bring out the seriousness in people. Every time I approached someone, they looked at me as if I was carting around the plague. My sister had to raise her head a little so she could see from under the black baseball hat I'd stolen for her. Dro had scolded me about reverting to our old, wicked ways, but she was a beautiful, memorable young woman, and she needed to be concealed as much as possible while we were on the run.

Besides, it wasn't my fault the guy just left the hat in the back of his truck before he jaywalked across the street. The way I saw it, we were squared.

"Warrick is ready to pay," I reported blandly. "Max, why don't you help him?"

He pouted, lifting the basket. "This stuff isn't as light as it seems. I don't want to keep carrying it around."

I raised my eyebrows at him. "And here I thought you were a chivalrous gentleman."

"I am," he countered. "But I'm not a luggage boy, either."

"Carry enough of those and maybe you'll start getting muscle definition," Warrick teased.

I tensed again, cursing myself for not hearing him

come up behind him. I needed to pay more attention. Next time it might not be a friend who snuck up on me. I forced myself to relax, and wished he wasn't so damn close. But also wishing he would get closer.

"Yeah, but that means a lot of work," Max pointed out. "I think I'll stick with being the brains of the group."

Warrick chuckled and reached around me to take the basket from Max. The movement caused him to lean in until his chest was brushing my shoulder. It was impossible not to feel the warmth of his body and smell his musky, pine scent. I stayed very still, trying not to remember how comfortable his arms had been, or how his lips had tasted.

"Meet you guys outside?" he asked me.

"Sure," I replied, quickly moving away from him and concentrating on Dro instead. "Come on, let's get some air."

Dro nodded and walked out of the store with me. She glanced back at the guys, but I never did. Having Warrick in our group was a huge relief, but sometimes I wished he weren't so damn attractive. Or compassionate. Or patient. Or loyal. That he didn't make my heart ache every time I saw him. It was a huge distraction.

Once we were out of the store, I turned into the alley and rested my back against the wall. I pushed my hood back and looked across the street, hoping I didn't look too much like a drug dealer anymore. It was mid-morning on a weekday, so the street wasn't very busy. There were a couple people walking by, but they were moving too quickly to notice me watching them. Everyone had a tense, uncomfortable stride these days. It was getting harder and harder to figure out who was possessed and who was just cranky. The Possessors were getting smarter.

I rested my hand on the hilt of my hatchet, hidden under my black military jacket, and looked down the sidewalk closest to me. There were some businessmen, a couple walking a dog, a bicyclist, and a man in a dirty coat shouting at them all. I kept my eyes on him until I knew he was just a crazy preacher.

"Repent! Demons walk amongst us! Repent and be saved by the angels!"

I sniggered to myself. If only that greasy bastard knew what angels were really like.

The autumn sun was still out and warming the concrete, but it was colder in the shadows. The alley smelled like stale bread, but Dro and I had been homeless for about four years. We were used to the smell.

Dro stood across from me, giving me a sour look. "We really need to work on your relationship skills, big sister."

"Yeah, I'll put that on my list of things to do, right under wearing a frilly pink dress and a tiara."

Dro folded her arms over her chest. "You're way too stubborn."

I glanced at her. "Fine. If I say that Warrick is smoking hot and a terrific fighter, will that be enough for you?"

She grinned a little, brushing a strand of snow-white hair behind her ear to hide under the baseball cap. The length of her hair was tied in a ponytail and tucked into the back of her denim jacket so it could hardly be seen.

"It'll do. There's still hope for you, Con."

I stifled a laugh and looked out onto the street again. My eyes went back to the crazy street-preacher.

"You must save yourselves! Beg forgiveness of the Lord! Ask His angels to bring you to Heaven! Do not submit to the lure of demons!"

My thumb ran up and down the hilt of my hatchet. I looked away from the preacher and focused on my sister. Max and Warrick would be back soon, and I didn't know when I was going to be able to talk to her alone again. Her eyes scanned mine. Her smile started to fade as she saw how grim I was.

We looked as opposite as possible. My skin was darker, my black hair short and down to my chin, my face, lips, and nose thinner, and my body athletic instead of curvy. However, Dro and I were closer than most sisters. We'd been through Hell and back ever since I found her as a baby in the middle of a forest. I'd been four years old when I made my parents adopt her. I never regretted my actions, even with all the horrible things happening to us, but being so close to me for so long meant that Dro could tell when we were about to have a conversation she wasn't going to like.

"Dro, back at the warehouse..." I started dumbly, and couldn't finish the rest of my sentence.

I believed in giving and getting hard truths from everyone, except Dro. My sister wasn't weak, but the world was against her. Despite it all, she never complained, never threw tantrums or whined about how we didn't stand a chance no matter what we did. She stayed brave and strong, kind and sympathetic, determined and hopeful. If anyone in the world deserved to be saved, it was my sister.

Dro looked down and rubbed the sleeves of her jacket. "I don't know what happened in the warehouse, Con. I just reacted." Her eyes lifted to meet mine. "I feel different, though. Stronger. I have all these powers, and it's like they're amplified now. I can sense thoughts and emotions from greater distances, I can heal people faster," she hesitated, "and I guess now I can control the hellfire."

"Do you feel like you have a lot more control? That the nightmares can stop?"

She shook her head. "They haven't stopped, Con. I still have them." A bleak shadow came over her face. "I still see myself hurting and killing people. I'm burning angels and doing disgusting things with demons."

The shadow turned into fear. Her hand slid into her jacket and stopped at her right side, exactly where her rib was missing. "Other times I have Lucifer's voice telling me to kill Warrick and Max. He says that you're holding me back, that my suffering is your fault and I should eat your beating heart."

A shiver ran down my spine, but I kept my face empty of fear. I couldn't think of anything to say. I was about to tell her that it was just Lucifer fucking with her head and trying to draw her out so he could make her his ally to take on the Heavenly Host.

But then my mind flashed to the image of my sister lying on a cold, stone altar, covered in blood and screaming in agony as her rib was torn from her body. If I had been stronger, faster, and smarter, it never would have happened.

If I had been able to protect her when I should have, the Gates would still be closed.

"What do you think, little sister?"

Dro's expression was strained. Her eyes went distant again, her mind starting to wander somewhere I wished it wouldn't go.

"Everyone wants me for something. The demons want to use nightmares to scare me over to their side. Angels keep prodding at my mind." She sighed and hugged her body. "I'm going to go insane before this is over."

I pushed off the wall and walked to Dro, putting my hands on her shoulders. "You won't. I'm not going to let anything happen to you."

She let out a shaky breath and hugged me tightly.

"Promise you won't let me give in. Don't let me lose myself."

I smoothed her hair. "I promise."

Someone screamed. I broke away from Dro and whirled around, grabbing the hatchet off my hip. She stayed behind me as I poked my head out of the alley.

Two businessmen stood over the street-preacher, who was crumpled in a motionless heap at their feet. They held bloody knives in their hands. Bystanders were running away. A random murder in broad daylight. Only one thing could cause that.

"Possessors," Dro breathed from my back.

My heart started pounding. I had been possessed once, before I got an anti-possession sigil tattooed on my chest. It only lasted a few hours, but it had been some of the most horrible hours of my life. I would never forget the helplessness and pain I endured during my possession.

Sirens blared. Red and blue lights were flashing.

People were shouting. I looked at Dro.

"Cops," I hissed.

I risked another quick look down the other end of the street. Warrick and Max were steps away from the alley with the bags of supplies. Their eyes were fixed on the murder up ahead, but they quickly found us. I flipped up my hood, touched Dro's arm, and tugged her out of the alley. I walked briskly in the opposite direction of the murder.

The shouts began to fade, but the sound of gunfire didn't. I jumped about a foot in the air when I heard the four shots and the screams that followed. I spun on my heel and grabbed the hilt of my hatchet. The cops had shot the two businessmen dead. People started screaming and pointing at the thick black cloud that funneled out of the dead men's mouths. The smoky demons flew down the other end of the street, far away from us.

I grabbed my sister's wrist and pulled her after me. The Possessors didn't seem to know we were here, probably distracted and high from their killing, but if they came back and saw my sister, we would be screwed. Possessors were hard to kill, and could easily report what they saw to their King.

People on the street were still screaming, but I walked as though I didn't have a care in the world. Violence came into my life at an early age. I learned to accept it, and was able to turn my back to it when the gun wasn't pointed at me...

It took us about a week to get to Ciudad Juárez after we survived the slaughter at Owl Creek. With our parents dead and no other family to turn to, I had to steal some money to bribe a smuggler for a seat on the truck going back into Mexico. My plan was to find someone my dad used to know before he came to America. He never talked about his old life, but he must have friends down here. Someone had to be willing to help us.

The smuggler didn't ask many questions, and kicked us out of the truck as soon as we were at the border. I had wanted to go deeper into Mexico. I'd heard stories about Ciudad Juárez on the news. They called it Murder City. Drug cartels ruled the streets and terrorized everyone they could. Anyone who stood in their way was ruthlessly murdered. I had heard of an entire family, including children as young as four, being stabbed to death over hundred dollar debts. Rape and the murder of women was an every day occurrence. Mass graves were found all the time. Heads literally rolled on the streets.

I couldn't imagine a worse place for a fourteen year old girl and her scared ten year old sister to be. But we didn't have anywhere else to go.

The houses of the city were crammed together and desperately needed paint jobs. The shops were rundown and heavily padlocked. Everything smelled like petrol and salt. Car horns blared angrily as traffic signs and pedestrians were virtually ignored. The heat made me sweat constantly. It really did feel like Hell on earth.

People wore cheap, ratty clothes and didn't offer us any help. Vendors shouted for us to buy meat that looked like charcoal. Thin stray dogs with molting fur lay in the middle of the streets, most of them not appearing to be breathing. I didn't want to attract attention, so I stole a shirt and gave Dro a hoodie to help hide her face and her hair. We tried to change her hair from white to black with hair dye a couple times, but the boxes I stole must have been cheap brands because the color washed out whenever we found a public washroom to clean ourselves in. Most of the people only spoke Spanish. I wasn't fluent in it, but Mom and Dad had taught me enough to get by. Dro barely spoke at all.

The first night was the scariest. We didn't have a place to sleep, and staying out in the open on the streets was dangerous. We managed to find some boxes and garbage bins behind a taco restaurant. We ate some of the thrown out food and used the boxes and bins for shelter. I kept my father's hatchet close, terrified that I would need to use it on a person one day.

We were trying to get some sleep when I heard the

fight. Taking out my hatchet, I kept Dro behind me and peeked out from the metal bins. Three men were beating up another man. It was too dark for me to see their faces and I couldn't hear what they were saying. I was watching a brutal shadow-puppet show on the wall. They kicked, punched, and stomped on him for what seemed like forever. Then two of the men lifted him up by his arms and held them out. The third man took out a machete. He used it to hack off the beaten man's arm.

His scream cut into my heart. I watched the shadows as blood gushed from his wound out into the alley. Dro was trembling behind me, covering her ears with her tiny hands. The man with the machete cut off the beaten man's other arm. More blood sprayed onto the stucco walls. He dropped onto the ground, bleeding everywhere. He tried to get up, but he had no hands to push himself to his feet. He never stopped screaming.

The man with the machete said something I couldn't hear. Then he raised the machete and brought it down on the man's neck. His head snapped onto his shoulder at a horrible angle. There was one more chop, and suddenly his screams stopped. After that it was way too quiet. One man picked up the severed head while another dropped something onto the corpse. Then they walked away.

I stared at the body, the entire scene stuck on repeat in my mind. One arm being cut off, then the other. Endless screams. His head being severed. The smell of blood.

Dro and I didn't sleep that night. In the morning, I covered her eyes and led her down the other end of the alley. I only looked back once to see what had been left on the chopped up body.

On top of the corpse that was still surrounded in thick pools of blood, was something that looked like a red rose.

We started sleeping in shifts. We moved around the city, finding out where the gangs were and doing our best to stay as far away from them as possible. We didn't beg, but I started stealing more, taking little things like food and clothes. We talked to vendors and merchants, but no one seemed to know our father.

It wasn't an ideal life, running and hiding and stealing, but after a couple days we had a system. Dro distracted people by looking lost and curious, and I pick-pocketed them. I didn't see any monsters and Dro didn't hear them, but I tried to watch for them as often as I could. All the gunfire and sirens made it hard to focus, but we kept going.

I stupidly thought our luck would last.

I was digging through garbage bins, trying to find food while Dro watched my back. We were a fair distance from gang territory, but I knew better than to think they'd stay in one place.

"Connie," Dro said urgently, grabbing the bottom of my shirt and tugging it.

I barely got out of the bin when the men arrived. They looked like giants, their muscles bulging from under their black T-shirts. One of them was bald, another had greasy, shoulder-length hair, and the third had a scar over his eye. All of them had the same tattoo on their body– a rose whose thorns looked like they were weaving in and out of the skin, dripping blood out of the wounds.

I'd heard of this gang. The Espanis de Sangre. The Blood Thorns. The deadliest, most feared cartel in all of Ciudad Juárez. They dealt more drugs and made more money than any other gang in the city. Thorns were everywhere, always buying weapons and dealing drugs. They even had an army of enforcers who brutally killed rival gangs and people who couldn't pay their debts.

My heart started to race. These could have been the killers from the murder I witnessed. If they were, I had no chance against them. Not even with my hatchet. These were the worst type of people I could imagine. I knew what they would do to young girls like us.

"Well, well, well, who do we have here?" the bald one asked me in Spanish.

I didn't answer him. I stood in front of Dro and took the hatchet out of the back of my pants. The men laughed at me.

"Careful, little girl. You might cut yourself." The bald guy grinned at me with yellow teeth.

"We don't want any trouble," I told him. "Just let us go. We won't say anything."

"Who's we?" He tried to look over my shoulder. "Who are you hiding?"

Crap. "Nobody."

"Lying to us isn't very smart, little girl." The bald man took a step closer to me. "So, I'm going to ask you again. Who are you hiding?"

I pressed my lips together. I didn't know what to do. They would hurt me if I lied again, but I didn't want them to see Dro. They'd do something bad to her for sure.

The man with greasy hair looked around me. "Damn, the other one's an albino." His eyes gleamed darkly. "She'd fetch a good price. Boss would have to see her to believe it."

Anger suddenly flared up in my chest. "Touch her and I'll kill you," I growled before I knew what I was saying.

The bald man and the man with greasy hair laughed at me. The man with the scar looked at me with confusion. Then his eyes widened.

"Holy shit," he gasped. "This is Luis's kid! She looks just like him!"

The other two men stopped laughing and looked at me with new eyes. I didn't waste time trying to lie. I spun and pushed Dro.

"Run!" I shouted.

She didn't need to be told twice, whirling around and taking off down the alley as fast as she could.

"Get them!" the scarred man shouted.

We didn't get very far before they caught us. Strong arms wrapped around my stomach and lifted me off the ground. I thrashed and kicked with all my might. I screamed at Dro to run. I heard a cry of pain and knew that she'd been grabbed. I hacked at the arm holding me with the hatchet.

The man let out a surprised bark when the blade cut

deep into his skin. He dropped me and I ran from him to get to my sister. The man with greasy hair had an iron grip on her arm. She was crying and trying to pull away, but he wouldn't let go.

Not until I slammed into him and knocked him away from her. I sliced at his leg with the hatchet. He cursed and tried to grab me, but I stepped back. I turned to find Dro, only to be punched in the cheek.

I'd never been hit so hard before. I thought someone had struck me with a baseball bat. I dropped onto the ground, tasting blood and feeling a huge bruise forming on my face. My hatchet was ripped from my hands. Then the man started kicking me in the ribs. Each strike crushed the air from my lungs and made it difficult to breathe. I curled into a ball and hoped it would end quickly.

Finally, the kicks stopped. My ribs ached. Some of them were probably cracked. I groaned, in too much pain to move. Dro was sobbing somewhere nearby. A hand twisted in my hair and pulled me to my feet. I blinked to clear my vision, seeing the angry bald man staring at me.

Fear went through me like an electric shock when I realized that they were going to kill me just like they killed that other man. They were going to cut off my arms and my head. Then they would do worse to Dro.

"You have some nerve, you little bitch. Just like your father. Emilio will have fun with you."

Before I could fight again, the bald man hit me in the face and knocked me out.

***

There was a bag over my head when I woke up. My body bumped up and down and I heard gravel crunching under wheels, telling me I was in some kind of car. My head was pounding, my ribs not much better. Every jolt of the car sent a spike of pain through me. My hands were handcuffed behind my back. I sat up and groaned. I tried to shake the bag off, but couldn't do it. I shuffled around, not sure who was around me.

"Dro?" I asked.

There was a choked sob on my right. "I'm here, Connie."

I followed her voice and soon pressed myself against her side. "Are you okay? Did they hurt you?"

She sobbed again. "No. I'm scared, where are they taking us?"

I wasn't sure, but we weren't going to like the destination. "I don't know. But I'll protect you."

Until they chop off my head.

Just as I thought it, the vehicle stopped. I heard car doors slamming and men talking. The doors beside us opened and we were pulled out of the car. I knew better than to fight back with a bag on my head. We walked outside for a few minutes (I could hear birds and smell fresh air and trees), before our captors started speaking rapid fire Spanish that I couldn't keep up with.

Then we were led up steps and into a building. I smelled roses and heard other people whispering. We were taken up a staircase and down what must have been a hall. The men stopped us, and one of them walked forward. I heard him speaking in a low voice to someone, but I couldn't hear what he was whispering about or who it was to. A piano was playing not too far away.

After a minute, we were pushed forward again. I heard doors open and we were brought inside another room. My heart began to beat rapidly when the doors were closed behind us. The piano was in this room, playing a beautiful, ominous song.

"I left a very clear message not to be disturbed," a man with a deep, rolling accent said from the direction of the piano.

"Our deepest apologies, Mr. Rocha, but I thought you would want to see Luis Ramirez's daughter."

The music stopped. It was quiet for a long time.

"What happened to you?" Mr. Rocha asked.

"Luis's little bitch attacked us with this," said one of my angrier captors. He must have been one that I cut with my hatchet.

I heard Mr. Rocha getting up and walking around. His shoes sounded expensive and sharp. He stopped directly in front of me. My heart wouldn't slow down.

"Show me."

The bag was yanked off my head. Strands of black hair covered my eyes. I looked past them to the man in towering above me.

He was tall and lean, dressed in a very expensive navy blue silk shirt and black pants. He wore a belt with a gold rose on the buckle. A gold chain necklace was visible under the collar of his shirt, resting against his bronze skin. His face was handsome and strong jawed. He had a black goatee peppered with grey. His hair was thick and black with streaks of silver, all of it smoothed over his head to the back of his neck. His eyes were narrow and incredibly dark. It was like looking at two black holes. He was staring at me so intensely I thought he was going to pierce my soul.

I looked away, trying to see the rest of the room. It was a huge den bathed in sunlight from the tall, paned glass windows on the left. I could make out the edges of a white stone balcony beyond the glass. A thick carpet with a Victorian design covered the floor. The walls were wide and painted sandy white, most of them covered in abstract paintings. In the corner on the left by the window was a huge, black piano. In the middle of the room was a wide, oak desk with a tall black leather chair behind it. The desk was meticulously organized, but there were no photos on it, only papers and pens. Behind the desk in the wall was a black, marble fireplace. On the mantelpiece were vases filled with red roses. On the right of the room was a wide shelf filled with books. In front of them were two wide, black leather sofas. A wide coffee table sat between them.

Seated on the farthest sofa facing me was a teenage boy. He was probably a couple years older than me, and he was very attractive. He was wearing a black shirt and black dress pants, his skin flawless and bronze. His hair was long and thick, loosely tousled over his head. His face was softer, but his eyes were wild and passionate. He looked dangerous, and almost identical to Mr. Rocha. He didn't take his eyes off of me.

"So," Mr. Rocha said in his alluring voice, getting my attention again. "You're Luis Ramirez's daughter. I saw you once, when you were first born. Constance, isn't it?"

I managed to hold his eyes, but I didn't say anything. Mr. Rocha kept staring at me, gently moving strands of hair off my face with his free hand. I looked at his other one, noticing that one of the thugs had given him my father's hatchet. My fingers itched to have it back.

"Your father used to work for me," he went on. "He was a falcon, one of my best runners. But you probably didn't know that. As soon as you were born, Luis was determined to change his lifestyle for you. Interesting that you would find your way back here, and stumble on my doorstep."

My heart skipped a beat. I knew that my father had endured a hard, treacherous life, and that he had done things he wasn't proud of. But I never expected to find out he had been a drug runner for the Blood Thorns. I was too stunned to speak.

Mr. Rocha moved his eyes over to my left. "And who else do we have here?"

I turned my head to the left when the bag on Dro's head was pulled off. She breathed in shakily, her icy blue eyes scanning the room until they found me. She relaxed, until she saw Mr. Rocha. Then she cringed away in fear. I tried to move in front of her, but someone's hand clamped on my shoulder and held me back.

Dro was trying not to shake when Mr. Rocha reached out and stroked the side of her face.

"A unique beauty I have never seen before," he said quietly.

"Leave her alone," I warned.

The bald man holding me gripped my arm and shook me. Mr. Rocha turned back, intrigued by my reaction.

"Who is she to you?" he asked curiously.

"She's my sister," I told him defensively. "And if

you hurt her, I'll cut you the same way I cut your loser friends."

The bald man holding my arm suddenly whirled me around and slapped me across the face. I saw stars and collapsed onto the floor. I shook my head and shuffled back as he stomped toward me.

"Enough," Mr. Rocha commanded.

The bald man didn't hurt me again, but he roughly hauled me to my feet. I caught a glimpse of the teenage boy watching me from the sofa. He hadn't moved, but I could see an unhappy expression cross his face. Strangely, his disapproval seemed to be aimed at the bald man instead of me. Shame the boy was a jerk that didn't care if a fourteen year old girl was slapped around.

The bald man spun me so I could face Mr. Rocha. He was toying with Dro's hair, examining it like he'd never seen hair before. She closed her eyes and was trying to stay calm, but she was so scared.

"Your sister, is she?" he crooned. "I never thought Luis would adopt another child. You aren't lying to me, are you Constance?"

I looked as strong as I could. I didn't know much, but I knew that if you showed your enemies fear once, they would never let you forget it.

"Not about anything," I answered coolly.

His pitch black eyes seared into me again. I didn't move a muscle. Then he smiled at me.

"What brought you back here, my dear? Surely your father didn't tell you who I was or where to find me."

This time I couldn't tell the truth. He would only think I was lying. I couldn't tell him monsters killed our parents, but I had to tell him something he would believe.

"Our parents are dead," I told him flatly. "We had nowhere else to go. Your meatheads found us. We weren't looking for you."

The bald man squeezed my arm hard enough to leave impressions in my bicep. I gritted my teeth but never broke eye contact with his boss. Mr. Rocha didn't look upset at all. He seemed more amused than anything.

"Shame. I would have loved to see the look on Luis's face if he knew you were here with me."

He slowly walked back toward his desk, leaning against it. He turned the hatchet over and over in his hands. The sight of it seemed to amuse him, and I couldn't help but wonder if my father ever used the hatchet when he was a runner. I tried not to think about that possibility for very long.

"He left me at a very, very bad time, you know. He cost me a lot of money. I'm still paying for his mistakes. Now that he's dead, I can't use you as leverage against him. So what do you think I should do, Constance? Are you willing to pay for your father's failure?"

My temper surged, but I forced it down. I didn't want to make the leader of the Blood Thorns angry, even if he was lying about Dad being a failure. I couldn't say no. If I did, he would kill us. We were nothing to him. Mr. Rocha smiled, his dark eyes gleaming bright. He knew that he had caught me.

"I'll work it off," I suggested. "I'll take Dad's old job. Whatever he did, I'll do."

"Why should I trust you? If you are your father's daughter, you'll simply run off at the first chance you get." His eyes slid back to Dro. "Of course, I wouldn't recommend doing that. Unlike him, you have something to lose."

The greasy-haired man and the scarred man closed in on Dro, starting to obscure her from my sight. I tried to move for them, but was yanked back by the bald guy. I swiftly looked at Mr. Rocha.

"I promise, I won't run until my father's debt it paid," I announced to everyone in the room. "I won't betray you. I know how to stay away from cops. I'll prove myself."

I hated sounding so weak and so desperate, but there was nothing else I could do to keep my sister safe.

"Please," I begged. "Give me a chance."

The next few moments were very tense as everyone in the room watched me. I didn't look at anyone but Mr.

Rocha. His smile widened.

"Very well. If you have nowhere else to stay, you can board in the servant quarters here. I'm not your father. I look after my children."

I bit my tongue to keep from saying anything rude to him, tensing again when Mr. Rocha straightened up from the desk and addressed his thugs.

"You let yourselves get wounded by a little girl," he stated coldly. "Am I to understand you are that weak?"

"It was a fluke, sir," the bald man said. "She wouldn't have gotten away."

"Like Marius got nearly got away?"

They said nothing. Mr. Rocha walked around the desk and pulled open a drawer. "I appreciate you bringing me his head, but he talked before you caught him. Fortunately for me, the cops he spoke to are on my payroll. Unfortunately for you, I'm not in the mood for forgiveness today."

He pulled out a gun and shot the man behind me. There was no hesitation. Two more gunshots cracked through the air and two more bodies dropped onto the ground. Dro screamed. The scent of blood filled the room. I turned to stare at the corpses in horror. The holes in their heads were small, but I was stunned at how much blood pooled out from behind their skulls. It seeped into the carpet, a stain that could never be cleaned.

No one came running in. The boy on the sofa was staring at the bodies without any recognizable expression. This was normal *in this house.*

"That's right, Constance. Keep staring at them," Mr. Rocha said from behind me. *"Get a good look at the blood and the bodies. You'll be seeing more of both."*

I turned my head and found myself staring up at him. He was only inches away from me, holding my father's hatchet loosely at his side. I was now truly afraid of him.

"You took away a lesson from this, didn't you, my dear?"

Oh, I had a lesson, all right. I learned that if I

crossed or disobeyed the leader of the Blood Thorns, he would shoot me if he were feeling charitable. I didn't want to think about what he would do if he were truly angry.

"Yes, Mr. Rocha," I whispered.

He chuckled. "My dear, you're part of my family now." He curled my hand around the hatchet, then tightened his fist over mine.

"Call me Emilio..."

Chapter 3

After the street-preacher's stabbing and the Possessor sighting, the demons decided to show themselves in full force. Everything turned so much worse.

It hadn't been two days before the first ghoul demons broke out of a portal in Santa Fe and ate three people. Reds were spotted darting around at night and grabbing unsuspecting victims. There was even a rumor that a hellhound had been set loose in a small zoo and killed all the animals before moving onto the late night staff.

The government was failing at containing the situation. News stations were having field days. Religious zealots were praying and shouting "I told you so" at the non-believers. Satanists were performing ritual suicides and willingly giving themselves over to Possessors. Gun stores were running out of weapons and bullets. Everyone was praying to the angels, but the angels never gave any sign they were on earth.

After the stabbing, we kept moving north. I thought we were getting away from the horror the more we drove, but it was hard to tell with so much chaos around us. It seemed that with every mile, people were filing into churches or cars, looking for comfort and escape. Street-preachers were out in armies, shouting at anyone who hurried past them. The actual army was everywhere, protecting whoever they could even though they didn't know what they were protecting them from. It was worse at night, when the demons had more power. Looters swept through the streets like a plague. There were too many assaults and murders for the police to keep up with. I could have been grateful to assume I wasn't very high on their priority list anymore, but even I'm not that selfish. Besides, every fast moving shadow made my hands tighten on the hilt of my hatchet.

Most people were taking the main exits to get out of the city, but we heard that the army was checking every car to make sure no one was carrying a bomb with them. Chaos was the perfect chance for terrorists to show the world how righteous they were by killing hundreds of people.

Luckily (and with a bit of psychic help from Max) we found an abandoned highway that would take us out of Oklahoma. Nobody was on this road but us.

Rain poured heavily on the stolen car as Warrick drove us down the road. He talked discreetly into his phone, which I would have teased him about if I hadn't been so tired. I was resting my head against the passenger side window, looking like I was asleep. I was basically closing my eyes and drowning out everything around me.

Warrick tried to be quiet for the sake of everyone in the car, but I wanted to know what was going on. The other demon slayers were constantly hounding him, though I couldn't help wondering if he was talking to a Federal Marshal in secret.

Warrick stopped talking, so I opened my eyes a crack to watch him. He stared at the road, looking exhausted and depressed. Suddenly I felt guilty about thinking he was only in it for the money hanging over my head. I never liked seeing him this way. He'd chosen to help us, but it hurt me to see him so unhappy when he should have been fighting somewhere else. I wasn't making it easy by not trusting him, but that wasn't the sort of switch I could randomly flip on and off. Still, I could pretend for a while. I raised my head slowly.

"What happened?" I asked him.

"Nothing." He sighed. "The rest of the slayers just want to kick my ass."

"Why?"

"They're pissed that I'm not fighting with them. All these possessions and attacks are overwhelming them and they want to know why I haven't reported in."

I snorted. "This from the same people who didn't believe you when you said you needed help in Texas?"

He grinned weakly at me. "The same." His smile disappeared. "They want to know where I am so we can meet up and fight together, but I told them no. I said I was on a mission, but I didn't say anything about Dro."

I glanced in the backseat. Max's head was resting in the crook of Dro's shoulder, his hand in one of hers. Her head was pressed against his. She was awake, but he was fast asleep.

"Thanks for that," my sister whispered. Warrick looked in the rearview mirror to smile and nod at her.

"Why didn't you say anything?" I asked. His eyes moved over to me, and I had to remember to breathe. *Damn bright green eyes.* "Do you think they'd try to hurt her?"

He looked uncomfortable. "Of the six slayers in North America, I only trust one now. We aren't the most noble characters."

"Says the one who collects government bounties to put bad people behind bars," I said.

I winced as soon as the words were out of my mouth, because I was one of those bad people who should be behind bars, and Warrick made most of his money by collecting federal bounties.

Which is what he's going to do to you when all this is over. Twenty-five grand is a lot of cash, and after this, he's going to want that more than he wants you.

"True," he admitted, glancing at me when he sensed my unease. "But I've recently learned that some people deserve a second chance."

He held my eyes for a long time, as if he could ask me to trust him with them. Damned if it didn't almost work. His eyes shone brightly against the grey light coming from the windshield. They were the color of leaves under a summer sun. It didn't help that they were attached to a rock hard body and a strikingly handsome face. It wasn't a perfect face– there was a scar under his left eye and he desperately needed a shave– but it was strong and confident, unrelenting and steadfast. It was a face that was too easy to dream about.

I didn't how to be careful around Warrick. Every time I looked at him, I felt myself starting to fall and not really caring. He looked at me with admiration, respect, and something else I didn't want to identify. He got under my skin, and I liked it.

But I'd been caught in that trap once before. I'd trusted and loved, and suffered because of it. I wasn't going to go through that again. I couldn't focus on it anyway, not with endless demons and indifferent angels hunting my sister. I liked Warrick, liked him a lot, but the risk was greater than the reward. It always was.

Warrick kept glancing at me, waiting for me to keep talking to him, but I turned my head away. Thankfully, Max woke up and broke the awkward moment.

"Are we there yet?" he yawned.

Dro smiled. "Max, we don't have a destination."

"Yeah, but I was hoping that would have changed in the last few–"

Dro inhaled sharply and snapped her head toward to the windshield. I twisted forward, and watched a man appear out of thin air. He landed in a crouch, stabbing a silver broadsword into the hood of the car, making it scream.

His head was hanging low. I couldn't see his face, but I knew who– and what– he was.

Rain soaked, bleach blond hair dripped in front of his face. He wore a long, white trench coat that snapped with the wind. The sword embedded in the car kept him in place. Warrick slammed on the brakes, but the man didn't slide off. The car skidded along the slippery road, and we had to brace ourselves as Warrick tried to gain control. After doing a one hundred eighty degree turn, the car finally stopped. The man lifted his head.

I recognized his pale grey eyes and stern, unforgiving face. The same face that had been horrified and outraged when he learned that my sister was the half angel, half demon child of Lucifer.

Rorkiel's eyes could have frozen a lake. But he wasn't looking at me.

"Get down!" I screamed.

Just as I was shouting, Rorikel lifted his sword out of the hood of the car and drove it straight through the windshield.

Glass shattered around us. I covered my head with my arms, twisting my body so I could see if Dro had missed the sword. I breathed easier when I saw that she and Max had ducked out of range. The sword jerked back out of the windshield, screeching along metal and glass.

I grabbed the hatchet off my hip and pulled open the car door. The rain was coming down in torrents. It soaked me the moment I was outside.

Rorikel stepped off the hood of the car, taking his sword with him. The blade was half as tall as I was. I'd seen Rorikel fight before, and knew exactly how dangerous he was. He was a Seraph a soldier of the Heavenly Host. He was humorless and cold. Despite our past alliance, he truly believed that Dro deserved to die just because she existed. He would have no problem cutting me in half to get to her. He'd probably enjoy it, simply because he hated me.

I spun my hatchet in my hand, the weight of it reassuring me. I might not stand a chance against Rorikel, but I could lie to myself before I died.

"Rorikel!" Warrick shouted through the rain. Out of the corner of my eye, I could see him standing near the front of the car, holding his sawed-off shotgun at Rorikel's head. "Don't do this!"

The angel ignored him. He was feet away from me. I got ready.

"Rorikel! Please! Don't–"

Warrick suddenly shouted in pain. I couldn't see what happened to him, because Rorikel swung his sword at me. If I hadn't ducked, he would have taken my head off. I took a step closer, knowing it would be a little harder for the sword to hit me. I slashed at his chest with my hatchet, but he blocked the strike with his wrist. I tried to kick him in the ribs, but he was able to twist away and make me stumble forward. I ducked again before as his sword swept over my head. Rorikel drove his knee up into my chin. My brain rattled in my skull from the hit, but I dropped down and swept my leg out to catch him off balance.

He was too fast for that. He stepped back, raising his sword to slash down at me. I rolled away, hearing the sword cut through the back of my lucky jacket. The tip of the metal sliced through my shirt, and I knew I had to be faster. I wouldn't get that lucky again.

I got up in a crouch and grabbed a silver throwing knife from inside my jacket. I threw it at Rorikel, only to see it batted away by his sword. I got to my feet as he swiped the sword at me. My hatchet hooked the blade to keep it from going into my face. Rorikel spun our blades around with so much force that my hatchet flew out of my grip. I was going for another knife when he kicked me in the chest and knocked me onto the road.

I pushed myself up as he walked away from me. He was walking toward Dro, who was being held captive by an angel I didn't know. Max was next to her, another angel holding his arms behind him as he struggled. The new angels had come out of nowhere, and now we were outnumbered two to one.

Rorikel never slowed as he approached my sister with his sword. I ran for him, getting one step before someone wrapped an arm around my throat. Leather creaked as it choked me. I kicked and thrashed, but whatever angel was holding me had an iron grip.

Dro shoved against the angel trapping her, but it was no use. Rorikel lifted his sword, ready to kill her.

As soon as I saw what he was going to do, I reacted faster than I ever had in my life.

I grabbed a knife inside my jacket with my free hand and stabbed it into the angel's arm. He barked in pain and let go of me. I stepped forward and hurled my knife at Rorikel's back.

The blade sank into his spine, causing him to stumble and screw up his strike. Dro ducked, the sword missing her completely and nearly slicing open the neck of the angel behind her. Rorikel whirled angrily, focusing all his rage on me. I saw my hatchet on the road and raced for it. A blast of gold light flared behind me, slamming into my back.

It was like I had been caught in a tornado of fire. My skin felt as if a million angry wasps were stinging it. The heat was so intense I thought I was going to turn into a pile ash. I cried out and dropped onto the ground, inches away from my hatchet. Dro screamed my name.

The heavenfire ended as quickly as it had come, my entire being swimming with pain. I had been hit with heavenfire before, but last time my brain was kind enough to shut my body down. This time I wasn't so lucky. Every inch of me throbbed ruthlessly. Every time I breathed, the wasps were back in full force.

Despite the agony, I tried to move. My body hated me and screamed for mercy, but Rorikel was still here. He would still try to kill Dro. I stretched my fingers out as far as they would go, straining for my hatchet.

I couldn't lift my head, but I managed to see Rorikel's white leather boots stop in front of me. My silver knife clattered onto the rain-soaked pavement a couple inches away. He kicked it and my hatchet out of reach. *Bastard.* His feet twisted, and another set of white boots came into view.

"She is quite resilient, for a human," a new angel said. This one's voice was lighter and more cheerful than Rorikel's monotonous voice, but that didn't make him less of an enemy.

"She is subdued. She will not be a problem." Rorikel paused, and I could hear my friends and my sister screaming for me. "Would you like to do the honors, Commander Gabriel?"

Gabriel. As in the archangel, second in command to Michael. *Oh no.*

I tried to move faster, but my body just wouldn't

allow it.

"It was you who found them with your subtle tracking of the hybrid. I trust you can do what needs to be done, Rorikel. You may proceed."

No! I pushed myself up, my arms shaking as I tried to support my weight. I got to my knees and started scanning the road for my hatchet. Someone stalked toward me. I lifted my head, and found myself looking at Gabriel.

I knew it was him. He was tall and beautiful, his skin perfectly tanned and flawless. Long, sandy blond hair cascaded in waves down to his shoulders, the rain shimmering through it like water in a shallow creek. His face seemed kind, his bones, nose, and lips so delicate that he almost looked like a child. But his eyes gave his true self away. They were shimmering hazel, so bright I swear they were glowing. He tilted his head, and then pushed himself into my mind.

I shut him out as best as I could. I didn't like supernatural beings going through my head. The last one to do it was Lucifer, and while Gabriel wasn't nearly as strong as he was, the archangel still caught glimpses of my darkest fears and deepest secrets. I gritted my teeth, but couldn't completely shut him out. He knew how much the demons terrified me, how destructive and ruthless I had been in the past, and how desperate I was to protect my sister.

Gabriel suddenly broke the connection, twisting his head to the side. My entire body sighed with relief, though there was a dull ache in the back of my skull from when Gabriel had torn himself out. I lifted my head again in Dro's direction. The angels had suddenly backed away from her. Max was lying on the ground with his hands over his head.

Dro had broken free of the angel that was restraining her. She held her arms out in front of her, and sent a blast of gold light at Rorikel and Gabriel. They blinked out of existence, avoiding her power in time. I watched in amazement. I'd never seen Dro use heavenfire before. The angels standing next to her and Max were stunned, and didn't move fast enough when she turned her wrath on them. The light hit them like a punch and sent them flying off the road.

The angel behind me drew his sword and ran for my sister, but she swung another blast of light at the angel, flinging her arm out to the side and sending him flying into the car. There were shouts and another blast of gold light to my right, and then someone was beside me, pressing their hand onto my back.

"It's okay, Con," Dro whispered in my ear. "I've got you."

Pins and needles coursed through my body as she began to heal me. I couldn't stop the small scream that escaped my lips. The heavenfire had been awful, and no matter how good her intentions, Dro was hurting me as much as she was helping me. But she pressed on, slowly numbing the pain and piecing me back together. More footsteps sounded beside me. Warrick and Max.

The uncomfortable tingles stopped and I opened my eyes again. I took a breath and pushed myself up. Dro and Warrick moved to support me, but I brushed them off. I might have been almost burned alive but now that I was healed, I could fight again.

Max handed over my hatchet and the knife I had thrown in Rorikel's back. "Thought you'd want these."

I took them, unable to smile. "Thanks."

I gripped the knife and hatchet tightly. I looked at Warrick next. He was standing, but he'd been roughed up. There was a deep cut under his eye, his lip was split, and his nose was bleeding.

"Are you okay?" he asked.

I raised my eyebrows, about to tell him how dumb that question was since I was healed and he had been pulped by an angel. But then Max breathed in sharply, and I twisted my head to look forward.

Gabriel and Rorikel were back, standing in front of us with their swords drawn. A new group of angels were standing behind them. I didn't see the angels she attacked earlier, but these new ones looked just as furious and stone cold as Rorikel did. Gabriel didn't look angry. If anything, he seemed entertained.

Spinning my hatchet, I took a step toward them. Dro held out her arm and pushed me back. I blinked at her, but she was completely focused on the angels. She was holding her breath, power blazing in her intense blue eyes. She took a single step forward and swept out her arm, drawing a line of hellfire between them and us. I knew it was hellfire this time because of the flames. Nothing else in the world was hot enough to evaporate water three inches before it hit the flame.

I cringed a little under the intense heat, not sure how Dro was controlling it but trusting that she could. I had no desire to be set on fire again.

For the longest time, I thought we were going to be trapped in a group stare-down. Then Gabriel spoke in his light, delicate voice.

"You're more than what they said you were, Andromeda. It is almost as if you are pretending to be human."

"We're trying to close the Gates," she insisted, ignoring the jab. "We should be helping each other. We're after the same thing."

Gabriel smiled, shaking his head. "I do not think so. You are the spawn of Lucifer, the result of an angel's violation. You do not have Heaven's interests in mind."

If Dro's hellfire line hadn't been there, I would have tried to kill him. No one disrespected my sister without getting a taste of my fist. If Dro was bothered by the comment, she didn't show it. She stayed still and strong.

"Lucifer is the enemy here," she tried again. "Not us. We don't need to do this."

"Give yourself over to us, and your friends shall not suffer. Enough humans are dying now that the demons are set upon Earth. I do not care for further bloodshed, and neither do you."

"Fuck you," I spat violently. Being attacked and burned brought out the worst parts of my temper. "She's not going to be killed by you flying motherfuckers. Go back to your puffy white clouds."

Max coughed uncomfortably. "Not helping, Constance," he muttered.

I shot him a look so murderous that he held up his hands in mock surrender and took a step back. "Okay, okay, sorry."

I looked at the angels again. Gabriel's amusement was vanishing quickly. Rorikel's anger was ready to explode.

"Do not taunt the power of Heaven, Constance Ramirez," Gabriel warned. "You know nothing of which we can unleash."

Rorikel noticed something behind me, his mouth opening in surprise. Something dropped heavily on the hood of the car at our backs, causing us all to spin.

Another angel had landed, dressed in the same white trench coat, white pants, and white boots as his brothers. This one had curly, auburn hair and bright blue eyes. Unlike the other angels, this one didn't want to kill us. He looked at Gabriel and the other angels fiercely.

"They do not," Sephiel said, pulling a small, golden tube out of his jacket. "But I do."

Rorikel and Gabriel rushed to stop him, but Sephiel leaped down from the hood of the car and got close to us. Max grabbed Dro and pressed her close to his chest. She grabbed my hand on reflex. I reached back and grabbed Warrick's hand as tightly as I could. Sephiel clutched Warrick's shoulder then twisted off the top of the golden tube and raised it above our heads.

There was a sudden snap of gold light and a roar of thunder that popped my eardrums. Then I felt like I imploded. A sudden, sharp pressure contracted my body in on itself, like a giant had taken hold of me and was trying to bend me into a harsh V-shape. I squeezed my eyes shut, feeling someone crush my hand in theirs.

My feet left the ground and the world rushed around me. A massive noise roared in my ears, the sound of a hurricane. My hair flattened around my face as I rocketed to wherever I was going, but I didn't open my eyes.

Everything was too tight and moving too quickly, like I'd been wrapped in Saran-wrap and fired from a cannon. I didn't know what Sephiel was doing to us, and part of me didn't want to know. I just wanted it to be over.

Seconds later, the thunder around me dulled to a low rumble. My ears continued to ring, but my hair flew out loosely around my face. The blinding light faded away. The pressure left my body and I felt like I was back in one full, proper piece again. I sighed heavily and opened my eyes.

The rain was gone, and now I was in a desert. Up ahead was a wide highway road with tall white street lamps on either side. There was a small town at the bottom of the hill. Beyond it was a wall of dark brown sand, a mountain range beyond it. The golden sun was beginning to set behind the mountains, turning them into jagged, black shadows.

I looked at the sign on my right. *Entering Bullhead City. Elevation 504. Founded 1964. Population 39,540.* The name sounded familiar, and after a moment I knew why. Bullhead City was one of the first places Dro and I went after we ran from the Blood Thorns. I looked at Dro. Her hand was resting on Max's back as he bent over, trying to either breathe or throw up. She read the highway sign behind me and slowly remembered where she was. Her eyes met mine, making sure she wasn't the only one who recognized this sign. She set her jaw and turned to look after Max.

I didn't realize I was still holding Warrick's hand until he steadily pried it free. I glanced at him. He was still bloody, and probably felt anything but comfortable.

"Still with us?" I asked.

He grinned, and my heart sighed. "In one piece, for whatever that's worth." He ran his hand through his soaked, oak-colored hair. He looked around. "Where the hell are we?"

"Arizona," I answered.

His head quickly turned to mine. "Seriously? Are you sure?"

"Yeah. Dro and I moved around here for a while. Why?"

He frowned. "The other slayers aren't far from Phoenix."

Damn it. "Then we just won't go into Phoenix."

I tried to act casual and not think about how close he was to me. I started to sloppily brush my short black hair with my hand, then gave up. It would settle in its right place eventually.

"You should get Dro or Seph to heal you," I told him. "You've looked better."

Warrick smirked. "Nice of you to say."

I stifled a laugh. "Don't let it go to your head, Warrick."

Just as I was about to walk away, he moved closer and brushed some pieces of my hair behind my ear. I stayed very, very still. His touch was as light as a feather, his fingers sending delicious chills down my spine when they grazed my skin. The tenderness in his bright green eyes rooted my boots to the sand. They softened more, turning into an expression close to guilt.

"I was trying to get to you, but that damn angel came out of nowhere and held me back," he trailed off, quickly glancing at me again. "Are you sure you're okay?"

Moving very slowly, I took his hand away from my face. My heart was pounding, wanting him to touch me again, but my brain just wouldn't let me trust him. I'd been betrayed too many times in the past to think that Warrick would treat me any differently, even though my heart was saying otherwise.

"Dro healed me, remember? Besides, I know how to take care of myself."

Warrick put his hand back at his side, a gentle smile crossing his lips. His eyes glittered like emeralds, and made my stomach flutter. *Damn it. I wish he would stop doing that to me. Whatever 'that' is.*

"You're right. You can."

If I hadn't seen someone walking over to us, I would

have forgotten where I was. Warrick had a bad habit of making me lose focus. Sephiel stood next to us, so I pushed the sexy demon slayer out of my mind and went back to being myself.

"Where the hell were you?" I asked aggressively. "We thought you were kidnapped or killed."

The damn angel didn't even blink at me. "Stealth was required for my mission. I did not want to risk revealing any of you by opening up a connection to Andromeda." He looked remorseful. "I apologize for any fear I might have caused you."

"We're just glad you're okay, Sephiel," Dro said quietly, now appearing at my side.

He smiled at her sadly. I wondered how much of Dro he was really seeing, or if he was looking for traces of her mother, Everiel. The angel Lucifer captured and used to create Dro was the love of Sephiel's life.

"I'd like to know what the hell we're doing in a place called Bullhead City," Max said, seeming to have recovered from the awful teleporting experience. "It doesn't sound like the most easygoing place ever."

"Your query shall be answered shortly, Max," replied the angel, tucking the golden tube into the pocket of his trench coat. "For now, it is best if we make our way into the town. We do not look like the most subtle group."

That we did not. A man in a long white coat, a pale girl with long white hair, a skinny teenager, an angry woman wearing a man's coat, and a bloody demon slayer would catch the attention of even the most disinterested truck driver.

Sephiel strode toward the city. Dro and Max linked fingers and followed him. I stayed away from Warrick and watched the sun disappear. It was a beautiful mix of orange, yellow, and gold settling behind the black mountains, a new stretch of navy and dark blue overtaking the highest parts of the sky.

But as I watched the darkness smother the light, I couldn't shake the feeling of déjà vu in my stomach. Dro and I hadn't been safe the last time we were here, and now we were in more trouble then than ever before.

Chapter 4

"No, you aren't going anywhere yet," I told Sephiel. "Not until you tell us where the fuck you went, and what the fuck you used to get us to goddamn Arizona."

It hadn't been a fun walk to our latest motel. Sephiel was fine, but the rest of us were aching and sore. My feet were promising blisters for days. I only had my knives and my hatchet with me. Warrick had rescued his sawed-off shotgun, a pair of Beretta handguns, and two combat knives. Dro had two silver throwing blades tucked in her boots. Max had the clothes on his back. We lost all of our new supplies after having them for maybe twenty-four hours.

Sephiel was on his way out with Max to get more, but I refused to let him leave without an explanation. Being sore, angry, and exhausted was not a good combination for me to be in front of a warrior angel. Thankfully, Sephiel was extremely patient. I'd never seen him truly angry; only slightly annoyed.

"I went in search of information," he replied, slowly reaching into his pocket and pulling out the strange golden tube, "as well as this."

I looked at the weird tool. Up close, it was detailed with strange text that didn't look like any other language I'd ever seen before. Not even the writing in Manny's reference books looked like this. I swallowed the lump in my throat when I thought about my dead mentor, looking up to see his son standing on the tips of his toes to peek over Sephiel's shoulder.

"Holy crap," Max exclaimed, "is that a *movens caeli*?"

Sephiel grinned a little. "Indeed it is, Max."

"What the fuck is a *movens caeli*?" I asked. I didn't

have a quarter of Sephiel's patience.

"It means 'heaven mover' in Latin. It's a special tool that angels use to teleport large groups of people. Huge, like for..." he trailed off and looked at Sephiel with serious eyes. "Like for armies."

The cheer was gone from Sephiel's face. He silently walked to the door and began moving his hand around, testing the protection wards he had set up when we arrived.

"The Heavenly Host is readying themselves to descend upon Earth. When I discovered this, I made haste to steal the *movens caeli*. It shall delay the entire Host, if not the archangels."

"But how did you get into Heaven?" Dro asked from where she was sitting on the bed. "I thought you said you would be killed if you went back there."

"I did not go to Heaven, Andromeda."

He turned to face us. "I came across a pair of Seraphim. They recognized me, and unfortunately we came to a disagreement." His bright blue eyes were sad. "I regret that they gave me no option but to end their lives."

Sephiel mourned for a second, then looked up again when all traces of guilt were gone from his face. "One of them was carrying the *movens caeli* with them. He was looking for a suitable place for it to be used as a beacon of invasion. The Heavenly Host is preparing to move against Hell."

"To do what, start a war?" Warrick said from the table in the corner where he was taking apart and cleaning his guns. He looked a lot better now that Sephiel had healed him.

"Precisely," he continued. "Most of Heaven believes that humanity is bound to sin, particularly now that the Hell Gate has been opened. They have been desiring to cleanse Hell of the damned, enforcing new rules to deter new sinners here on earth."

"I thought that was what Hell was for," I said. "A place where you were punished for all the evil things you do topside."

"It used to be," answered the angel. "Though we have received word over the centuries that Lucifer has been slipping his rule and letting chaos reign. The Royalty of Hell is constantly at war, though no one dares to challenge their King himself."

I tightened my arms around my chest, remembering a catastrophically beautiful creature with four bat wings, long white hair, and abysmal black eyes. I remembered the waves of power that flowed off him, making me want to scream in fear and cry with desire. I completely understood why no one would want to brawl with the King of Hell.

"And Hell wants to take over Heaven," I said quietly.

Sephiel nodded. "There will be bloodshed on both sides, and I fear that humanity shall be caught in the crossfire." He looked down sadly. "Most supernatural creatures care little for collateral damage."

"Then we need to get the Gates closed," I said. "Max hasn't seen them and Dro can't risk alerting the angels, but you're back now so you can take us to the Heaven Gate."

"I fear that is not possible."

I narrowed my eyes. "Why not?"

Sephiel sighed. "I do not remember where it is."

We all stared at him, waiting for him to go on. Sephiel lifted his head, his azure eyes looking heavier than usual.

"The only way we can descend to earth is if we obtain permission from Michael. He opens the Gate for us, then immediately closes it to protect our home. When we take our human vessels, our memory is cleansed of the location of the Heaven Gate. Only archangels distinctly remember where the Heaven Gate resides."

His eyes were distant, as if he was drawing on his memories. "Sometimes when I think of Heaven, I recall a beautifully serene forest. A place where I could feel the magic surging through me. Other times I wonder if it is a dream or a fantasy."

I kind of regretted being so snappy and demanding. When Sephiel sided with us, he gave up his chance to go home. If he ever went back, he would be killed. I'd only ever lived in one place that I'd truly called home, but I hardly thought about it anymore. I had too many problems to be homesick. I couldn't imagine how bad it must hurt Sephiel to know he would never see his home again.

"What happens if the Heaven Gate closes?" Warrick asked quietly. He was good at reading people. He knew exactly when to help them, and when to change the subject.

"Heaven itself is not affected. The angels residing there will remain as they are. But the angels on earth shall lose their forms, and be trapped in their vessels," he answered. "They shall settle into their host's soul, and become human. That is why the archangels are so adamant and ferocious about keeping the Heaven Gate open. We cannot enter Heaven again once the Gate is closed."

Damn. I thought being forever banned from your home was bad enough. If we closed the Heaven Gate, the angels would never forgive Sephiel. They wouldn't rest until his head was on a spike and the rest of us were charred ashes on the ground.

"What about the Hell Gate?" Warrick tried. "Do you know where that is?"

Any heartache Sephiel was feeling was quickly covered up. He was a soldier of the Heavenly Host. He was good at hiding his emotions and focusing on what needed to be done.

"I do not. But my assumption is that it will be far more difficult to locate. Lucifer is clever and will have tricks to guard it. My suggestion is to focus on closing the Heaven Gate first. Every moment it remains open is another chance Lucifer will find it. If he does, he shall monopolize it and doom us all."

"You don't think Michael can take him?" I asked.

Sephiel looked at me with a hardened expression. "Michael is the commander of the Heavenly Host and the most powerful of all the archangels. But Lucifer's magic is beyond comprehension. It would be an even match, but I cannot predict who the victor would be."

The angel turned his head to my sister. "I have confirmed that you are Michael's chosen vessel, Andromeda. Has he tried to make contact with you?"

Dro shook her head. "No, not yet."

He was suddenly in front of her, his hands gently wrapped around her arms. I was a bit alarmed by his sudden movement, but I knew Sephiel would never hurt Dro. Despite her being Lucifer's daughter, he still intended to keep her safe in honor of her mother.

"You must not give in to his pleas when they come," he urged. "No matter what he says or promises, do not listen. Michael's intentions for you are not ones of compassion."

She winced, nodding carefully.

"Is he on earth?" I asked suddenly. We didn't even know how to beat Lucifer. Michael was another problem I wasn't ready to think about.

"No, he remains in Heaven for now. But if he becomes desperate enough to come to Earth, he could make use of another available vessel. His powers are beyond discernment, and he will use them if necessary. Michael is not an angel you want to agitate."

"But you did," Dro said softly.

His gentle, sad smile returned as he took his hands from her arms. "Not all angels are as disobedient or as foolish as I am."

My sister tried to smile, but it didn't reach her eyes. "But why does he want me? I thought all the angels considered me an abomination."

I cleared my throat and glared at her. Dro glanced my way and shook her head. She accepted what the other angels called her. I didn't.

"We choose our vessels carefully," Sephiel explained. "Michael selected you as his own even before the Gates were opened. Despite the turn of events, he shall not alter his choice lightly. With your powers, he would find it reasonable that your combined strength would be enough to destroy Lucifer."

I scowled. Dro was the toy in the playground that everyone wanted, and they weren't willing to share unless she was torn in half. Dro took a moment to process what he said, then looked at the auburn-haired angel anxiously.

"Sephiel, those angels, back on the road..." She swallowed nervously. "Did I kill them?"

We all waited patiently for the answer. Dro had never intentionally killed a person in her whole life, but she had killed. In our early years of running in the States, Dro would have nightmares given to her by demons. They would make her scream and burst into hellfire. It only ended when she woke up from the nightmare, and usually that was the point when the entire building was on fire. I trained myself to be prepared after the first time it happened, to be fully awake at the first smell of smoke, but not everyone had my reflexes. We would look on the news and see the blackened motel or car park, as well as bodies being taken away in black bags.

Dro hadn't been able to control her powers before. I didn't know why she was able to do it now. But I did know that when the Shredder was about to kill me, and those angels were ready to cut me to pieces, she hadn't even hesitated. She just reacted. And now she was ready to face the consequences.

"No, you did not," Sephiel announced, relieving us all.

"But–"

"When I arrived, I saw them rising from where they had fallen. Albeit slowly." His lips quirked in a proud smile, but it left as quickly as it came. "Your powers have been changing since the Gate ritual, have they not?"

Dro nodded. "In the warehouse, we were attacked by demons. Con... She was pinned and I was able to use hellfire on a Shredder, while I was awake. I could control it." The very idea scared her.

Sephiel still looked proud. "Your abilities must have been amplified by the opening of the Gates. Your mind must be subconsciously separating your angel powers from your demon powers. You are becoming much stronger, Andromeda. I fear I can do nothing to assist you in harnessing your demonic abilities, but I can help you improve the strength of your angelic powers. I predict you shall be in need of them shortly."

"What can you show me?" she asked curiously.

"You can already use your healing ability to its near full extent. You are learning to manipulate heavenfire, which is what you used on Gabriel's guard. If you had used hellfire, you would have destroyed them. But you meant them no harm, and that must be what differentiated the fire. All that remains for you to learn are telepathy and mind control."

Dro frowned. "I'm not so sure I want to concentrate on either of those."

"They can be quite useful. You can discover what your enemies are thinking, no matter what they are."

She bit her lip and looked at me. I didn't trust it. "Won't using her powers alert the angels to where she is?"

"That outcome is extremely rare," he said, showing me the gold tube in his pocket. "The *movens caeli* also cloaks our location for a time. It can shield us from all Seraphim, and can delay the less powerful archangels."

"So Michael won't be able to talk to me?" Dro confirmed.

"Not unless you choose to seek him out. If you give me permission to help you train your mental capacities, you shall be able to quell the potency of his calls to you. There is no way to stop them, but you can learn to overlook them."

That was when I knew he had her. The idea of Michael taking her over and destroying her from the inside out terrified her, just as much as the idea of him killing her outright.

She glanced at me. I frowned, not thinking it was a good idea. It seemed like more exposure to me, the very last thing we needed right now. But I couldn't make Dro's choices for her when it came to her powers. She read my eyes and knew that I would support any decision she made, whether I agreed with it or not.

Dro looked at Sephiel. "All right. I'll do it."

They started talking about how he was going to begin teaching her control, but I wasn't listening anymore. I was thinking about the consequences of what she was doing, trying to imagine if they would help her or hurt her in the end...

It was easy at first, sneaking through the shadows and getting information on rival cartels and police raids. I got to know all the runners and falcons like me, who operated which corners, where the best deals went down, and who could be mostly trusted. Dro and I lived in the servant quarters at Emilio's hacienda, which was a separate apartment on the grounds that was constantly watched by his personal guards. He wanted us to be comfortable, but he wanted us to remember that we belonged to him now.

The staff at the hacienda kept a careful eye on me, but they loved Dro. She was their angelito– their little angel. While I was out spying on the streets, Dro did work in the kitchens, helping the cooks prepare food. She used to cook all the time with Mom, and the kitchen staff was eager to have her as a protégé.

I didn't like leaving her alone in a house filled with murderers and people I refused to trust, but Dro couldn't come with me. It was too dangerous. At least she wouldn't be hurt at the hacienda. Emilio wouldn't allow it. Unless I stepped out of line.

I worked hard to impress the Blood Thorns, giving up all my earnings to work off my father's debt. I was paid by the value of information I brought back, so I kept my eyes and ears open to everything that the enemies of the Blood Thorns were doing.

But I also saw what the Blood Thorns did to them.

I once brought back information on where an exchange was going to be. One of Emilio's men had been turned by the Fuego Cartel, their biggest rival. I'd had to stay in the dumpsters behind a rundown warehouse to get all the details, but it had been worth the atrocious smell. The traitor had given up details on Emilio's operation and what his expansion plans were. The ex-Blood Thorn was a falcon like me and while his knowledge of Emilio's operation wasn't as thorough as mine, he was still betraying his employer.

He should have known better.

When I told Emilio, he said little. He hadn't screamed or shouted or thrown something. He had calmly asked me when and where this meeting was taking place, and that I take him there. I did as he asked, going with him and the El Mirar– *The Watch. Emilio's private army.*

I sat in Emilio's car with his most trusted guard, Hernandez, and Emilio's son, Mateo, the quiet boy I'd seen in Emilio's office the day I was first brought to them. We pulled up to the warehouse where three large, black Jeeps were parked. I looked around, seeing another four vehicles pull up beside us. More of The Watch. They stepped out of their trucks and Jeeps, dressed in black uniforms stolen from dead riot police. All of the men were armed with guns.

Emilio gave me a bouquet of two dozen roses. He told me to stay with Hernandez, to say nothing and not move until he or Mateo returned. Then they and The Watch left. There had been two minutes of shouts, followed by five minutes of gunfire. Then there had been screams. Mateo came out of the warehouse and walked toward us. Like the rest of the Watch, he was dressed in a black tactical outfit, carrying a large automatic rifle in front of his chest. Blood splattered his face, but none of it was his.

Mateo had been instructed to take me into the warehouse with the roses. I walked in silence with him, and saw my second massacre.

Blood coated the sandy floor and the far metal wall. It pooled under bullet-riddled corpses and painted the boxes of plastic wrapped cocaine. There must have been a dozen bodies. One of them was collapsed on his side, a bullet hole clean through his head. The back of his skull was cracked open like an egg, red blood and grey brain spreading out behind his cranium. His dead eyes stared at me, unseeing but stuck in my direction.

Mateo told me to place one rose on every body. His eyes were serious, yet sympathetic. He stayed close to my side and watched me diligently. I shook with every step, feeling my stomach churn as I stared at the bullet riddled corpses. The metallic smell of blood and sour rot of death made me gag. But I placed the roses on the bodies.

Then Emilio asked me to come over to where the last traitor was standing. It was the falcon I had ratted out. He was bound to a post with his hands behind his back, his eyes wide with terror. He'd been beaten by The Watch, his bruised face as bloated and swollen as a drowning victim. He looked at me with so much fear that I stopped walking. I clutched the last rose and felt the thorns bite into my palm. Mateo put his hand on my back and pushed me forward. I barely felt myself moving.

Hernandez grabbed the falcon's head, prying open his mouth. I nearly screamed when Emilio took out a knife and sawed off the falcon's tongue. The man gagged and choked on blood as Hernandez held him in place. Emilio turned back to me, looking into my eyes when he took the rose from my trembling fingers. He walked back to the falcon. He took out a gun from inside his jacket and shot the traitor between the eyes. Blood and bone exploded out from the back of his skull, splashing onto the metal post. His eyes rolled up into his head, and then he was still. Hernandez kept the dead man in place as Emilio put the rose in the falcon's bloody mouth. Emilio looked at me, his dark eyes cold and merciless.

"We send messages, Constance. You will never be respected if you do not make them remember you."

I barely remembered Mateo's hand on my elbow as he led me out of the warehouse, or how he promised it would get easier. I didn't remember the drive back to the hacienda. All I remember was going into the room I shared with Dro, and the worried look on her eleven year old face when she saw me. I burst into tears and dropped *onto the floor. Her little arms had held me as much as they could, her familiar voice telling me that everything would be all right.*

***

After the massacre, I went back to work. Months passed, and soon I was coming up on my sixteenth birthday. I was getting colder, more detached. I was becoming faster, stronger, and more dangerous. I took more risks. I paid off more of the debt. I kept an eye out for monsters. But I never forgot what I had seen in the warehouse. My nightmares didn't fade. I simply tried to keep my screaming to a minimum so Dro could sleep.

I was almost glad to go on my latest run. One of the Fuegos was planning to ship a huge amount of heroin. Emilio planned to intercept it and steal it. The shipment was worth one hundred thousand American dollars, and it was my job to find out where the drop was going to be.

I stayed in the shadows, watching my target. He slipped out of a dark alley and waited at the far corner. By now, I knew most of the streets downtown. I turned and sprinted down another alley. I squeezed between the narrow stone walls by the street shops, feeling the metal bars of the windows press against my back. I made it through the narrow crevice into the alley he walked down. Barely looking past the corner, I saw my target, a man named Horatio Juarez, standing six feet away at the mouth of the alley.

He wasn't a very tall man, only a couple inches taller than me, but he was fairly broad. He wore black pants and a black military jacket over his big shoulders. He looked back again, but didn't see me. The sounds of honking horns and shouts from the street faded as I focused on Horatio. He stared at the intersection ahead of him, sliding his hands into his pockets. Two minutes later, a black car pulled up. A man got out and walked toward Horatio.

"Tuesday, south border desert, 11:25."

It was faint, but I heard everything I needed to hear. That was all the man had to say. He turned, got back into his car, and drove away. I started to slide back through the crevice. It was a tight squeeze, but if I made it once before, then I could make it again.

A hand suddenly clamped on my arm and dragged me out from between the buildings. I was thrown onto the alley floor, landing on my ribs. I whirled onto my back. Horatio was standing over me, a furious look in his eyes.

"So you're the one who's been following me," he growled. "You're not as sneaky as you think, you little bitch."

I backed up and tried to get away. He was faster than me. He grabbed my ankle and jerked me back. I cried out and tried to kick at him, but he was already reaching down and grabbing my throat. He lifted me off the alley ground and squeezed. I tugged at his hand, trying to get it off me so I could breathe, but he was too strong.

Horatio twisted and threw me into the wall. My face crashed against it. Blood burst from my nose and my head was filled with a sharp, throbbing pain. I shook my head and tried to move away, but Horatio pressed himself against my back, crushing my chest into the wall.

"I know who you are," he snarled, his stale breath hot in my ear. "You're Rocha's little whore. The quick little bitch running around giving him all the info he wants. You think the Fuegos wouldn't find out about you?"

My heart pounded behind my ribcage, beating against the wall. I tried to slide my hands to where my hatchet was hidden, but I couldn't move them to my back. Horatio grabbed a fistful of my hair and jerked my head back. I gritted my teeth and tried not to cry out. No one would help me if I did.

"I'm gonna make my own message out of you. Give Rocha something to think about."

He pulled me by my hair until I stood in front of him. Then he backhanded me across the face. I spun onto the ground, landing on my front. Blood dripped from the cut on my lips and my bleeding nose. Everything was spinning. I pushed myself up just long enough for Horatio to kick me in the ribs. I landed on my back, and then he was on top of me.

I panicked, struggling and shoving against him. I had to get my hatchet. I arched my back, sliding my hand toward the back of my belt where I'd hidden it. Horatio used one of his hands to punch me in the cheek. My head snapped to the side, filled with new pain. He trapped one of my hands by my side and used the other one to slide under my shirt and cup my breast. I winced as his fingers pinched and twisted my flesh. An uncomfortable bulge pressed against my hips. His breath smelled like old meat and cheap tequila. My fingers found the hilt of my hatchet. Horatio fumbled at the button on my jeans. I pried my hatchet from my belt, feeling its awkward shape against my back. I twisted my arm out from under me as Horatio tugged at my pants. He leaned in, biting my ear hard enough to make it bleed.

I screamed and slammed the hatchet into the side of his neck.

Horatio stopped moving. Blood squirted out from where the blade had stuck in his skin, splashing onto my collarbone. He slumped heavily against me, pressing the air out of my lungs. He was heavier now than he had before. My heart was straining painfully in my chest. I struggled to control my breathing. My entire body shook.

I wrenched my hatchet from his throat. It made a squelching sound as it was torn from his flesh. More blood dripped onto me. It took all of my strength, but I pushed Horatio off me. I scrambled back and looked at the body.

His head was twisted in my direction, his shoulder blocking his mouth. I could see the dark red stain on his neck, the blood oozing out onto the ground around his head. His eyes stared forward, glazed over in death. My hand shook so badly that I lost my grip on the hatchet.

I had killed him. I had killed a man. I'd done the worst thing a person could do to someone.

I tried to tell myself that he would have done the

same to me without hesitation. That he was going to rape me and beat me to death, leaving me as nothing but a warning for Emilio. But the tears wouldn't stop. There was an ache in my chest that was threatening to eat me alive.

I had killed someone. Dro would never be able to look at me again.

I lost track of time as I sat in the alley with Horatio's body, crying until I was certain I was going to dehydrate my body. After a while, there were no more tears. I couldn't be weak anymore. I had to keep my little sister safe, even if she would hate me. I needed to be stronger. I was lucky this time. I had to become something else if I wanted to survive in the life I'd chosen.

I had to be a monster.

Feeling numb inside but shaking on the outside, I crawled over and took Horatio's jacket off his body. I tucked the bloody hatchet into my belt, pulling my arms through the jacket. It smelled like blood and was too big for me. Maybe I would grow into it. I was going to keep it as a reminder of what had happened here. What I had turned into.

It took me a couple hours to hike back to the hacienda. I had missed my ride, and I wanted to clear my head. Emilio would be angry with me for being late, but he would appreciate weakness even less. I couldn't cry in front of him. I had to be strong. Cold. A stone.

When I finally made it back to the house, the guards didn't ask where I had been or why I was covered in blood, but they still let me through the gates. They all knew me by now. I trudged through the gardens and into the house, hearing the maids, gardeners, and guards whispering about me. I didn't care.

I found Emilio, Mateo, and Hernandez in the dining room having breakfast. Dro was with them. She looked up from her barely eaten food, gasping when she saw me. I felt my heart crumble even more at the sight of my eleven year old sister. I wasn't looking forward to her despising me, but I wouldn't blame her.

"Connie!" she cried, jumping out of her seat and running for me.

Mateo looked up and gaped when he saw the mess that I was. Emilio and Hernandez stared, but I could read nothing in their eyes. Dro threw her arms around me and hugged me tight. I put my hand on her back, grateful that she was here, but still too broken to move.

"You didn't come back," she whispered into my chest. "I was scared you were kidnapped or hurt." She squeezed me tighter. "And you are hurt."

"I'm okay, Dro," I breathed. "I got trapped and had to do something bad." My voice caught in my throat. "Something really, really bad."

"I know. I can see it. I feel how sad you are."

I swallowed, trying to look strong in front of Emilio and Mateo. Emilio got up from his chair. There was an uncomfortable tingling in my body. Dro was healing me.

"I'm just glad you're home," she said softly.

Right then, I knew she wasn't going to be angry with me. She wasn't going to see me as a monster. At least not yet. The long walk had given me time to think about how to make myself tougher, and I came up with one conclusion. After what I was about to ask Emilio, I wasn't sure she would keep thinking so highly of me.

"You're wearing Horatio's jacket," Emilio noted.

I lifted my eyes to meet his. He was only a couple feet away from me with Mateo and Hernandez close to his back. I peeled Dro off my chest and moved her behind me. Emilio's eyes scanned mine. It wasn't long before he knew.

"You killed him," he stated.

"He knew I was following him," I explained. "He attacked me. I defended myself. The jacket is my proof."

Emilio's stare was vacant, and a little scary. "Hernandez, get a lead on Horatio. Make sure that he's dead."

The big bodyguard left the room. I took a deep breath. Here goes nothing.

"I want to be an enforcer, Emilio," I said.

Mateo took in my request with silence and an empty stare. I could feel Dro looking around me, tugging on my hand. I focused on Emilio. He stared blankly at me.

"I'm tired of doing the small jobs with pointless risks. I want to know how to fight back. I can get you more information. I can pay off more of the debt. I've earned it."

He took a slow step toward me. "Have you?"

"Yes. I deserve to—"

The loud smack of his hand across my face subdued me, cutting through the air like a knife. Dro shivered and clutched my hand tightly. She wanted to defend me, but knew there was nothing she could do against a stone-cold killer like Emilio. I wouldn't ask her to. The pain was bad, but nothing I couldn't deal with.

"You deserve nothing," Emilio growled. "Not unless I decide it. You are the one who came crawling to me, begging for help because you weren't strong enough to take care of yourself. Never assume otherwise, Constance."

I stayed still, frightened that I might do something to push his rage further. I knew about the things Emilio did. He might have let me live in his house and eat at his table, but he wouldn't hesitate to kill me if I displeased him. Something I had obviously done.

"With all due respect, father, I think she has potential."

Emilio turned to look at his only son. Mateo held his ground, strong and confident. Unlike his father, his dark eyes glimmered with passion.

"I've been watching the reports. Constance has brought back more information than any of our other falcons. I think she's ready."

"Being an enforcer is not for the weak, Mateo. Do you think she'll be able to handle the things an enforcer must do?"

"I'll train her myself," Mateo answered. When his dark eyes found mine, they were almost as severe as his

father's. He grinned coldly. "She'll be able to do it."

At the time, I was grateful that Mateo stood up for me. He was handsome, confident, and strong. I noticed the way he'd been looking at me, felt how he made my heart beat a little bit faster when he walked into the same room I was in.

But if I had known what he would turn me into, I would have stopped him...

Chapter 5

We had to share the two-bed room of the motel, but it was nice to stay in one place for a couple days. Even if the motel did smell stale and the hot water lasted for five minutes. We'd gotten more supplies and heard nothing of the angels or demons after us. I stayed in the motel and rested, actually managing to sleep more than four hours for once. I shifted on the bed, blinking my eyes open and sitting up. I ran a hand through my hair and sighed. I glanced around the hotel room, seeing only Max sitting at the dining table with some takeout food and a laptop.

I swung my legs out of the bed and quickly walked toward him. His dark eyes lifted from the computer screen to me. I opened my mouth to speak, but he raised his hand to stop me.

"Dro is fine," he said. "She's out training with Sephiel. Warrick is watching them and getting his ear talked off by the other slayers."

I relaxed and dropped into the chair across from him. He pushed the bag of food across the table to me. I reached inside and grabbed a huge chicken wrap and some crispy steak fries. One of the best things about the Southwestern states was the food. To them, there was no such thing as too much food. I unfolded the paper around the chicken wrap while nodding to the laptop. "Where'd you get the computer?"

"Sephiel," he answered. "I swear, there's nothing that angel isn't willing to steal."

"Don't suppose anyone had a breakthrough regarding the Gates?" I asked as I ate.

"Not yet. Every time I try to look forward, it's like a wall goes up in my head. The angels must have warded it against psychics." Max smirked a little. "I hope it's near a beach."

I rolled my eyes as he concentrated on the screen again. Once I was finished chewing, my next question was, "What are you looking at?"

Max shrugged. "Just the news." He frowned. "If I say the world's going to Hell in a hand basket, is that too foreboding?"

I stifled a laugh. "Nah. For once that phrase is fitting. What's going on?"

"Mass demon attacks, reporters broadcasting it all, churches asking people to pray, half the country demanding answers while the other half demands protection." He looked at me with worried eyes. "It's getting bad out there. Constance. Really bad."

I slowed my eating, barely tasting the chicken wrap anymore. He didn't need to tell me things were getting worse. I was all too aware.

"I've been looking for Drake, too."

I went still, losing my appetite. Max's eyes were heavy and sad. "I haven't been able to find him."

I dropped my food onto its paper and placed my hands on my arms, thinking about the same thing Max was. His father, Manny, had been a demonologist who'd taken Dro and me in for a time. He let us stay in their house and taught me everything he knew about demons. He tried to help us uncover what my sister was when we didn't know. He'd been my mentor and my friend, able to stand against my temper and willing to overlook my past to help us.

Then a ruthless bounty hunter named Drake Talbot barged into his home, looking for me. He killed Manny before shooting Max and capturing my sister and me. I could still see the bullet entering Manny's chest, his body crumpling onto the floor, the color of his blood soaking into the carpet. I remembered Max's heartbreaking scream when he saw his father's corpse.

Max didn't blame me for what happened, but I blamed myself. Drake was hired by the Blood Thorns to capture me. If I hadn't been there, Manny would still be alive. It was hard to believe his death had only been a few months ago. Sephiel had taken Max back to bury his father's body, but I never got to say goodbye to him. I still missed his sharp brown eyes, intelligent smile, understanding kindness, and his stubborn will.

Across from me, Max's pain was worse. I knew what it was like to lose both parents, but there was nothing I could do or say to comfort him. Not unless it involved me stabbing Drake in the eye.

"I want to kill him," Max whispered. "I want to kill him before he hurts anyone else. Before he gets to Dro."

We all had our reasons to want Drake's head on a platter. He killed Manny. He kidnapped Dro. He raped and murdered Warrick's sister. He stabbed me twice and left me for dead. All of us wanted to take him apart, piece by bloody piece. But only two of us had the rage and the stomach for it.

I reached across the table and touched Max's hand. I let him feel all the anger, sorrow, regret, and understanding I had in me. Max could see deeper into a person through his psychic gift, sensing emotions as much as the future. He looked at me with grief-stricken eyes.

"We'll get him, Max," I said. "I promise you that. But you won't be the one to kill him. Leave him to me and Warrick." He was ready to protest, but I wasn't done. "When you kill someone, you kill yourself too, Max. A part of you dies. You become a monster. Manny wouldn't want you to be that way. Neither does Dro."

Max exhaled, as if in pain.

I gave his hand a gentle squeeze. "Dro will never hold anything against me, but she loves you because you don't have a bad bone in your body. You would never hurt anyone. You make her feel human." I pulled my hand back. "Don't take that away from her."

Max had loved my sister from the first moment he'd seen her, and she loved him back. He was everything she wanted, and she was everything he needed. But like the rest of us, the desire for revenge was tearing him in half. He ran his hand through his curly black hair, keeping his eyes low. He fought back tears.

"I miss him, Constance," he said with a tremor in his voice. "I miss him so much."

Heartache dug into my chest. "So do I."

We sat there in mournful silence until the door opened. I lifted my eyes, hand slipping to my hip and brushing against my hatchet. It hadn't been closed all the way, making it easy for Warrick to hear our conversation before he walked in. One look in his remorseful green eyes told me he'd done just that.

Max turned in his chair, picking himself up and pretending he wasn't grieving for his murdered father.

"Man, how did you sneak in like that?"

Warrick grinned at him. "I'm a demon slayer. We have practical skills."

I pushed away from the table and stalked to the other end of the room to where my lucky jacket was. I reached inside for some of my throwing knives. Now that I was feeling bitter, I could train, and stop thinking about Manny.

"How's Dro?" Max asked.

"She's fine. Still working with Sephiel. But she might do better with you out there supporting her."

Max laughed. "That might be a bad idea. My devilish good looks are only going to distract her. But I could use some air."

I spun one of my knives in my hand and heard Max get up from his table. I turned and watched him leave the room. Max was gone, but Warrick was still there, like he was waiting me.

"Are you coming?"

"Where?" I asked.

"Outside. You look like you're getting cabin fever, too."

I kept spinning the knives in my hands. "I can break it by training."

Warrick smirked. "Well, it's better if you do it outside. Sephiel might want his security deposit back."

I suppressed a laugh, looking at Warrick and

weighing the options. My mind had been traveling down dark roads, and I needed to fight it out of my system. Spending time with a fiercely attractive demon slayer wasn't a bad idea, either. I grabbed my lucky jacket and threw it on.

"Fine. Let's go."

***

Warrick led me behind the motel, not very far from where Dro was training with Sephiel and Max. The psychic was sitting at a picnic table with my sister, the Seraphim warrior standing beside them. Dro didn't notice me, too focused on using her powers on Max with Sephiel's advice. Max's hands were gripping hers, Dro's eyes bright and focused. She looked calmer than I'd seen her in a while.

I watched her until Warrick walked me into a patch of forest and she was gone from my sight. I shrugged out of my jacket, and tossed it onto the dirt. I put all my weapons beside it. I looked up and saw Warrick standing in front of me. His brown leather jacket was on the ground and his hands were loose at his sides. It was hard not to admire the well sculpted biceps under the short sleeves of his grey T-shirt, or the way his shirt hugged the broad muscles of his shoulders and chest.

"What are you doing?" I asked, trying not to let my eyes drift too far down.

Wickedness gleamed in his bright green eyes. "Helping you train."

He darted for me before I was ready. I twisted at the last second, feeling his arm brush past my waist. My body snapped into action. I swung a roundhouse punch at him, but he ducked and got in close again. He brought up his elbow to catch me in the ribs, but I bent away, kicking for his knee. He stepped back and punched at my chest. I twisted, knocking his arm away. I snapped out my fist to jab him in the nose. Warrick grabbed my wrist and pulled me into him. I skidded to a stop and drove my knee into his stomach.

He buckled and moved back. I wondered if I'd hurt him, but he raised his head and showed me the sly grin playing across his lips.

"Spar rough, do you?" he said.

This time I smiled. "Nah. Just to win."

Warrick laughed, then rushed me again. This time he fought me at a distance. Fighting up close and dirty was my forte, but distance and mid-range was more of a challenge for me. Warrick caught onto this quick, sweeping wide kicks and roundhouse punches that I had to block.

One of his kicks nearly slammed into my head, but I blocked it with my arm. He grasped my wrist and took the chance to dart closer and drive me back into a tree trunk. I knocked against it, about to push him off, but he carefully pressed his forearm to my throat. His face was inches from mine, my chest bumping his when I exhaled. His eyes were piercing, matching the color of the leaves above my head.

"What was that about winning?"

I growled and pushed him back. Warrick chuckled and leaned away from my foot when I kicked at his head. I pressed harder, staying on the offense and making him eat his words. He wasn't looking so damn smug anymore. He swung a punch at my jaw, but I leaned back from him, catching his wrist when it was away from my neck.

I swept up an uppercut, but he caught my hand and stopped the strike. I shoved forward, hooking the back of his foot and toppling him off balance. He pulled me down with him. I landed on his chest and quickly pushed up before he could roll me.

Before he could move again, I lowered myself onto his chest and grabbed his wrist, pinning it next to his head. I felt his other hand move, but knocked it aside with my knee and trapped it against the forest floor. I pressed my free hand to his throat, letting him know I had won. I smiled proudly.

"Nice try, John," I said.

His face softened when I used his first name. His reaction sent a flush of warmth into me, relaxing my body and my mind. I felt his hard muscles underneath me. His heart was pounding just as quickly as mine. His pulse raced under my hand. I moved my knee off his wrist and told myself to stand up, but I didn't. I couldn't take my eyes off him, or get rid of the desire to kiss him again.

It happened once before, when he chose to be a distraction so Max and I could rescue Dro from the Gate ritual. Warrick was certain he was going to die, and wanted to go out with a good memory. Kissing me was what he'd wanted more than anything else at the time.

Ever since we'd survived the ritual and began running again, Warrick had been trying to get closer to me. I kept pushing him away because I didn't want either of us to be hurt. The opposite side of the coin was that I didn't want to be alone for the rest of my undoubtedly short life. Sephiel was a heartbroken angel who would never love again, and Dro had Max.

Warrick... Well, Warrick was everything I wanted. Strong, smart, quick, confident, a fearless fighter. When I wasn't constantly worrying over something, my thoughts drifted to him. Remembering how many times he saved my life and my sister's life. How tenderly he'd held me when Dro was taken. The way he refused to let me go after pulling me out of a cave-in.

The way he was looking at me now didn't escape me, either. That gentleness was back in his eyes, the steady desire that seemed to be there only when I was near him. Like me, he had seen and endured many horrible things. Like me, he wanted to find someone who would understand it all and help take the nightmares away.

That must have been why I was moving closer to him, letting my hand trace up his neck to his cheek. His heart beat faster against my chest. Or maybe that was mine. I couldn't tell, because I was too distracted by the tender way his hand combed through my hair to rest on the back of my neck.

All of that longing had to be the reason I kissed him.

This wasn't the last, desperate kiss we had shared when he used himself as bait and I thought I'd never see him again. This was complete awareness, complete desire. His lips were soft against mine, his musky pine scent making my emotions go haywire. He was passionate, but wasn't rough or aggressive. He didn't try to tear my clothes off then and there. Warrick just kept his lips on mine and held me close. He made me feel normal, and suddenly I wanted to tear down all the walls I had put around myself. I deepened the kiss, pushing my tongue into his mouth. Warrick breathed into me, his face so close to mine that I could feel his eyelashes on my cheek.

It had been a long time since I'd felt this alive. I wanted to open my heart up to him, give it to him unconditionally and have him accept all my good, bad, and ugly.

It was the kind of kiss that made me want to be in love again.

But the last man I loved nearly destroyed me, emotionally and physically. I didn't want to take the same chance with Warrick. If I let myself love him, he could hurt me worse than Mateo had. He was a fierce warrior, but gentle with people he cared about. Gentleness was something I was used to with Dro, but not with anyone else. The walls weren't ready to come down.

I pushed away from Warrick suddenly. I slid out of his arms, and tried not to think about the hurt I saw in his eyes.

I grabbed my hatchet and hooked it through my belt loop. I walked away from Warrick, going for my jacket.

"What the hell?" he said from behind me.

I heard him getting up, but didn't look back. I was leaving when he grabbed my arm. He wasn't rough, but I jerked away from his hand. He stared at me, waiting for an explanation I wasn't sure I could give.

"Mind telling me what that was all about?" he asked impatiently.

"It was nothing," I muttered.

"Didn't feel like nothing," he said with a touch of

bitterness.

I turned and started walking away again. He quickly got in front of me. I made sure to avoid his eyes.

"Move," I warned.

"No. Not until you talk to me."

"There isn't anything to talk about. We kissed. End of story."

I tried to move around him. He blocked me. I clenched my fists at my side. I wasn't going to hurt Warrick, but I wanted him out of my way. I wanted him to stop imagining that something would happen between us.

The thought hurt me more than I realized.

"What are you afraid of, Constance?" he asked.

Damn it, Warrick, stop caring. "I'm not afraid of anything," I shot. I breathed evenly to control my temper. "You aren't what I'm looking for."

I was a good liar. I'd made a career of it once. But my practice must have been slipping, because Warrick didn't believe me.

"Right," he scoffed. "You kissed me, Constance. Not the other way around. If this is about that Marshal reward bullshit, you might as well drop it. I'm not going to turn you in. Not now, not when this is through. You don't deserve it."

He really believed that, and it made me want to kiss him again. But I needed to push him away, not bring him closer.

"Yes I do. You have no idea the things I've done."

"So what? You think my hands are cleaner than yours?" He took a step closer to me, and I couldn't find the strength to back away from him.

"I've been around a lot of bad people, Constance. I know the worst from the worst. And that isn't you. Everything you did, everything you will do, is because you care."

"How do you know?" I snapped.

"Because if you didn't care, you wouldn't have Max along," he fired back. "You would have tried to use Sephiel. You never would have let me stay."

I wanted to tell him he was wrong. That he, Seph, and Max didn't matter to me. Except that I would be telling the biggest lie of my life. I needed to be cold, to harden myself so I wouldn't get distracted by thoughts of a future that would probably never happen. One where we all survived and got the things we wanted. It was better– easier– to focus on the problem directly ahead. I couldn't do that if I started going through a list of 'What-if's' and 'I hope's'. But I didn't want to be that way. Maybe that was the whole problem.

Maybe lying wasn't what I needed to do. Maybe it was time to tell the truth.

"I loved someone once," I said. "I thought he was everything I wanted. He was kind of like you. Tough, clever, loyal. At least until he turned on me."

My mind wandered, and suddenly I was back at the hacienda, doing everything I could to escape.

"It went to shit after that. He tortured me, I killed someone close to him, and he shot me."

I raised my head, steeling myself and looking into his neon green eyes. He was caught between horror and sympathy. I was halfway there. Time to nail the coffin.

"This ends here, Warrick. I'm not going to be broken again."

A stricken look crossed his face, but he pulled himself together and seemed undaunted. "I'm not your asshole ex, so stop thinking that I am. I would never hurt you."

There he went again, saying all the things I wanted to hear and making me ache for him all over again. He deserved way better than me. Warrick should have someone who wouldn't cause him any pain, but care about him just as much as I did. I swallowed and kept up my wall.

"You already are."

I might as well have punched him in the chest. He looked confused and crushed, not understanding what he was doing wrong. Except that the problem wasn't him. It was me.

Warrick tried to say something else, but I wasn't going to listen. I couldn't risk giving him a chance to talk me into another state of mind. It was better this way. He didn't stop me when I brushed past him this time. I walked as quickly as I could, never looking back, though I could feel his eyes on me.

I couldn't be in love again, and certainly not with someone as unselfish as Warrick. I wasn't a good person. I would drag him down. He would die because of me. He was only on this insane trip to get revenge on Drake. I had been good with the idea that he would leave as soon as Drake was dead.

Now my heart was sore, and I wasn't sure about anything.

When I pushed through the clearing, Dro was sitting alone at the picnic table. Sephiel was talking to Max a couple feet away, gesturing as though he was giving the psychic some training as well. I straddled the bench across from my sister, making sure my back was to the forest so I wouldn't need to look at Warrick when he came through the trees.

Dro turned her head and smiled at me, but quickly sensed my mood.

"Are you okay, Con?"

"Yeah. Fine."

She frowned, glancing at the forest. "What were you doing in there?"

I played with the edge of my lucky jacket. "Nothing."

Dro was still looking past me. "Uh huh. Does it involve the tall, handsome, green-eyed nothing walking out of the trees?"

I twisted my head on instinct, then stopped halfway. I couldn't give in to my heart's desires. Keeping Dro safe came first. It always had, and it always would. But sometimes I missed the things I would never have.

"You told him off?"

I glanced at my sister as Warrick walked past. He didn't look at me, thank God. "You read my mind?"

She grinned sheepishly. "Sephiel told me to practice. It was just a peek, Con. Honest. But seriously, why did you push him away?"

I put my elbow on the table and leaned my head into my hand, blowing out some air. "There are a lot of reasons."

She prodded into my mind again. She was my sister, so I let her. Dro's eyes narrowed. "He's not Mateo. He would never do that to you."

I dropped my hand and straightened my head. "Doesn't matter. He'll be safer away from me."

I wished I sounded a little more carefree, instead of sounding like I'd just destroyed my only chance for happiness.

Which is why Dro couldn't let it go. "That isn't true, big sister. You haven't seen what I've seen because you aren't looking. Do you have any idea how much he cares about you? How close he is to—"

I looked at my little sister desperately. "Don't, Dro. Please."

She read my eyes, dropping the accusation when she felt how much pain I was in. It was raw, it was my fault, and I didn't want to think about it.

"Tell me what you learned from Seph."

Dro frowned deeply, something not suited for her beautiful, saintly face. But she could tell I was finished with the subject of my trust issues and how I would rather isolate myself from a man who wanted me than to go after him. She sighed, but straightened her back.

"He showed me how to draw on heavenfire instead of hellfire. It's less dangerous, since it's mostly light. Obviously it would still hurt our enemies, but I would rather use it than hellfire." She frowned again. "It feels more like a force of good, I suppose."

But she didn't want to hurt anyone. Having been burned by heavenfire, I knew just how much pain it could cause.

"The mental powers are a little harder to control," she went on. "I have to really concentrate on blocking everything out except the person in front of me if I want to read them. I used to just get bits and pieces when I read others, you know? If I want to read full thoughts, I have to basically stare at a person and push apart their mind. It feels like poking Jell-O, which has turned me off of it forever."

We both stifled a laugh. Dro had loved Jell-O as a kid, constantly eating it even when it made her sick. Who'd have thought it was mind reading that would erase her desire for her favorite childhood treat?

"Sensing and seeing the future is a little harder to do. When I push too far forward, it feels like I'm trying to drive a finger through my brain. That's why Max decided to get more training from Sephiel with it. I guess he wants to feel more useful."

Dro glanced over her shoulder at her boyfriend. Softness crept over her face, making her look happy and alive. Max had no idea how much he was helping our group, or my sister.

"I think he's doing just fine," I said. It was true.

"He is," she agreed. Dro stared at Max for a moment longer, then turned back to me. "The only thing I didn't want to try was the mind control. I really don't feel comfortable controlling someone. That seems like the kind of thing Lucifer would do."

We both fell silent at the mention of his name, no doubt considering all the terrible things he could– and probably would– do if he ever found us.

"I don't think we should stay here much longer," Dro said. "I think something bad is coming."

"Any details you can share?"

"Not really, but it's like there's a darkness spreading over this place. Like a calm before a storm."

That was all I needed to hear. "We'll get out of here then. Tonight. Seph will have to work that little magic teleporting thing." *Which will be about as fun as shoving myself through a drainpipe.*

"There's something else," Dro hesitated. "It's about Lucifer."

Frigid fingers slid down my spine. "What about him?"

She pulled her knees tighter to his chest. "I can hear him when I'm awake now. His voice will just suddenly be in my head, telling me that the angels are going to kill us all. That he can get me into Heaven if I help him find the Gate."

I snorted. "What a fucking hypocrite."

Dro barely heard me. She bit her lip and looked away, fighting scared tears. "I can't shake the images he's putting in my head, Connie. He says they're going to keep getting worse, and that if I don't let him help me, it's going to get all of you killed. I feel like I'm losing my grip on reality, like one day I'm not going to be able to tell the dream from the truth, and I'm going to hurt one of you." She sighed and ran her hands through her hair. "Maybe I'm finally going crazy."

Dro was as tired of running as I was. I could hear it in her voice and see it in her eyes. She wanted the same things I did. To live a normal life, to be safe, and have a home. To be in love and know you weren't going to lose the person to a horrible fate.

"You're not going any crazier than the rest of us, little sister. I promise."

But the rest of us weren't a combination of human, demon, and angel. The rest of us didn't have angels whispering ill intentions into our heads, or demons creating volatile dreams to make us scream in the middle of the night. The rest of us weren't part of whatever the Devil had planned, or the chosen vessel for the general of the Heavenly Host. That was more than enough to make anyone insane, even before all the wild superpowers were dumped on. It was a miracle Dro was holding herself together.

The same might not be said for me. I would never let anyone hurt my little sister again, but fighting demons and angels while pushing away all human contact was wearing me down. Dro might not go crazy, but my own mental state was up in the air.

I shuffled closer to her. "I'll keep you anchored to the real world, Dro. I won't let you drift away. We'll stop Lucifer."

Dro flinched and shook her head, able to tell where my thought process was going. "You can't do that, Constance. He's too strong. You can't fight him."

Her comment didn't offend me. I'd witnessed a decimal of Lucifer's power. I knew I wasn't stronger than him. I was human. He could snap me like a toothpick. But toothpick or not, I refused to let him take Dro away. I would find a way to make him pay for torturing and nearly killing her.

"You're right. I can't. But *we* can. No one's invincible. There's got to be a way to either stop Lucifer's plans or to lock him up in Hell again. We'll find it, and we'll do it. Together."

That put Dro at ease. She visibly relaxed, even managing a weak smile for my sake. For a minute, she could pretend all her problems were simplified.

"Together."

She was quiet for a moment, then pinched her eyebrows together.

"Dro? What's wrong?"

"There are Possessors at the motel."

She pushed off the bench and walked toward the side of the motel. I quickly followed her. Sephiel, Max, and Warrick saw us moving and hurried after us. Dro pressed herself against the side of the motel wall and looked around the corner. I was taller, and looked over her shoulder.

A cop car was in the middle of the parking lot. Two fully uniformed cops were talking to the motel owner. I stiffened, certain they were here about me. I had been careful to keep my hood up when we got to the motel, and Sephiel made sure to register us under a fake name. I doubted the motel owner had recognized my face, and we didn't see any other renters. That left one option...one I hated to consider.

"The policemen are possessed," Dro said,

confirming my fear. "They must have followed me."

I shuddered and looked at her. My sister's eyes shimmered with power. She wanted to charge and stop the Possessors before they hurt the motel owner. It was something she wouldn't have a problem doing.

"We must not act rashly," Sephiel whispered, noticing how tense my sister was. "Remember that all Possessors are connected to Lucifer. An attack on one of them could bring him upon us."

He barely finished talking before one of the Possessors grabbed the motel owner by the throat and lifted him a foot off the ground. Dro surged forward, but I grabbed her arm and stopped her. She turned and fixed me with a frosty stare. I almost flinched. Dro never looked this angry.

"Sephiel's right, Dro," I told her cautiously. "We can't give Lucifer a chance to find you."

"So we're just going to let an innocent man die? I can stop them. You know that."

"Maybe they won't kill him," Max tried. "Maybe they just... oh."

We looked into the parking lot again. The motel owner was lying on the pavement, his neck bent at a sickening ninety degree angle. He wasn't going to move again. Dro was nearly shaking with rage. I kept my eye on her as she watched the two Possessors get back into the police car and drive away. It was a long time before she spoke again.

"I could have stopped them," she said. "I could have saved that man's life." She spun and focused her rage on us. "Why did you hold me back?"

Her eyes blazed with blue fury. Sephiel was speechless. Warrick was wary. Even Max didn't know what to do. I was the only one calm and confident enough to take a step closer to my sister.

"Because he was going to die no matter what we did. If the Possessors didn't kill him, Lucifer would have shown up and done it instead. We're not ready to fight him, Dro. I'm sorry, but we're not, and there's no way I'm going to let you do it alone."

Her hands balled into fists at her side. I kept still. I didn't know what she was going to do or what was pushing her into this sudden anger, but I would never raise a hand to my sister.

Dro blinked, and the anger began to fade. Her eyes flicked between us, and she knew how aggressive she was being. She shrank back.

"I'm sorry," she whispered. "I didn't mean to..."

I put my hand on her shoulder. "Don't apologize. You didn't do anything wrong."

"Yeah, pretty girl," Max consoled with a grin. Any unease he felt about his girlfriend was abruptly gone. "You were getting mad for the right reasons. Constance just gets mad at everything."

I looked at Max. "You do realize I'm standing right beside you and fully armed, right?"

He smirked at me. "Come on, you know you like me to much to stab me."

I raised my eyebrows. "That so?"

"Yup. Now, if you don't mind..."

Max put his hand on the back of Dro's neck and kissed her. Just like that, no fear, no hesitation, nothing to make her worry that he would be afraid of her. My sister melted into his arms, pulling him closer and letting her anxiety slip away. It was sweet, and almost made me think that things would work out the way they were supposed to.

Then I turned around and saw the tender sadness in Sephiel's eyes before he looked at the ground. Warrick quickly averted his gaze and started to walk away. I frowned. We were all happy for Dro and Max, and I hoped that fate wouldn't rip them apart.

But the rest of us knew what reality was like, and that heartbreak always came when you least expected it to.

Chapter 6

We ditched the motel before the real, human cops showed up to investigate the owner's death and walked deeper into Bullhead City to look for a car. We didn't have a destination yet, but we decided to keep traveling north. The southern half of the country was going crazy. We heard that most of Texas was under quarantine from flesh-eating demons that sounded a lot like ghouls. People scrambled around us, taking as much as they could carry and stuffing it into their cars. It wasn't long before the roads were clogged with people trying to escape.

Sephiel walked at the front of our group, watching the roads and examining every vehicle he set his sights on. Wherever we intended to go, it would be faster to drive. Teleporting all of us at once used a lot of energy from the *movens caeli*, and we needed to reserve it in case out next fight went downhill.

Warrick and Max followed behind him, chatting easily. I had to beg Dro to keep me company instead of being with Max. I felt guilty because he relaxed her so much, but I wasn't ready to be close to Warrick again. So I let her pout and resigned to pay for it later.

It wasn't easy to take him off my mind, though. I wished I had it in me to apologize, but every time I got the courage, Warrick's face turned into Mateo's. My ex-boyfriend had been the definition of tough love...

"I'd get up if I were you."

I pushed myself off the mat, glaring at my trainer. Mateo stood above me, his black hair tied into a short ponytail at the nape of his neck. He was dressed in a black tank top and black sweatpants. His muscles glistened with sweat, his broad shoulders rising and falling as he breathed heavily. There was a grin on his face and trouble flashing in his eyes.

He looked smoking hot.

I ignored the naughty thoughts making their way into my head, and got onto my hands and knees. Mateo didn't even wait until I was standing before he attacked me again.

He kicked for my face. I raised my arms and blocked him, shooting out my foot to trip him. He backed away and I rose to my feet. He jumped and kicked at my chin. I batted his foot away and kicked at his ribs. He blocked me with his elbow and shoved his palm toward my sternum.

I grabbed his wrist and turned out of range. He tried to pull his arm back, but I had a good grip on it. I twisted his wrist until his arm was under my control. I made him turn his back to me, and he jabbed me in the stomach with his other elbow. My grip on his wrist slipped, and he spun around. His elbow slammed into the side of my head.

I stumbled to the side, watching the training room spin. I blinked to clear my vision, seeing a horrified look on Mateo's face. It was gone as soon as I raised my fists again. I was sick of him kicking my ass. Mateo charged me and aimed a kick at my head. I blocked it with my arm. He used his other hand to try and punch my stomach. I brought my knee up and knocked his foot away. I kicked his inside knee and drove my fist into his chest. He stumbled back as I grabbed his arm and held his wrist again. I stepped back so he couldn't reach me, then kicked his other foot out from under him.

As soon as Mateo was down, I put my foot on his chest. It had taken an hour and countless bruises, but I finally won. I was sore, exhausted, and damn proud.

"All right, all right, this is your round, don't break my arm," he said.

I grinned. "Why not? You were smacking me around."

"Not on purpose. You know that."

He gave me puppy dog eyes, and I knew I couldn't stay mad at him. Pain was just part of training. Better I feel it now and prepare for it later. After all, he was right.

Mateo hadn't done it on purpose. He was my friend. He would never hurt me.

"I guess I can cut you some slack," I teased, releasing his arm and stepping back.

Mateo let out the breath he'd been holding as he rolled to his feet. I couldn't stop myself from admiring his body again. We'd been training for almost three months now. He was coming up on his nineteenth birthday, and every day he looked stronger and much more handsome.

It was even better when he glanced at me, his dark eyes holding all kinds of mystery and promise. More than once, I'd fantasized about being pulled into those muscular arms and feeling his warm lips touch mine.

But as soon as I had those thoughts, I pushed them away. Mateo was Emilio's only son, the heir to the Blood Thorns. He was one of the leaders of The Watch. Getting involved with him was a whole new definition of bad.

Then again, maybe that was why I wanted him so much.

"Did you hear what I said?"

I snapped out of my trance. "Yeah, of course."

He grinned and walked closer to me. "I don't think you did."

I crossed my arms, hoping he wouldn't see my heart getting ready to jump out of my chest and into his hands. Was this how all sixteen year old girls acted when they had crushes?

"Care to repeat it?"

Mateo's smile turned sympathetic. "I said I'm sorry I hit you. I tried to control myself, but you know how it is in a fight. Sometimes you get so caught up in it, and..." His shoulders slouched. "I'm really, really sorry."

I shrugged. "It's okay. We were training."

"No, Constance, it's not okay. Doesn't matter if we were training. You have to let me make it up to you."

I tilted my head. "How?"

His warm, dark eyes matched his mischievous smile. My stomach fluttered in response.

"Let me take you out for dinner."

I blinked stupidly. "Dinner? Seriously? Why?"

Now he was the one who was confused. "What do you mean why? You're the toughest girl I've ever met, you don't take shit from anyone," he was inches away from me now, "and you're absolutely stunning."

I nearly laughed, since I was bruised, soaked in sweat, and my hair was a mess. I was far from attractive. But that didn't stop Mateo from putting his hand on my waist and pulling me closer. He kissed my temple where I'd been hit. His lips stayed there longer than necessary to work magic on me. I wasn't even aware of the throbbing pain. All I felt was his hard, sweat-slicked body close to mine. His hot, musky scent drifted over my like a fog.

Mateo took his lips away from my head and cupped my chin. My body responded with a racing heart and a heat that stretched from the top of my hair to the tips of my toes.

That should have worried me. I knew a little bit about hormones from school, but was this just my body responding to him? Was I supposed to be this out of breath, or was I still tired from sparring? I'd never had a boyfriend before. I tended to beat up anyone who touched me without permission. But this felt different. I wanted Mateo to keep touching me. It felt good. Gentle. It was almost too much to handle, but I didn't ask him to stop. I couldn't speak. I wanted to know what he would do next.

His thumb stroked the bottom of my lip, teasing me in the worst way I could imagine. I was completely under his spell, and I didn't care at all.

"This is a bad idea," I whispered. "Your dad would kill me."

Mateo grinned. "No, he wouldn't. He likes you."

I winced. He backed up a little, scanning my eyes. "What's wrong?"

"Nothing," I said too quickly. "It's... I just don't want to piss him off. You know how he gets when he's mad. All murderous, and stuff."

Mateo frowned. For a second I thought he was upset. Then he took my face in both his hands. The warmth of his skin sank into my face and made me a little dizzy.

"I won't let anyone hurt you, Constance. Not even him. I promise."

My heart skipped. Of all the Blood Thorns, Mateo was the most loyal to his father. He never questioned orders, never gave more than a few second thoughts. To him, Emilio's word was law. Anyone who crossed it ended up dead or worse. I walked on a high wire when it came to Emilio, but Mateo was willing to follow me across it. Knowing how deeply he cared put a flutter in my stomach and a sweet ache in my chest. Mateo dipped his head lower, bringing his lips closer to mine–

"Mr. Rocha, sir!"

"God fucking damn it," he cursed, backing up. He glared at the guard who had just run into the training room. "I'm kind of busy right now," he snarled.

"Sir, I'm sorry, but, there's a problem in the kitchen, and your father isn't here–"

I pushed past Mateo and rushed the guard. "What problem?" I demanded.

The guard glanced from me to Mateo, then back to me again. "There's been a fire in the kitchen–"

That was all he managed to say before I shoved him aside and ran up the basement steps. Once I hit the top floor, I followed the smoke that was billowing out of the swinging double doors at the far right of the hacienda. The smell of burned food and smoke funneled out toward me. I shouldered my way through the doors. The kitchen staff was running around with fire extinguishers, dousing the flames coming from the stove. Windows had been opened to let out of some of the smoke, but the blaze was huge, and three men were needed to put it out. One woman stood off to the side with her friend, clutching her blackened hand to her chest and screaming bloody murder.

I ignored all the shouts and curses, looking for my sister. I found her sitting in the far corner by some shelves. She huddled her knees to her chest, tears streaking down her face. I ran down to her side and put *my hands on her shoulders.*

"Dro, what happened? Are you okay?"

She choked on a sob and threw her arms around me. I hugged her tightly.

"It was me," she whispered. "Valentina was being mean to Lucy and I told her to stop, then she got angry and started calling me names, and she was standing by the pot and I just got so mad that I grabbed her hand..."

Dro crushed me closer to her. "I didn't mean to do it, Connie, I don't know what came over me, I didn't know I was gonna hurt her–"

"Shh, hey, it's all right, little sister."

"What the hell happened?" Mateo's voice from behind me.

I looked over my shoulder at him. He was standing next to Valentina, the woman whose fingers were burned. By now, the fire was put out, but half of the stove was melted.

"That little witch burned me!" Valentina screamed, pointing at Dro with her good hand. "She touched me and set my hand on fire! She's the Devil's child! Putita del Diablo!*"*

Mateo slapped her across the face. The entire room fell silent. He looked at Valentina with so much fury I almost cringed.

"Don't accuse a little girl for an accident, Valentina. Not when I know how careless you are in here."

"But, but Mr. Rocha–"

"Did anyone else see Andromeda burn Valentina?" he asked the staff.

The cooks looked away, too scared to meet Mateo's eyes. No one spoke up to defend her, not even the friend standing at her side. He turned his eyes back on Valentina.

"That's what I thought," he snarled. "Don't even try to justify yourself. Andromeda and her sister are family. Be grateful I'm not going to tell my father about this."

Valentina shuddered and looked away. Mateo turned and addressed the rest of the nervous kitchen staff.

"Someone get Valentina to the hospital right now. Tell them I sent her, and give her the best care. The rest of you, clean this up. I'll order another stove and have it replaced before my father comes back from his business trip."

The kitchen staff hurried to get to work. Mateo watched them all to make sure no one was wasting time, then turned his attention to me and my sister.

"Is she gonna be okay?"

"Yeah," I said, smoothing Dro's hair. "She's just rattled. That's all."

Mateo smiled kindly. "Well, if you need anything, I'll be in my dad's office."

I smiled at him and watched him walk away after Valentina left. I thought about everything I had just seen him do. Mateo was dangerous. There was no question about that. But the more I thought about how he'd handled this situation and how gentle he'd been in the training room, the more I reasoned that he would make good on his promise. He would stand up for us against anyone. He would keep us safe...

I'd been so lost in my memories I didn't know Sephiel stopped walking until I nearly collided with him. He was looking up, watching dusk begin to fall. Dark clouds spiraled up from the far side of the city. Dark clouds I quickly recognized as plumes of smoke. Dro fell silent beside me.

"Sephiel?" Warrick asked. "Are you all right?"

"Someone is burning a house of God."

There was a strange lack of emotion in his voice that put me on edge. A fire was a fire, and I wasn't really surprised that Sephiel would know where a piece of holy ground was. But he continued staring at the smoke, and was so stiff he could have started a career as a lamppost.

"All right," I said, hoping we could move on, "so we're not going that way."

Blaring sirens zipped past me. I quickly turned my back to the road, in case some of the sirens belonged to cop cars. Being arrested was really going to hinder my ability to fight in a supernatural war.

"Come on, we need to get out of here before more cops drive by."

I started to move to the head of the group, trying to remember old streets and shortcuts to get out of the city. Everyone but Sephiel followed me. I glanced back. He was still watching the smoke.

"I can feel the consecration in the ground being stripped away," the angel went on, "This is the work of demons."

"Seph, we need to leave."

The auburn-haired angel stayed where he was. I walked over to him, clutching his arm. Sephiel's bright blue eyes shifted over to my dark brown ones. For the first time, I could see the age in them. I didn't know how old Sephiel really was, but he always managed to look human. He was one of the few Seraphim who respected mortals. If it weren't for his vanishing acts and his spells, I would think he was just a very strange man with a white leather fetish.

I wasn't seeing the humanized Sephiel right now. I was seeing Sephiel the angel, a guardian and warrior for Heaven. A stoic, immoveable, and fierce soldier. That was when I got an idea of what he wanted.

"You can't do anything there, Sephiel. It's too late."

His eyes narrowed, the muscles in his jaw clenching tightly. "They are violating a house of God. A place where lost souls find salvation. They have destroyed a place of hope."

Sephiel sounded as angry as he did sad. He was the only angel I knew who wanted to save humanity, not barrel over them to restructure Hell. I wasn't sure what he loved so much about humans. His ex-partner, Rorikel, hated us and sometimes it was hard for me to remember what made us so special. But then I looked over my shoulder at Dro, Warrick, and Max, and understood what he was trying to save. I looked at Sephiel again.

"No," I told him. "They destroyed some blessed earth and a building. Real hope only gets destroyed if you let it."

I wasn't known for my words of wisdom to anyone but Dro, and on the rare occasion, Max. I was a walking cynic. I didn't completely trust Sephiel, didn't fully understand his motives, but I needed him on my side. I wasn't strong enough to fight both Heaven and Hell alone. Besides, I liked him. He was a good fighter and he would help me protect my sister. He was also the only angel I knew who would actually have a conversation with me and not bring in a superiority complex.

When I felt Sephiel prod into my brain, I didn't immediately shut him out. I let him see that I believed what I said before I pushed him away. He relaxed, the soft, almost human look coming back into his bright blue eyes. This time, the look held respect.

"You are equitable in this, Constance. I am sorry for my outburst."

I shrugged. "We've all had one. It was just your turn."

Sephiel smirked and took the lead again. Dro offered him a kind smile as he passed, no doubt hearing what I'd said. She turned the smile to me and took Max's hand before following the angel. Which left me with Warrick and his gorgeous, piercing stare. He read my eyes like he was trying to see beyond them, maybe hunting for the soul beneath. I don't know what he was looking for, but after a while he seemed to be satisfied with whatever he found. He gave me a small smile, then started after the rest of the group. He didn't wait for me, but at least he wasn't avoiding me anymore.

I sighed, and wondered when I became so damn compassionate.

***

It was a good thing I had my conversation with

Sephiel when I did, because when we arrived downtown, there was a riot.

All of the shops and cafes were burning, and half the cars were on fire. Broken glass littered the streets. People were screaming and running from the chaos. Kids in dark hoodies were throwing bricks through windows and stealing from buildings that weren't on fire. Police locked themselves in their cars and shouted for backup. Street preachers and lost believers waved cardboard signs saying the end was nigh.

We hadn't meant to go this way. We were pushing for the edge of the city until Max used his gifts to tell us the military was arriving to establish quarantine. Roadblocks were set up on all the major roads out of the city. Nothing could get in or out.

We darted into an alley. Sephiel and Warrick stood at the mouth of it, watching the quickly emptying street. Warrick drew his sawed-off shotgun from the lining of his jacket. I got my hatchet out from my hip. Sephiel hadn't drawn his sword from thin air yet, but he was probably itching for it.

"Tell me again why we aren't using that damn teleporting thing?" I asked angrily.

"The *movens caeli* is what humans may refer to as a battery," Sephiel explained without looking away from the alley. "Its power can be drained, no matter how it is used. Until then, I can only transport two people at once, and each extra person can wear on my abilities."

"I seriously doubt we have time for that, Sephiel," Warrick said. Another burst of flame lit up the street, making him cringe and settle back into the shadows.

"Guys," Max said with some impatience, "I just got a flash. The army is closing in. We kinda need a decision, here."

I glanced from my sister to Max, weighing the options. We couldn't go forward, and we couldn't go back. There wasn't really a good decision. Sharp green eyes and smooth blue eyes fixed on me when I spoke. "Seph, take Dro and Max and get them to safety. Then come back for us."

"No," Dro countered immediately, giving me a hard look. "Take Max and Warrick, then come back for Constance and me. We'll be okay here, you just need to–"

She suddenly gasped, doubling over and pressing her hand to her chest. I kept her from falling by holding her shoulders and waiting for her to breathe normally. Max stood beside her, putting a hand on her back and looking nervous. Sephiel watched anxiously, leaving Warrick to focus on guarding the alley entrance.

"Dro? Talk to me, what's wrong?"

Her breath was shaky, and when her eyes finally did meet mine, they were filled with sheer terror.

"Night... wretches," she shuddered. "They have wretches with the night!"

I had no idea what the hell she was talking about. My sister might not be human, but she wasn't crazy. She was trying to explain something to me, but she was afraid of it. Max didn't seem to know what she was talking about either. He closed his eyes the way he often did when he was trying to use his psychic gift. I looked at Sephiel. He had gone completely rigid, and seemed paler than before.

He knew what she was talking about. And it terrified him.

Beside him, Warrick looked just as uneasy. He walked over to us. Warrick gently put his hand on my sister's shoulder.

"Dro, are you absolutely sure that's what you sensed?"

She straightened and looked at him with the same scared expression. She held her breath and nodded quickly. He dropped his hand and stepped back.

"*Fuck,*" he breathed.

"Can someone give me a fucking clue here?" I demanded.

Warrick was moving to the front of the alley, looking more serious than I had ever seen him. Sephiel was still frozen in a panic-stricken state that worried me. Finally, he answered my question.

"She is not indicating it as you may assume, as in 'the dark of night.' She indicates the word *knight,* as in a demon Knight." His eyes were grim. "They are the most elite of Lucifer's soldiers. The assassins for Hell."

I didn't need any further explanation. I knew earth-shattering bad news when I heard it.

"Do not engage the Knight," Sephiel continued. "It is too strong."

He reached behind his back. I saw a subtle gold glow from his hand, which quickly elongated into the gold hilt of a sword. Sephiel drew the long broadsword over his shoulder, looking stern and formidable.

"Focus on the Wretches," he instructed. "You may survive their attacks longer."

He disappeared before I asked him what the fuck that meant and where the fuck he was going. I was going to kick his ass twice for that. I looked at Warrick again.

"What the fuck are Wretches?"

"Angels that were captured by demons and taken into Hell," he said, glancing out of the alley again. "They were tortured into madness and became rabid pets for Royalty." He hesitated, then added, "Kind of like hellhounds."

I didn't need further explanation there, either. I'd faced a hellhound once before, and was almost torn to pieces by it. If Wretches were even a little bit like hellhounds, we were about to be well and truly *fucked.*

"We have to get to the edge of the city," I said. "Fuck the quarantine."

"What about Sephiel?" Max asked as I left Dro in his arms.

I tried not to look too angry and or too nervous. "You tell me where he went, we'll go find him. But he took off, Max. We have no idea what he's going to do."

He gave me an unhappy look. I was just as upset, but I didn't have time to baby him.

"There's nothing we can do for Seph right now, but he wouldn't have left so quickly without a reason. We won't leave him behind, all right?"

That seemed to satisfy him, though not very much.

"If we're going, we have to go now," Warrick said, glancing out of the alley. "There are people walking with the Wretches."

"More Possessors," my sister whispered.

Which meant they would be much harder to fight. Since Max was able to console my sister by himself, I walked toward Warrick to get a better look at what we were dealing with.

"Ever fought one a Wretch before?" I asked as I made my way to his back.

"No," he replied, not budging an inch. "But I've heard of them. I prayed to God that I would never see or have to fight one."

I stood by his side and peered out of the alley in the direction he was looking. Beyond the heat waves seeping off burning cars, past the few people running for their lives, I saw the Possessors moving through the street with the Wretches.

They were about fifty feet away so most of the details were fuzzy, but the possessed humans looked normal. Construction workers, mechanics, and businessmen, judging by the neon vests, coveralls and suits they wore. The only way to tell they were possessed was by getting in their face and seeing the pitch-blackness of their eyes. Usually that was the same time they decided to beat you to death.

There were about six of them, and they were all gripping leashes they could barely control even with supernatural strength.

For a moment I thought the two things they were holding were pasty hellhounds. Then I saw the broken bones sticking up and out of their backs. They had a hunched, shambling gait, moving like crippled spiders. Long hair hung in strips from their heads. They were impossibly pale. But then again, I doubted they ever saw the sun in Hell.

Every time something raced past their line of sight, even if that something was a billowing plastic bag, the tortured angels would thrash and scream, tugging at the leashes around their throat. Their screams were raspy, as though they had been screaming all their life. My heart ached at the sound and sight of them. They truly did look wretched.

A hand landed on my shoulder. I nearly jumped, twisting my head to look at Warrick. He shook his head sadly.

"Don't think of them as angels, Constance. They're monsters now. There's no way to save them."

But he sounded like he wanted to. If there were a way, he would have. I listened to the Wretches' tortured howls one more time, then turned and walked back into the alley. Max had his arms wrapped around Dro, whispering something I couldn't hear. I glanced at her as I jogged past them, knowing they were going to be right behind me.

I retraced my steps, away from the worst of the chaos. I stopped at the end of the alley and looked around it, unable to see anything. I started forward, making for the alley across the street. I skidded to a stop when a car nearly ran me over.

It was a minivan racing for downtown, apparently not knowing the madness was worse down there. I checked to make sure no more cars were looking to mow me down, then ran across the street.

The screech and crunch of metal stopped me in my tracks. I heard broken glass and a human scream. I looked down the street, seeing the minivan had been in an accident. But not with another car.

The Wretches had been set loose. One of them jumped on the roof of the van and was pounding its fists down onto it. The other Wretch climbed onto the hood and was punching at the windshield. Inside, I spotted a family shielding whoever was in the backseat. I couldn't see them but if I had to guess, I would say that it was kids.

Warrick and Dro moved past me before I could stop them. They were the only people in our group who would always put their lives on the line for strangers. Max was quick to chase after them. Even if I could tell them that it was a dangerous idea, that we didn't have time, that the family was going to die regardless, and that the Possessors weren't far behind, it wouldn't matter. They wouldn't have listened to me.

Then I heard a little girl scream, and I knew I wasn't going to run either.

I dashed ahead of Max, making my way toward Dro. Warrick turned his head, and saw the Possessors coming closer. They spotted us, and were starting to run in our direction. Not good.

Warrick tucked his sawed-off shotgun into his jacket and drew one of his handguns, which were better for distance shooting. He took cover by a car that wasn't burning, keeping watch over Dro. My sister came to a stop, raising her hands and throwing out a blast of hellfire. The burst consumed the Wretch on the hood of the minivan, the blaze so hot that it was melting the fiberglass. The insane angel screeched and fell off the van, writhing in pain. She controlled the blast as much as she could, but it was taking a lot of focus.

She didn't see the second Wretch crouching on the top of the van, ready to pounce on her.

But I did.

It was already leaping for her when my hatchet left my hand, spiraling through the air and slamming into the Wretch's neck. Dro released her hellfire and stepped back, letting me bolt past her. The Wretch scrambled into a crouch, and I finally saw just how horrible it really was.

Its bare skin glistened with perspiration and was so thin that I could see the blue veins underneath, once I looked past all the stab and whip scars. The angel was naked, but it had nothing to prove what sex it was. Just ugly scars where the parts were supposed to be. Its hair was all but gone, nothing more than a strand or two on the sides of its head. Cracked, yellow nails poked out of skeletal fingers. Its teeth were blackened and decaying from not being looked after. The two bones that came out of the back of its shoulders were snapped and cracked. If it had wings once, they had been torn off. But the worst part was the crazed angel's eyes.

The whites had turned a sickly yellow, the irises bleached and the pupils half purple, like they were filled with blood. They were consumed with a madness I couldn't comprehend and didn't want to face. They were inhuman, feral, blind to the world around them. It was like someone had taken out their brains and replaced them with a rabid pit bull's.

Those insane eyes fixed on me. I barely held back my shudder. The creature was oblivious to the hatchet embedded in its neck, even as dark blood dribbled down its chest. I barely had time to draw a throwing knife before the Wretch moved with alarming speed and tackled me onto the ground.

My back crashed into the pavement, the leather hilt of my weapon pressing against my chest. The Wretch screamed with tortured madness as it grabbed my hair and dashed my head on the road. Pain filled my skull, everything blurring in front of my eyes. I stabbed up with my knife, catching the Wretch in the throat. It stopped trying to crack my head open, giving me a chance to pull out my hatchet and knife. I twisted my hips and threw the monster off me.

The weight was gone, but I could hardly see straight. I twisted and rolled to my feet, swaying under the wave of dizziness in my skull. I jumped when I heard the crack of gunfire, whirling to see Warrick shooting at the Possessors who had caught up with us.

All of them drew out handguns from their belts or jackets. They started firing at Warrick, who flinched and was forced to return the fire. There was no such thing as a quick exorcism, and with so many Possessors around him, Warrick had no choice but to shoot back. He shot one of the Possessors in the kneecap and winged another. The other four scattered for cover behind cars while Warrick chased them with bullets. The Possessors who had their vessels crippled were forced to leave, spiraling out of the human's mouths and rocket into the night. The humans suddenly began to scream and clutch their excruciating injuries.

As Warrick was reloading, Dro stepped up. She pushed out her hands, but used a blast of gold heavenfire at the four Possessors that were still shooting. Her magic hit two of them in the chest, sending them tumbling down the road like they'd been tossed out of a moving car. I didn't know if they were alive or dead, but they sure as hell didn't get back up. The last two Possessors were staring at Dro with hesitance, and before they could decide what to do, Warrick twisted around the car and shot at them.

On the other side of me, Max was helping the shrieking family out of the minivan. They looked scratched and traumatized, which must have been hell on the emotional level of his gifts, but he gritted his teeth and got them out. I jerked back into reality when I noticed quick movement out of the corner of my eye.

I jumped aside as the furious Wretch threw itself at me, its fist slapping across my ribs. I grunted at the bruising pain, but was grateful the creature didn't have claws. I spun on my heel and kicked the Wretch in the face, knocking it away from me.

I got into a fighting stance as the Wretch got up. Max sent the family across the street to relative safety. Dro was sending out blasts of gold heavenfire to the remaining Possessors, keeping their shots away from Warrick. I could hear shouts and gunfire coming from his direction. It was only seconds before the Wretch screamed and raced toward me, ready to get its revenge.

A blast of blinding white flame roared in our direction, hitting the back of the Wretch, so bright it nearly blinded me. I moved so my back was to the van, and listened to the shrieking Wretch. The hoarse cries were lost in the angry hellfire. I couldn't see an inch of the tortured angel in the hunched, flaming shape. I looked over my shoulder.

Dro was holding her hand out to the Wretch, her eyes grim and determined as she controlled the demonic flame. It circled her arm almost to the elbow. Stars seemed to dance in her icy blue eyes as the Wretch burned to a crisp.

It was so brief I almost missed it, but I swore there was a gleam of satisfaction in my little sister's eyes. As if she knew the Wretch was beneath her, and that it would be an easy kill. The flicker stopped suddenly, and the fire left Dro's hand. The hellfire began to die down, leaving the Wretch as nothing but a heap of smoldering ash. Dro made her way toward me, then looked at something down the stretch of road. She came to a stop and stared with horrified eyes.

I turned my head to see what was scaring her, and saw my nightmares.

They walked down the street like they owned it. I wasn't sure they didn't.

The man on the left was built like a linebacker that drank steroids for every meal. He was at least six foot three, his entire body made up of bulky muscle. He still wore his black duster and dark pants, but they did little to hide all the guns and knives he carried. Dark stubble was on the top of his head and his chin. His eyes were pits of black.

The man on the right was younger, but I recognized him all the same. He was still handsome, though his hair was shorter, stubble was growing around his mouth, and his eyes were much colder. They didn't hold the same passion I once adored. Now they only looked furious and dangerous. He looked bigger than the last time I'd seen him, his muscles straining his black tactical uniform. His gloved hand was wrapped around a machete.

My knees almost buckled when I saw the man in the middle, out of fear as much as lust. He was the most stunning creature I had ever seen. Even more beautiful than Dro. He was seven feet tall, with pale, flawless skin that looked almost marbled. His broad, muscular body was hidden under a perfectly smooth white suit that hid his four bat-like wings. Glorious white hair streamed down his back He was wearing so much white that he was like a beacon of light. *Like the true Morning Star.* The only darkness about him was his eyes. Solid black from lid to lid, shining like obsidian.

Drake Talbot, the man who had stabbed me twice, tormented my friends, and killed my mentor. Mateo Rocha, my ex-lover who betrayed me and shot me when I left him.

Lucifer, the King of Hell. The being that wanted to take over Heaven, who ripped my little sister's rib from her body for a ritual, and would do anything to have her back.

The monster who was Dro's father.

Chapter 7

Terror made my heart expand and contract so sharply I swore I was having a heart attack.

This can't be real, I told myself. *This has to be a nightmare. This isn't happening.*

Lying to myself was no use. They were here, and they weren't going to leave until Lucifer took Dro and the rest of us were dead at his feet. There was no point in running. I wasn't even sure I could move yet.

A loud snap made me jump. I looked to see Warrick standing beside me, the sawed-off shotgun in his hands and a furious look in his bright green eyes. He must have taken care of the rest of the Possessors before coming over here. He didn't even see Mateo or Lucifer. All he could focus on was Drake. The big bounty hunter smiled at his enemy.

"Still kickin', Johnny-boy? That's good. I would've been pissed if someone offed you before I did."

Drake's cruel voice pulled me into reality. I put myself in front of Dro so it would be harder for Lucifer to see her. The King of Hell looked right through me. A shudder wracked my body. He wasn't even trying to push power onto me. I was human, and I could still feel it twisting around me like smoke.

I was frightened that he would annihilate me. But I also wanted him to. There would be a strange, sick satisfaction in being destroyed by something as powerful as Lucifer.

Stop it, Con. Don't let him get to you.

The three of them stopped walking about ten feet away from us. The next couple moments felt like hours, each side waiting for the other to make its move, and sizing each other up until it happened. Every second that ticked by made me even more nervous. What were they waiting for? Something about this wasn't right.

Seph, get back here, we could really use that teleporting thing right now.

I turned my head to Mateo. It was impossible to remember why I loved him in the first place. He looked icy and furious, and I knew that there wasn't any good in him. Not where it mattered. Not anymore.

"So you made good on your promise, huh?" I said with a heavy amount of disdain. At least it made my voice sound steady. "Went to work for Satan after all?"

Mateo didn't blink. He just stared at me with a frozen hatred that would never thaw. I looked at Drake next, carefully keeping my eyes away from Lucifer, though I could feel his tempting and terrifying power rushing through me like a wave. I gripped my hatchet so tight it hurt.

"You too?" I asked Drake. "Thought you might move down in the world?"

Manny's killer grinned at me. It was the same smile he'd given me before he slid his knife into my ribs.

"Working for the Devil pays better." He lowered his chin, his eyes looking almost as black as his master's. "And it's a lot more fun."

"Persuasion was not a necessary tactic," Lucifer said. His voice was beautiful, deep, and seductive. Nothing in the universe sounded as exquisite as the Devil. "Drake Talbot was all too eager to join us. But Mateo Rocha did not need to be asked. You caused him deep grief when you killed his father. When I told him you were still alive, he immediately gave himself over to me. All he had to do was wait for my return."

I knew Lucifer's obsidian eyes were on me as I spoke, but I pretended not to hear him. A very hard thing to do when your mind and soul are being smothered with a power that makes you want to beg for mercy while howling for pleasure. Since the topic had switched to Mateo, I turned my attention to him. He was the easiest one for me to concentrate on.

"But you couldn't even wait for that," I told my ex-lover bitterly. "You hired Drake to find me."

"Don't make this worse, Constance," Mateo snapped, barreling right over my statement. "Hand Dro over, and you might live."

I shook my head. "You still think asking me that is going to work? I thought you were smarter than that, Mateo."

"I am. But I figured I would give you a chance. Then you wouldn't have to go through this."

He turned his head to the right, looking at the top of the buildings. We all looked with him.

It jumped just as I finished turning, moving faster than anything I'd ever seen. It landed on the hood of the car Warrick had been beside earlier. Metal crunched and glass exploded onto the pavement it as the demon landed, breaking the vehicle nearly in half. It slowly picked itself up, and suddenly I understood why Warrick had been nervous and Sephiel had been afraid.

The Knight was about six feet tall and nearly as broad. It was covered in black, metal armor that made it look like an onyx Templar. The armor was pieced together like a snake's scales, inscribed with endless, jagged symbols. Two wide black bat wings protruded from its back. It held a tall, serrated scythe in the gloved gauntlet of its right hand. A pointed helmet similar to a medieval jouster's covered its face, the lower half completely hiding its mouth, leaving two small slits on the upper half so the demon could see. Smoke billowed out of the eye slits and crevices of the helmet. Beyond them were two burning red eyes that blazed as the Knight stared at us, powerful and horrific.

Its eyes stopped on my sister.

I kept her behind me, holding my hatchet firmly in my hand.

The Knight jumped off the car, flapped its gigantic wings once, then landed four feet away from us. It was so close I could see the crude, dark red symbols etched onto its armor. Warrick stood close to me, turning his shotgun on the Knight. His shotgun blast was probably going to be as useful as a shot of elastic bands, but the thought was nice.

The armored demon took one large step forward, dragging its scythe along the ground. Metal screeched over concrete as it got closer. I tried to focus on its armor, to see if there were any cracks I could exploit, but all I could think about was how easily it could cut me down, how one swipe would slice both me and Warrick in half, and that there would be no one to protect Dro and Max–

He blinked into existence right in front of us. He snapped up his hand and fired a shot of gold heavenfire at the huge demon. It struck the creature in the chest and knocked it back.

Bloodstains and open wounds covered the back of his white coat, like he had been ruthlessly whipped, but none of that would stop Sephiel. I didn't have to see his face to know his bright blue eyes were filled with defiance.

The Knight shook off the blast and raised its scythe. A puff of dark smoke filtered out of its helmet, red eyes burning like coals. It crouched, about to spring.

A harsh noise filled my ears, so awful I winced. Someone might as well have shoved glass into my eardrums. That was what demon-tongue sounded like when Lucifer spoke.

The Knight instantly pulled out of its crouch, resting the curve of the scythe on the road again. Sephiel watched it, holding his broadsword with both hands. He wasn't going to turn his back on it for a single second.

Then Lucifer spoke English.

"An angel that willingly fell. Such a thing is unthinkable to the Host. Yet here you stand, Sephiel, with three humans, and mine and Everiel's child."

I didn't know what an angry Sephiel was like. With us, he was always patient, kind, and understanding. The most he ever got was annoyed or concerned. He hadn't even been angry when Rorikel betrayed and tried to kill us.

But Rorikel wasn't Lucifer. He wasn't the one who captured, raped, tortured, and caused the death of the woman Sephiel had loved for thousands of years. He wasn't the one who was standing there taunting Sephiel about leaving Heaven for us. He wasn't the one claiming Dro belonged to him.

Sephiel twisted his head to Lucifer. Blood covered his chest and face, but there was no fear or exhaustion in his eyes. Only a pure, unfiltered rage.

"Do not speak her name, demon," Sephiel threatened in a voice that scared even me. "Do not *dare*."

The rest of us, even Drake and Mateo, stared at the angel and the Devil. We were all subdued by the sheer *fury* in Sephiel's voice. On my worst day, I could never sound that pissed off. I knew he was beyond angry with Lucifer for what he'd done, but I didn't think that anger could border on such a ruinous level. Sephiel sounded like he was ready to cut the world in half if it meant killing his mortal enemy.

This of course, only amused Lucifer further. His pitch black eyes sparkled with malice and cruelty.

"You are brave for speaking against me. But surely you cannot think you can obtain retribution. You are not strong enough. You are not fast enough. That is why you could not save her."

Sephiel started shaking. I took a step to the side, not sure if he was going to actually explode.

Lucifer's lightless eyes fixed on the angel, the malice gleaming even brighter now. He looked like a hungry spider who knew he had a fly trapped in his web. "How long did you search for her, Seraphim? What did you expect to find?"

He looked at Dro. I felt her shrink back behind me and touch her missing rib. Lucifer turned his eyes back to Sephiel. Everiel had been nothing to him, and he wanted Sephiel to know it.

"Why do you protect her? Does it not cause you pain to look upon her everyday and see Everiel's eyes?" He tilted his head a little. "Or have you forgotten what they looked like?"

Sephiel's control snapped like a twig. He charged Lucifer with a thundering war cry, raising his sword to stab it into Lucifer's heart. He moved with a speed that made him a blur to my eyes.

But he wasn't fast enough.

The angel's sword slashed across the Knight's chest as it appeared in front of its King. His blade screeched across the metal chest plate. Sephiel raised his hand and threw out a blast of heavenfire that knocked the Knight back a couple feet. Lucifer took a single step back to avoid being hit. He watched the desperate fight with a bored expression.

Sephiel was holding his ground, but he was fighting out of anger. He was out of focus, and it was going to get him killed.

The Knight was winded by the heavenfire, but still standing. It twirled the scythe and laid it across the back of its shoulders, spinning low and flinging out the weapon. Sephiel dipped his sword and knocked the scythe away from him, only to give the demon an opening. He darted in close to Sephiel, punching him hard in the ribs with a metal-gloved fist. I saw Sephiel wince in pain, but he didn't stop fighting. Fear gripped my heart and squeezed as I tried to find a way to get into the fight, but Sephiel got in the way of each opportunity I saw. Warrick and Dro must have had the same problem, because they stood there and watched with the same terrified expressions, unable to help their revenge-crazed friend. Every step I took turned into a missed chance, and filled my chest with dread. I felt like I was watching beyond glass, helpless to intervene.

Sephiel blocked the scythe before it could sink into his neck, pushing it up so he could duck underneath it. Sephiel spiraled to get away from the demon, but it was quicker. It twisted and sliced the scythe along Sephiel's back. I saw blood spray up behind him as his face contorted in agony. The demon swung its weapon up across the angel's chest, sinking it into his front shoulder. He shouted painfully as blood poured from the top of his arm. The Knight tugged on the weapon, creating an even larger cut on Sephiel's chest. He used one hand to grab the edge of the scythe to push it out of him. His other hand reversed his sword and shoved it back into the demon's stomach.

The monster buckled and gave Sephiel the chance to tear the scythe free. Blood fountained out from the wound and stained his already ruined white coat. He turned and was kicked in the chest with so much force that he landed on his back on the road. He kept a grip on his sword, raising it in a block when the demon hammered down with its scythe. The curved weapon hooked the angel's blade, and ripped it from his hands. The demon planted its foot on Sephiel's chest and raised its scythe, ready to cut open the angel's throat. I was already running as fast as I could.

But she was faster than me.

I didn't know Dro was running until she pulled to a stop in front of me, feet away from Sephiel and the Knight. It lifted its head to look at her at the same time she raised her palms. Two streams of white-hot hellfire shot from her hands like napalm. They soared over Sephiel and enveloped the Knight. It stepped off Sephiel, who rolled out of range. Dro walked forward, continuing to blast the Knight away from the angel.

White fire illuminated the street, forcing me to squint. It was so bright that I couldn't even see the Knight anymore. She tilted her hands down as the Knight began to die, disintegrating.

I helped Sephiel to his feet. He clutched his shoulder with one hand, reaching for his fallen sword with the other. He tried to push me off and go for Lucifer, who was watching Dro with an interested expression. Sephiel jerked wildly like he was trying to get rid of a stubborn fly, but I held him back. He turned his furious blue eyes on me. I honestly thought he was going to punch me, but I made him focus.

"Not now, Seph," I commanded over the fire. I looked at my sister. "Bigger fucking problems."

The half conscious, bleeding angel turned his head

to Dro, and his anger started to break a little.

Dro was still burning the Knight, and she wasn't having a problem with it.

Finally, she let go of the fire. She took a shaky step back, but she didn't stumble. All that was left of the Knight was a charred Rorschach on the road. I couldn't even see a hint of ash. Dro took a deep breath to steady herself, then looked at the creature that created her.

I'd never seen such a dark expression on her face before. Lucifer was pleased by it.

His lips curled up, turning into a smile that made me want to scream in horror, and cry with lust. Intensity, power, beauty, and chilling serenity seemed to wrap around him in a blanket that suffocated everyone around him. He was simply too perfect. It was easy to see why so many people gave into him, one way or the other.

"You have grown powerful," he purred. "I am proud of you, my daughter."

Dro clenched her fists, white-hot hellfire crawling up her curled fingers to her elbows.

"I am not your daughter," she hissed. "I will *never* be your daughter. Don't ever think otherwise."

And here I thought Sephiel was the angry one. My little sister, the picture of a snowy angel, sounded even more dangerous than the vengeful Seraphim. She didn't sound like she would cut the world in half. She sounded like she was ready to burn the universe.

Her tone made my body temperature drop until I was sure I would never be warm inside again.

Lucifer stared at Dro, but didn't move. I would have thought he turned into a statue if I didn't see the subtle night wind moving through the long, white strands of his hair. I couldn't tell what he was feeling, but darkness was moving through his eyes like exploding stars.

"Seph," I whispered in his ear, "use the *movens caeli* and get us out of here."

He didn't reply, but he started moving his injured hand toward the inside of his destroyed jacket.

"I shall forgive your rudeness because you are my

child, Andromeda," Lucifer said, oblivious to us. "But make no mistake– you belong with me. You will never be one of them. Take your place at my side, and I shall see that no harm comes to those you cherish. They will not know suffering or pain as I make the transition. You can save them."

Dro swallowed. I could see the gears working in her head as she considered it. I watched her, ready to get between her and Lucifer if it came down to it. No matter what Dro wanted, I would never let her give herself up to the King of Hell. Not after what he had done to her.

Evidently, she had the same idea.

"So you can let the rest of the world suffer? I don't think so."

He didn't move an inch. He didn't even blink. But the stars were still exploding.

"You mistake my actions, child. I wish humanity no harm. I want to deliver them from hardship. I understand human beings. They seek peace and reprieve from pain and sorrow. I would bring them beyond the Heaven Gate, never let them endure the torments of my Kingdom. All are bound to sin, as the angels believe. But it is that flaw that makes humans so unique. I would not punish them for being what they are. I would see them unrestricted. Liberated."

"By twisting their minds and lying to them," Dro shot back. The hellfire was rising up to her shoulders now. "By sitting back and watching them torture themselves, letting them blacken their souls by killing everyone around them."

Sephiel shifted beside me, getting ready. I looked at my sister, bending my knees so I would be able to sprint to her.

"No," Dro said venomously. "I won't let you do that. I'll die first."

I went even colder when she said that, because I knew she meant it. She was ready to fight Lucifer to the death. My sister was stronger now, but Sephiel told us over and over again that only Michael was strong enough to defeat Lucifer. I didn't want her to test the limits of her power on the fiercest creature in the universe.

Which is why Sephiel drew out the *movens caeli* and started our escape.

Lucifer saw the movement out of the corner of his eye. He flicked out his hand, and suddenly Sephiel was gone from my side. He slammed into the broken van behind me, his back breaking the glass of the window while his sword flew from his grasp. He dropped onto his front, but Lucifer twisted his hand and flipped him over.

Then Sephiel started screaming. I stared at him, not seeing what was wrong. There were no new wounds, no strange bruises or burns or anything to indicate how he was suffering. But his screams just went on, and they were so horrible that my heart split at the sound. It didn't matter that I couldn't see what was happening. Lucifer was going to torture Sephiel to death.

The angel arched his back like he was trying to break it. He clenched his fists at his side and screamed until I thought the veins bulging in his neck and temple were going to burst.

"*Stop!*" Dro yelled.

She shoved out her hands and threw all of her hellfire at Lucifer. The King of Hell snapped his head over to her and held up his hand. All the hellfire absorbed into his palm, twisting until it was a bright, white ball of flame against his skin. The heat and light didn't bother him at all. Then he threw it back at her. Dro cried out and swept the blast away from us with her hands. It twisted over her like a crescent moon that evaporated overhead.

I ran for Lucifer. I didn't even think about what I was doing. I focused on attacking him, and nothing else.

Which is why Mateo nearly killed me.

A quick shadow and a glimmer of silver flashed on my right. Instinct made me duck. I felt and heard the air rush over my head as the machete cut through it. I twisted around, trying to straighten myself. Mateo kicked back, catching me in the chest and sending a bruising pain through my collarbone. I winced, but stayed on my feet and caught my breath, just as he swung his machete at me again.

I turned away at the last possible second. The blade kissed along the side of my arm, nearly going into my sleeve. I aimed a knee at his exposed side, but he drove his elbow into my temple. Pain erupted in my skull as I stumbled. I shook it off and saw Warrick running for Mateo and aiming his shotgun. Until Drake got in his way.

He kicked the shotgun out of Warrick's hands and punched him square in the jaw. It wasn't long before they started swinging at each other, both of them equally matched. Warrick got punched in the back, but he drove his knee into Drake's ribs. He jabbed Drake in the face, only to be kicked and kneed in the stomach.

On my other side, Dro was still throwing hellfire at Lucifer. Every time she did, he flicked it away and took a step closer. She made pillars, walls, mountains of hellfire, and Lucifer knocked them aside like specks of dust. His face was a stone. I couldn't tell if he was annoyed, impressed, angry, or proud, and it didn't matter. I had to stop him from hurting her. If I could keep my ex-boyfriend from slicing me to pieces first.

He was so much stronger than I remembered. Every time he swung the heavy blade at me, it was meant as a killing strike. Mateo wanted me to die a bloody death, like his father had.

I leaned away from the machete before it could slash open my throat, then got off the defensive. I let him finish swinging his machete before kicking down on his wrist. Mateo was jerked off balance, giving me the opening I needed to kick him in the chin. I rushed forward, slashing down with my hatchet. He moved back before I could kill him, but the blade still left a slice across his collarbone and chest.

Mateo turned his wrist to drive the machete into my side. I used my free hand to grab his arm and pull the weapon away from me. Unfortunately, Mateo still had one free hand. He punched me in the face then fisted my hair. He wrenched my head back painfully, raising the machete again.

I used the crook of my hatchet to catch the weapon before it could decapitate me. I pushed with all my strength, my arms trembling as he tried to press the machete blade into my throat. I felt it start to press against my neck. Mateo jerked on my hair again like he was going to tear it all from my head. I gritted my teeth and growled as he tried to snap my neck backward.

I kicked Mateo's knee, making him stumble. His grip loosened and I was able to push the machete back. I spun away and roundhouse-kicked Mateo in the side of the head. I reached into my jacket for a silver throwing knife, ready to launch it into his throat.

Dro's sudden cry of pain stopped me. I whirled around.

Lucifer was standing three feet away from my little sister, who was almost completely engulfed in hellfire. But while she was holding up her hands, it wasn't her fire. It was his. She buckled to one knee, turning her face away from the blaze as it licked around her. Every time she winced, my despair rose. I forgot all about my murderous ex-boyfriend and ran for Lucifer.

I skidded to a stop when I was in perfect range and hurled my silver knife at Lucifer. He turned up his hand, whipping his head at me. My knife stopped in midair, six inches from his face.

Goddamn it, not again.

But this time, Lucifer threw my knife back at me. I twisted sharply, but the blade still nicked the top of my shoulder. I winced at the stinging pain, then gripped my hatchet and turned back around.

To find myself face to face with the Devil.

His face was even more beautiful up close. There were no words for its exquisiteness. Roman statues had nothing on Lucifer. Every time I breathed, I smelled smoke and roses. Flashes of light sparked through his obsidian eyes. They were the kind of eyes that could show you all the wonderful and dreadful secrets of the universe.

His incredible power wrapped around me, and

suddenly I couldn't move. He was close enough to strangle me, close enough to kiss me. Either way, he was going to make me his. He would make me bleed and scream, then have me crawl back for more.

But out of the corner of my eyes, I saw another person with snow-white hair. She was lying in a heap on the road, exhausted from overusing her power. She was hurt, and the thing in front of me had been the one to hurt her. Seeing her took away the fog in my head and sharpened my sense of purpose.

I swung my hatchet up. Lucifer was still looking at my face when he caught my wrist. He twisted it sharply, snapping the small bones inside it. I cried out sharply, then did the first thing that came to mind.

I punched at him.

Obviously it didn't work.

Lucifer didn't even have to grab my fist or block me. My hand stopped in mid air, two inches from his cheek. It was like I had punched quicksand. I was unable to pull my hand back. My fist was shaking in mid air.

Before I could try kicking him, Lucifer shoved the heel of his palm into my chest.

I flew back and landed hard on the road. I coughed, clutching my chest, certain that he'd punched a hole through me. My heart stumbled, trying to get back into the right beat. Before I could get to my feet, he returned, and picked me up by the throat.

His fingers seared my neck as he squeezed, like burning tongs. I kicked and threw punches at him, but all I was hitting was air. Lucifer slammed me hard onto the road. Bruising pain filled my spine and my head even as he released my throat. I was dizzy and seeing two of everything. It made Lucifer standing over me all the more terrifying.

"Did you truly think you would harm me, mortal?" He held out one of his hands. Invisible ropes coiled around my body, pinning me onto the ground. His other hand filled with hellfire. "Or that there would not be consequences for your actions?"

He didn't give me a chance to respond. He just pushed the hellfire down onto me.

I thought I knew what pain meant until that moment. Turned out I was way off.

Every inch of me felt like it was melting off, scalding skin peeled away so the nerves and muscle beneath could be torched. My bones splintered and cracked under the heat. Blood boiled in my veins. I smelled burning clothes and scorched hair. My eyeballs felt like bees were stinging them. I breathed in smoke and tasted fire when I screamed. My entire body was rigid, unable to move as it was turned to a black cinder.

The roar of hellfire in my ears was so loud I couldn't hear my cries. I couldn't tell if my eyelids were burned off or seared shut because everything was blindingly white. There were no visible flames, no trace of the place where I was. Just an unending whiteness and an agony I never knew existed.

Now I knew what Hell truly felt like.

It went on and on and on. The unbelievable heat, the incomprehensible pain. I'd thought that being possessed and exorcised was the worst pain I'd ever endure. Not the case. Even heavenfire was a vacation compared to this.

I screamed until my voice was raspy and broken. Then I screamed some more. I only stopped when my vocal cords welded together and my tongue felt like coal. Lucifer didn't show me any mercy. He wanted to kill me in the most painful way possible.

It was working.

There were shouts. Angry screams. A sweeping wind over my body.

Then it was over. The fire was torn away from my body, leaving me trembling on the ground. I could smell my burning skin, and was suddenly glad I couldn't open my eyes. I felt like a piece of charcoal. A gentle breeze caressed my body, and I almost screamed again. Every piece of me was opened and raw to the dirty world. Each slight motion caused me incredible pain. I wasn't going to survive. If I did, I was going to be useless. Lucifer had given me a few seconds of his hellfire, even though it felt like an eternity. My heart broke when I knew I wasn't going to see Dro again.

Someone screamed in utter agony. The air heated over me, and I cringed in fear. The light that appeared above me was so bright I could see it through my closed eyes. I was in too much pain to even think about what was going on. A minute later, someone dropped to their knees beside me and started crying.

More voices surrounded me. I didn't know who they were, but they were either going to watch me die or kill me out of sympathy. I hoped it was the latter.

"Damn it, Connie," a girl who sounded like Dro sobbed. "Sephiel! Help me!"

"We have to get her out of here," a strained, deep voice said. It might have been Warrick.

"She must be healed first," Sephiel said. Or I think it was Sephiel. My ears were filled with crispy, flaking skin and filling my brain with a low, cracking sound. "She will not survive otherwise."

"I'm ready when you guys are, but sooner would be better," Max's voice urged.

They didn't hesitate. Knife-like pain erupted along my body, and I arched my back. A raspy wheeze tore from my charred throat. I was too damaged to scream normally anymore. My body was on fire again, as if every nerve was exploding. I couldn't take the pain of Dro and Seph healing me anymore than I could take Lucifer burning me. At least I told myself that was what was happening. If this was some new torture of Lucifer's, I was going to lie to myself. It was something I was good at.

It went on forever, the spikes of healing magic stabbing into my raw flesh. Tears slipped from the corners of my eyes. I winced as they slipped into the cracks on my burned face. The salt from them sent sharp bites of pain over my exposed wounds. But if my tear ducts were being fixed, then the rest of me was being fixed, right?

Wrong. You're an idiot, but you're not stupid, Constance. You know you can't survive this.

The agonizing stabs of magic stopped, and my body slumped against the road. My head felt like lead, and I nearly passed out. Arms scooped me up as gently as possible. I still moaned. It was a sad, pathetic sound, but the only one I could make to react to the pain. I was held against a body that smelled like pine. More bodies pressed around me.

"Shit!" someone yelled. It sounded like Max.

Someone else yelled, a war cry of pure rage. Heat smothered the air beside us. I peeled my eyes open to see what was happening.

A wall of hellfire stood menacingly between Lucifer and us. It cut a line through the road, standing nearly as tall as the King of Hell. He narrowed his eyes at the fire. The wall began to decrease in size. Dro shouted again and pushed out her hands. More blinding flames tore from her hands and fuelled the wall.

"Impressive," Lucifer called over the hellfire wall. "It takes incredible strength to create a hellfire barrier capable of resisting me. But you placed too much power in the first wall. Then you exerted an excessive amount to heal that human." His eyes flashed dangerously. "This wall is weaker, my child."

To prove his point, Lucifer stepped forward. Dro threw out her hand again, but this time the flames weren't blazing white. They were the sharp, merciless gold of heavenfire. The burning wall shuddered with intensity, though it remained solid and strong.

Lucifer stood in place, a frown creasing his lips.

"You cannot run from me, Andromeda," promised Lucifer in a blistering tone. I shivered, and the person carrying me held me closer. "I made you, and you are mine."

"I will never be yours, *Devil*," replied my sister in a tone that could have poisoned the world. "But I will make you pay for this. I'm going to turn these powers on you, and erase you from the earth."

That was the last thing I heard before a crack of thunder and blinding light smothered me. My body condensed before we started flying. Air rushed around me, filling my head with dizziness. We were moving too fast for me to feel any more pain. Then just like that, it was over. We landed on the ground. I didn't open my eyes to see where I was. I thought I heard some people shouting, but I didn't know who they were. I wasn't able to find out either. My head spun one more time, and I passed out.

Chapter 8

I knew the dream was a memory, but it felt as though I was reliving it...

I had beaten the shit out of the guy. Blood pooled under him, painting his remaining teeth. He hadn't expected a seventeen year old girl to slip out of the shadows and knock him out, but he knew where he was when he woke up and saw us. He knew who we were as soon as I showed him the rose tattooed behind my ear and Mateo showed the matching one over his heart.

Mateo moved out from the shadows, stood close to me, and folded his arms over his muscled chest. I spun the lead pipe in my hand, red drops spiraling off it.

"What do you say, Raymond? Are you going to say you're sorry, or is she going to have to hit you some more?"

"Please," Raymond blubbered. "Please, I didn't mean to steal it—"

Mateo laughed. "Right. You didn't mean to steal a bag of cocaine worth five grand. No addict ever means to do that." He turned his head to look in my eyes. "What do you think, baby? Did he mean to do it?"

I shrugged. "I think he hasn't apologized yet."

I took a step forward, raised the pipe, and swung it into Raymond's kneecap. Two more strikes were needed before I heard a sickening crack and he screamed in pain. I swallowed my disgust, grateful my back was to Mateo. I raised the pipe again and used it to shatter his other kneecap. His tortured howls echoed off the warehouse walls.

Remember why you're doing this. You chose to be stronger. To be stronger, you have to be colder.

I stepped back, my face devoid of emotion as Raymond cried his apologies. "I'm sorry! I'm sorry! Please, I don't want to die!"

Mateo looked at me. I shrugged yet again. I was in charge of beating the apology out of Raymond, but killing him was Mateo's job. He was the leader here, ever the boss's son. He had to keep Espanis de Sangre's ruthless reputation up to par. It was all going to be his one day.

My boyfriend hammered punches onto Raymond's stomach and ribs, then slammed his fist into his jaw. I stood back and watched it all.

I was used to the sight of blood. I had been an enforcer for a couple years now, but that didn't make this easier. It didn't mean I wanted to see more people hurt. I damn sure didn't enjoy hurting them.

But I chose this. I wanted to be an enforcer, trained under Mateo himself. The bruises and hard lessons had made me stronger. I was dangerous, making a name for myself. All of that came with the price of blood. I could hold onto the guilt, remember Raymond's face, and have nightmares about it later. Right now, I had to look utterly ruthless. Inhuman. These days, it was getting way too easy.

Mateo finally finished pulping Raymond. He was breathing heavily, his energy spent on the man who was now barely alive. The only indicator was the slight whistle coming from his mouth. One of his lungs must have collapsed. Mateo took his machete off his hip.

"Apology accepted," Mateo said.

He swung his machete with both hands, slicing into Raymond's neck. Blood shot out as arteries split in half. His head lolled grotesquely to the side. The next cut clashed with the bones in his neck, scraping across them. Blood painted Raymond's neck and chest. One more strike, and then it was done.

The head landed on the ground with a thump about a foot away from me. Mateo slowly evened his breathing. We were out in the middle of nowhere, so he had time to calm down. I tried not to look at the head very much. It *was a bit ironic. The first decapitation I'd ever seen horrified me beyond all belief. Now I was standing there and watching them happen. The sight wasn't scaring me anymore. I'd stopped feeling ill. It was wrong of me, awfully wrong, but I couldn't focus on the act.*

So I tried to think about his family and friends, the faceless people who would miss Raymond. I forced myself to remember that he was a person, maybe not even a bad guy, and that someone had loved him. It would make it easier for the nightmares to come.

There was another bit of irony: I wanted to have nightmares about the people I watched die so I could keep my humanity.

Once his adrenaline slowed, Mateo turned and looked at me. From the neutral, even expression on his face, it was almost impossible to tell that he had just decapitated a human being.

"Can you help me with him, babe?"

I did, not thinking about how I was helping my boyfriend chop up another corpse. How we were going to connect the parts with strings and thorny rose stems, or how we were going to leave a message in blood that said: Pay the whole, or be in pieces.

After we left the warehouse, Mateo was still riding on the edges of adrenaline. He loved getting a rush of any kind as often as possible, and he was hungry for his next one. His hand skimmed my thigh the entire drive back, inching higher up my leg as we got closer to the hacienda. He gave me a squeeze and I held my breath.

I wanted to tell him I wasn't in the mood, but then I looked over and I saw the naughty smile on his face. He looked at me as if I was the center of his world. I matched his smile and reached over to twine my fingers in his.

Mateo quickly got his own idea. He drove the car off to the side of the road, shut off the engine, then pulled me into his lap and kissed me. Mateo's lips crushed against mine roughly, his hands snaring my waist and bringing me closer into him. I breathed in his woodsy cologne, completely lost when his tongue snaked through my lips.

Mateo's hands slid under my shirt and lightly trailed up my back. I shivered, and had to back away to take a breath.

"We don't have enough time," I sighed, struggling to control my beating heart. "Emilio wants the report."

"Relax, babe," he purred, his lips placing gentle kisses on my neck and taking me deeper under his spell. "Dad trusts us." His hand slid further up my spine, resting at the clasp of my bra. "He'll give us time."

My heart thumped against my ribcage. I loved the feel of his hands on my skin, and it wasn't the first time Mateo made it clear he wanted to move onto the next stage of our relationship. A stage that involved a lot less clothes.

I held my breath and reached behind my back. I clasped his wrists and drew them away from my bra clasp. My shirt collapsed in tandem with Mateo's smile.

"I'm not in the mood, Mateo," I told him sternly.

His expression darkened. I couldn't think of anything to say to lighten it. I was tired and felt a knot in my chest. I didn't know if I was ready for sex yet, and even if I was, I couldn't do it after a murder. Not when I kept hearing Raymond's screams in my head and seeing his blood on my clothes.

Mateo shifted abruptly. He didn't throw me off his lap, but he made it clear that he didn't want me close to him anymore. A stinging pain snapped in my chest as he started driving again. I watched his face, saw the tension in his jaw. I reached between us and pried one of his hands from the wheel, carefully so he wouldn't swerve off the road. I wound my fingers through his.

The attraction between us had been there the day we started training together. When we started dating, it became lust. I had been with Mateo for almost two years now. It had become love.

Mateo sighed and squeezed my hand gently. The gesture was warm and comforting. His eyes weren't.

Two hours later, we were back at the hacienda, about to split off from each other. I told Mateo I was too exhausted to talk to Emilio, which made him smile. He kissed me and said that he would give the report to his father and find an excuse for me. I didn't say that the real reason I wanted to get away was so I could see my sister. I told him I loved him, and that was enough.

Dro was brushing her hair in our room when I opened the door and walked in. She was fourteen now, looking less like the small, quiet girl I grew up with and more like a beautiful teenager. She twisted in her chair at the vanity table to look at me, her eyes going wide when she saw the blood on me. I was grateful that Dro never got used to it.

"It's okay, little sister," I assured her, closing the door and kicking off my boots. "None of it's mine."

She frowned at me. "That better not be an attempt to comfort me."

I shrugged out of my black jacket and tossed it on the chair. I unstrapped my knives and hatchet from my body.

"Well, it's true."

I could feel her eyes on my back as I washed the blood from my hands in the bathroom sink. When I was done, I walked back out into the main bedroom and dropped onto my back on the bed. I slid my hatchet under my pillow and put a knife on the nightstand. Dro's eyes were still on me, waiting for me to open up and talk. I wasn't in the mood.

Dro left the vanity table and lay down on her stomach on her bed next to me. She propped her chin in her hand and waited. I glanced over at my little sister. She looked just as gentle and as comforting as always. She knew me too well.

I sighed and looked at the ceiling. "It was awful." My voice was as tight as my chest.

"Did you kill him?" she asked.

I shook my head. "Not this one. Mateo did. I had to help with the body again."

"Not the most romantic thing you guys could have done on your anniversary."

I laughed bitterly. "Boss's orders. Not mine."

Dro was silent at that. I glanced over to see her clasping her elbows with a troubled look on her face. "Are you sure you can't go back to how it was before?" she asked hesitantly. "Be a falcon again instead of an enforcer?"

"Emilio doesn't demote anyone. They disappoint him, and he kills them. Or he tortures them if he still kind of likes them."

Dro was biting her lip. I rolled onto my side to face her. "We talked about this, Dro. This is the only way the Thorns will let me train. I have to get stronger to keep away the monsters."

Her head lifted, a flicker of fear going through them. "Did you see one?"

"No, but that doesn't mean they're gone. I want to be ready when they come back."

Dro exhaled heavily and held the sides of her head. "I don't want you to keep doing it, Connie. It's not you."

"You think I like it?"

"Of course not," she told me sharply, "I know you don't. But we could run. We could leave it behind, like Dad did."

My heart ached when I thought about my father, his blood spraying out from his throat onto his killer's hand. Dro was probably thinking the same thing. I swallowed the pain before I spoke again.

"This is still our safest option, little sister."

She started shaking her head.

"We haven't seen any monsters in years–"

"I can't do it, Constance!" she suddenly cried.

I froze, my eyebrows rising up my forehead. Dro didn't yell. Ever. She was the politest, most decent person I had ever met. For her to freak out like this was a clear sign something was very wrong. I stayed silent until she settled down and collected herself.

"I can't do it. You don't see what I see. This place, everyone in it, they've got darkness in them. Even the maids and the cooks." She hesitated, then added, "Even *you."*

Dro pushed herself up and rested her back against the wooden headboard. She wrapped her arms around her knees, looking small.

"It's everywhere here. The monsters don't need to find us. We're living with them."

I was still struggling for something to say. Dro saw things I couldn't understand or comprehend, no matter how hard I tried. I didn't know what she was, if it was possible to take away the things she saw. I could handle myself waking up screaming from nightmares created by my memories. It was just a reminder of my black little truth. But I couldn't take it when I heard them from Dro. I sat up.

"Do you think I'm a monster?" I asked, very serious. Afraid of the answer.

Dro looked at me with heavy eyes. She shook her head. *"No, of course not, Connie. You're my sister, and I love you. But you deserve a better life. You're better than these people, and..."* Tears formed in her eyes. *"And I'm scared of what they're going to turn you into."*

I thought back to the endless faces of people I had beaten. The ones I had stabbed. The two that I drowned. The one I had shot. All the times I stood back and let Mateo or another Blood Thorn torture and murder someone. I enforced my rules– no kids, pets, pregnant women, or innocents– but not every member of the Espanis de Sangre shared my morale code. Not even Mateo did.

I tried to remember Raymond's face. The way his head lolled to the side, gushing thick blood onto the walls. But it was a blur in my head, a fading photograph of something that seemed like it happened five years ago instead of five hours.

Dro was right. The longer I stayed with the Thorns, the less I would care. The fewer nightmares I would have. I would become a monster, one that even Dro would see.

But... *"It isn't that simple, Dro."*

She looked up at me, scowling a little. *"Because of*

Mateo?"

I tried to say he had nothing to do with this, but that would make me a liar. Despite the terrible things he did, he had a soul. He did all these terrible things because he had to, not because he wanted to. He must have a heart, because he loved me. He was sweet to Dro. He was a good son. He promised to protect us. Mateo wasn't any different from me.

Right?

"He's a bad person, Connie," my sister said. "I know you love him, but he's not right for you. There's an evil in him. Something you can't fix."

I must have given her a sharp look and not realized it, because she shrank back to the wooden headboard of her bed. Any annoyance disappeared. She was my little sister, the most important person in the world to me. I didn't want to upset her.

I shuffled off my bed and crawled onto hers, shifting so I could sit beside her and drape my arm over her shoulder. Dro rested her head against me, instantly relaxed. I put my cheek on her head. No matter where I was, Dro always smelled like home.

"Don't worry about Mateo, little sister. And I think the first step is to set up a place to meet."

She twisted her neck to look at my face, chilly blue eyes shining in the darkness. "Meet? What do you mean?"

"You're right, Dro. We shouldn't be here. If you don't think it's safe, then it isn't. I'm not at the house enough to tell. So we'll find a way to leave, Dro."

"How? They're never going to let you go. People don't quit the Blood Thorns."

I sighed. "I don't know. But we'll figure it out." I paused, then figured out where we could go. "We can meet at the warehouse where they had the Fuego massacre a couple years ago. No one goes there anymore." I looked down and smiled at her. "I hated that place. They'll never think to look there."

Dro wasn't smiling. She put her head back on my shoulder and snuggled closer to me, the way she always did when she was scared.

"I wouldn't ask this if I didn't have to, Connie," she said, as if she needed to explain herself to me. "I just... I can't let you get hurt. I won't survive if anything happens to you."

I put my other arm around her and rubbed her bicep.

"Nothing's going to happen to me, little sister. I promise..."

I was getting sick of waking up in places I wasn't familiar with. At least this time I was decently comfortable. I shifted against the mattress, which was softer than I was used to. I tried rolling onto my side, but that didn't help me get back to sleep. I was awake, and I had to figure out where I was.

I sat up, then regretted it. Forcing myself to open my eyes, I looked down at the damage done to my body. Except there was none. I was fully healed, my skin no longer charred and cracked. There weren't any patchy burn scars. I touched my head and face and found that I even had my hair, eyebrows, and eyelashes. Dro and Sephiel had done wonders on me, but there was still a dull throbbing in my body, and my skull felt like it was splitting in half. Still, it was better than feeling like an overcooked piece of bacon.

"You shouldn't move," a rumbling voice said.

I twisted, shocked that the person in my room wasn't my sister. Warrick was sitting across from the bed by a flat desk. The tall, hooded lamp in the corner shadowed the far half of his face, but illuminated the rest. It brought out subtle highlights in his oak-colored hair and made his eyes sparkle. Dark circles were under his eyes, and his face was the definition of bleak. He must have been awake for hours.

"Where's Dro?" I rasped. I touched my throat. It was healed enough to speak, but my throat was parched and my tongue was as smooth as sandpaper. I wondered how long I would sound like a veteran smoker.

"She's fine," he answered, getting up from the chair and slowly walking over to me. "She spent the whole day healing you with Sephiel, making sure you looked like yourself again. Her body just couldn't take more exertion, and she needed rest. I promised to stay here and make sure you were okay."

He knelt down next to the bed and took a glass of water from the nightstand. He handed it to me. "Sephiel said you'd need another night to heal. You should sleep."

I downed the entire glass in a couple gulps. "No," I told him, starting to sound a little more like myself now that I had something to drink. I could have drunk a full pitcher, but there wasn't one in the room. Warrick probably didn't think I would wake up yet. Besides, water could wait. I needed answers first. "Not until you tell me where I am and what happened."

Warrick sighed, and I felt a twinge of guilt. Dro might not have slept until recently, but Warrick didn't seem to have slept at all.

"We ended up in Phoenix," he explained. "About a block away from where the slayers were, actually. You passed out just as they ran over to us. Dro was screaming at them to help you. It took Max forever to calm her down. I managed to persuade them to let us stay here. It's a secure location underground and Sephiel warded the shit out of it. The *movens caeli* can shield us from Lucifer for a bit. We'll be safe for a little while."

"Are we at the main slayer base or something?"

He nodded. "It's been a rough couple days. Everyone's pissed off. The slayers are mad at me for dumping all this on them, I'm mad that they're being so stuck up, Max and Seph are mad that they're not telling us anything, and Dro's mad..."

Warrick trailed off. I read between the lines.

"She's mad at me," I confirmed.

His eyes were sympathetic. "She's just worried about you, Constance. We all thought you were going to die." He looked away, as if the memory was playing through his head all over again. "You didn't see what we saw. One moment you were standing up to Lucifer, the next you were..."

I was being burned to death.

For a second, all I could think about was the scalding heat. The blinding light that burned my retinas. The hoarseness of my voice as pieces of skin flaked off my body. I gripped the glass tighter as a trickle of sweat went down the back of my neck. I breathed evenly, blinking a couple times to make sure I was really sitting in a bed with Warrick next to me, and that this wasn't a final death-dream.

I looked at the demon slayer. He didn't notice my anxiety because he was looking away. He was lost in his own unforgiving memory.

"There was so much fire that I couldn't even see you," he said very quietly. "I thought you were gone."

I stared at Warrick as that sweet ache crept back into me. Dro was right. He did care about me. He watched me nearly die, and now he was out of sorts. It hurt to see him so miserable because of me, and suddenly I didn't want to push him away. I was almost ready to let him break my heart. Maybe it wouldn't be as bad as when Mateo had broken it.

Then again, maybe it would be worse.

I didn't want to give Warrick hope that would be crushed later. But I couldn't bear seeing him this way, either.

I put the water glass back on the nightstand then reached over and clutched his hand. He felt alive and real, which is exactly what I wanted right now. I needed something to anchor me to here and now so I wouldn't remember what Lucifer had done to me. Even this was enough to make my heart race. Warrick's bright green eyes met mine and I forgot to breathe.

"Thanks for sticking around, John. Really. But I should go see my sister." I looked away. "I need to fix things."

Warrick rose up so he could sit on the bed next to me. He clasped my hand. His palm was rough and callused, but also warm and gentle. I didn't pull away.

"Dro will forgive you, Constance. She knows you did what you did to protect her." The pad of his thumb skimmed the top of my hand. My heart was running a mile a minute.

"I fought with Emma all the time," he said with a tragic smile. "One night I got her in huge trouble. She was supposed to be studying for her finals, but I saw her sneak out to party with her friends. I waited up until she came back, then locked her out of the house. I stayed on the other side of the door to watch out for her, but I never let her in. She slept on the porch."

He grinned. "Mom and Dad were pissed, and she had the worst hangover of her life in the morning. When she got back in the house I thought she was gonna kill me. Emma didn't talk to me for three days after that. I apologized, did all her chores, but none of that helped. Not even our parents could make her talk to me. I was worried she wouldn't take me to tae kwon do like she promised. Fourth day came along, and she picked me up after school and drove me to my lessons."

"How did you get her to do that?"

He raised one shoulder, then lowered it slowly. "I didn't force it. She remembered that she was my sister."

Warrick looked at me. "You've given up everything for Dro, Constance. She won't stay mad at you for that. Just let her rest for the night, and talk to her tomorrow. It's all going to work out. I promise."

I knew it was crazy, but I actually believed him. Dro and I went through everything together. I might have gotten myself hurt when I decided to take on Lucifer alone, but I would do it again. We weathered the harshest storms together, because that was what sisters did. We needed each other to stay strong.

"Yeah, I guess you're right," I said, slowly prying my hand from Warrick's and resting my back against the headboard.

"Wow, never thought I'd hear you say that," he teased.

I stifled a laugh. "Don't get used to it, Warrick. Dro's heard it, Max has heard it, now you. Once I have Seph crossed off my list, I never have to say it again."

He laughed. It was a comfortable, deep timbre that made me want to move closer to him. I watched his face, taking in the details of it. His thick, brown hair was starting to grow to his ears. His beard was trimmed down to short stubble. The mark under his left eye from where Drake had scarred him was almost invisible against the light from the lamp in the corner. The more I looked at him, the more perfect he seemed to be.

He turned his eyes toward me but I looked away.

"So," he said after a while. "That guy with the machete. Was he your ex?"

I groaned and thunked my head against the bed frame. "Goddamn it, how much did Dro tell you?"

"Only a little. He's a real asshole."

"He wasn't always," I mumbled, picking at the bed sheet that was bunched up around my hips.

Warrick paused, then said, "Do you still love him?"

"Fuck no," I said harshly. "He tried to kill me multiple times. He's going to keep trying. Why would I keep loving someone like that?"

The demon slayer raised his hands in surrender. "I just wanted to make sure." He put his hands back on the bed and gave me a dangerous look. "That way I can kick his ass next time I see him."

I grinned for a second before reality showed its ugly face. "Lucifer will be with him next time. So will Drake. And fuck knows what else."

Warrick pulled his long legs up onto the bed and shifted closer to me. I didn't move away, but I hoped he wouldn't see my heart pounding its way out of my chest.

"I can't promise that nothing will hurt you again. I think we both know that's inevitable. But I will promise to do whatever I can to keep you safe."

He was so close now I could feel the breeze from his breath on my face. Bright green eyes sparkled despite the dark of the room. I inhaled the musky pine scent from his body.

"You don't need to," I croaked out.

Warrick moved even closer. "No. But I want to. I see you fighting all these demons and psychos by yourself, and it drives me crazy. You're the bravest woman I've ever met, Constance. But it kills me to watch you fight alone. So I won't do it."

His lips were almost brushing against mine. Warrick's body was half pressed against me. He was warm, real, and totally inviting. I was painfully close to kissing him again. He might not make a move unless I wanted him to, especially since he was beginning to understand just how badly Mateo had hurt me. But Warrick wouldn't give up, either. He wasn't the type.

Yet something held me back. We had so much to do, so many enemies to fight. I'd just proved that we could very well die in our next battle. I was *crazy* about Warrick, and it was clear that nothing I said or did would make him leave. He'd become another person I was scared to lose.

"I..." I whispered, barely able to think straight. He was drowning me in comfort and tenderness, and I was sinking like the stone that I was.

"This isn't the time, Warrick," I pushed out.

There might not ever be a time, I kept to myself.

He read my eyes, then leaned back. The room suddenly felt much colder.

"You're right. I'm sorry. I don't know what came over me. I guess I'm just tired." He started to slide off the bed. "Jackson's got a cot for me in the living room. Get some rest, Constance."

"Screw the cot. Stay here."

I blinked, hardly believing the words were out of my mouth. But I didn't try to take them back. Warrick looked at me from across the bed.

"Are you sure?"

This time I thought about my answer. "Yes."

He smiled gently, his eyes seeming to glow brighter. He kicked off his boots– but kept the rest of his clothes on, gentleman that he was– and slid under the covers of the bed next to me. I rolled onto my side, putting my back to him and tugged the sheets up to my shoulders. My heart was still doing laps behind my ribcage, so I didn't think I'd get back to sleep. Especially since I could feel his body inches away from mine.

"Are you sure this is okay?" he asked again.

"Yeah. Just don't get mad if I kick you in my sleep. I get nightmares."

Warrick shuffled under the covers again, carefully pressing his chest to my back. He slowly and put his arm over my ribs, laying it on my stomach. His other arm slid under my neck and over my shoulder, resting along my chest but not making any awkward grabs.

"Will this help?" he whispered into my hair.

Warrick's body heat was sinking into me. I was wrapped up in strong, secure arms. His breath was a gentle, relaxing wind in my hair. The heartbeat at my back was steady and hypnotic.

"Maybe," I whispered back.

I should have been tense and paranoid. I didn't like other people touching me, let alone spooning me. Even Mateo had never been this gentle with me. It could have been the perfect trap.

But I felt Warrick drift into sleep behind me. He stayed here when he should have been resting. He'd stood by me when the Knight appeared. He'd saved my life countless times. He really did care.

It wasn't long before the soothing heat of him and rhythm of his breathing made my eyelids heavy. I shifted back and pulled his arms tighter around my body.

I could add benefit of the doubt to the list of things I owed John Warrick.

Chapter 9

Sleeping in Warrick's arms didn't keep me from dreaming. As soon as I gave in to sleep, another memory dug its way into my brain...

Mateo was up to something. I could tell, because he'd barely talked to me all day. Everything was one or two word replies. He wouldn't tell me what was wrong, getting snappy when I brought it up at all. He said it was a meeting, and none of my fucking business. Finally, I couldn't take his attitude anymore and stormed off.

At least that was what he thought I was doing. In reality, I decided to climb the hacienda roof and wait until nightfall. Then I could drop down toward Emilio's office. He kept the windows open during the hot summers, so I would be able to hear this meeting. Every meeting was held in Emilio's office and my boyfriend went to all of them, but I wondered what would make Mateo so antsy about this one.

As soon as the sun went down, I crawled along the roof to Emilio's balcony. I reached the corner of the house and looked down, making sure that no one was standing on the balcony. I turned and dropped down, hanging on the ledge tightly. I skittered down until I reached the concrete edge. I crouched like a gargoyle and peered through the open window.

None of the people in Emilio's office could see me at this angle, but I could see all of them. Hernandez the bodyguard was standing by the door with his large hands clasped in front of him. Emilio and Mateo were leaning against the desk, both dressed in their best suits. They were looking at the other person in the room. It was a woman. I focused on her face, then nearly fell off the balcony.

She was in her thirties, and absolutely gorgeous. Her long black hair was pulled up into a high, sleek ponytail. She was thin with murderous curves, and she knew how to exploit them by wearing a skin-tight black dress with small red beads attached to a lace trim. I could see the shiny black pumps with razor thin heels as she crossed one leg over the other, revealing a well toned thigh. Lace gloves covered her hands. Her eyes were circled in dark shadow and eyeliner, and her pouty lips were the color of blood.

My heart pounded in my chest, and I struggled to control myself.

Isabel. The woman who had stalked my little sister. The person who brought monsters to Owl Creek.

The bitch that killed my father.

I nearly lost it. My fingers were itching for my hatchet or a throwing knife. Isabel was a fair distance away, but I could hit her. I could kill the fucking skank.

Though as soon as I did, Hernandez, Emilio, and Mateo would see me. They would send every guard in the house to find me. I wasn't sure Dro and I could escape if we were caught.

But I did know we were leaving tonight, as soon as I figured out what the hell Isabel was doing here. I edged close to the side of the house.

"You're sure of this?" Emilio asked. His voice was faint, but there was no wind tonight so I was still able to hear what everyone was saying.

"My master has told me so," Isabel answered. "Your son has been chosen by the King himself. He would not send me here if young Mateo was not worthy of his purpose."

"And what purpose is that?"

Isabel smiled. Anger grew like a bonfire in me. I knew that smile. I wanted to carve it off her smug, fucking face.

"You'll know soon enough, I assure you. But let me give you a word of advice." Isabel leaned closer, looking *at Emilio and his only son. "Declining such an offer would bring all kinds of unpleasantness to your door."*

"Do not threaten me or my son in my home, witch," Emilio said venomously. "I will only warn you once."

Isabel wasn't the least bit intimidated. She reclined back on the dark leather sofa and relaxed comfortably. All she was missing was a wine glass filled with blood.

"I wasn't making a threat, Mr. Rocha. Though I do need Mateo's decision right now."

I looked past Emilio to the man I loved. At this angle, I could barely see his face.

Don't do it, Mateo, *I mentally begged.* Please, whatever she's offering, don't take it.

Mateo took a step forward and looked directly at Isabel. "I accept."

My heart slumped in my chest, turning into a weight too heavy to hold up. I pushed away the throbbing pain, and focused on the meeting.

"Is there something I need to do?" Mateo asked.

That evil smile spread across Isabel's face again. She pushed herself off the couch and model-walked toward my boyfriend.

"I'm so glad you asked. As it happens, I'm looking for someone very, very important. She's a little girl, and would be fourteen years old now. Pale skin, bright blue eyes, long white hair. You wouldn't forget her if you saw her. She goes by the name Andromeda."

My heart was pounding so hard it hurt. He won't do it, *I told myself.* Mateo likes Dro. He loves me. He won't turn on us. He would never–

"Yeah, I know Dro. She's a kitchen helper here. What do you want with her?"

I felt like I had been stabbed in the chest. A huge, raw pain dug itself into my heart like a knife, twisting and shredding every piece of hope I had. My vision blurred and a heavy lump formed in my throat. It hurt to breathe. I tried to tell myself it was a lie, that Mateo was just stringing Isabel along, but he had spoken too easily. There hadn't been any hesitation. He just gave in.

I clutched the side of the hacienda and the balcony railing, forcing myself to concentrate and push away the pain burning in my heart. I would feel it later. I held my breath and blinked to clear my vision, looking at the woman who ruined my life and the man who had just shattered the rest of it.

Isabel smiled again. "Don't worry about that. But if you bring her to me, you will be greatly rewarded." Isabel considered Mateo. "I trust that bringing Andromeda won't be difficult?"

"No, but," Mateo hesitated, "she has an older sister. Constance. And Constance won't give up her sister without a fight."

Isabel laughed. "I'm sure I can handle one temperamental girl."

Mateo stared at Isabel for another long minute, then turned his head toward Hernandez. "Bring Andromeda here. But don't hurt Constance."

That son of a bitch, *I thought hatefully.* Still acting like he cares.

It didn't matter now. I had to get my sister and get out of here. We couldn't wait. It would take Hernandez five minutes to walk to the servant house once he got out of the hacienda. Which meant I had ten minutes to get my sister and escape.

I gripped the railing and dropped down. I clutched the bricks and made my way down as quickly as I could. I slipped a couple times since there wasn't a lot for me to hang onto, but I kept going. Focusing on Dro made me faster, and once I was close enough to the ground, I let go.

My boots thumped hard into the grass, shock vibrating up my legs. I pushed myself up from my crouch and looked up. None of the guards had seen me. I shot to my feet, whirled on my heel, and sprinted toward the servant houses.

The little apartment building was tucked in a curve of trees on the left side of the hacienda. It had never seemed too close before. It would only take me five minutes to walk to Mateo's room whenever I wanted to see him.

My heartstrings twisted at the thought of looking in his eyes after what he had done. So I thought about Dro, and ran faster.

The door to the servant house was always unlocked, so I was able to shoulder my way in. I didn't even bother to see if anyone was awake and wondering what the hell I was doing. I didn't have time to care. I swung myself around the railing and stormed up the stairs.

"Dro!" I shouted. "Dro!"

She pulled open the door before I reached it. She was dressed for bed in navy blue sweatpants and an oversized sky blue shirt. Her long white hair was braided over her shoulder. Her eyes looked drowsy from sleep, but the moment they fixed on me, she started to wake up.

"Connie? What's wrong?"

I clutched her shoulders and forced her back into our room. "We have to get out of here, now," I urged.

I slammed the door shut and twisted the lock. I yanked the chair from the desk and shoved it under the doorknob.

"Connie, what's going on? You're starting to scare me."

At least I'm not the only one. *I pulled away from the door and looked at my sister.*

"Isabel. She's here."

Dro backed up, eyes going wide with fear. She started shaking her head. "No, no, that can't be—"

"I saw her, Dro" I said, grabbing the rest of my weapons and strapping them to my body. "She made Mateo an offer, and he took it. He sold us out."

I walked to the window and slid it up so we could climb through.

"Oh, Connie, I'm so sorry."

I flinched when heartache stabbed me again. Despite all our recent problems, we had loved each other. Or I thought we had. Things had been going good. I should have known better.

"We need to get out of here," I said as evenly as I

could. I pulled myself out of the room and hung on the windowsill. "Hernandez is on his way. They don't know what I heard, so we have a little more time. Come on."

Dro hesitated, then scurried over. She didn't have anything she needed to take. She climbed out of the window beside me and started making her way down. I reached up with one hand and pulled the window closed behind me.

I skidded down the walls while Dro made her way down the white lattice. We used to climb trees all the time as kids. Who knew the skill would come in handy later on when we needed to run from a traitorous gang and an evil witch?

I made it to the ground first, dropping onto the grass. Dro landed behind me, rushing to my back. I jogged to the corner of the apartment and looked around it. There were no extra guards. No one had been told to stop our escape, since they didn't think we would be making one. I looked at the line of vehicles across the front yard.

"Do you know who keeps their car unlocked?"

"Ricardo does," Dro informed.

"Which is his?"

She pointed to a pale green Mercedes Benz across from us by the gate. I looked between it and the security booth beside it. I glanced at the hacienda again. Hernandez wasn't out here yet, but he had to be close. I looked over my shoulder at my sister.

"You remember when Dad taught me how to drive?"

"Yeah, but I can't drive, I've never done it."

"Pull the handle to D to put it in drive. The left pedal means stop, the right pedal means go. I'll take care of the guards."

"Con, that's too risky! What if you get caught?" Her eyes glistened. "You know what they'll do to you?"

Oh, I knew all too well. They paid me to do the same things.

"They have to catch me first," I said. I reached

around my back and handed her my hatchet. She looked at it nervously. "Hang onto this until I get back in the car. Are you ready?"

"Yes," she lied.

I checked around the corner of the apartment building again and made sure the coast was clear. Then I turned and started running for the Mercedes. I moved at a brisk pace to avoid attention, but looked back and forth to make sure no one was following me. Dro had to jog to keep up with me. I reached inside my jacket and slid out one of my throwing knives. I tucked it up the sleeve of my long shirt so it would be ready when I needed it.

"Constance! Andromeda!"

I stopped in my tracks and whirled around, pushing Dro behind me. Hernandez was walking briskly toward us, his face completely deadpan. His jacket was open, ready to get a gun if I gave him trouble.

"Get in the car, Dro," I whispered to her.

She hurried to do so. Hernandez started jogging. He looked over my shoulder at Dro as she eased the car door open. I kept my hands loose at my sides and tried not to look severely pissed off.

"What's your sister doing?" Emilio's bodyguard asked when he was only a foot away from me.

"Ricardo forgot something in his car," I said. "He asked Dro to get it. Seemed fishy, so I came with."

"Huh," Hernandez grunted, clearly not buying my story. "Well, Emilio wants to see her. It's important."

"That so? What does he want?"

"Didn't say, and it doesn't matter." He leaned to look past me. "Get out of the car, Andromeda."

She started the car instead. Hernandez gave me a menacing glare. "Tell her to get the fuck out of the car," he growled.

"No."

His lips peeled back into a scowl, and he reached for the gun inside of his jacket. I palmed my throwing knife and hurled it into Hernandez's chest just as he pulled his hand back. His dark eyes widened in shock. He opened his mouth to scream, but I leaped on him. I yanked the knife out of his chest and shoved it into his throat. Blood squirted out from his neck, splashing against my hands and face.

There were some raised voices, the other guards asking what was wrong with Hernandez. I lifted my head and looked at the two guards manning the booth. I stood up, taking my knife with me. I looked at Dro and signaled her to move the car.

I dashed toward the guards as one of them lifted a radio to his lips. The second guard fumbled for the gun on his hip. I slowed down just enough so I could hurl my knife into his chest. He screamed and collapsed. The guard with the radio dropped it and reached for his gun. By the time he got it out, I was in front of him. I knocked the gun away and punched him in the throat. He chocked and gagged. I spun a wide roundhouse into the side of his head and knocked him out.

Then I heard new voices shouting. I looked over my shoulder. More guards were pouring out of the hacienda. Isabel, Emilio, and Mateo were among them. I grabbed the fallen guard's gun, then ran for the security booth. Dro was idling the car in front of the gate. She refused to go anywhere without me.

I stormed into the booth and looked at the controls. I flipped the switches to turn them on. The gate started to slide open–

Crack!

I jumped when the first bullet shot through the booth, splintering the glass window on my left. I ducked on instinct, but there was nowhere I could run. Two more bullets slammed into the wall and desk behind me. It stopped, and the shouting resumed.

"Don't shoot, you fucking idiots!" Emilio screamed. "We need them alive! Get the girl!"

I got to my feet, raised the gun, and started shooting at the guards. They cringed and scampered for the little cover there was by the other cars. It was all a blur, and I lost sight of Isabel, Emilio, and Mateo. I could only hear

Isabel and Emilio screaming. As soon as I stepped out of the booth, a sharp kick knocked the gun from my hands. I looked to my right. A fist crashed into my face.

The hit knocked me onto my ass. I shook off the dizziness, and looked up at the face of my boyfriend. My ex-boyfriend, now.

I scrambled back, glancing over my shoulder at the car. Dro had driven out of the gate and was waiting for me. She was hanging out of the driver side door, staring at me urgently. With Mateo stomping toward me, there was no way she could escape before someone else caught her.

"Go!" I screamed at her.

Mateo punched down for my face, but I rolled away and kicked him in the jaw. He grunted and stumbled. I hooked my leg around his arm and twisted until he was on his front and I was controlling his arm. I gave it a sharp tug, and yanked it out of its socket.

As Mateo screamed in pain, I looked back. I was about to be swarmed by Blood Thorns. There was no way I could make it out. I looked at Dro.

"Go! I'll meet you!"

My little sister shook her head, tears sparkling in her eyes.

"I promise! Go!*"*

That was the last thing I managed to say before Mateo jabbed his other elbow into my ribs. I was thrown off him, but ignored the pain as I got to my feet. I ran for the booth again, swinging into it and flicking the switch to get it to close. I looked out of the window and saw Dro driving away. As soon as she was gone, I reached under the desk and yanked out all the wires. Hopefully one of them would keep the gate locked–

A hand twisted in my hair and pulled me out from under the desk. He hurled me against the wall. I slumped against it, and he slammed a boot into my chest. My cry of pain was a broken gasp, but it didn't make him stop. His heel connected with my jaw, sending a flurry of pain through it. As soon as I landed on the floor, the kicks started.

Sharp, pointed boots jabbed themselves into my ribs and stomach, crushing the air from me. I used my far hand to reach for another knife, but he hooked my elbow. He twisted it until I rolled onto my back, desperate to relieve the searing pressure.

Emilio looked more furious than I had ever seen him. I'd killed his bodyguard, injured his son, and let someone important escape from him. He'd killed people for less.

But he wasn't going to kill me. That would have been far too kind.

"I should have known you were just like your father," Emilio sneered. "Trying to be noble and do the right thing, but a traitor to the very core."

Emilio leaned down, twisting my arm until I thought he was going to break it. I winced, but he stepped on my chest so I couldn't move.

"I never got the chance to make him pay for what he did. So I'll just have to make you pay for his betrayal, as well as your own."

Emilio's fist shot down into my head, snapping it to the side. My eyes fluttered closed, and soon I was drawn back into a pain-filled darkness...

Someone grabbed my shoulder. I jerked out of the dream and swung my fist at them with a roar. The man caught my wrist before I punched him in the head. I tried to pull away, but he wasn't hurting me. It took me a second to realize I'd nearly hit Warrick.

He stared at me with concerned green eyes. "Hey, relax, it's just me."

I jerked my hand back, unwinding a little. I sighed and started to sit up, rubbing my eyes with the heel of my palm.

"What time is it?"

"About three in the afternoon."

That explains why I'm so damn hungry and why I desperately need to pee.

Hunger and bladder aside, I was feeling much better.

All that sleep had been magic for my body. There wasn't any hint of pain or tenderness. Which meant I could start getting stuff done.

"Looked like you were having a hell of a dream," Warrick said, stepping back from the bed as I swung myself off of it. "Do you want to talk about it?"

"Nope. What's going on?"

Warrick frowned, but dropped the topic. "Everyone else is awake. The slayers want to meet with you. We need to talk about our next step, Constance."

"Wow, don't make it sound too fun," I muttered.

I raised my arms over my head and stretched them. They were a bit sore from two days of not being used, but they would be functional. I turned around and nearly bumped into Warrick, who had been watching me intently.

Goddamn it, he needs to stop doing that.

"Are you sure you're okay?" he asked.

Okay, maybe he can do it sometimes.

"I'm fine," I insisted. "I'll meet you in the kitchen. There is a kitchen, right?"

The worry eased itself off Warrick's face as he smiled. I practically melted.

"Yeah, go left down the hall and then turn right. I'll see you there."

I nodded and waited for him to leave the room. I finished stretching, used the bathroom, and picked out a set of clothes I found in the dresser. They were made for a woman about my size, so the black sweater and green cargo pants would fit me just fine. I started stripped and swapped clothes, pausing when I looked down at the bullet hole scar in my right shoulder.

Even with all her healing abilities, that was one mark Dro couldn't take away. It was a constant reminder of Mateo's betrayal, and if it had been three inches to the left, I would have died.

I thought I had left him and the Blood Thorns behind. But no matter what I did, it seemed like my past was all too happy to catch up with me.

Chapter 10

I thought I would like the demon slayers when I walked in the kitchen and saw the huge lunch they'd made us.

There were mouthwatering pulled pork sandwiches with crisp coleslaw, a hearty roasted zucchini and potato dish, a sweet-as-Heaven chocolate mousse pie, and fresh iced tea to wash it all down with. My stomach rumbled with anticipation. I was more than ready for an overly filling meal.

Then I looked at everyone in the room, and saw how pissed off they all were.

Sephiel was standing near the farthest wall with his hands crossed behind his back. He was staring at the ground, though he didn't seem hurt. I couldn't see his eyes, but I imagined he was caught between grief and anger. On his right, Max was sitting on a navy blue couch. He was slouched over a coffee table, slowly eating his lunch. He glanced at me and gave me a weak smile, but his eyes were distant.

At the kitchen island directly across from me, I spotted Warrick sitting with three other people. The one he was directly beside was a bald, bulky, kind faced man with onyx skin, wide lips, and big dark eyes. He was dressed in a grey shirt and military cargo pants.

Next to him was a blonde woman in her early thirties. Her hair was tied in a sleek ponytail that made her look cold and severe, but it didn't take away from her beauty. She had high cheekbones, pouty lips, sculpted eyebrows, and bright blue eyes. She raised her head when she saw me walk in. Her eyes went down to my clothes, and she grimaced. Well, at least I knew whose wardrobe I'd raided.

On the other side of the pissy woman was a man in his late fifties. For a guy his age, he was in fantastic shape. Hard muscles could be seen under his black shirt. The man was about as sturdy as a piece of concrete. Grey hair was cropped close to his head in a buzz cut. My gut told me he must have been a military man at some point. His lips were turned down and his eyebrows were pinched together, as if he spent all his time accusing people.

Which must have made him the leader of this little group.

I looked to my right when I saw white hair moving near the stove. Dro was focused on putting a couple plates together, her snowy hair pulled into a simple braid down her back. My heart sighed gratefully, until I saw the tightness of her lips. I took a resigned step toward her.

"Sit," she said sharply, not even turning to look in my eyes.

I stayed there for a moment, not wanting to keep things this way, but not getting another choice. We had to figure out what to do next. Then I could get her to forgive me. Hopefully. I turned back to the kitchen island and took the last chair next to Warrick. He gave me an understanding smile that I didn't return.

My sister dropped a mountain of food in front of me, and was gone before I could thank her. I pretended it didn't bother me and grabbed the pulled pork sandwich. I took a bite and focused on the barbecued bliss. The pork was tender, the bread was warm, and the coleslaw was tangy. I immediately knew that Dro had made it. She tried to cook when she was cranky or upset. I kept eating, but it felt like I was just going through the motions and fuelling my body.

"So you guys are the other demon slayers, huh?" I said, not caring how snarky I sounded.

"Yeah," snapped the woman across from me. "You're welcome for saving your life, by the way."

Warrick cleared his throat. "Constance, this is Jackson," the big, black man waved to me. He smiled a nice, sincere smile.

"That's Elle," Warrick continued, pointing to the scowling blonde woman. His finger went to the man on my right. "And that's her father, Carver."

Carver stared at me. I stared back.

"Carver's the one who recruited me," Warrick said, getting my attention. "He's the leader of the slayers. He's kept it secret for years."

"Something we had every intention to continue doing," Carver said. His voice was even deeper than Warrick's, which made his indictment sound even harsher.

The green-eyed demon slayer glared at Carver, but held his tongue. I showed less restraint.

"We'll make sure to stay quiet the next time Lucifer and his band of psychotics show up and start torturing people."

Carver shot me a look that could have cut glass. I stared unflinchingly.

"You've been unconscious for two days, so you have no idea what your actions caused Bullhead City."

"Do share."

His blue eyes were piercing. "It was destroyed."

I didn't have anything smart to say to that. The words sank in slowly. I thought about the sign before we had entered. *Population 39,540. Jesus Christ.*

Maybe it had been less than that when Lucifer finally arrived, but how many more people had died once we escaped? If Warrick was right and the King of Hell couldn't find us, did he really take it out on a city of innocent people?

Once glance at Warrick told me all I needed to know.

"When John told us where you were coming from, we tuned in the radio to see what was happening," said Jackson, pushing himself up from the kitchen island. He seemed a little more sensitive. "It took a few hours, but by then the news vans were there."

Jackson walked over to the coffee table and picked up the remote for the TV hanging in the top corner of the room just above where Max and Dro were sitting. She was picking at her food with one hand, and holding her boyfriend's with the other. Max was pressed against her arm, whispering gently and gesturing to her food.

The TV flickered to life to a news station that was running a live story. The screen was split between a middle-aged man in a newsroom, and a pretty brunette reporter standing in front of a warzone. I couldn't even see buildings. It was just a wall of flame.

"Alan, I'm standing in front of the remains of Bullhead City, where an unknown explosion has completely devastated the area, despite it being under military protection."

"Do we know what caused the explosion yet, Shannon?"

"I'm afraid not. Firefighters are still trying to put out the blaze with water bombers, but so far the attempts have been wasted. I'm standing three hundred feet from the city's border, and even from here I can feel the fire on my back..."

I curled my fingers into fists. I knew firsthand what Lucifer's fire felt like. I remembered how it blistered and cracked my skin, the way the smoke tasted as it scorched my throat and burned my lungs, how my blood simmered until I thought it would melt in my veins–

I jumped when something touched my knuckles. It was a hand. Warrick's hand. I glanced at his concerned green eyes and gave him a nod to let him know I was fine. He didn't seem convinced, but still took his hand back. I focused on the reporters when they started talking again.

"Do you think this could be a terrorist attack, Shannon?"

"Well, government officials are looking into all possibilities at this time," said the brunette reporter, "but no terrorist groups have come forward with demands. A lot of people are thinking this is either connected to the strange, supernatural attacks that have been occurring in all the southern states, or to the unusual group that appeared outside of Bullhead City shortly after it was attacked."

The footage cut to a dozen men in white trench coats stood in front of the burning city with their backs to the camera. Whoever was holding the camera was using the crappy zoom on their phone, but I could still make out the faces of the angels when they turned around.

I spotted Rorikel and Gabriel. In the center of the group was the tallest, toughest looking angel. I'd never seen him before, but even in the camera-phone video, he looked incredible. Not as heart wrenchingly beautiful as Lucifer, but very, very close. Golden hair curled down to his broad shoulders. His face was perfectly sculpted and strong. I couldn't tell what color his eyes were, but they burned like the fire behind him. He wore a white metal chest plate similar to the ones the ancient Spartans used to wear. On the middle of the plate was a gold sigil that I recognized, because I had it tattooed on my chest.

The sigil of archangel Michael.

I wasn't even listening to what the reporters were saying anymore. All I could look at was Michael. I knew it was him. My head snapped to Sephiel. His eyes were on mine, and he nodded sadly.

Damn it. God fucking damn it.

Jackson shut off the TV and looked at me. I didn't have any answers for him. I wasn't even sure this wasn't another fucked up dream. My appetite was completely gone, and I'd barely eaten half the sandwich.

"We know that those men were angels, like your friend over here," Carver said, gesturing to Sephiel and keeping that accusing tone in his voice. "We also know that Lucifer was the one who destroyed Bullhead City. Warrick has told us that he's been hunting you and your sister, but he never said why. She must be important, because I know she isn't human."

I narrowed my eyes at Warrick, who opened his mouth to speak.

"Don't try blaming John, Ms. Ramirez," Carver said. "The moment we found you, I saw your sister healing you with magic." He turned his intimidating eyes on Dro. "She's been very stubborn and has refused to answer any questions, let alone say more than three words. So I'm going to ask you. What is she, and why does she matter to Lucifer?"

"What she is isn't important," I said, amazed at how steady my voice was. "Lucifer is."

"Well, Lucifer is looking for her," Elle said sarcastically. "So why don't you tell us what her secret is?"

I glared at her. "Lucifer's a fucking sadist who wants to gather up anything supernatural for his army. Happy?"

Elle's lips curled back. "You're a fucking liar."

I balled my fists. "I've had a really shitty week, bitch. Don't push me."

"Uh, whoa, okay, calm down ladies," Jackson said. "This isn't the time for a cat-fight."

It wouldn't be a fight, I thought to myself.

"Listen, Constance, we can't help you if you don't give us something."

I looked at Jackson. He seemed straightforward and nice. He must have been the one demon slayer that Warrick said he'd trusted. Not that it encouraged me.

"Lucifer wants something more than my sister," I admitted. "He wants to get into Heaven."

That confused the demon slayers enough to forget about Dro.

"Why would he want that?" Jackson asked.

"Because he believes it is time for the damned to be granted salvation," Sephiel said, making us look at him. "Hell has become overrun with the sinful, and Lucifer wishes to lead their souls to Heaven and increase his power."

"But you angels are supposed to stop them," Elle pointed out. "That's what you do, protect humanity and stuff."

Sephiel was shaking his head. "Perhaps you remember a few months ago when these supernatural events first began occurring in Texas. That was when both the Gates of Heaven and Hell were opened. Heaven has long waited for the opportune moment to cleanse Hell of damned souls. They believe humans are destined for sin, and they wish to restructure Hell."

"But, that would upset the balance of the universe, right?" Jackson said. "And they would have to cross paths at some point."

Sephiel nodded this time. "Yes, Jackson Everhart. They would confront each other the moment war appealed to them. I fear that such a battle would be devastating to mortals." He looked at us seriously. "My hypothesis is that none of you would survive."

Silence was a heavy cloud in the room after that. *Ugh. I hate when he sounds so right about everything.*

"We need to find and close the Gate of Heaven," I said to get us back on track. "If we do that, then we can guarantee that Lucifer won't take over Heaven, and it will take the angels off our tail."

"The angels are trying to kill you, too?" Jackson said. He looked at Warrick. "Damn, Ricky, what the hell did you get yourself into?"

"Believe me, Jack. I ask myself that every time I have a chance to think."

He gave me a teasing smile. I couldn't even roll my eyes at him.

"You're an angel," Elle said to Sephiel. "Shouldn't you know where it is?"

"I am a soldier of the Heavenly Host," he answered simply. "But I fear my memory has been cleared of the Gate's location so that it may be protected."

"How convenient," she muttered.

That bitch was really getting on my nerves. "Look, you want to stop the demons? Closing the Heaven Gate is how we start to stop the demons. If you'd listened to Warrick in the first place, this might not have happened."

"Warrick withheld information from us," Carver said sharply. "He was helping an unnatural creature and–"

"Don't call her a creature," I warned.

My threat would have worked better if he'd actually been intimidated by me. "Look me in the eye and tell me that all of this would have happened if there weren't supernatural creatures in the world. If angels and demons had stayed in their territory."

I tried to think of an argument, but I didn't have one. The son of a bitch was right. If angels and demons had left well enough alone, the world wouldn't be falling apart. Bullhead City would still be standing. Nearly forty thousand people would still be alive. Sephiel would be with Everiel. Warrick might still have his sister. Manny would be alive to spend time with Max. I wouldn't have turned into a criminal. My parents wouldn't have been murdered.

Dro would never have existed.

There were a lot of things I wished I could change, but that wasn't one of them. Maybe it was because I had been beside her my whole life, but I just couldn't imagine a day without my little sister. I wouldn't be half as strong as I was today. Dro wouldn't be around to lift people up and take care of them.

I wouldn't truly understand what hope meant.

"Wake up, Carver," I said bluntly. "This is the way the world is. It's full of demons and angels and shitty situations, and that isn't going to change. But don't you dare blame it on my little sister."

A muscle twitched in Carver's jaw. He narrowed his eyes. "You said Lucifer is hunting her, but you're purposefully blind to what she really is. Look at what he did to Bullhead City when he couldn't get her. How much suffering will you let her cause before you accept that she's a monster?"

My hand was on the knife by my plate before I could think about what I was doing. Warrick grabbed my wrist and trapped my hand to the table. I shot him a look that could have killed. I was ready to shout and curse and beat the shit out of Carver.

I wasn't ready for what my sister did.

"*Enough*," she commanded.

The entire room turned to look at her. Max had moved a couple inches away from her. Dro's blazing eyes were everywhere at once. For the first time, I could feel the power radiating off of her. It was heavy and all encompassing, like Lucifer's. When I was possessed, the demon controlling me had thought that Dro was one of the most powerful creatures in the universe.

I was starting to think he was right.

Her jaw was set, eyes burning with passion. This was how Dro looked when she faced off with Gabriel and his angels, when she destroyed the demon Knight. She looked this way when she spoke to Lucifer.

Strong. Confident. Impressive. Dangerous.

Deadly.

"This isn't high school," she snapped. "We don't have time to be petty. I'm grateful that you sheltered us and let me heal my sister, Mr. Carver, but I am not going to sit here and let you judge me based on something I couldn't control. I want Lucifer destroyed more than any of you. So instead of spitting venom, why don't we focus on something we can actually do?"

No one interrupted her. Dro took a deep breath.

"Max can't see where the Heaven Gate is, and Sephiel can't remember. I won't risk looking in case Lucifer senses me. The best option we have right now is to look at locations that have a high supernatural frequency. Max can use his gift when we go there using Sephiel's teleporting magic. That will keep us hidden from both the angels and the demons for a little while. Unless someone has another idea."

Nobody did.

"All right. Then we should get a map and get started."

"Um, we might have something better than a map," Jackson started.

"Jackson," Carver warned.

"Sorry, sir, but she's right. We don't have a lot of options, and he might know."

I looked between Carver and Jackson cautiously. "Who might know?" I asked.

Carver didn't want to answer. Warrick turned to face

him directly.

"Carver, we don't have time for secrets regarding the Heaven Gate. We need to close it if we're going to start helping people."

The leader of the slayers stared at Warrick for a long time. I wondered what it must have been like to train and work under this guy. It must have been about as fun as walking on broken glass.

After another minute, Carver pushed himself away from the kitchen island. He got out of his chair and started walking away. Elle pouted, then followed her father. Next was Jackson, after he clapped Warrick on the shoulder. The rest of my group followed. Warrick and Sephiel left the room. I tried to walk with Dro, but she clutched Max's hand and kept her eyes down. I sighed heavily and followed them out of the kitchen.

Carver and his gang turned down another grey hallway, entering a code into the keypad next to a huge steel door. There was an angry buzz before the door could be pulled open. We all filed through the hallway that held four locked doors. It reminded me of a solitary ward in a prison.

Carver stopped at the last door on the right, turning as if he was giving us a tour.

"We picked him up after the Bullhead City Burning, as the media's now calling it," he said. "He hasn't said a word to us, but maybe you can get him to give up something useful."

Carver punched in another code by the door. It buzzed open, and we looked inside.

The room was nearly pitch black except for a dull yellow glow from the tube lights in the ceiling. There was nothing in the room except a steel chair and a man bound to it. His head hung to his chest. Dirt and blood covered his white clothes and jacket. He heard us come inside, and raised his head.

His tanned skin was broken and bruised, his sandy blond hair was mussed and wild. Hazel eyes blazed with anger.

I didn't even know it was possible to capture an angel, but I never thought the slayers would be able to capture Gabriel.

Chapter 11

"Brother Gabriel?" Sephiel said, clearly as surprised as we were.

The archangel smiled playfully. "Brother Sephiel. It is good to see you again."

Gabriel looked like he'd been thrown down a rocky hill. His white trench coat and clothes were covered in brown and grey dust. His skin was just as dirty. His left eye was closing over, there were two yellow and purple bruises forming on his right jaw and cheek. Blood dripped from his broken nose, split lip, and the cut on his left eyebrow.

I'd seen beatings before. I'd given and taken them. But this shocked me. An archangel had been captured and tortured. Something sacred and holy had been damaged. It made me sick, but I wasn't as vocal as the rest of my group.

"What the fuck is this, Carver?!"

"I demand that he be released immediately."

"You guys are fucking lunatics!"

"He needs to be healed."

I stared at Gabriel, who watched the whole scene with an amused expression. I wondered if he was in pain, and why he hadn't healed himself. My eyes went down to the cuffs on his wrists, which were covered in strange symbols I couldn't read. His chair stood inside a spray-painted circle on the floor around his feet. The same symbols on the cuffs were on the floor. It didn't take me long to understand what the slayers did.

They had created a trap.

I did the same thing once when I was trying to get information from a demon. We never really focused on angels in the beginning. I didn't know they could be captured and bound, let alone trapped.

"When we found out that angels were starting to run around, we knew we needed to get one for information," Carver explained once everyone stopped shouting. "They're hard to find and put up one hell of a fight. But this one got overwhelmed by some demons," he pointed to Gabriel. "As soon as we had him, we bound him with anti-seraph spells. The cuffs prevent him from doing any sort of sorcery. He can't hurt anyone."

"But he can't heal himself either," Dro repeated.

"He doesn't need to be healed," Elle said. "Not until he tells us what he knows about the other archangels and how to defeat them."

"You cannot defeat the Heavenly Host," Gabriel said in his elegant voice. "We are a legion beyond mortal comprehension. Michael alone could crush thousands of you in the blink of an eye. And make no mistake, humans; he will search for me. When he learns what you have done, he shall take revenge upon you."

Gabriel's sharp hazel eyes turned to Dro. "And then he shall take possession of his chosen vessel."

Dro flinched and squeezed Max's hand.

"No one is taking Dro anywhere," I said, crossing my arms and walking deeper into the room. "But if you tell us where to find the Heaven Gate, we'll let you go."

"That is not your decision to make," Carver growled.

"Ask me if I give a shit," I snapped. "You kidnapped and tortured an archangel because you hate the supernatural. You're not what I would call a rational person."

"You fucking bitch," hissed Elle.

She might have said more, if Gabriel didn't start laughing.

His laugh was sweet and gentle. It would have made me smile if I didn't know exactly how lethal Gabriel was.

"Humans are so emotional and short-tempered." He slid his hazel eyes over my shoulder. "I understand why you enjoy their company, Sephiel. Angels are not nearly as galvanic as mortals are."

"Gabriel," Sephiel said, taking a step into the room. His bright blue eyes were heavy with pity and sadness. "Brother, please, you must help us find the Heaven Gate. You have seen the destruction Lucifer has wrought. This madness is of spiritual design. Humans should not suffer for it."

Gabriel laughed again. "Truly, you have spent time with the wrong species, brother Sephiel. Your allies are a burdened demon slayer, a lost prophet, a murderer, and the unholy spawn of Lucifer."

I spun my head over my shoulder, watching the other slayers as they eyed Dro suspiciously. Warrick moved himself in front of Dro, ready to protect her. Max never let go of my sister's hand.

Jackson flashed his eyes between Warrick and Carver. Elle was bordering on confusion and anger. Carver looked so tense I thought he was going to snap in half. He turned his face to mine, and focused all his rage on me. I looked away from him, scowling at Gabriel. The damn archangel was smiling.

"They did not know who she was birthed from, did they? Such a shame."

"Tell us where the Heaven Gate is, Gabriel," I said, making sure I had a solid hold on my temper.

"Why? So you can destroy my kin? Tear the wings from our backs and make us fall? Your demand requires too high a cost."

"How high is it going to be if Lucifer gets into Heaven?"

Gabriel's smug expression started to vanish. "You have no idea how powerful the Heavenly Host is, mortal. Lucifer and his minions are no match for it."

"Really? If you could have crushed him so easily, why didn't you just do it the second the Gates were open? Humans are just tiny ants under your boot, right? Why not step over us and get the inevitable out of the way?"

Gabriel set his jaw and glared at me. If the anti-seraph cuffs hadn't been binding him, he probably would have jumped out of the chair and strangled me.

"Lucifer's stronger than you thought, isn't he?" I didn't ask it as a question.

"Because of *her*," the archangel said viciously, narrowing his eyes on my little sister. "She is the turning point. Under Lucifer's control, her power would be calamitous. That is why she must give herself to Michael. He can absorb her powers and defeat the beasts of Hell."

"And kill the entire human race in the process?" I snorted. "I don't fucking think so."

"Your desire to save your race is the exact thing that ensures its demise!" he suddenly roared. "Inflexibility and inability to see the greater good is what will cause your downfall!"

"You seriously need to spend more time around humans," I said.

Gabriel laughed cruelly. "Why, so I may become like him?" He jerked his head at Sephiel. "The angel who chose to forsake all his beliefs for the child of his dead lover?"

Sephiel stared blankly at Gabriel. I couldn't tell how much his brother's words hurt him, but they had to sting. Every time someone brought up Dro's dead mother, Sephiel either went tense with anger or slumped with grief. Right now, he looked tired more than anything else.

"Sephiel may find humans noble," Gabriel went on after Sephiel didn't react, "but after what I have seen and endured, my assumption is quite different."

"We didn't know what was happening to you," I said. "If we did, we would have stopped it."

Gabriel scoffed. I crossed my arms tightly around my chest. "Dro offered to help you. Don't get bitchy just because you said no."

"Constance," Sephiel said wearily. "I fear we shall not obtain any information from Gabriel. He is a resilient angel. We can do no good by arguing with him."

I looked at Sephiel, then opened my mind to let him into my thoughts.

They're just going to keep torturing him.

I am aware. But there is nothing to be done for it. Time is short. If Gabriel will not help us, then we must explore other options.

I pushed him out and snapped my mind closed. I might not like Gabriel, but I didn't want to leave him in the hands of Carver and Elle, either. But what choice was he giving us?

I sighed heavily and turned, walking out of the room. Sephiel followed me.

"That's it?" Max said, looking between Gabriel and me. "We didn't get anything."

"In case you missed that whole conversation, Mr. Angelic Asshole isn't going to tell us anything. If you have any other ideas, drop them on us, Max."

The dark eyed psychic gave me a hard look. He turned his head to his girlfriend. Dro was watching Gabriel with sad eyes. She wanted to help him, but there was no way we would let her get near him. I sure wouldn't allow it, even if he was in pain and tied to a chair with enchanted handcuffs.

Max was still holding Dro's hand, making up his mind about something. I glanced at their hands. There was such a contrast to their skin. His was the same dull gold as mine, and hers was paper white. But it didn't look unnatural. It looked meant to be, like white-hot fire melting into a pot of gold. Their fingers meshed together, his larger hands perfectly aligned with her delicate ones.

Max's touch comforted Dro in ways I never could, though I wondered what it was like for Max. He had a lot of control over his powers, and touching someone as powerful as Dro never seemed to bother him. He'd been surprised when his fingertips first brushed hers and he got a sense of how strong she was. All that power should have alarmed Max, but it only made him want to get closer to my sister.

Maybe that was why he trained with Sephiel to control the senses and emotions that came with his unique magic, and why he was working on honing his precognition. He wanted to keep them under his control.

Max's powers were sporadic sometimes, but he knew how to use them. More importantly, he knew *when* to use them.

Max looked over my shoulder at Carver. "Those wards are secure, right? He can't get out of the bonds or the circle?"

Carver shook his head, narrowing his eyes on the kid. "Not unless we release them, which we have no intention of doing until we have answers."

"Max?" Dro said.

He looked at his girlfriend. His face softened when he smiled at her, like all his problems could be taken away by staring into her eyes.

"It's okay, pretty girl. This will work."

"What will work?" Warrick asked.

Max grinned at the demon slayer. He pried his fingers from Dro's and showed Warrick his palms.

"Magic hands."

"Max," I said, starting to understand his plan.

"Seph said that the archangels know where the Heaven Gate is. If I look into his mind, I might be able to see where it's hidden."

"An archangel's head isn't like a human's head," Warrick pointed out. "Looking into one seems like a huge risk."

"Well, yeah, it's risky, but that's why it might work." He looked at Dro. "I don't want you to do it, pretty girl. It'd be too dangerous."

Dro bit her lower lip. "But what if he does something to you?"

Max just shrugged. "I doubt he can. Like the slayers said, he can't do any of his magic outside the bonds and the circle. There isn't a way for him to hurt me. If there was, he'd be out of that chair and burning our eyeballs out."

None of us laughed. Max sighed and stood in front of his girlfriend, taking both her hands in his.

"This will help, Dro. I know it will. I'll be careful. Anything feels off, I'll back out. I promise."

Dro hesitated again. Max must have felt her worry,

but he kept his face neutral and calm, as if her uncertainty reminded him of how much she loved him.

"The angel is my prisoner," Carver said angrily. "I haven't given you permission to do anything to him." He turned his cold blue stare onto Warrick. "You never told me he was a supernatural."

"No disrespect, pal," Max said, "but what I am isn't your business."

Carver tensed and tried to take a step forward. Jackson put his hand on the man's shoulder to stop him. Carver twisted his head around, looking at Jackson icily. The large man took his hand back.

"Sir, maybe we should let them try this. We haven't been lucky with our tactics."

Carver's eyes narrowed until they were slits. Then he turned his blistering eyes on Max.

"You have five minutes. Use them wisely."

Max rolled his eyes. "You can't rush talent, you know."

Steam was practically shooting out of Carver's ears, but Max ignored it. I swear, no living human being could intimidate that kid anymore.

Max kissed Dro's hand and walked past me into the cell. Sephiel followed right behind him. Dro watched her boyfriend nervously. I put my hand on her shoulder before I walked back in the cell.

I wouldn't let anything happen to Max, and not just because he meant the world to my sister. Max was a good kid, stubborn and fearless. He had been nervous about me when we first met, but it didn't take long for him to get used to me. He was the only person in our group who had enough sense of humor to keep us smiling, no matter how bad the situation was.

Max stopped in front of Gabriel. The archangel tilted his head, trying to push himself into Max's mind. He frowned when it didn't work.

"You must have some sort of magic," Gabriel guessed.

"Yup. Don't worry. I don't think this will fry your

brain."

Max took a step closer to the edge of the circle, reaching out to touch Gabriel's hand.

"And you love the hellspawn."

Max's hand froze in midair. He stared directly into the archangel's eyes. "Yeah. I do. So watch what you say about her, bird-brain."

Gabriel looked at Max with total confusion. "How?"

"How what?"

"How can you love her? Surely your magic must show you the darkness surrounding her. You must feel it with every touch. How can you cherish something so evil?"

Max's eyes narrowed. "Because I'm not blind. I can see what she is. Her power nearly knocked me on my ass the first time I touched her. It's a tidal wave in my head whenever I touch her now. Some days I think it'll drown me. I don't have any illusions as to how powerful my girlfriend is.

But there's something stronger underneath that power. I can dig past it and see the goodness in her. The strength and courage she never knows she has until she uses it. Nothing evil loves and cares as much as Dro does."

Max bent at the waist to look directly into Gabriel's eyes. I was amazed that the angel had stayed quiet.

"Her origin might be evil, but her soul is as bright and as clear as it can get. It's this blindingly warm feeling that makes you think you can touch the sky. It's perfect and pure, and that's who Dro is. She makes me think anything's possible, because I know she can literally do *anything*."

Max leaned back. "How can you not love someone like that?"

We were all speechless. I knew Max loved my little sister and would stand up to her, but I never expected him to tell us what he saw when he touched her. She was his adrenaline rush and his hope. The beacon that gave him strength. No wonder he was head over heels for Dro.

I almost asked him if he knew how much he would love her when he first met her. If he'd had a vision of her before they met, and if the feelings were stronger than he thought they would be.

It was a mystery I was happy not knowing. Max would never hurt my sister, and that was the only thing I really needed to know.

The archangel read Max's face, seemingly too stunned to speak, like some of what the kid said actually resonated with him.

"Well," Max sighed as he straightened his back, "now that the truth's out there in the open, let's get this party started."

Before Gabriel could protest or flinch, Max reached out and touched the top of the archangel's hand.

The slayers and I couldn't see anything happening. We were all non-magical humans. Dro and Sephiel were the only ones who could see the supernatural. Max's shoulders were tense, his eyes squeezed tightly shut and his mouth was in a thin line. Gabriel stared at him unblinkingly and without emotion. I turned to Sephiel.

"What's going on?" I asked.

"Max is trying to break past the barriers Gabriel has placed in his mind," he answered, watching the scene carefully. "Angel minds are meticulously warded to prevent demons from breaking in and stealing Heaven's secrets."

"Can Max do it?"

"Perhaps. Gifted humans are exceedingly rare, and therefore most angels have not protected their minds from them. We never sought the need. This may not have worked on Michael, but with the right motivation, I believe Max can obtain some information."

Sephiel looked at me. "And now we understand the depth of his motivation."

That we do. I loved my sister with all my heart, but there were things I couldn't give her. I couldn't hold her at night and make her feel like she was the center of the world the way her boyfriend could. The love I felt was the love of a sister, which was completely different from the tenderness of a lover. I was overprotective of Dro. It was the one switch I couldn't turn off. But Max was perfect for her, and I would never take that away from them. It only made me want to fight harder. My sister had found the happiness she was missing with me. I was determined to let her keep it.

I watched Max carefully for the next two minutes. His body got more strained every second that passed. He began to tremble slightly. His eyes and lips were pinched so tight I could see tiny wrinkles forming around them. His breathing was becoming labored. I looked at Sephiel.

"He must have found a way through. Patience, Constance."

Five seconds later, Max gasped sharply. I took a step forward, but Sephiel put his hand on my stomach to keep me from breaking his concentration. Though the angel was ready to move if he had to. Gabriel sat in the chair, looking as blank as ever. I would have thought he hadn't moved at all, except that his hands were now tightened into fists.

A flicker of shame darted through Gabriel's sharp golden eyes. He blinked slowly, and then looked down. Max collapsed immediately after.

Sephiel and I caught him before he hit the concrete, carefully putting him into a sitting position on the floor. Dro and Warrick rushed into the room. The slayers stood outside, watching tensely.

Max's face was twisted in with pain. His eyes were shut so tight they looked almost sewn together. His lips were turned down into a grimace. Thin trails of sweat beaded down his forehead. He breathed through his teeth.

Dro knelt beside me and put her hands on her boyfriend's face. They began to glow a moment later as she healed whatever was in his head. I gave her some space and stood up. I turned to glare at Carver and clenched my fists at my side.

"I thought you said he couldn't do any magic in that circle," I growled.

Carver stared me down. "I did the wards precisely as my research instructed, but this is the first time I've ever captured an angel. Let alone an archangel. Mistakes can be made."

He might have been right, but I still wanted to knock his teeth out. Then again, maybe it wasn't Carver I should be getting ready to punch, but the creature that hurt Max. I turned my fury on Gabriel. The archangel sat on the chair and looked at the ground, as if he were defeated.

"What the fuck did you do?" I snapped, walking closer to the prisoner.

"Angelic wards always have a failsafe," he answered, surprising me, "in case our minds are broken into."

"What kind of failsafe?"

This time he looked up at me. "They are meant to erase the memory of all the intruder has seen. It is impossible to steal the mind of an angel."

"Forest always green waterfall dahlias stream willows trees," Max was breathing out craziness that meant nothing to us.

The gold light in Dro's hands grew brighter. He finally slumped, exhausted. Dro pulled her hands back and sat on her heels. She watched her boyfriend's face as Warrick and Sephiel kept him steady. Max groaned, then blinked his eyes open.

"Well," he sighed. "That was an experience."

He grinned weakly when Dro took his hand. He relaxed again. "Are you okay?"

"Yeah," his smile faded, "but I think I got a legendary headache for nothing."

"You can't remember anything?" Warrick asked.

"No, I can, but it's all images. I was telling you guys everything I could, but I think it was seeing what Sephiel saw."

The angel looked at him. "Your jargon sounded most accurate, ironically."

Warrick took Max's hand and pulled him to his feet. "You might want to take it easy for a bit."

Max was standing straight, but he looked exhausted. He put his arm around Dro's shoulders not just to hold her close, but to keep from collapsing again. He used his other hand to point at Warrick's chest.

"I like the way you think."

Warrick grinned and stepped back so Dro and Max could leave the cell. My sister didn't look back at me. The rest of us followed them out, standing in front of the slayers. I didn't like the way they were watching Max. Carver looked like his head was about to burst.

"You should have told us you had a psychic with you," he growled at Warrick.

"Max is harmless," he defended. "Which is more than I can say for us if you try to do something to him."

Carver tightened his jaw. I don't know what his past relationship was like with Warrick, if he used to be the favorite or was the troublemaker he could never control, but at that moment all he seemed to want was to punch Warrick's lights out.

Thankfully, Jackson was quick enough to stop Carver from doing anything he would regret.

"So," the large man said awkwardly, "what are we going to do with the angel now?"

We all looked at Gabriel. He still hadn't raised his head.

"If he isn't going to tell us anything, then he's useless," Carver said. "We might as well kill him."

Warrick's jaw dropped. Sephiel's eyes blazed with rage.

"I will not witness the murder of my brother," he said seriously.

"We can't let him go," Elle pointed out. "He'll kill us the moment he's released. Do you honestly think he'll show mercy to you? He made it pretty clear that he doesn't really think of you as family."

Sephiel's fists were white-knuckled. He was ready to punch Elle into the next universe. Carver reached for a knife from his hip and took a step toward the cell door. I stood in front of him and blocked his path.

"Get out of the way."

He made sure I could see the huge knife he was carrying. I crossed my arms, uncomfortably aware that I had no weapons. My knives and hatchet were missing. I didn't know if they'd been recovered after the fight with Lucifer or if I'd lost them again. It made me sad to think I might have lost another special weapon. Sephiel made the hatchet to replace the first one I lost. It was a light, silver bladed weapon with a leather wrapped hilt. On the edge, he engraved the words *'Anima potentis, cor sororis.'* In Latin, it meant 'Soul of a warrior, heart of a sister.'

I'd become accustomed to the new weapon, though it wasn't the original hatchet I had taken from my father the night he was murdered. It was the last piece of my family, and it was lost in the cave-in when we were rescuing Dro from Lucifer. I didn't like the idea that I would be losing things I was getting attached to, even if they were just things. I didn't even think about losing the people I was attached to.

Still, I kept my face neutral as I stared down Carver. He wasn't the first large fighter I'd faced. There was nothing he could do or say that would scare me.

"Killing him is a bad idea," I said.

"I'm not going to tell you again," he threatened.

"Then I'll spell it out for you. How long do you think this bunker will be shielded from Michael? You think he won't come looking for his second in command? What do you think he'll do when he finds out that you haven't just tortured him, but murdered him, too?"

Carver didn't immediately attack me, so I kept going.

"I'm not saying Michael will be kind or merciful if he finds you." I looked into the hallway. "I've only known one angel who's both of those things."

Sephiel inclined his head gratefully. I looked at Carver again.

"But I think it's a safe bet to say that Michael won't immediately come after revenge if you leave Gabriel alive. You guys aren't the ones he's after."

"You think you know how an archangel's mind works?"

"Oh, I know I don't. But getting on an angel's bad side is the last thing you want to do." I cringed as I remembered the heat of heavenfire at my back. "Trust me."

Someone stood next to me. I didn't have to look to know it was Warrick. I was all too familiar with his warm, musky pine scent when he stood close to me.

"She's right, Carver. We've seen what angels can do. They're just as ruthless and deadly as demons are. You can't take back killing Gabriel, and Michael isn't very forgiving to his enemies."

For the next couple minutes, Carver and Warrick were completely focused on each other and oblivious to the rest of us. Warrick looked as honest and uncompromising as ever. Carver looked like he wanted to put a hole though the wall. Or through someone's head.

Then a miracle happened. Carver sheathed his knife.

"We let him live for another few days until you figure out this damn Gate thing. If I think he's going to be a danger to us, then I will do whatever I have to do."

Warrick cringed a little, then nodded. He took a step forward until he was inches from Warrick's face.

"This is the last favor I'm giving you, John. I won't let any of us be killed because you care too much. We both know what happens when you start doing that."

Carver turned and walked away before Warrick could say or do anything. Elle followed her father like a hungry puppy. Jackson gave Warrick a regretful look, but followed them too.

"You were right," I said when they were out of earshot. "These slayers are assholes."

I looked at him, grinning to make him feel better. Warrick stared ahead hopelessly, like he was trapped on an island and watching his rescue boat go up in flames.

"Warrick?"

He didn't even blink. I touched his arm. He jumped a little and looked at me.

"Are you okay?"

He slumped and took a step away from me. I had the crushing urge to grab him and pull him back.

"I'm all right," he muttered. I didn't believe him for a single second. "I think I'm gonna go train for a little while."

"Do you want me to come with..."

Warrick was already walking away. He turned out of the door and was gone. I sighed, rubbing my forehead to take away the headache beginning to grow in my skull. Why did everything have to be so fucking complicated?

I was walking out of the room when I felt eyes on my back. I looked over my shoulder.

Gabriel was sitting in the chair watching me. He didn't look as conceited as before. His hazel eyes were locked on mine in an earnest way, almost like he understood me. But that couldn't be possible. Gabriel liked watching humans run around in circles and get into trouble. He didn't want to understand us. He just wanted to remind us that he was better than we could ever dream to be.

I turned my back to him and started walking away again. For some reason, I stopped when I was in the hallway to look at him one more time.

That strange, understanding expression was still on his face. He held my eyes for a long time, and I was suddenly grateful he was bound in the circle. I didn't want him jumping into my head right now.

Gabriel dipped his chin, then raised his head at me.

I was stunned. Did he just nod at me? Why would he nod at me? What did it mean?

I had no clue, and I didn't trust it. But even as I closed the door and pulled the door handle it to make sure it was locked, I couldn't help but think that the archangel was debating on switching sides.

Chapter 12

Sephiel was the only person waiting in the hallway after I made sure Gabriel was locked up. Heavy sorrow covered him again. Maybe he'd been too lost in his own thoughts to move. The last few days had been a wild ride for Sephiel. It was amazing he hadn't completely snapped yet.

"Sorry about what he said, Seph," I told him quietly.

"Your condolences are appreciated, Constance, but unnecessary." His voice was lifeless.

True, it should have been Gabriel who was apologizing, but seeing Sephiel broken down made me sorry for him. The angel had turned his back on his home and his brothers and sisters to protect a girl he should have hated. He saved our lives and always seemed like nothing could faze him.

Then Lucifer appeared, and all that changed.

"We should return to our domiciles," he said.

"Yeah. I feel like I can never get enough sleep these days."

We were silent as we walked down the hallway. My mind kept going through ways to talk to Sephiel, but everything seemed too wrong. I couldn't even think of a random topic to take his mind off everything happening to him. His family was trying to kill him. His spiteful brother was being tortured. His lover was dead. His archenemy had returned and nearly slaughtered him.

People going through all that drama didn't exactly talk about the weather.

"I am indebted to you for standing up for Gabriel," the angel said after a long time. "I am aware how protective you are when it comes to the well being of your friends."

I snorted. "Gabriel's not a friend."

"No," Sephiel said, stopping in the middle of the hallway to face me. "But I am."

I stared at the auburn-haired angel. He didn't even doubt what he said. I wasn't a nice person. I wasn't easy to get along with, and I didn't give out my trust easily. But Sephiel had done a lot for us. I owed him more than I could ever repay. Whether I wanted to admit it or not, he was a friend.

"Don't hang onto that sentiment too much," I replied with half a grin. "I'd still like to give Gabe a smack for talking to you the way he did."

Sephiel lowered his eyes. "It is not Gabriel who angers me." His voice became much, much darker. "It is Lucifer."

I kept my mouth shut, thinking back to the way Sephiel had reacted when he saw his lover's rapist and murderer. There were no words to describe how hateful Sephiel had looked. It scared even me.

"We had no reason to suspect it was he who stole Everiel," the angel said out of the blue. "Michael and the others assumed she had fallen of her own accord. But I knew better. Everiel may have loved humans, but Heaven was her home."

Sephiel paused, lingering on the bittersweet memory.

"I searched for her, receiving Michael's permission to leave Heaven and discover her whereabouts. It was not long before I encountered demons."

He flexed his hands, turning them into fists. "I did things to them that I am not proud of, but I obtained my answer. They said I would never find her. That Lucifer was already using her for his own ends, and that she showed promise, despite her resistance."

I felt sick. Rape was common in Juárez. Men tried to rape me all the time when I was getting into fights against rival cartels. Every single one of them got a taste of my hatchet.

It was impossible for me to imagine the pain and

suffering Everiel had endured under Lucifer. All of that power forced onto you in Hell would break the strongest woman.

"The demons would not tell me the location of the Hell Gate, so I returned to Heaven and pleaded to Michael to launch a full scale rescue. He did not accept. He said it was foolish to risk the entire Host and provoke Lucifer into war. He believed Lucifer would not be able to produce a child from Everiel."

He was very fucking wrong.

"I turned my pleas to other angels, desperate for help in my search. No one would test the will and wrath of Michael. So I searched alone. I spent a century on earth looking for her, living among the mortals and opening up all the channels to hear her."

That explained why Sephiel was so sympathetic toward humans. He'd lived with us for a hundred years.

"Finally, I put out a call, and I heard her voice." Sephiel took a deep breath. His eyes glistened. "I followed her cry across the world. She needed me more than ever. When I arrived, Andromeda had already been born."

I was very careful when I asked my question. "You saw Dro when she was a baby?"

Sephiel nodded, but didn't look at me. "I urged Everiel to return with me to Heaven, but she was so weak..."

He paused to take another steady breath. "She pleaded that I watch over the child. She had the gift of foresight, and told me the child would have a fierce protector, but they would need another to watch over them. It was a promise I could not deny."

Sephiel stopped again. I didn't push him or tell him to end the story. There was no reason for him to tell any of this to me, except that it might ease all the misery he was enduring. How did a person live with all that pain locked inside? How could they keep it all together? Maybe Sephiel had a method of keeping himself in one piece, but I couldn't even imagine how hard it was.

"She would not have wished that I seek revenge for

her. I tried to honor that wish. I have demonstrated obedience and temperance my whole life," Sephiel went on. "I am willing to forgive any faults of my kin or of mortals. I have forgiven Michael for forbidding the search, all the angels who would not help me, and I have even forgiven you for restraining me when I saw the Archfiend."

He lifted his head. That terrifying, blistering hatred was back in his eyes. They glowed blue with rage. It was the kind of look that made me remember exactly how malevolent Sephiel could be, and that getting in his way was a very, *very* bad idea.

"But I will not forgive Lucifer."

It was a promise. If Sephiel had the chance to kill Lucifer, he would do it. I wouldn't stop him again, but I knew he would die. Sephiel was blind with sorrow and hatred. It would get him killed.

"Lucifer will get his, Seph," I told him. The lie was smooth and sincere. "But you can't run off after him alone. He's stronger than you."

"Do you assume I am not aware of this?" he said sharply. "I have observed the results of his power countless times, Constance. I was witness to his Fall, the Sin of Eve, everything. All he has done, I have seen. But Death will come for Lucifer, by my hand or another's."

"Then let it be another's," I offered. "Killing for revenge doesn't bring you peace. I killed Isabel, and I still feel the same pain I felt after she killed my father." I kept my hands loose at my sides before adding, "Revenge won't bring our loved ones back."

I honestly thought he was going to hit me. Sephiel's animosity oozed from his whole body like lava. If he attacked me, I would put up a fight, but I wouldn't be able to stop him. Partly because he was stronger than me, and partly because he was one of my only friends. I didn't want to hurt him.

But Sephiel didn't move. The anger twisted into sadness so agonizing to see it made me want to cry for him. I wouldn't wish his pain on anyone.

Except for Drake, Mateo, and Lucifer, of course.

I took a careful step toward the grief-stricken angel. "Look, don't do anything to get yourself hurt. It would crush Dro."

He raised his head again.

"She loves having you around. You're her mentor and her friend. The last thing she wants is for you to suffer and die." I took one more careful step. "You don't have to worry about honoring Everiel's memory, Seph. You already are by keeping Dro safe. I might not have known Everiel, but I'm willing to bet that you protecting her daughter would mean more to her than martyring yourself."

Sephiel slumped against the wall, closing his eyes. He sighed heavily, like his heart was sinking with every breath.

"Yes," he finally whispered. "It would."

It was another minute before Sephiel opened his eyes. There was still a deep misery in them, but I could see a hint of closure. As if he was finally ready to accept that revenge wouldn't get him anywhere. He wasn't ready to let Everiel go, however. Something told me he never would. At least this was a start.

"I am grateful for your kindness and attention, Constance. I did not know how dearly I needed it."

I shrugged. "Don't mention it. You're the only person who wants to talk to me right now."

Sad but true. Which means I need to talk to my sister.

"Perhaps I should leave you to tend to Andromeda," Sephiel said.

I raised my eyebrows. "Did you read my mind?"

He smiled sadly. "I fear there was no need. I shall seek conference with Max to give you more privacy. We will try to uncover the location of the Heaven Gate."

I nodded. Sephiel bowed slightly then turned and started walking down the hall. I watched the angel turn down the corner and disappear from sight. Half of me was glad that Sephiel had gotten all of that off his chest. The other half was remembering what it was like to be broken hearted, and suffer because of it...

He nearly knocked my head off with his latest punch. The entire world was pain to me. My head was pounding. Smears of blood and puffy bruises covered my cheeks. I could hardly see out of my left eye. My chest and stomach felt like elephants had stomped on them. I was wheezing every time I breathed.

And Emilio thought his son was being too soft on me.

"Tell us where she is, Constance," my employer said. "Mateo has all the patience in the world for you, but mine is running thin."

I stared at Emilio's shiny black shoes because it hurt to lift my head. I was unconscious when they dragged me into the basement to interrogate me, so I learned later that Isabel had left in a rage, storming away to start her own search for Dro. I was worried about my little sister, but she was smart. She would be able to sense Isabel coming and find a way to hide. She would be safe.

The same couldn't be said for me.

Mateo's harsh slap woke me up from my trance. I choked on a cry as the blow stung my battered face, making the open cut on my cheek burn even fiercer. The right half of my face felt like it was on fire.

"Stop dragging this out," Emilio said, taking a step closer, "otherwise we're going to have to get creative."

I forced myself to scowl and push my eyebrows together, pretending to be angry. The truth was that I was fucking terrified. Beating the life out of people wasn't amusing for Emilio. Not when he would burn, drown, stab, hang, electrocute, or dismember them. Nobody created suffering quite like Emilio Rocha.

I kept my lips closed. It wasn't that hard, since my blood was making them stick together. I still had my voice, for whatever that was worth. I'd been to enough 'interrogations' to know that everyone had a breaking point. All it took was the right leverage and the right motivation. I wasn't stupid enough to think I wouldn't snap sooner or later. The goal was to get out of here before then.

So I just stayed silent and stared hatefully at the father and son. Emilio didn't have a mark on him. There wasn't even a speck of dust on his fancy black pants. Mateo looked a little rougher around the edges. His shoulder was back in place, but his dark hair was mussed and sticking out, dirt and tiny scratches covered his black suit, and a bruise was forming on his jaw from where I'd kicked him.

Mateo stared at me with a mix of disappointment and distress. It only made me angrier. He wasn't the one who had been betrayed. He had no right to feel anything at all. As I looked at him through one and a half eyes, my sore heart thumped slowly. I couldn't tell if it was because he'd broken my heart, or because I hated him down to the core of my soul.

"This isn't going to work," Mateo said, flexing his knuckles and staring at my blood on them. "She isn't going to give Dro up."

"Yes she will," Emilio said. "She just needs to understand how serious this is."

He walked toward the left wall and started rifling through items left no the table. I listened to the heavy clatter of tools and sharp blades as Emilio looked for something more his style. I tilted my head down as gently as I could, my sweat-soaked hair sticking to my forehead.

The zip ties around my wrists and ankles were so tight I was almost losing circulation. They'd already cut into my skin from where I'd pulled on them, and I couldn't risk severing a vein. There was no way I could escape.

The light clip-clop of Emilio's shoes made me lift my head. A sharp bolt of pain ripped down the back of my neck. I winced at it, my eyes starting to widen as I saw the hacksaw and the c-clamp. All my pain turned into fear. I'd seen this torture before.

He would take the hacksaw and start to slice off an appendage. Usually, he started with the hands. He sawed slowly, making sure the victim felt the pressure and wrenching agony of the saw. It was impossible not to see the flesh being savagely shredded away, dark blood squirting and gushing out as veins and arteries were severed.

But he didn't cut all the way to the bone. Not to start. He stopped after a couple cuts, and then the clamp came into play. He would tighten it around a finger or toe, then pull as hard as he could.

Usually it wasn't enough to rip the hand off, but the victim wouldn't know that. All they would feel is the searing agony as Emilio pulled their skin hard. It wouldn't be long before he pulled too much, and dislocated a finger from its socket.

If they still didn't talk or were too busy screaming, it was back to the saw.

Emilio reserved this torture for people he wasn't just angry at. This was something for people he despised. The ones he wanted to suffer with every waking breath.

I didn't know if I could take it.

I turned my head away as he slowly walked closer, each step sending new waves of terror through me. I squirmed in the chair, no longer caring that I might cut myself on the zip ties and bleed to death. It would be better than what Emilio was going to do.

I froze when I felt the jagged edges of the hacksaw on my wrist, just above where they were tied to the arms of the chair. My heart smashed against my ribs so hard it made my entire body shake. I couldn't control my breathing. Emilio was as calm and as cool as a stone.

"This is your last chance, Constance," he warned flatly. "Tell me where your sister is."

The smart thing would be to tell the truth. Torture broke everyone sooner or later. But I knew Emilio. I'd been working for him for four years. The second I told him what he wanted to know, two things would happen. First, he would send all the Blood Thorns to find Dro. And they would find her. His network was enormous.

Second, he would torture me to death. Giving him

information wouldn't keep him from punishing me for killing his bodyguard, attacking his son, and letting my sister escape.

There was no way to win.

He pressed the hacksaw down on my wrist until the jagged tips were pressed into my flesh. I winced as new blood flowed out around the zip ties. He tightened his grip on the handle of the saw. His eyes were black holes in the dim light of the basement.

"Remember that I gave you a choice," Emilio whispered. His voice held promises of pain.

My breath hitched as a scream built in my throat.

"Wait."

We both looked at Mateo. He was staring at my hand, desperation in his eyes. He looked at his father, that desperateness quickly fading away.

"I have an idea."

"You had time for ideas, Mateo. We're going to do this my way now."

Emilio pressed the hacksaw harder into my wrist. I winced as the serrated edges sank in, like a vampire slowly sinking its fangs into its prey.

"There's another tactic we haven't tried yet," Mateo said quickly. Emilio and I looked at him again. "Let me talk to her. Alone."

Emilio scowled. Then he straightened and walked over to his son. I slumped with relief as the hacksaw came out of my arm. My entire hand was covered in streams of blood and throbbing like it had just been smashed with a hammer, but it was still intact.

My chest heaved rapidly, unwelcome adrenaline making my ears pound. I tried to steady my breathing, but I couldn't focus.

Mateo looked at the wall near the door, a sign that he wanted to talk to his father where I couldn't hear. I groggily dropped my head, letting them assume I was too focused on my pain to listen to what they were saying. I felt their fierce glares on me, then heard them walk across the room and start to whisper. Their voices were so faint *that I had to lean forward in my chair to hear them.*

"You really think talking will work with that traitor?" Emilio remarked quietly. "She isn't the type that can be reasoned with."

"Not by you," Mateo replied. "But with me."

Emilio stifled a laugh. "I doubt that. Your judgment is clouded when it comes to her. Your feelings will get in the way."

He took a step closer to his father and lowered his voice. "No, that's exactly what will make her talk. Trust me, Dad. I'll make her understand. I can do this."

Mateo looked at me. I dropped my head before he could see I was listening to what he was saying. Rage went through me like an electric shock. He still thought I cared about him enough to give up my little sister because he would ask nicely.

The bastard never knew me as well as he thought.

"Fine," Emilio said impatiently. "Try it your way. But when she refuses to tell you anything, I'm going to do it my way. And you will not interfere."

Mateo paused. He was the only person in the world who could actually negotiate with Emilio, but even his son knew there was a point where he couldn't stand in front of his father.

"Yes, sir," Mateo said.

Emilio shoved the torture devices against Mateo's chest and stormed out of the room. It suddenly seemed too quiet. I kept my head hung low as he walked back to the left wall. He dropped the tools onto the table, then fumbled around for something. Mateo might want to talk to me, but torture wasn't beyond him either.

I was mildly surprised when he put a chair down in front of me with a white cloth and a first aid kit. I said nothing as he opened the kit and took out a bottle of peroxide. Mateo poured some of the peroxide onto the cloth and reached up for my face.

"Don't fucking touch me," I hissed.

He pulled back a fraction, looking hurt. For a second, he looked like the Mateo I had loved, heartfelt and emotional. Then his dark eyes hardened, and he became the Mateo I hated.

"I'm trying to keep you from getting an infection," he shot. "Why do you have to make everything so fucking difficult?"

"Don't blame me for this. It wouldn't have happened if you hadn't ratted Dro out to that bitch."

Mateo flinched, now knowing I'd heard him talking to Isabel.

"What did she promise you? Power? Strength? A harem of fuckable teenagers? All of the above?"

He glared, clutching the peroxide-soaked cloth tighter.

"I can't believe you bought into that shit, that you're some chosen one for a divine purpose. You don't know a lie when you hear one– ah!"

Mateo shoved the peroxide soaked cloth onto the cut on my cheek. I winced as the peroxide seared my open wound. It was a torture in of itself. I was able to breathe through it until it was over, though my eyes were watering when I opened them.

I turned my head to meet Mateo's eyes. He frowned, reaching out to grab the nape of my neck. I tried to pull free, but he jerked me closer. His grip was an iron vice on my neck. I flinched again as he wiped away blood and spread peroxide around my face.

My entire head started to burn. Tears spilled down my cheeks before I could stop them. I gritted my teeth until it hurt, trying to tear myself away from his hand.

"Stop moving, damn it," Mateo growled. "I'm trying to help you!"

Hatred filled me again. I was done with all this pain and his lies. My sister was out there alone and worried sick. I had to get to her before she decided to come looking for me. I snapped and tried to bite Mateo's hand.

He jerked back before my teeth could get him. He stared at me with shock, his face turning darker as he grimaced. His fingers curled into a fist, and he arched his arm to hit me. I stared at him and waited for him to do it.

Mateo sighed and dropped his arm instead.

"Why the fuck are you making me do this, Constance?" he whispered. "I hate hurting you. Stop making me."

Mateo sounded so pitiful I almost felt bad for him. If I'd seen him like this yesterday, I would have done anything and everything to comfort him. But that had all changed now. There was no forgiving what he'd done.

"Nobody's making you do anything, Mateo," I replied. "You're doing this because you want to."

His head snapped up. "I have orders—"

"Which you break all the time," I reminded.

I didn't expect my voice to crack the way it did. That was when I had to know why he'd done it. Why he'd been so eager to give my little sister to Isabel.

"Why?" I forced myself to ask.

Mateo looked at me sadly. He knew exactly what I was talking about. He just didn't want to answer me. When he reached out with the peroxide to clean my face again, I let him.

"She said I was chosen to serve her master, and that if I did as he wished, we would have the future we all wanted," he answered. "The Thorns would take control of Mexico, we would move the organization up into the States. Dad would have no restrictions. No one would be able to touch him. And I..."

Mateo raised his eyes and I remembered why I'd fallen in love with him. Deep, dark brown eyes glittered with strength, passion, and life. He refused to let anything or anyone stand in his way. Not even me.

"She said I would be able to make you mine forever. You'd only love me, and no one else."

Breath squeezed out of my lungs. My heart started cracking again.

"You were going to give up my sister because you thought I would stop loving you?"

"Dro never liked me and never trusted me," he argued. "She wanted you to see the worst in me. She wanted to break us. I couldn't let her do that, Constance. I

DARK DIVINITY 186

love you too much."

He meant every word. I was the reason he woke up in the morning, what he dreamed about at night. I was his whole world. Any other time, I would have killed to hear those words.

Now I just felt hollow.

"Look me in the eye and tell me you never would have left," he said.

I could see the pleading in his eyes. This was him asking me to give up my sister. This was his attempt to save me from more pain. He was angry with me, but he was willing to forgive it all if I gave in. After everything he'd done to me, he still thought I would love him enough to forgive him. Mateo had complete faith in me.

So I destroyed him.

"You're right," I admitted. "I would have left. Dro didn't like it here, and I would go because she asked me to. But I would have taken you with me, Mateo. There would have been time for her to see the good in you. We could have made it work. But instead, you were selfish. You were blind and jealous. You forgot how much Dro means to me, and you betrayed all the trust I ever had in you."

Mateo leaned away slowly. I watched the pain spread across his face. I was breaking his heart. Good. It was the only way I could get him out of my life. I wasn't anything like him. I wouldn't betray someone I loved to get ahead in life. Even if I could stomach it, Emilio wouldn't buy my story for a second. He'd hound me until he discovered what I was up to, and then I would be tied to this chair again with no one to stop him from cutting my hands and feet off.

"I loved you, Mateo. I would have given you that dream you wanted. But not anymore. I will never love you again, and when I get out of here, I'm going to rip all your dreams to shreds."

He was frozen in the chair, clutching his chest like it was wounded. I knew how badly he was hurting, but none of it changed my expression or made me feel sorry for him. Mateo was prepared to let my sister suffer so he could have me to himself, completely forgetting that she was the biggest part of my life. He disrespected me in the worst way imaginable, and acted like it wouldn't matter if she were gone as long as we were together.

If he'd had a younger sibling, maybe he would have been different. But it didn't matter now. I wouldn't take back what I said. He searched my eyes, hopelessly trying to find anything that might prove I still loved him.

Except that I didn't. I looked at him blankly, without any emotion. Finally, the reality set in. Mateo closed the first aid kid, refusing to look me in the eyes. He stood up from the chair and began to walk out of the room. Just when he was at the door, he stopped and turned his head to the side.

"My father is going to kill you, Constance," he said heavily. "He's going to torture you to death. I don't know how, but he'll make it last. You're going to beg for me to save you."

Mateo turned to look at me. His eyes shimmered, but his face was hard.

"And I'm not going to be there."

The man whose heart I demolished walked out of the room, slamming the door shut behind him. I couldn't feel anything. I tried, but there was an emptiness inside me. It would never be filled again. I wouldn't let it.

That was fine, because I wasn't going to live much longer...

Chapter 13

I ran into Max just as I got to the room where Dro was staying. He was shocked to see me, and his cheeks turned red. I crossed my arms.

"Do I need to be concerned about my sister's honor? Because I promise you, I'm ready to fight for it."

Max flinched, then shot me a pointed glare. "Give me a break, Constance. It wasn't like that."

I scanned his eyes, looking for guilt. There was none, at least not from him. Max loved and respected Dro. He would never push her into doing something she wasn't ready for. I felt a little bad for the harshness of my teasing, but if Max wasn't used to my attitude by now, he never would be.

Rather than apologize, I went with a standard icebreaker. "How are you feeling?"

He shrugged. "Oh, you know, nearly having my head explode is a feeling I'm starting to get used to," he grinned.

I wasn't able to smile. "Look, Max–"

He waved me off. "Forget it. I didn't do it for you."

That got me smiling after all. I glanced at the door. "She's inside?"

Max hesitated. "Yeah, but she's asleep. You might want to come back later."

I shook my head. "She's awake. Dro can't sleep when she's mad."

"Are you sure it's a good idea to see her, then?"

No. "I'm not having this go on longer than it has to, Max. It's between us. Seph's waiting for you in the training hall."

Max paused, like he didn't want me to see my sister, but he knew by now that nothing would keep me from her.

He held the door open for me so I could walk into the room. My little sister was sleeping on her side, her long white braid draping down her back.

"Good luck," Max said quietly.

"I'm not going to hurt her again," I said.

"It's not her I'm worried about."

I turned my head to Max, but he was already closing the door and leaving us inside. The room was dark except for the lamp in the corner. This room looked identical to the one I was borrowing. I took a deep breath and walked toward the bed. I kicked off my boots and climbed on top of the sheets, resting my back against the headboard next to her.

After a long time, I asked, "How mad are you?"

She didn't say anything, but I saw her tighten her arms over her chest. "On a scale of one to ten? Eleven."

I sighed. "I'm sorry for whatever I did, okay?"

"No you're not."

I looked at her as she finally rolled over to face me.

"You say that, maybe you even believe it, but you're not really sorry. You always put yourself in danger when you know better."

So that's what she was mad about. Me literally putting myself in Lucifer's line of fire, and almost dying in the process.

"I'm your big sister. I'm supposed to do stuff like that."

She shot up into a sitting position, icy blue eyes furious. "Don't use that as an excuse."

"It isn't—"

"Yes it is," she snapped. "I had it under control. I didn't want you getting hurt."

"It didn't look like you had it under control," I muttered before I could stop myself. I winced at Dro's harsh expression.

"Because you did so much better. What was your plan, big sister? Stab the Devil and hope he would die before he could strike back?"

I held her eyes. "Honestly, I wasn't planning on

doing anything but keeping you alive."

Dro's temper faltered for a second. She took a deep breath and gathered herself again.

"I'm not a child anymore, Constance," Dro said as patiently as she could. "You can't fight all my battles for me, especially not these ones."

I narrowed my eyes. "Well, I'm not going to sit here and twiddle my fucking thumbs, either."

"Goddamn it, Con, I'm not joking around!"

"Neither am I!"

We stared each other down. We were as different as sisters could be, but we had one trait in common:

Stubbornness.

"Look, I didn't mean to shout," I told her honestly. "But what do you want me to do?"

Dro's eyes softened, but the intensity remained. She took a deep breath.

"When we come up against him again, I want you to let me fight Lucifer."

For a moment I thought I misheard her. Then I saw the seriousness on her face.

"Absolutely fucking not," I said flatly.

Her eyes turned to stone. "This isn't a negotiation. I'm fighting him. Not you."

"Andromeda—"

"No," she interrupted. "This is how it's going to be. You're the strongest, toughest, bravest person I've ever met. You're the best big sister in the world. You've fought for me since before I could stand. But this isn't a street brawl. These aren't the Blood Thorns or demons. This is *Lucifer*. The King of Hell. The Original demon."

Dro held her breath. "And you're human."

There it was. That damn word again. *Human*.

My loss for words gave Dro the chance to speak again.

"I'll find a way to do it, Con. I don't know how, but I will. You showed me how to defend myself. I won't give up or run. But it's going to be a battle with powers and magic... And you don't have those."

"Because I'm human," I said aloud.

Dro looked at me sadly, her resolve beginning to break.

"Please don't think it's a bad thing, big sister. I love that you're human. You keep me feeling normal. You scare off demons and monsters and prove that anyone can be a champion. But you don't know what it was like for me to watch him burn you. I heard you screaming and I knew you were so much pain, and..."

She trailed off as the awful memory choked her. Dro shook her head, snow-white braid swishing against her back.

"I've spent the last six years watching you nearly die. I stand back because you tell me to, because you've always been the one to protect me. But I can't do it anymore, Connie. I can't keep letting you treat me like I'm made of glass."

Her words hurt me more than I expected. Did Dro really think I saw her as someone who was weak? I didn't have a chance to ask, because she looked at me again and spoke before I could.

"The things that worked for us on the run aren't going to work anymore, Con. It literally is us against the world. If we really are going to fight together, you can't keep pushing me back. You've been my shield for way too long."

I'd been guarding Dro for so long that it never occurred to me that I was hurting her as much as helping her. It was just instinct. If something tried to attack my little sister, I killed it. That was the way it had always been.

But Dro grew up when I wasn't looking. She was getting stronger every single day. I couldn't hold her back from herself.

"I can beat him," she repeated, bringing me back into the world. "But you have to promise that you'll let me. If I worry about you and lose focus, he'll kill us both." She winced. "Or worse."

It would definitely be worse. Lucifer's hellfire had

been the most horrible thing I'd ever felt, and I was willing to bet that he could get experimental in his tortures. Nothing would break Dro and I faster than watching him torture one another. She would do anything he asked, and he would enjoy my pain.

Watching Lucifer tear out Dro's rib was a memory that haunted me every minute I was awake, and every second I slept. Even now, with her sitting inches from me, breathing, looking healthy and completely alive, I could see was his hand jamming into her side. I could see her back arching as she screamed and screamed and screamed...

I looked down. "I can't make that promise," I admitted quietly.

She watched me without speaking for a long time. "You have to," Dro said firmly. "You're going to. Or so help me, I'll knock you unconscious, drop you in Mexico, and go on alone."

The commitment in her voice hit me like a punch in the stomach. Dro and I didn't lie to each other. If she thought knocking me out and ditching me would keep me safe, she'd do it. After all, that's what I would do.

"Promise me, Con."

I looked at her. Angel face, long white hair, bright blue eyes. My little sister didn't seem so little anymore.

Trapped facing choices no one should face. Hunted by the Devil just because she was existed. Fearing her powers and the damage she could do to the people she loved.

I didn't know how to stop protecting her from all those things, let alone Satan himself.

I opened my mouth and nothing came out. I dropped my head and shook it, short black hair hiding my face.

"I... I can't, little sister."

"Promise me," she demanded.

Dro wouldn't take no for an answer. She was going to fight Lucifer alone. I couldn't help but feel like I was getting a taste of my own medicine. Dro had been following my lead since the time she could walk. As she got older, she got tougher. She made her own judgments. She watched how hard I fought and how fearless I made myself. I never let anyone take control in a situation when I didn't have to.

But this situation was out of my control. A choice I couldn't– and had no right– to make. My sister didn't get upset with me very often. When she did, it was for a good reason. If I took another risk when she begged me not to, it would take weeks for her to talk to me again. If she ever did.

My heart felt too heavy, like it was a boulder I was pushing uphill with every breath. There was no happy end to this. If I ignored my sister's wish, I would die. If I gave in, we might both die. Either way, we would lose.

It hurt to breathe, but I inhaled, steadily raised my head, and said the two hardest words of my life.

"I promise."

I didn't wait for Dro to confirm my expression. She knew my word was my word, especially to her.

I wanted to leave, but I couldn't move. I wanted to argue, but I couldn't speak. It felt like something had been cut out of me. Something was lost between us, and I didn't know what it was.

Dro threw out her arms and hugged me. I tried to understand what just happened. How had it come to this? Why did I say yes? Had I done something wrong? Didn't Dro trust me?

As if she heard my thoughts, Dro hugged me tighter.

"I love you, Connie. Don't ever change. Please just let me do this."

I folded my arms around her and waited for the tightness in my chest to ease. I couldn't even pretend everything would be okay. There was only one thing I could take comfort in.

No matter what happened, Dro would always be my little sister.

"You're okay, right?" she asked when she broke away.

"I will be," I said. It almost sounded true. "Just wish

we could go back to being kids again."

Dro grinned sadly. "Yeah. Everything was easier then, wasn't it?" Her grin faded. "Con, about Mateo..."

"Don't worry about it," I mumbled. "I'll deal with him when the time comes."

"I never thought we would see him or Lucifer," she went on. "I didn't even bother to ask Max to look."

"He wouldn't have a lot to go on. Besides, we were kind of busy running for our lives," I said with a dry smile.

Dro's smirk was awkward, and didn't stay on her face very long. "I'm nervous to open my mind again," she went on. "The moment I start using my powers, Lucifer will sense me."

"Then don't use them."

"I have to. How else are we supposed to close the Heaven Gate?"

"I don't know," I confessed. "But you told me to make sure you don't lose yourself. At the motel you wanted to kill those Possessors. You incinerated that Knight. Seems like every time you use your demon powers, you become more..."

Dro and I were close enough that I didn't have to finish that sentence. She pulled her knees up to her chest and looked at her feet.

"I know. I hate that feeling, but demon powers are just so much easier to use, and I don't see any other options. Max and Sephiel can't pinpoint the location, and Gabriel isn't going to tell us anything." Dro shook her head. "I wish there was something we could offer to have him change his mind. I wanted to heal him. They should never have hurt him like that."

I watched my sister's eyes. We were both coming off an edge and trying to get rid of bad memories. We needed something to cheer each other up. If there was one thing that would make Dro feel better about a bad situation, it was helping someone.

"Do you still want to heal him?" I asked.

My sister looked up at me. "What?"

"Gabriel. Do you want to heal him?"

Dro bit her lower lip. "Of course, but wouldn't that make Carver mad?"

I waved the comment away. "Who cares? Carver shouldn't have been trying to capture angels in the first place. Who knows, maybe Gabriel will feel more chatty if we help him."

I started sliding off the bed and walking to the door. Dro followed me.

"What makes you say that?"

I paused, turning to face Dro. "Before I left the room, he gave me this weird look. Like he was ready to trust us."

Dro squinted, confused. "Why would he do that?"

"No idea." I opened the door. "So let's get the guys, and we'll find out."

***

Warrick, Max, and Sephiel didn't hesitate to come with us when we told them we were going to see Gabriel. It eased my mind the closer we got to the cell door. The archangel might have been spelled and bound, but I didn't trust him not to try anything when Dro came in.

"Shouldn't we be asking Carver's permission?" Max asked.

"Don't tell me you want to have him boss you around," I said.

Max stifled a laugh. "Not at all. But he'll probably have a hissy fit if he finds out."

"Carver's asleep," Warrick said. "So is Elle. Jackson's taking a break. This is the only chance we're going to have. If Carver does find out, I'll say we were going to ask more questions."

Max and I looked at him. "Won't he go berserk on you?"

Warrick stopped in front of the keypad and sighed. "One problem at a time. Let's get Gabriel healed first."

The demon slayer still seemed a bit off. I wasn't

going to ask him about it yet. He probably wanted to avoid the issue anyway. I certainly would.

"You know the code?" I asked.

He nodded. "Every few months we would get together and have a meeting about places that had a heavy demonic presence. Carver would reassign us to another state to cover it until the supernatural threats were decreased or gone. I haven't been to a meeting in a few months, but Carver is predictable once you know how his mind works."

Warrick punched in the code for the door. Sure enough, the door buzzed and clicked. Warrick pulled the door open and waited for the rest of us to file in. He stood by the door, glancing down the hall to make sure no one was going to catch us off guard.

Gabriel was still awake and staring straight at us. That same weird, understanding expression remained on his face. His hazel eyes traced over each one of us, stopping the longest on Dro. He grimaced a little as she got closer. We all stayed close to her back. I was wearing my new hatchet and knives under my lucky jacket, borrowed black shirt, and cargo pants. Sephiel managed to find a new hatchet for me, and Warrick brought me a new set of throwing knives that our angel made sure to bless. My other weapons had melted when Lucifer burned me. I wanted to be sure that Gabriel would be able to see all my sharp new toys, so he would think twice about trying to hurt my sister.

Dro knelt down until she was eye level with the archangel. He watched her, not sure what she was doing.

"I'm sorry for what they did to you," she said honestly.

Gabriel kept staring. Dro lowered her head.

"We might not agree on how to stop Lucifer, but no one should be captured and tortured."

"What is this?" Gabriel asked. "An effort to appeal to my sympathies and earn my permission to destroy the door to my home? Do you know how many angels will fall if you close the Gate?"

"I can hear all the angels if I want," Dro said, a hint of coldness in her voice. "So yes. I do know."

Gabriel narrowed his eyes. My sister sighed. "I understand why you don't like me. If I were in your position, I wouldn't like me either." She raised her eyes. "But closing the Gates is the only way to prevent unnecessary war."

He grinned cruelly. "You do not seem like the type to condone the sacrifice of many for the lives of a few."

"I'm not," she replied. "And believe me, I'll grieve for every fallen angel. But unless you have another way to defeat Lucifer, then we don't have a choice."

His smirk faded. Dro shifted a little closer to the chalk circle. She never broke eye contact with the angel.

"But I didn't come here to argue. I came here because I wanted to heal you."

Dro slowly raised her hand and eased it toward Gabriel. I wrapped my hand around the hilt of my hatchet. Sephiel moved to Gabriel's side, standing just on the edge of the white chalk circle. The archangel never flinched or blinked.

My sister's pale hand rested on top of his tanned one. A moment later, a gold glow came from her palm. Her healing magic seeped into Gabriel's skin. He couldn't move his hand away, so he just looked at my sister without emotion. I could only imagine what was going through his mind as his bruises began to fade and open cuts were closed. In a couple minutes, Gabriel looked perfectly fine. The only evidence he'd been beaten up at all was the leftover blood on his face and clothes.

Dro took a deep breath. She pulled her hand back and stood up. Max was at her side, placing his hand at the small of her back and giving her a gentle smile. Gabriel watched her, stunned.

"Why did you do that?" he asked. "I tried to have you killed."

Dro looked at him seriously, a knowing smile coming over her face. "I know. But no one else was going to help you."

She slid her hand into Max's, then glanced at Sephiel. He inclined his head gratefully. She turned and met my eyes, giving me a gentle smile. I didn't fake the one I gave her. Dro would feel a little better about everything now that she'd used her powers for something good, even if Gabriel was on a mission to kill her. The four of us turned and started walking for the door, where Warrick was still waiting.

"You stole the *movens caeli*, Sephiel."

The auburn-haired angel turned, meeting his brother's hazel eyes. "I did. And I do not plan to return it."

"Good," replied Gabriel. "Then you can use it to aid us in escaping this place."

I turned, crossing my arms over my chest and resting my fingers on the head of my hatchet. "You make it sound like you're coming with us."

"If you wish to find the Heaven Gate, you will require my assistance, and therefore I must be released."

"I don't think so," I said. "I'm not letting you get in arm's length of my sister."

"You will not find the Heaven Gate without the support of an archangel, and I am the only one who will provide the help you require."

"Wow, that sounds like an awesome idea," Max snarked. "Can you make it sound more like a trap, please?"

Gabriel shot him a withering glance. "Have you forgotten that the *movens caeli* conceals the location of its users for a time?"

"Doesn't matter," I said. "You'll kill us all the moment we free you. There is nothing you can say that will make me believe you."

Gabriel looked me directly in the eyes. "I swear on the sword of Michael, archangel and Commander of the Heavenly Host, that I shall take you to the Gate of Heaven, and I shall harm neither you, the fallen angel, the prophet, the demon slayer behind you," his eyes fixed on Dro, "or the hybrid of Lucifer and Everiel."

We all stared at him with disbelieving eyes. Gabriel

had just spoken the Oath of Michael. I'd only heard it once before, while I was under possession. Sephiel swore the Oath to promise I would survive my exorcism. It was the most sacred Oath an angel could make, and was never made lightly. I didn't know what would happen if the Oath were ever broken, but Sephiel once said that defying Michael meant you were likely to be vaporized.

I looked at Gabriel for a long time. Sure, he wanted to be free, but at what cost? Would he face any consequences if he broke the Oath by killing us all? Or would Michael give him a pat on the back and move him up a rank?

On the other hand, we had no way to find the Heaven Gate. Gabriel was offering us the chance to. His eyes were focused, determined, and yet again, understanding.

"Why?" I asked. "What's stopping you from calling Michael and the Heavenly Host the second we let you go?"

"Nothing," he answered truthfully. "But I shall not do so." His eyes went to Dro and Max. "I have recently begun to discern that the situation is not as I imagined. I felt no evil in the hybrid's touch. She means to harm nothing and no one. As the prophet said, her origins are evil, but her spirit is pure. It is perplexing, but the spirit matters more than its creation."

Gabriel looked at me again. "If it appeases you more, I shall permit Sephiel to place a spell upon me preventing my betrayal."

"What kind of spell?" Dro asked.

"It is called the Oath-Binder. Once it is placed upon me, I am sworn to maintain the Oath I have made unto the death of my vessel."

I looked at Sephiel, who might as well have just heard Lucifer's plea for surrender. Complete and utter shock filled his face, followed closely by a sense of triumph. Sephiel looked at me, giving a slow nod.

I was conflicted about trusting Gabriel, but I did trust Sephiel. He wouldn't let Gabriel hurt Dro any sooner than I would. Now that the Oath of Michael was made, it didn't seem like something we should skip on.

Still, I took a step closer to the archangel. His expression never changed, even when I grabbed a throwing knife from inside my lucky jacket. I stopped in front of the chalk circle, bending at the waist so my face was inches from Gabriel's. His expression still didn't change.

"Betray any one of us, and I'll kill you much slower than Michael will."

This time, Gabriel did sneer. "Slower, maybe. But not as painfully."

I grimaced, then stepped into the chalk circle. I didn't start screaming in agony, so the spell must not have affected humans. I walked around Gabriel to the back of the chair and used the edge of my knife to undo the cuffs, releasing Gabriel from the chair. He stood up slowly, groaning and stretching his legs.

"I have forgotten how stiff these human vessels can become."

He turned his head and waited for me. I sighed and walked to the edge of the circle. I stomped and kicked the chalk line until it smeared, then stepped out of the circle. Keeping my knife in my hand, I crossed my arms and waited for the archangel to step out.

Gabriel looked at the broken circle carefully, as if he was making sure there wasn't a spell that would fry him the moment he stepped out of it. He extended one of his long legs, stretched it over the smudged line, and planted his foot on the concrete floor. Nothing horrific happened to him, so he swung the second leg over the line. Still nothing. Gabriel grinned and started walking toward us.

He frowned when he saw that none of us were smiling.

"Perhaps I was wrong in assuming that being human would be simple and entertaining."

Sephiel began walking toward him. Dro was the only one who was able to smile hesitantly.

"Thank you, Gabriel," she said.

"Thank him when he gets us there," I said bitterly as I watched Sephiel stand in front of Gabriel.

The archangel looked at his brother, then placed his palm over his heart. Sephiel held his hand close to Gabriel's and starting speaking in what I guessed was angel-tongue. As he spoke the elegant, musical language, his palm began to glow a dull gold shade. The light turned into a funnel that left Sephiel's hand and went into Gabriel's. The archangel's hand glowed with the same light, but he didn't seem to be in pain as it moved into his chest. After another minute, the glow faded from Sephiel's hand. He lowered it to his side, looking at Gabriel directly. The other angel lowered his palm, and Sephiel gave him the slightest nod. He looked at me.

"The Oath-Binder has been placed on Gabriel. He shall lead us to the Heaven Gate and will bring us no harm, lest he wishes to suffer the consequences."

I wondered what those consequences were, but something in Sephiel's bright blue eyes told me not to ask. If I had to guess, I would say it revolved around death.

One spell now completed, Sephiel reached into the pocket of his white trench coat and began to draw the *movens caeli.*

He began started speaking in angel-tongue again, this time using magic to likely take down the wards he'd put up when we came here. I never knew the wards were powerful enough to block even the *movens caeli*'s magic. Having a powerful, clever angel definitely had its bonuses. I felt someone walk up behind me. I tensed until I knew it was Warrick.

"Do you think this is a good idea?" he asked once he was standing at my side.

"No," I replied. "But that's why I carry sharp things around."

Warrick grinned, and I had to force myself not to smile back. Sephiel looked at us, holding the *movens caeli* with Gabriel. We all walked forward until we were hanging onto each other. I took Dro's hand and then Warrick's. I squeezed my sister's hand and winked at

Warrick.

The world exploded into thunder and gold light, and then we were gone.

Chapter 14

We staggered to a stop when our feet hit the ground. While the four of us were dizzy and gasping, Sephiel and Gabriel were completely relaxed and walking without a problem.

Damn angels.

I straightened, let go of Warrick's and Dro's hands, and took a deep breath. Crisp, morning air filled my lungs. The scent of a lush forest followed. I let myself refocus, and was staring down at the most amazing view I had ever seen.

We stood on a hill, looking at sloping, green mountains covered with tall, thick leaved trees. Thin lines of cloud masked the dull gold light of the rising sun. The trees in front of us were perfectly green, but the farther we looked, the more blue the landscape became.

It was breathtaking.

My sister took a step forward. Gold sunlight splashed across her face, weaving through her snow-white hair and making it glow. She looked like she had just stepped out of a fairytale.

"It's beautiful here," Dro breathed. "Where are we?"

"Mortals know this place as Olympic National Park," Gabriel answered. "Once the Gates were opened, the magic hiding under those trees was awakened. The forest is irresistible to all those who cross its path. What you are looking at is the Heaven on earth we have created."

"Let me guess," I said. "The angels guarding it will know we're coming anyway?"

Gabriel shook his head. "There are no angels guarding this place. They are all searching for the daughter of Lucifer. But there will be illusions. Images to prevent you from destroying the Gate of Heaven."

Well, that sounds fucking great.

"All right, so where exactly is the Gate?" I asked.

Gabriel stared at me. "You are looking at it."

My eyes went from him to the vast, sweeping mountains that stretched to the horizon. I whipped my head back at him.

"Wait, there's no actual physical door? *All* of this is the Heaven Gate?!"

He nodded. "This place was created to be one of spirituality and belief. It was made for those seeking serenity and peace. You cannot find those things in steel and iron. They must surround you, comfort you, and fill you. That is what powers the Heaven Gate."

"How the hell are we supposed to shut it, then?"

The archangel looked at me with sad, heavy eyes.

"You must burn it all to the ground."

We stared at Gabriel with horror. I looked at the landscape again. The sunlight was starting to burst through the thin clouds, spilling gold light onto the blue tinted mountains. It was like the forest was waking up, yawning and stretching as the dawn's light warmed it. The smell of crisp pine needles and fresh air soothed my lungs. I wasn't a very calm person, but even I could feel this forest working its magic on me. It would break my heart to see it destroyed.

But it would hurt me even more if Lucifer got his claws into it.

"Do not fear for mortal souls," the archangel went on. "I assure you that the entire area is cleared of innocent life. It was shielded from human eyes upon its opening. Even the animals are beginning to flee. They sense the abnormality of this place, and have no desire to continue residing in it."

That didn't make me feel better.

Dro started shaking her head. "There must be another way," she said. "There has to..."

She trailed off when she saw Gabriel's regretful face. "There is not."

He took a step away from us, clasping his hands behind his back as he gazed over the mountains and trees.

"The Heaven Gate is a structure made by angels, and can be broken as easily as a structure made by man. All you need to do is find the weak point."

Gabriel paused for a long time. I couldn't see his face, but I wondered what he was thinking. He was bound to the Oath of Michael and couldn't hurt us, but that didn't mean he wanted to go along with it. This place obviously meant a lot to angels. He couldn't want to see it turned into a pile of ash.

"You will find a waterfall near the middle of the forest," Gabriel finally went on. "It is in a clearing surrounded by a pool. The pool is enchanted with heavenly magic. You must set the water ablaze with heavenfire. The fire will then spread quickly through the rest of the forest. It will consume it to the borders, and shall not stop burning until the entire Gate is scorched."

Gabriel turned back to us, no emotion on his face. He walked back to Dro. "Focus on using your angelic abilities, if you can. They shall lead you directly to the pool. Do you think you can conjure enough heavenfire to ignite the water?"

Dro bit her lower lip, looking like she wanted to cry. "I... I think so."

He watched her face for a minute, then reached into the pocket of his coat. I jerked my hatchet off my hip and got ready to throw it. Gabriel held up his hands. One of them held a clear glass tube about three inches long with golden caps on the ends.

"Peace, Constance Ramirez. I am not revealing a weapon to use against you."

When it became clear that I wasn't going to lower my arm or relax, Gabriel began to move in slow, controlled motions. He unscrewed the cap on the top of the bottle, then filled his free hand with heavenfire. This time we all tensed up. Even Sephiel, who placed the Oath-Binder spell on Gabriel, shifted his feet in case he needed to fight his brother.

Instead of using the heavenfire to torch us, Gabriel turned his hand, putting the gold light into the bottle. He filled it until the bright gold fire consumed the entire bottle, then screwed the gold cap back on. The heavenfire in his hand snuffed out. He looked at the gold flames licking and dancing the edges of the glass tube. It was like a contained bonfire. Gabriel held the bottled heavenfire out to us.

"If you find your heavenfire is not powerful enough, use this. As it was created by an archangel, there is no possibility it shall fail."

Dro looked at the bottle of heavenfire hesitantly. She didn't want to touch it. I took a couple steps forward and took it from the archangel's hand. I waited for it to burn me, but all it felt like was a warm glass tube. I looked at Gabriel again.

The archangel gave me a sad, resigned nod. He bowed his head to Sephiel, looked at Dro one more time, then started to walk away. He moved past us without saying a word. I turned on my heel and looked at him.

"Why are you finally helping us?" I asked. "Can you get back into Heaven once we close the Gate?"

Gabriel stopped walking. "No. None of us will be able to. Not even Michael. If you close the Heaven Gate, all of us will fall and remain on earth in our human bodies until we die and pass through Saint Peter's Gates."

The archangel turned. Sunlight warmed his face, making his tanned skin look truly gold. It brightened his sandy blond hair. His eyes were even more radiant, turning into two golden suns themselves. I finally saw how glorious of an archangel he was.

"Once, I would have followed Michael to the end of time. I believed in everything he said and did. He promised us the Heaven Gate would never be opened, and Lucifer would never be able to defeat the Heavenly Host." He looked at Dro. "Then we heard of the hybrid. We were told she was a monster, a fiend straight from Lucifer's seed. I was willing to believe it, until she healed me and I saw the pureness of her spirit. It is unparalleled, and unquestionable, as is your love for her."

Gabriel slumped. "Being an archangel has become too complicated and confusing. I no longer feel the strength or authority I once felt. I do not believe that Michael can stand against what Lucifer has created. I have watched over humans for thousands of years, and have come to one definite conclusion."

A sad smirk crossed his lips. "They are better adapted to deal with complications."

Then he was gone. Gabriel blinked out of existence. Warrick looked around, as if he expected him to return. Max wrapped his arm around Dro's shoulder and pulled her closer to him. Sephiel stared blankly at the mountains. I looked down at the bottled heavenfire.

The gold flame danced around the glass, teasing and aching to be released. It didn't seem like much, but it was from the second most powerful archangel known to exist. With Dro's heavenfire, I didn't think we'd have to use it, but I wasn't going to throw it away. I tucked it in the inner pocket of my lucky jacket, right above my knives.

"Come on," I said. "We should start walking down the hill."

Sephiel was the first one to move. His steps were sluggish and silent. Warrick started after him. Dro clutched Max's hand as they followed him.

I hung back, taking a final look at the beautiful, dreamy landscape. A heavy sadness filled my heart. The next time I saw this place, it would be nothing but fire and smoke...

Shortly after Mateo left, the guards came in. They knocked me out so I couldn't fight. I didn't know why, until I woke up in a steel bathtub.

I blinked my eyes open, feeling the water under me soaking my clothes. The steel was cold against my spine and the back of my legs. The tub was about as long as I was and filled up to my arms with lukewarm water. I was still trapped in the basement, so the steel tub must have been brought in while I was unconscious. The zip ties around my hands and feet had been replaced with thick rope, probably because Emilio didn't want me bleeding out before he had his fun. I tugged the rope acting as handcuffs on my wrists, which were trapped behind my back. I bent my hand awkwardly to feel the knot with my fingertips, the rope chafing my wrists as I twisted my hand. The knot was secure, far too tight for me to loosen. I writhed in the tub, trying to push myself out of it. I tried rolling hard to dump the tub over, but it was too heavy for me.

"At last," a deep, accented voice crooned. "You're awake."

My body tensed and went cold. I looked up, seeing Emilio standing over me. He was dressed in a black suit with a white shirt. He wore his belt with the golden rose buckle, and had a red rose pinned to the breast pocket of his jacket. The only things off about his outfit were the thick electrician's gloves he wore.

There was no smile on his face, nothing but rage in his dark eyes. The desire to hurt me, to make me scream for mercy, then hurt me some more.

He took the same chair Mateo had sat in and dropped it next to me. From where I was lying, I could only see his head and shoulders. He stared at me with more hatred than I'd ever seen from anyone before. It took all of my courage to hold his gaze, but I did it. Mostly because I wanted to do one more brave thing before Emilio murdered me.

It seemed like forever before he said, "You broke my son's heart."

The words were spoken so blandly I almost laughed. He said it the same way he would say, 'The sun is shining today,' or 'I wish this person wouldn't scream so much.'

But I didn't laugh. Emilio wasn't finished yet.

"You betrayed my loyalty. You took away a substantial profit from me. You disappointed me."

My heart beat faster as he bent lower, shadows crawling over his face. "I treated you like a daughter, and you turned out to be no different from your father."

Emilio pushed his arm over the rim of the steel tub. My eyes widened when I saw the thick electrical cord in his gloved hand. It was cut off at one end, revealing a mess of copper wires. I sucked in a breath, edging away and pushing against the wall of the tub. Emilio put the copper part of the wire in the water.

For the first second, I was numb. Then it was like someone had flicked on a switch and replaced the world with pain. Sharp, snapping agony cracked around my skin. Blood churned and broiled in me. My lungs and heart thrashed violently. My eyes and brain felt like they were going to explode. I could even feel the pain in my teeth. My body arched and thrashed rapidly, splashing water everywhere. I was trapped in a huge static shock.

As soon as it started, it was over. I didn't realize I had been screaming until I inhaled and felt the rawness in my throat. I couldn't tell if I was shaking because of the pain, or because I was terrified.

"That's for not accepting my offer, my dear," Emilio said. "All you had to do was give up your weak little sister, and you wouldn't have to suffer all of this."

I moved the binds around my wrists, flicking the knot with my fingertips and trying to tug it loose. The knot wouldn't budge. I'd pulled it impossibly tight when I was being electrocuted. I twisted my hand again, struggling with the knot–

Water slid into the open cuts on my wrists. I forgot the knot and moved my wrist.

The knot was hopelessly tight now. Whoever tied me up focused on making sure I couldn't untie the bind itself. They didn't focus on the actual loops around my wrists. The knot was tight, but there was a little bit of give at the intersection of the bind. I gave up on the knot pulled my hands apart, working to tighten the knot and slide my hands free of the loops.

Come on, come on–

He moved the wire again, this time hovering it just over my left breast. He let it hang there, watching as my chest heaved. I tried to calm down, but I was breathing *too quickly. My chest rose and fell, teasing the wire. I yanked my hands farther apart. The rope dug into my skin. Water stung my wounded hands. My arms trembled as I struggled to pull my hands out–*

Fire exploded in my chest as it was filled with piercing, sizzling pain. The shock went straight to my heart, making it beat faster than I ever knew it could. My nerves were on fire, agony rushing through my veins and arteries until I thought they would burst. Electricity crackled through my brain, like someone was snapping flaming elastic bands on it. This time I knew I screamed, because it was the only way I could breathe.

Emilio held the wire there for what felt like forever, even though it must have only been a couple seconds. When he lifted it from my chest, I heaved and dropped onto the bottom of the tub. My body quivered, throbbing with pain and sending jerky ripples through the water. Tears slipped out of my eyes. I felt numb, hardly able to feel my fingers. The ropes seemed a little looser than before, but what good was that going to do if I was half paralyzed?

Think about Dro, *I told myself.* You have to get out of here if you're going to find her.

"That was for my son," Emilio said. "At first, I was skeptical of your relationship. Then I saw how much he loved you. It was beautiful to see him that way, with that glow only young lovers have. But you crushed him, Constance. You took that beautiful piece of him, and you ravaged it. I never thought you would be so selfish."

I dragged my arms across the bottom of the tub. The move was sluggish. I thought about my sister's face, turned my will into strength. I didn't want to die. I wasn't going to die. I pressed my fingers together and tugged my arms apart as far as they would go. The ropes bunched with tension, but there was more give than before. I compressed my fingers and pulled up, feeling the binds slide off my wrists, catching on the top of my knuckles–

Emilio put the wire in the water directly next to my head.

While my body went completely taut, a sharp buzzing filled my ears. It sounded like a thousand angry bees zipping through the water. I completely forgot about the noise when the pain started again.

It raced down my body like a wildfire, turning my nerves into lightning bolts. My entire head felt like it was being punched nonstop. My heart turned into a whip, cracking against my ribcage. Even my bones were aching.

A static buzz snapped along my skin. I was shaking worse than ever, every shiver sending a wave of pulsing agony through my body. Tears were flowing down my cheeks, completely out of my control. My head was spinning the way it did when I was about to pass out.

"That was for taking all the gifts I gave you, all my trust and respect, and throwing them away. I believed in you, Constance. I should have known better."

He leaned over the tub and grabbed my throat, lifting me up. I winced and let out a hoarse cry as he half dangled me out of the tub. Water dripped from my hair into the tub, the only other sound besides my raspy breathing. Emilio was inches away from my face now. I smelled the musky rose cologne he always wore, and saw the ferocious contempt in his eyes.

"Don't go unconscious now, Constance. I'm only getting started with you. That was five minutes. You have at least fifty-five more to go."

Despair filled me. I couldn't take one more minute of that pain, let alone a full hour. No one was going to save me. No one would take pity on me. I don't know what else Emilio had planned for me, but it would be worse. I couldn't stand to think about anything more horrible than this.

Don't you dare think it, Connie, my sister's voice said sharply. Don't you dare give up. Get out of here. Survive. I can't do this without you.

That was what my sister would say if she knew what was happening to me. She was out there, alone and scared and worried half to death. Isabel and the Blood Thorns were looking for her. I didn't know if she'd made it to the warehouse. I hoped she did– I told her exactly where it was the night of the massacre, and Dro knew the city as well as I did– but anything could have happened. I had to find her and make sure someone else hadn't captured her along the way. And if they did, I had to find them and show them exactly how big a mistake they made.

Just like that, all the rage I'd been holding in began to rise. It filled my body the same way the electricity had. I thought about everything I'd done under Emilio's orders. The people I'd beaten and killed. Raymond, Horatio, the man who'd turned on Emilio, the three men he'd shot in front of me, the victim I'd watched Blood Thorns dismember. I thought about what he was putting me through now, how he didn't think I would survive it.

Then I snapped.

I swung myself back toward the water. Emilio's grip was so tight on my throat that his arm slid down with me, splashing into the water. He threw the wire away before he could be electrocuted with me. I bent myself in half, my knees knocking Emilio in the head. He grunted and jerked his hand off me, his skull crashing into the side of the tub with a metallic thunk.

While he was dazed, I gave the ropes one more violent tug. I nearly dislocated my wrists, but I pulled them out of the loops. I punched up, catching Emilio in the face. I did it again, and again, then twisted so I was squished up against the far wall. I kicked with both my feet, catching him directly in the nose. Cartilage crunched inward, blood gushing out on either side of my boots.

Emilio tumbled out of the tub. I pushed myself onto my knees and rolled out of the container. I landed hard on Emilio. The movement knocked the air from his lungs, but I was gasping for breath, too. My limbs felt heavy, aching from pain and aftershock. I crawled on top of him, pinning him with my weight since I couldn't do it with my hands. I used my free hand to punch him in the face over and over. Each impact sent a stinging shock through my torn wrists, but I didn't stop. I knew that if I stopped, he wouldn't toy with me anymore. He would kill me swiftly, efficiently, and *brutally.*

His nose broke and his lip split under my fist. Once I was sure he was disoriented, my fumbling hands felt around his jacket. I took out his handgun and grabbed his pocketknife. I cut the binds off my ankles. I pressed the pocketknife to his throat.

"You can't call for help before I cut your throat open, so don't try. Understand, my dear?"

Emilio stared at me, fury in his eyes and blood on his face. It dripped from his smashed nose into his teeth, staining them red.

"Good," I said. "Now, this is what's going to happen. You're going to get up, and we're going to walk out of here. Try anything, and I'll have to choose between shooting you in the knee or stabbing you in the back. Both options appeal to me, so choose wisely."

"You bitch," he spat. "I'm not doing anything you say."

"Oh yes you are," I told him coldly. "Because if you don't, I'm going to have to try out some of those tools on the table. I don't know what I'm in the mood for, but I'm sure I'll come up with something."

I pressed the knife deeper into his neck, drawing a thin line of blood. "After all, you taught me so well, Emilio."

He growled, looking like a wild animal instead of a man. But I caught the reluctance in his eyes. I stood up slowly, getting away from him and making sure he couldn't attack me. I didn't want him to see that I was tackling the last of my strength. I took out the gun and pointed it at him. It made me feel a little bit stronger. Emilio tightened his fists, his shoulders going up and down as he seethed. He was a live volcano about to explode. I had to be careful. I would only have one chance at escaping.

Finally, he turned and started walking for the door. I followed close behind him, keeping the gun at his back. I made sure he didn't put his hands in his pockets to go for a phone or a radio. The last thing I needed was him calling for backup. I still didn't know how to get past the guards that were going to be around the hacienda and in the parking lot.

One thing at a time, Constance, I thought to myself. Get out of the basement first.

When he was at the door, I pressed my back to the wall. I took out the pocketknife and pressed it to his neck. Emilio glared at me. I dug the gun barrel into his ribs.

"Tell the guards to get out of the hallway. Don't try using any codes or eye signals. I know them all."

Emilio peeled his lips back in a snarl, then slid the peephole open. The slot was only wide enough for the guards outside to see his eyes. They wouldn't see the whole of his battered face and realize something was wrong.

At least, that was what I hoped.

"Sir?" I heard one of the guards say.

"You might as well take a break. I'll be in here a while. The bitch is being a pain in my neck."

Smart-ass.

Emilio slid the peephole shut after watching the guards walk down the hallway. He reached down and opened the door. I kept the knife and gun close to his neck and back. I checked down the hallway. There weren't any Blood Thorns waiting to attack me. So far, so good.

Now we just had to get outside.

The basement was built like a dungeon. Half of the doors were filled with supplies and wines. The other doors were connected to torture rooms and cells. The left half of the basement hallway led up into the hacienda. That was the exit I didn't want to use. Not unless I wanted to walk into a mansion filled with gun toting gangsters and a pissed off, homicidal ex-boyfriend.

I turned Emilio to the right, leading him toward the cellar exit. I checked over my shoulder every once in a while, nudging Emilio to keep him moving. No one came running down the hall to see us, and soon we were on the steps. I pressed the barrel of the handgun to the back of his knee so he wouldn't turn and push me down the stairs.

Emilio fiddled with the lock until it was unlatched, then pushed open the door.

We walked out of the cellar, and were now outside standing on the grass by the side of the house. I kept the gun on Emilio and stayed behind his back. I pressed the gun into the base of his neck, glancing over his shoulder to make sure we were still out of sight. I tucked the knife into the belt loop of my jeans and reached into his suit jacket's pocket to grab his car keys.

"I did train you too well," Emilio grumbled.

"That's your fault, not mine. How many guards are out here?"

"More than you have bullets for."

I shoved the gun barrel into the back of his neck. "Then it looks like you have to be my meat-shield for a little while longer. Move."

Emilio did as instructed, walking toward his car. I moved to his side, glancing back to check out the guards. There would be two at the front of the house, but the entire front gate had been removed. I must have really wrecked it, because it looked halfway through replacing.

Which was perfect for me. Once I was in his car, all I had to do was drive straight through. We were almost at Emilio's black Lexus. I couldn't see any other guards walking the grounds, and I was keeping to the tree line so the guards at the front of the house wouldn't see us. A couple more feet and I could–

"Dad?"

Fuck! Fuck, fuck!

I wrapped my arm around Emilio's neck and put the gun to his head. Mateo had just come out of the house. He stopped mid stride and squinted, trying to see me in the dark of the night. He finally made the connection, and a violent rage passed over his face.

"Let him go, you bitch," my ex-boyfriend growled, reaching for his gun on his hip.

"Ah, ah, don't do that, Mateo," I warned as I pulled Emilio back with me. "I plan on letting him go, as soon as I'm in that car and driving out of here."

He stopped going for the gun, resting his hand loosely at his side. His anger never dissipated. I bumped against the driver side door of the Lexus. Now came the tricky part– getting the car unlocked without someone fighting me.

"You're not getting out of here," Emilio said matter-of-factly.

"If you want to keep your head, you better make sure that I do."

I loosened my hold on his neck and started fumbling at the door behind me. Which button unlocked the damn–

Emilio's elbow drove into my stomach, pushing all the air out of me. I gasped and doubled over, just as he whirled around and slammed his fist into my jaw. I fell onto the grass, clinging to the gun for dear life. My ex-boss pounced on me and started beating the life out of me.

Punch after punch rained down on my chest and face. It wasn't long before I was seeing stars and tasting blood. I gripped the gun and slammed it across Emilio's face. He pitched to the side and fell off me. I sat up and shoved him away, kicking him hard in the ribs with the tip of my foot. I aimed the gun at Mateo, who was charging for us. I could hardly see, but I took a shot. Mateo suddenly bellowed and dropped to the ground, clutching his leg. I didn't know if the bullet grazed him or went through his calf. I just hoped the pain would be enough to keep him down for a couple minutes.

I reached up and jammed the key into the car door. Screw the fancy buttons. It was an awkward angle, since I was shooting the gun with my right hand to keep the guards back and unlocking the car with my left. I kept twisting until I heard the door lock click. I stayed low when I yanked the door open and crawled into the driver's seat. I slammed the door closed and slumped until I was basically lying on the floor of the car. I shoved the keys into the ignition and brought the car to life.

The door was suddenly wrenched open. Emilio stood over me, blood covering the lower half of his face. His hair was wild. He looked like a demon from Hell. He *reached forward to grab me and pull me out of the car.*

I didn't hesitate. I lifted my gun a few inches higher until it was just under Emilio's chin, and squeezed the trigger.

Bone and brain cracked through the top of his head, blood misting over his hair. Emilio stumbled back, stiff and awkward. Then he collapsed onto the ground. He didn't get up again.

The heartbreaking scream kept me from driving away right then. I knew that voice. I had just taken the only thing Mateo had left in the world. I couldn't help but feel sorry for my ex-boyfriend as he crawled to his father's corpse, shaking his shoulders and crying his name.

My heart was in my throat, but I had to use the precious time I had to escape. I slammed the car door shut, put the car in gear, and sped for the gate.

Bullets cracked the back window. I stayed as low as I could, trying to keep the car straight. I was almost there, almost out–

A brutal pain punched into my right shoulder. I screamed at it, my grip slipping on the steering wheel. I nearly drove into the security booth, but wrenched the car back on track. I floored the gas and sped down the gravel road. I glanced in the rearview mirror.

Mateo was on his feet, holding a gun at the back of the car. His body was getting smaller and smaller the faster I drove. I couldn't see his face, something I was enormously grateful for.

I didn't look down at the gunshot wound until I knew the hacienda was behind me. Blood was pouring out of it. Way too much blood. The pain was excruciating, pulsing aggressively with every heartbeat. I took one hand off the steering wheel and pressed it to the wound. I kept pressure on it, but warm blood was still seeping through my fingers. It was hard for me to steer straight and I had to blink to keep my vision clear.

I'd finally done it. I'd escaped the Blood Thorns and survived. Now all I had to do was stay that way until I found my sister...

Chapter 15

It only took us almost two hours to make it down the hill. When we reached the bottom, I thought we had entered a dream.

The tall trees had thick trunks, their branches sagging under the weight of the healthy moss growing on them. Ferns and small clumps of green grass covered the forest floor. Pink, purple, and yellow wildflowers grew out of the heavy brush. The air was humid, but not uncomfortable. Everything smelled fresh and pure. Sunlight glittered through the treetops, shining through some of the trees like spotlights.

I didn't deserve to be here. This forest, the Heaven Gate, it wasn't meant to be touched by mortal hands, let alone bloodstained ones like mine. I shoved my hands in my pockets, keeping my eyes on the ground.

Not that it helped. The ground was just as gorgeous as the rest of the forest. The soil was fresh and soft under green grass. Tiny white flowers sprouted up in some areas. My scuffed combat boots looked blasphemous against the earth, and I was afraid to step anywhere. I didn't want to harm this forest. It hadn't done anything to me, and all this beauty ought to have been honored and preserved.

I looked over my shoulder at the rest of the group. Sephiel was in bliss, wandering around the forest and studying it. Recognition would cross his face every once in a while, like he was going back into a happy memory.

Warrick stared up at the trees like a little boy who was amazed at how tall they could grow. He touched some moss hanging over his head, a clever smirk playing on his lips. He ran his fingers through the moss, liking the feel of it. His eyes went back and forth over the branches above him, as if he was thinking about climbing them. Warrick finally noticed me staring at him and met my gaze

His eyes were electric, identical to the color of the bright leaves around him. My heart stopped at the sight of them. Just as it got back on track, he smiled. It was the warm, playful, brilliant smile I'd become dangerously attached to. The one he didn't give to anyone else.

Something went through his eyes when he saw me, a look that melted my heart and put a warm feeling in my stomach. I tried to smile, but I looked away instead. Gabriel said that this place was magical, literally and figuratively. There was no way to tell if Warrick was looking at me that way because he wanted to, or because the forest was playing tricks on me.

I turned my head to where Dro was standing with Max. They were next to a bush growing some ruby red dahlias. Most of them were opened in full bloom, but the kids were standing in front of one that wasn't. Dro hesitated, then reached out and touched it.

The petals peeled open, the dahlia blossoming to life before their eyes.

Dro gasped happily, a huge smile coming over her face. My heart lifted at the sight of it. For a minute, she looked like the carefree little girl I grew up with. The one who would always trail after me when I wandered into the forest outside our camping spot at Owl Creek. We would come back covered in mud and grass stains, then give Mom a bouquet of wildflowers so she couldn't get mad at us for getting dirty. Dad would roll his eyes and say we were worse than two boys. They would tell us not to do it again, but I never listened, and Dro would always want to see the new places we could explore.

Max said something that made Dro smile. She cupped his face and kissed him. I looked away and let them have their moment. I couldn't remember the last time I'd seen her so happy. It had been too long. These days, her smiles usually held traces of fear or worry, and sometimes rage. I would have given anything to make a time machine and take her back to when things were simple. When we were both innocent, and didn't know what she was. When we hadn't cared.

I trudged forward. I could have stayed in the clearing forever, but the longer we admired this place, the more motivation we would lose. I took out the bottle of Gabriel's heavenfire. I focused on it, watching the flames twist under the glass. My heart drooped at the thought of what it would do to this place. I bit my tongue to keep my eyes from watering.

Someone walked up to my side. I looked at my sister. She was completely under the forest's spell.

"Did you see that?" she said, smiling blissfully. "I've never had a flower bloom under my touch before."

"Yeah, it was pretty," I muttered. I turned the bottle of heavenfire over in my hands a couple times. There had to be another way to close the Gate. Didn't there?

No. Gabriel would have said so.

I sighed. "Dro..."

"I know, Con. I can see all the power here, and I know that everything I'm seeing and feeling about it is just an illusion," she replied sadly.

I met her eyes over my shoulder. The grief was back, and I instantly regretted saying anything. Still, my sister managed a weak smile.

"At least I'll have one good memory to hang onto."

Leave it to Dro to see the bright side of anything.

She touched my arm before turning to grab her boyfriend. I held my breath and tucked the heavenfire back in my lucky jacket. I shoved my hands in the front pockets of my jeans and started forward again.

I led the group for what must have been an hour. I kept my eyes on the ground and tried to ignore everything around me.

It was impossible.

There were no words to accurately describe how this forest made me feel. The air was warm and relaxing. Every smell was clean and sweet. A lazy wind made the leaves rustle softly in the breeze. I wanted to touch everything I saw. I could have walked here for hours, making myself get lost so I could see it all.

I didn't stop walking until I heard a flowing river. I pushed aside some heavy fern branches and walked down a slope to the riverbed.

The water moved quickly against moss covered boulders. The water was sky blue, white rapids crashing against the rocks. It smelled crisp and natural. I wouldn't try and swim in the rapids since I couldn't see the bottom of the river, but I was willing to bet the water was soothingly warm. I felt the rest of the group come up behind me.

"The rocks are too far apart," Dro said. "We can't get across this way."

"There's a fallen tree over here," Warrick called from our left.

He was standing by a huge tree trunk that had collapsed naturally across the river. It wasn't as mossy as the rest of the trees, but it looked sturdy enough to support our weight. Dro and Max started walking toward him. I looked over my shoulder at Sephiel.

The angel was crouched by the edge of the water. He dipped his hand in it, letting the water flow through his fingers.

"Seph? Are you okay?" I asked.

He nodded. "I am beginning to recollect my memories of this place. It is more beautiful than I remembered."

I guiltily thought about the heavenfire in my pocket. We were going to destroy the door to Sephiel's home. This was the last time he would ever see it.

"Maybe you shouldn't be here."

The blue-eyed angel looked at me, standing up slowly.

"You remember what we're doing, right? We can't take it back when it's done."

Sephiel's eyes were heavy with sorrow. "I have not forgotten our quest, Constance. Gabriel was not deceiving us when he said this was the only way to close the Gate to Lucifer. I shall mourn for the Heaven Gate and my fallen brothers. But I shall keep my priorities in line."

Sephiel inclined his head, then walked after the rest of the group. I tried to say something else to him, but nothing came to mind. I stared at the water as it flowed by, suddenly compelled to touch it. I knew it would feel like no other water in the world. I wanted it to slip through my fingers. I wanted to be reckless and jump into the river, letting it carry me to wherever it was going.

"Constance!"

I snapped out of my trance and looked over my shoulder. Warrick was still waiting at the edge of the tree. Sephiel was striding toward him. Max was about halfway across, and Dro was watching me from the top of the makeshift bridge. I started walking for them.

By the time I reached the fallen tree, Max and Dro were across. Sephiel was about halfway over the bridge. I frowned at the tree trunk. It was about a head taller than I was. I wasn't a short woman, but it would be a challenge to get up to the top.

"Need a lift?"

I looked at Warrick. Even when he was smug, he looked gorgeous.

"No," I told him stubbornly.

I jumped for the top of the trunk. My fingers and boots scraped along the moss and bark, but I couldn't get traction. I could feel myself slipping, until hands cupped themselves under my feet and pushed me higher. I crawled onto the top of the tree trunk, getting into a crouch. No one else seemed to have noticed my clumsiness, but I didn't know for sure. I looked down at Warrick, who was grinning from the ground. I narrowed my eyes.

"Don't say a word."

He laughed, drawing an 'X' over his chest. "Cross my heart."

Warrick stepped back and jumped for the trunk. He was taller than me, so he didn't need anyone to boost him. Still, I helped pull him up until we were both standing. He didn't let go of me once he was on the trunk. His hands were warm and gentle as they slid up my arms to my biceps.

A ray of sunlight filtered through Warrick's short, oak-colored hair, tracing over his face and sinking into his eyes. I tried to tell myself that I was dreaming, but my heart was beating too fast. His neon green eyes pierced my dark ones, like he could see and comprehend everything I was trying to keep locked away. He started leaning in slowly, drowning me in his comfortable pine scent.

I turned my head, letting him slip into my hair. My heart screamed at me, but I told it to shut up. The magic here was made of dreams. It was all illusion. Whatever was between Warrick and me was being enhanced because of it.

Liar.

I told myself to shut up again, then pulled out of Warrick's arms. The air was warm, but I still felt cold. I kept my eyes down so I wouldn't have to see any frustration or hurt on his face.

"We should keep going," I muttered.

He waited, hoping I would say something else. When I didn't, he sighed heavily. "Then lead the way."

I turned and started walking over the tree trunk. I concentrated on where I was stepping, even though the tree trunk was secure and there was no way I could fall off. I watched the blue river water flowing under it. The sight didn't make me dizzy. It made me want to leap in the water all over again. But it turned out I was excellent at resisting the things I wanted.

I jumped off the edge of the tree trunk when I reached the other side, bending my knees to catch my fall. I walked through the clearing where the rest of the group was waiting, hearing Warrick land on the ground behind me.

We kept wandering through the trees, our senses drowning in its beauty. The deeper we went, the more perfect everything seemed. The amount of love and care the angels had put into creating the Heaven Gate was unbelievable.

The overgrown grass mixed with ferns and softly brushed my shins. Old, strong trees stood proudly, stretching on for miles. Warm pockets of sunlight illuminated every leaf. A warm breeze lifted the hair on either side of my face, kissing my skin. I smelled musky oak and sweet tree sap. I was ready to fall onto my back and lie in a bed of grass, staring at the treetops and forgetting everything else. I reached into my jacket and touched the heavenfire. It was the only reminder that could keep me anchored to the reality of what had to be done.

"We're almost there," Dro said. "I can feel it." She stopped. "There's something else."

My hand went to my hatchet. I walked briskly until I was beside her. "Something that's going to try to kill us?"

"No," she said, scanning the thick forest with confused blue eyes. "Whatever it is, it's not evil. It's almost, lonely..."

Dro trailed off, then turned her head to the trees on the left.

Someone was standing in them.

She was about twelve feet away from us, and I could see that she was stunning. She was a few years older than me, probably in her early thirties. Thick, dark brown hair touched her shoulders in light waves. She was wearing a dark green T-shirt and beige jeans. A stunning smile came across her pink lips. Her eyes were a brilliant, bright green. A color that belonged to only one other person I knew.

"Emma?" Warrick said from the back of the group.

His big sister smiled even wider, looking radiant.

"No," breathed Dro.

Warrick never heard her. He started went directly to Emma, as if he couldn't believe she was here.

Because she isn't. She's dead.

But when I blinked, she was still standing there, looking as real as my own hand. When Warrick hugged her, she hugged him back.

Something was very, very wrong.

I turned to Sephiel. "What is this?"

The auburn haired angel wasn't looking at me. He

was staring at something north of him. I moved around Max to see what he was focused on.

The most beautiful woman I'd ever seen was standing next to a tall pine tree. She was dressed in a long, white trench coat, white pants, and a white shirt that showed her perfect frame. Her skin was pale and flawless, glowing under the sunlight. Smooth blonde hair was falling out of a loose bun at the nape of her neck. Her face was kind and soft, her flower shaped lips forming an incredible, tender smile. Icy blue eyes glistened as she looked at Sephiel.

He was walking toward her before Dro could stop him. He said something in angel-tongue so I couldn't understand him, though I did catch the only word that mattered.

"Everiel."

Sephiel held her, brushing his fingers over her cheek and whispering things I didn't hear. Like Warrick, he couldn't believe that he was with her again. Like Warrick, he couldn't remember that she was dead.

Max's hitched breath had me turning to the right. I followed his line of sight, and found myself looking at Manny.

He looked exactly the way I remembered him. A gentle, weathered face, dark grey hair with patches of white at his temples. He had the same eyes, lips and nose that Max did. Manny was wearing the same grey sweater and black dress pants he'd worn the day he was shot, except there were no bloodstains on them.

Max took off like a bullet from a gun, not stopping until he was in front of his father, hugging him like he would never let go. Manny's chuckle sounded as real as it had when he was alive, patting his son on the back. A loving smile filled his face. He'd found the piece of him that he was missing so much. Manny slowly opened his eyes, and looked at me.

My heart strained, a knife of sadness cutting through it again. I'd never forgotten Manny, but I forgot how much it hurt to know he was gone. He was my mentor and one of my only friends, a good, honest person who deserved to be alive. He'd sheltered us, trained us, and treated us like family. Seeing him now was a sweet poison filling my chest.

I tore my gaze away from Manny's comforting smile and looked at my sister. "Dro, what is this?" My voice was shaking more than I wanted it to.

She was close to tears. She took a deep breath. "This is the magic of the Heaven Gate," she whispered. "This is what protects it. People will see the beauty of the forest, but they'll also see the people they love the most, and keep them from going any further."

While she was explaining it to me, I noticed two people over her shoulder. A man and a woman holding hands. She was a kind looking woman with gold skin, curly black hair, and loving eyes. He was tall and strong with the same tanned skin, short dark hair, and strong dark eyes. They smiled when they saw me. My breath couldn't catch up to my heart.

I started to move past Dro. She grabbed my wrist and yanked me to a stop. Her eyes were desperate.

"Don't Connie," she begged. "Please, don't."

"But it's Mom and Dad," I pleaded, sounding like a child.

Dro shook her head, tears building in her eyes. "No. It isn't."

I stared at her. "How can you say that?" I said, shocked. "Don't you see them?"

"Of course I see them," she replied sadly as a single tear slipped down her cheek. "But I can see further than that, because I'm part demon. I'm Lucifer's daughter, and I can see the layer of illusion over all of them."

Dro squeezed my hand tighter. "They're not real, Connie. None of them are."

I looked back again. My parents smiled at me. Mom held out her hand. Dad's eyes were filled with pride.

All my old wounds seemed to rip open at once. It was so sudden and so fierce I thought I was tearing in half. My heart seemed to fall out of my chest, leaving me with a dull, hollow ache. Tears pricked my eyes. My breath caught.

I missed them so fucking much.

Dro pulled me back and put her arms around me. She hugged me tight, the same way she had after I took my first life. When I was breaking down after Mateo's gunshot. Every time she thought I was going to die.

I hugged her back, desperate not to fall apart. The pain was more than I could bear. I knew Mom and Dad were gone and were never coming back. I missed them, but I had let them go. Except they were here now, wanting to see me. They wanted to talk to me, listen to the stories of my life, catch up on all the years they missed.

I fastened my arms around Dro with more pressure than I should have, but I needed to know she was here. I needed to know I wasn't losing myself to memories and false dreams. Dro didn't protest or cry out. She let me crush her to my chest. Maybe she needed the same assurances I did. I took a deep breath, trying to drag myself out of the misery I had fallen into. Sweet smelling hair tickled my face.

Dro was the real thing in my life. She wasn't an illusion. She was here, keeping me secure the way she always did.

"Can you make it stop?" I whispered into her hair.

Dro stiffened, then nodded. She pulled back from me, squeezing my arm. I fixed my eyes to the lush, green ground as she walked behind me and touched the back of my head. It felt like someone was peeling a thin layer off my mind. Everything seemed clearer, and I could no longer feel my parents eyes on my back. Once her touch was gone, I turned around. The clearing was empty. My parents were gone. A fierce blow of heartache hit my chest. I compressed my lips and shoved my hand into my jacket and clutched the heavenfire.

It didn't take away the pain, but it distracted me from the sadness in Dro's voice as she explained to Max that Manny wasn't really there, that Sephiel wasn't really holding Everiel, and that Warrick wasn't really talking with Emma.

I don't know how she was able to do it. I would never have found the strength to. We were all suffering from the same sickness. We'd lost people we loved, and would do anything to have back. Dro didn't want to make us endure this cruel, heart-wrenching agony, but the more we gave in, the more lost we would become. She was trying to save us, and that meant she had to hurt us.

I finally lifted my head, turning around and seeing Dro kneeling behind Sephiel. She had her arms wrapped around his back, hugging him to her chest. There was no other angel beside them.

There was a quiet sniffling on my right. I looked at Max, who had his back to me. There were only trees in front of him now. I could see him rubbing his eyes. I took a step forward and put my hand on his shoulder. He turned around and threw his arms over my neck. He was hurting too much to care that I wasn't Dro. I rubbed his back, letting him sob into my shoulder. I missed his dad too, but nowhere near as much as Max did.

After a minute, he pulled back and wiped the tears from his cheeks. "Sorry. Wasn't thinking clearly."

"It's okay," I said honestly.

I wanted to tell him that I understood, that I wanted Manny back too, that at least we knew he was in Heaven, but all it would do was cause him more pain.

Instead, I said, "Dro's over there with Sephiel."

Max nodded and started walking toward his girlfriend and the brokenhearted angel. I let him pass before turning around and walking back into the clearing. Warrick was still standing in the same place, staring at the vacant trees ahead. I made my way over to him. He heard me coming and faced me.

He looked like a man who had seen a glimmer of hope before reality smothered it. I couldn't think of a single thing to say. I couldn't even tell him that my heart was breaking for him.

Warrick's bright green eyes met mine. They were a little redder than before. He almost looked relieved that I was there, and that I wasn't a dream. But it didn't take away his pain. He took a step closer, and this time I didn't back away. Warrick lowered his head until his forehead touched mine.

"I fucking hate this," he whispered. "All of it."

"We'll be out of here soon," I said quietly.

He nodded. Then Warrick's fingers brushed along my cheek, gently grazing down my face until they reached my chin. Then his hand dropped and he lifted his eyes. He looked hopeless and beaten.

"Just for once, I wish I could have what I wanted instead of always dreaming about it."

My heart nearly burst when he said that, but I didn't know what to do. If I let him get closer, would it be because I wanted him, or because the magic here pushed me to want him?

He didn't give me the chance to find out. He took another deep breath, then walked toward the rest of the group. I watched his back with longing eyes, soon turning my gaze on the rest of the group. They were back together, silent and mourning. They had all lost their loved ones all over again, and my sister had forced them back into reality when I knew it destroyed her to do so.

For the first time since we arrived here, I wanted to burn the forest to the ground.

Chapter 16

No one spoke as Dro and Sephiel led us through the forest, guided by a magic I couldn't feel. We didn't see the visions again, either because Dro's powers were shielding us from them, or because the Heaven Gate didn't feel like tormenting us again.

Despite what she had done, none of the guys gave Dro contemptuous looks. They knew her well enough to understand that she was trying to keep them from living in a dream. The longer they stayed in it, the more they would have gone astray. The Gate would be burned, and they would never know until they were ashes.

I tucked my hands into my jacket and stared at the forest floor again. I walked like that for hours, glancing up every once in a while to make sure I wouldn't walk into a tree.

I slowed down when I heard water gently crashing in front of me. I lifted my head and watched Sephiel glide toward a curtain of hanging willow tree branches. They weren't touching the ground, so I could just barely make out a pool of water surrounded by rocks underneath it. He pushed the branches aside and stepped through. We followed him one by one, and found the most incredible part of the forest.

Every inch of it was magnificent, but this part was *exquisite*. All the trees circled the edge of this clearing so the sun could fill the entire space with its warm, golden light. Soft grass covered the area, batches of gentle white flowers decorating it every couple feet. Dandelion wisps danced in happy rings when the caressing breeze lifted them up. Before our eyes was a clear, blue pool. Behind it was a fifty-foot, cascading waterfall that rained crystal blue water. The sunlight made the water sparkle in a dozen places like winking jewels. Unblemished white rocks circled the pool, gleaming in the sun like freshly polished marble. It never overflowed, no matter how much water was poured into it.

My first thought was utter awe. This little patch of earth was as sacred as it was mesmerizing. It made me want to believe in God, that if He could make such a perfect place, others would be able to see the goodness in life. If only other criminals could find this clearing, they might fall down and weep for forgiveness. You wanted to live and breathe this place. There was nothing to care about, no stress or anxiety. No anger or grief. There was only dense grass, a clear blue sky, and a calming waterfall. You could die happy here, and never regret a second of the life you let pass by.

"This is the place," Sephiel said. His voice still carried the pain of seeing Everiel's illusion, but being here seemed to relax him a little more. "The lock, as you may call it."

Dro stared at the pool, swallowing heavily. I watched my sister.

"Are you okay?" I asked her.

She nodded too quickly. "Fine. It's just... I'm fine."

No she wasn't. I could read her as easily as she could read me. Dro's eyes were wide in astonishment as they moved along the clearing. She looked like she was walking in a dream that she didn't want to wake up from. Her expression was thoughtful, sleepy, and tragic. Dro appreciated nature in all its forms. She was falling in love with this place, and knew she was about to break its heart.

I faced my sister. "Dro, you don't need to do this. Gabriel gave me the heavenfire. I can do it."

She shook her head, icy blue eyes meeting my dark ones. "No. It has to be me. Lucifer used me. I'm the reason the Gates are opened. It's my responsibility to close them."

She sounded so convincing I almost believed her. I was tempted to tell her that none of what happened was her fault, but Dro wasn't the scared little sister I knew.

She wanted to make her own difficult choices, even though didn't need to prove how strong she was to anyone.

Dro blew out a breath, then walked toward the pool. We stayed back, not knowing how much heavenfire she would need to use to set the pool on fire. Dro stopped at the edge rocks, looking at the alluring waterfall, the glittering water, the smooth, alabaster stones. She took a deep breath and held out her hands. We all waited for them to glow with gold fire. But nothing happened.

As the seconds ticked by, I began noticing things. The tension in her shoulders, the shakiness of her breath. The way her hands were trembling.

It suddenly became too much for Dro. She dropped her hands, knees buckling under her until they were pressed into the grass. I rushed over, putting my hands on her shoulders and kneeling in front of her. Dro's sobs were heavy and heartbreaking. Tears streamed down her beautiful face. My chest twisted into a knot at the sight of her.

She clutched my hands and continued sobbing. She squeezed her eyes shut, more tears falling onto the fresh grass.

"I can't," she sobbed out. "I can't, Connie. I can't."

I pulled her to my chest. She fisted my shirt and kept crying. I rubbed her back, wishing I knew what to say to make her feel better.

"Do you want to?" I whispered into her hair.

Dro paused, then started shaking her head.

"You don't see it, big sister. There's a light coming from the pool. It's like an aura, the most precious one I've ever seen, and I... I can't turn it off. I don't want to see it go out. I can't do it."

I hugged her tighter, and looked at the forest around me. The tall, proud trees with crisp green leaves. The warm grass under my knees. The smell of wildflowers and fresh air. The strong pounding of the waterfall next to me.

This was paradise on earth. This was beauty, purity, and goodness.

We'd seen magic and wonder here. Loved ones we missed with every waking breath. She'd already seen through the illusions, saved us from them, and seen the most incredible light she'd ever seen. I looked at the pool and the waterfall. I didn't see what she did, but I had no doubt that it was there.

No wonder Dro couldn't find the strength to destroy it. She would never be the same if she burned out that light. It would damage and scar her soul for eternity. She would never forgive herself.

So she wasn't going to.

I gently pushed her back from my chest. Dro's eyes were red from tears. I wiped them from her cheeks and gave her a small smile. I didn't say anything as she read my eyes. I didn't have to. I took her hands and carefully helped her to her feet.

Max was suddenly there, putting his arms around Dro and pulling her into another hug. He whispered quietly to her, holding her close and probably saying how much he loved her.

My heart was heavy as I watched my fragile sister, but I knew what I had to do for her.

"I think you guys should stand farther back," I said.

Dro and Max looked at me. My sister's eyes were shining with tears. "Con, you don't know what it will do to you," she said. "How badly it will stain your soul."

I was already reaching into my jacket, taking Gabriel's heavenfire out of its hiding place. I looked at the bright gold flame.

"I wouldn't worry about that. It can't get blacker than it already is, little sister."

I turned around and started unscrewing the cap. A pale white hand covered mine. I looked at Dro. There were still tears in her eyes, but she looked stronger than she had a moment ago.

Much stronger.

"I can't do this on my own," she said, talking around a sob. "But I can do it with you."

We looked at each other for a long time. I was trying

to tell her that it was okay if she didn't want to do this. She was trying to tell me that she had to prepare herself if she was going to face Lucifer and his demons.

Eventually, we came to the same conclusion.

We were strong in different ways, but were unbreakable together.

Dro kept her hand on mine as we knelt down by the pool and twisted off the golden cap. The heat from Gabriel's heavenfire instantly went around my hand, making me want to jerk back and drop the damn bottle. But Dro kept her hand where it was, tilting the bottle until the heavenfire poured out of the glass into the water.

The second it touched the smooth, liquid surface, the gold fire scorched along the water. It was like we had just dropped a match onto a pile of gasoline.

The intense heat flushed against my face, making me scramble to my feet. I gripped Dro's arm and pulled her up, then pushed her behind me. I watched the heavenfire race until the entire pool was covered, moving quicker than a normal fire ever could. Then it started climbing up the waterfall until it was pouring golden flames instead of water.

It took half a minute for the heavenfire to reach the top of the waterfall. After that, it spread to the trees. Moss crumbled away, leaves turned to ash, tree trunks splintered under the intense heat. The fresh air was replaced with smoke.

This was a flash fire that was going to get out of control very, *very* fast.

But it was working. We were closing the Heaven Gate. We would keep Lucifer from entering Heaven and twisting paradise.

I was ready to count it as a victory, until Dro and Sephiel screamed.

I whirled around, catching Dro as she collapsed. Her fingers twisted in her hair, pulling it from the roots. My sister's face was pinched with agony. Max was right beside me, holding his girlfriend close and frantically trying to understand what was wrong.

Across from us, Warrick was kneeling by Sephiel, looking just as lost as Max was. I remembered he had the *movens caeli*, and raced toward him.

"Bring Dro over here!" I screamed to Max over my shoulder.

I looked at up, seeing the heavenfire igniting the trees like they were coated in lighter fluid. Thick, black smoke billowed up over us until I couldn't see the sun. The air was hot and heavy, so dense that I could taste it. We maybe had seconds until the fire made its way toward us.

I skidded to a stop and dropped to my knees by Sephiel's head. He was screaming worse than ever. Warrick was trying to prop him up, looking for injuries. I started rifling through his trench coat until I found the *movens caeli*. Warrick froze, looking at his hands. I lifted my head, and saw they were covered in blood.

Sephiel suddenly twisted and flipped onto his stomach. Two dark red bloodstains were soaking through the angel's back. They stretched from his shoulder blades down to his lower ribs. But there were no cuts in the fabric. Just a huge, red stain. Sephiel was losing blood at a terrifying rate, and I had no idea why.

Max half carried, half dragged Dro over to us. We all knelt together. I looked up again, seeing the heavenfire closing off our exit. We were completely trapped by the fire. I watched it start to scorch the grass, incinerating the twirling dandelion wisps and making the white flowers shrivel.

I shoved the *movens caeli* against Max's chest. "Figure out how to work this!" I shouted against the roaring fire.

He hesitated, looking at the golden tube like it was a stick of dynamite. His gaze went to Sephiel, and then his hand shot forward. He gingerly touched the angel's forehead and closed his eyes. His shoulders started shaking as he looked into the angel's mind, his breathing strained. But Sephiel was the only one of us who knew how to operate the *movens caeli*. If Max was going to use it to get us out of here, he had to look into Sephiel's mind to do so.

Dro was still awake, but barely. I grasped her hand and held on tightly. I took Sephiel's hand. It felt clammy and cold. Max opened his eyes again and swayed. He caught himself before he collapsed. Sweat plastered his dark curls to his forehead. He fumbled at the device with shaking fingers. Finally, he held it firmly with both hands. He looked at me with determined eyes. His nod was sharp and ready.

Warrick threw one of his arms around me and put his other hand on Max's shoulder. A second later, we were smothered in blinding gold light. Thunder roared in our ears. I squeezed my eyes shut and let the angelic device carry me to wherever we were going. It couldn't be far, since the thing had a limited battery life.

Sure enough, we crashed into the earth a couple seconds later. We all lurched, Warrick nearly banging his head against mine. I looked at Dro as Max cradled her. She blinked her eyes open, touching her fingers to her forehead. She winced, but sat up with his help.

"You okay, pretty girl?" Max asked.

She nodded and looked over at us. Her eyes dropped to Sephiel for the first time. They widened with horror. She gasped, then shoved out of Max's arms. She stumbled at first, then pushed past me and Warrick. She stopped when she reached Sephiel, gingerly touching his back. The angel didn't move.

"No," she breathed. "No, no, no, no!"

"What happened to him?" I asked, giving her space as she and Warrick started pulling Sephiel's trench coat off.

"His wings!" she cried. "His wings are gone!"

We looked at her, then at Sephiel. Given the way the wounds looked and him being an angel, it made sense that Sephiel had wings. But I'd never seen them. Apparently, no one else had either.

"He had wings?" Max asked carefully.

Dro nodded, staring at the blood covering Sephiel's

back. His white shirt was almost completely red and clinging to his skin. There still weren't any cut marks in the fabric. However, I didn't know many people who could lose that much blood and survive.

"They were attached to his aura," she explained. "That was why you never saw them." Her voice hitched. They were beautiful," she whispered shakily.

Dro's hands hovered over Sephiel's back. She must have seen where the wounds were, because she knew exactly where to place them. The familiar, steady glow of her healing powers filled her hands.

She suddenly gasped in pain and clutched her hands.

"Dro? What's wrong?"

"I don't know," she gasped. "It hurts when I use my angel powers."

From the grimace on her face, it hurt a lot. Dro breathed through it while Max rubbed her back, because he didn't know how else to help her. Warrick pressed his fingers to Sephiel's neck, giving me a worried look.

"His pulse is getting weaker," he told us gravely.

Dro sighed again, then reached for Sephiel's back. I thought about how much pain she'd just been in. Would healing him drain her powers? Or would it cause her so much pain that she blacked out? I didn't want to lose either of them, but if Dro passed out then Sephiel was going to die. The rest of us were too human to do anything.

There was also the very real possibility that Dro could get herself killed while healing Sephiel.

"Dro," I started, reaching for my little sister's hand.

She batted it away and gave me a fierce look.

"He's going to die if I don't help him!" she shouted at me.

I was ready to argue all my points, but I backed off instead. Dro was right. She was the only one would could save Sephiel. She needed me to believe in her.

"Just be careful," was the only thing I said.

Dro relaxed, then pressed her hands onto Sephiel's back. Light filled her hands and flowed into the angel. She squeezed her eyes shut and gritted her teeth. I watched my sister nervously. I tried to tell myself that she was putting herself in pain to save a friend's life, that her suffering was being done for the right reason.

Then I thought about the Heaven Gate, and wasn't so sure that I was the best person to give advice anymore.

Finally, Dro snuffed the light from her hands. She sighed and slumped. Max caught her and hugged her to his chest. He kept her upright, kissing the side of her face and whispering something I couldn't hear.

Dro nodded. "I'm all right," she murmured weakly.

I didn't believe her, but she was awake. That was the most I could ask for at this point.

We all looked at Sephiel, waiting for him to stand up. Warrick pressed his fingers to the angel's neck again. He lifted his head.

"Pulse is stronger."

As soon as he finished telling us the good news, Sephiel sucked in a huge breath, like he'd just come up from drowning. He coughed until he could breathe properly, then groaned and tried to sit up. Warrick helped him, gripping his arms instead of his shoulders. Sephiel's arms shook a little bit, but he was moving.

"Seph? Can you stand?"

"Perhaps with some assistance, John Warrick."

The demon slayer got to his feet, keeping his hold on Sephiel until they were both standing. Sephiel straightened his back, wincing. I tried to picture him with wings. Had they been the traditional white feathers? Did he only have two or multiple ones like Lucifer? Did they look different if you were a higher ranking angel? How long would he be in pain?

Sephiel staggered away from Warrick, wanting to stand on his own. His bright blue eyes found Dro.

"I am indebted to you yet again, Andromeda."

My little sister was still hanging on to Max, but she was more alert than before. I almost couldn't notice the beads of sweat going down her temples. She looked at him mournfully.

"But, Sephiel, your wings..."

The angel looked down. I didn't know what he was thinking, but it must have been painful. An angel losing his wings was probably as agonizing as a soccer player losing a leg.

"There was nothing you could have done," he muttered wearily. "I understood the implications of my actions. I am truly fallen now." He lifted his eyes and tried to smile. "You are not to blame, Andromeda."

For a moment, he almost looked like the old Sephiel again. But there was something different about him. He looked like himself, but he seemed smaller. His eyes weren't as bright. They used to glow with power and confidence. Now that was gone. I didn't know for sure, but I was starting to think that all of Sephiel's heavenly skills were gone. Everything that made him an angel was now torn away.

"Oh my God," Max breathed.

We turned our heads from Sephiel to look at the horizon. I almost couldn't tell that we were standing in the same place Gabriel had left us, because there was so much fire.

Night was starting to fall, but the sun was completely veiled by a smoke as black as night. It looked almost oily against the purpling sky. The mountains were covered in heavenfire, the flames spreading until the entire forest was a giant, golden bonfire. The air smelled like wood smoke and burning pine.

My chest was tight. I had done this. I helped destroy the Heaven Gate. I caused all the angels outside of Heaven to fall. I was part of the reason Sephiel's wings were gone. My heart broke as I remembered how beautiful the forest had looked, the way it smelled, the feel of the breeze on my face. It would never be seen again. This fire would never be put out until every inch of serenity was turned into a cinder.

Like everything I did, it hadn't really bothered me when I'd been doing it. Then I started thinking about my actions when it was too late.

Dro was standing beside me, watching the Gate of Heaven burn. We made the choice together, and we both thought the same thing:

Did we make the right sacrifice? Was destroying Lucifer's chance into Heaven worth trapping the angels from it?

"Sephiel," Max asked, his dark eyes still fixed on the fire. "What happens now?" He looked at the angel. "If someone innocent dies, where do they go?"

"Heaven is not closed to the dead, Max. The Heaven Gate was only for living angels to use. When a soul perishes, it shall ascend to the clouds to the Gates of Saint Peter. When our vessels die, that is where we go as well. It is another part of Heaven, but it is different from the home I knew."

Sephiel's voice was full of sorrow. I knew what it was like to miss the home you grew up in. To miss the person you used to be. But I was only twenty years old. Sephiel had been around since about the dawn of time. He'd always lived in Heaven. Now he would be shut away from it until he died. I don't know how he was able to bear all this anguish. It was enough to kill a person.

Dro gasped sharply. I turned away from the burning Gate and looked at her. She was staring at the hills behind us. I followed her line of sight. At first I didn't see anything. Then I blinked, and saw that we'd been discovered, and that we were completely outnumbered.

They had a small army this time; a dozen possessed people, six Wretches, six hellhounds, two Knights. Mateo and Drake stood in front of them. Lucifer was in the center.

They were still dressed in the clothes they'd worn in Bullhead City, but something was obviously different about Lucifer. His soulless black eyes were narrowed to slits, and I didn't need to read them very long to see what the problem was.

He was *furious*.

Chapter 17

For a moment, nobody did anything. We were too afraid to move. Then Lucifer started walking toward us, and we split into action.

I yanked the hatchet off my hip. Warrick pulled out a Beretta handgun from inside his leather jacket. Sephiel took out two short, curved blades I never realized he was carrying from his jacket. Dro filled one of her hands with hellfire. Max desperately grabbed onto her and me, trying to open the *movens caeli*.

The golden tube was yanked out of his hand. It hung in midair under Lucifer's control, until he made it explode into a million tiny shards.

Lucifer was only about ten feet away from us now. I gripped the hatchet tighter.

"You destroyed the Gate to Heaven," he said in his beautiful, paralyzing voice. "Why?"

"So you couldn't destroy it," Dro told him. The tremble in her voice almost couldn't be heard.

Lucifer turned his black gaze on her. "What you have done is irreversible. You have barred souls from claiming redemption. You have stripped all the angels on earth from their wings. They shall not have a chance to see Paradise. Why would you deny that to them?"

"We didn't do it to keep them out," I said.

Lucifer's head twisted to mine, his perfect, white hair moving ever so slightly. As soon as his black eyes hit my dark ones, I felt a delicious chill slither down my spine. It was pain and pleasure, fear and lust. I wanted to run from it as much as I craved it. I tightened the grip on my hatchet.

"We did it to keep *you* out."

The King of Hell narrowed his eyes on me again.

Something flashed through them, looking like a shooting star over oil. Then the pain hit.

I dropped to the ground, screaming in agony as a million invisible claws dug into my skin and tried to rip it from my bones. My flesh stretched like it was hanging on meat hooks, gripping tighter and tighter until it was in knots. I couldn't hear anything but my own screams.

Just as I thought I was going to pass out, I felt a rush of heat from my left. The pain snapped off, leaving me heaving for breath. My throat was hoarse, my heart and head pounding like hammers. Someone was picking me up. I swayed on my feet, but Warrick held me in place. I blinked at him until he knew I was fine. Then he was pointing one of his guns at Lucifer. I reassured my grip on my hatchet, and turned to see how I was saved.

Once again, my sister had gotten between me and the most dangerous enemy I could imagine.

"If you do that again, it's going to be the last thing you *ever* do," Dro warned.

Lucifer didn't scowl or start throwing poisonous words around. He just stood there, looking at his daughter. Even now, he still seemed astonished that she wouldn't drop everything and come running to his side.

But he was starting to learn that Dro's free will couldn't be manipulated as easily as he designed. I smiled and let myself feel a little smug, thinking that I was to blame for that.

"You think physical pain is the worst I can do, my daughter? That is ecstasy compared to what I shall bestow upon you. I shall strike you where it shall wound you the most, and you shall never know it was my intention. I will destroy you so intricately and so exquisitely, that you will believe you have brought it upon yourself."

His words seemed to freeze the air, and his eyes nearly made me beg to hear his voice again. Dro didn't say anything, but she never backed down. Hellfire covered her arms and was starting to spread to her torso. Lucifer didn't blink.

"Though we shall see how much physical pain you

and those you love can truly endure," he said coldly. "Kill them."

The demons didn't hesitate. The Possessors, Wretches, and hellhounds raced forward. Dro threw her hands out, huge streams of hellfire surging toward the beasts. The light was almost blinding, but she controlled it. I heard monsters hiss and howl in pain, though I couldn't see how many of them were actually being killed.

Then she was thrown back, half of her body crunching inward, like someone had just hit her in the stomach.

That someone being Lucifer, who wasn't even touched by her hellfire.

Dro landed hard on her back, rolling to get to her feet. By the time she stood up, we were all standing beside her. Sephiel was the first one to get into the fight. His wings might be gone, but he was still an incredible warrior. The first Possessor, who was a big man in a black T-shirt, curled his hands into tight fists. Before any punches could be thrown at him, Sephiel swung his blades at the Possessor like he was closing a pair of scissors. He moved his head back to avoid decapitation, but the weapons still sliced open his throat and it gushed blood.

A Wretch pounced for Sephiel's back, but he lashed out with a perfect sidekick that crashed into the ruined angel's head. Sephiel was moving quick and efficiently, but a dark armored Knight was rushing toward him with the scythe raised high. Sephiel's attention went to the bigger problem, which meant he didn't see the female Possessor lifting a knife from her belt to stab him in the back.

Which was kind of amusing, because she didn't see me. I drew a knife and threw it at her. The silver blade sank directly into her heart, making her scream and collapse. A Wretch howled and loped its way to me. It screeched as it curved its arm back to hit me. I stepped back so its swing went wide, then rushed forward and slammed my hatchet into the center of its face. The Wretch shrieked and tried to bat me away. I pulled my hatchet free and drew the blade along its throat. The creature twitched once before it began caving inward and crumbling to ash.

A sharp bark came from my left. I somersaulted out of the way as a hellhound launched itself in my direction. I kicked back to catch the demonic dog in the muzzle. It gave me the chance to turn and face it head on.

Hellhounds were the size of a small horse. Their lean, muscled bodies were hairless and oily. Each paw held five hooked claws. Their eyes were completely black except for the disgusting red veins. The lips were peeled back in a terrifying snarl to show off the sets of jagged teeth. Two small horns rested behind its pointed ears. I'd faced one a couple months ago in the tunnels where Dro was trapped, and it had absolutely terrified me. I hoped never to face one of these beasts again, but I couldn't say I was surprised at Fate's sense of humor.

The hellhound made a choking, barking sound before leaping at me. I twisted away at the last possible second so I was standing by its ribs. I wrapped one arm around the hellhound's neck to hold it in place, then started hacking down on its back with my blessed hatchet.

It seemed like a good idea, and it would have worked, if hellhounds weren't so damn *strong*.

The beast thrashed and wrenched its head from side to side until it wriggled away from me. Then it pounced on my chest.

I hit the ground hard, sharp black claws digging into my shoulders. I gritted my teeth against the pain and the awful smell of rotting blood and sulfur coming from its breath. I looked into its face, staring at pupil-less black eyes and bloody veins. The hellhound snarled and opened its jaws, aiming them at my throat.

A blast of hellfire struck the monster before it could bite me. The beast gave a surprised yelp as the white flames covered its body. The hellhound stepped off of me. I lurched into a sitting position and smashed my hatchet into the side of its head. The hellhound twitched and collapsed onto the grass, slowly dissolving into dark powder.

I got to my feet and looked in the direction of the blast. Sephiel was fighting as hard as he could against *both* of the Knights– was he *insane?!*– carefully jumping aside when their scythes got too close.

Dro was focusing on the remaining Possessors and some hellhounds. She pushed out with both hands, consuming the demons trying to rush her. The wall of white flame lit up the entire hill like a beacon. They stood no chance against her. I couldn't see Lucifer, but he was probably standing back, enjoying the show before he made his move.

Max was on Dro's other side, holding out his hand. She took a quick chance to yank the silver knife from her boot and slapped it into his hand. Max wasn't a very good fighter, but he did his best against a Possessor that swung at him. He stabbed the blade into the possessed man's stomach, stepping back to avoid being punched in the chin. Black smoke exploded out of the dying man's mouth, trying to smother Max. The smoky Possessor shrieked when he felt the barrier protecting Max, thanks to the sigil of Michael tattooed over his heart. The Possessor spiraled away into the night.

Gunfire cracked on my right. I jumped and turned in its direction. Warrick shot a hellhound that had been running for me. He was as calm and cool as water, keeping his aim focused on the speeding monster's face. Bullet after bullet drilled into the hellhound's face, until it finally collapsed onto the grass. While it was crumbling into ash, Warrick turned his head and focused on the beast he wanted to kill the most.

Drake.

Since he didn't have time to reload, Warrick tucked his gun away and drew his combat knife. Drake was grinning maniacally as he charged the demon slayer, taking out his own Bowie knife. The second were in arm's reach, they started hacking at each other. Warrick blocked Drake's knife with his free hand, reversing the grip on his blade to drive it into Drake's stomach. The bounty hunter was quicker, grabbing the knife and trying to rip it away. Warrick kicked Drake's knee and drove his knee into the larger man's stomach. Drake wrenched his knife-hand free and slashed at Warrick's face. The blade was so close I swore it nicked his cheek.

Warrick was so busy fighting Drake that he didn't notice the Wretch coming up on his right. But I did. I wanted to keep my hatchet, so I took another throwing knife out of my jacket. I hurled it at the tortured angel, the blade sinking home in the middle of its back. The Wretch shrieked and stumbled, whirling around to see what hit it. Sickly yellow eyes fixed on me, and then the monster started running for me on all fours, like a charging bear.

Something moved out of the corner of my eye. I ducked on instinct. A heavy machete blade cut through the air just over my head. I twisted while I was low, slashing the hatchet across my attacker's leg. He cursed and buckled. I scowled at Mateo's familiar voice. I flipped it in my hand, bringing the weapon upward to slice open his face.

Mateo caught my wrist just as the blade nicked his chin. His dark brown eyes were filled with total contempt, an inhuman snarl twisting his lips. He slashed the machete toward my ribs, but I turned around him before the weapon could slide into my body. The motion allowed me to wrench my hatchet free. I kept spinning until I was behind him. I jammed my elbow into the back of his head, then sent my boot into his face with a scorpion-kick.

I spun on my heel, ready to drive my hatchet into Mateo's back. Then I heard a sharp howl and turned my head to the right. The Wretch slammed into me, knocking me onto my back. I grunted and pushed up my knees so it couldn't crush me. It screamed and roared all its insanity at me. I glanced to the side, seeing Mateo shaking off my kick and walking toward me. He spun the machete in his hand, ready to drive it into me somehow.

A burst of white light filled the left of my vision. Dro was using her powers in the fight again, trying to push back Lucifer and all the other demons swarming her,

Sephiel, and Max. I needed to get over to them.

I slashed open the throat of the Wretch with the hatchet. The blade cut so deep I felt it scrape against neck bones. It shuddered and began corroding. I glanced to my right again. Mateo's boots were right there. I twisted and threw the crumbling Wretch onto his feet then rolled away. I got to one knee as he slashed the machete down toward my neck. I stopped it with the crevice of my hatchet, where the blade met the handle. The weapon nearly splintered in half.

The back of his fist cracked against my cheek. My head snapped to the side, the entire world spinning. I propped myself onto my elbows and shook it off, just before Mateo kicked me in the ribs. I winced as pain flared in my side, and landed on my back. I brought my hatchet up, aiming to catch him in the leg.

He kicked my wrist down and pinned it to the grass. I reached for another knife, stopping when I felt the tip of the machete touch my throat.

Adrenaline rushed through my veins as I looked at my furious ex-lover. I was hearing demonic screams and cries of pain from my friends, but I couldn't move.

"You don't know how long I've thought about this," he said in a dead voice. "It was the only thing that kept me going. I wish I could make you suffer more, but it would be a waste of time."

It was a mistake to provoke my enemies, but sometimes I just couldn't help myself.

"Yeah, you're right," I told him. "Your dad tortured me, and look what happened to him."

Watching Mateo's anger build was like watching a steadily growing fire. It started off small and relatively harmless. Then before you knew it, the fire was a towering inferno you couldn't run from.

His lips peeled back in a malicious scowl. He raised the machete to drive it into my neck.

Something caught his eye, just before he could kill me. He stepped back as a white arrow flew by his head. I reached into my jacket and grabbed another knife, rolling away from Mateo and getting to my feet. I stepped back to keep distance on him, then followed his line of sight.

About half of the demons were piles of ash, but Sephiel's clothes were covered in blood. He was barely standing. Max was clutching his ribs, hunched over and grimacing in pain. Dro was on her knees, one hand pressed into the grass and another over her heart.

Lucifer was standing with his back to her. He commanded his Knights to face the other side of the hilltop.

Where all the angels were.

There were around a hundred of them. I was staring at sea of white trench coats. All of them were armed to the teeth with swords, knives, bows, spears, and shields. I could even see one with a morning star.

Michael was at the front of the army. He held a sword in and shield in his hands, looking just as fierce and as powerful as ever. If he was in pain from falling, it was impossible to tell. His blue eyes fixed on Lucifer, but not with hate. Just with an unwavering determination to fight to the death.

Behind Michael, dressed in the same fashion as their leader, were the remaining archangels. Gabriel wasn't there. Rorikel seemed to have taken his place. He held a white recurve bow in his hands, a single white arrow nocked against the string.

"I must say, Michael," Lucifer said, casually taking a step forward. "I did not expect you to arrive, since you have now fallen. How did you come to this place?"

"It is not your concern, Lucifer," replied the archangel. He had a deep voice than demanded respect. "But do not think that this fall has completely stripped the archangels of power. You should know better than that."

While they were talking, I was making my way to my sister. I kept Mateo in my line of sight, and further back I could see Warrick and Drake were easing away from each other. They both looked exhausted, but they could see something major was about to happen. Their Battle Royale was going to have to be put on hold, again.

"See reason, Michael. There is no victory for you here. If you have not become human now, you shall be one soon. Heaven was your source of power. It will drain away from you, leaving you nothing more than a mortal shell. I am willing to let you surrender. It would be a shame if I were forced to slaughter every member of the Host."

"The centuries have kept your tongue silver, brother," the archangel replied. "But you waste your words. We shall not surrender. If we cannot return to our home, then we shall make a new one of earth. And it is not a place where you belong."

I winced. *That doesn't sound good.*

I was only a couple feet away from Dro when Lucifer turned his head toward us. I froze to the spot.

"Do not place your ire on me, but on them," the King of Hell accused. "It is they who burned the Gate to Paradise."

Michael's intense azure eyes met mine for the first time. They flashed with a blazing rage that could have probably incinerated us on the spot once. He *hated* us. We'd taken him away from his home, he probably couldn't move from the vessel he was currently in, and he was getting weaker with each passing second. Michael narrowed his eyes on my sister. The anger burned even brighter than before. Any chance of reasoning with him had flown out of the window.

Fallen or not, he was going to make it his mission to rip us apart.

"Heaven will have its justice. Make no mistake about that."

It was a cold promise. I clutched my hatchet and my throwing knife and stood in front of my little sister, completely obscuring her from his view. His eyes lifted and bored into mine. I didn't blink or turn away in fear. Instead, I gave him a promise of my own.

Go ahead. I'll be waiting.

The archangel didn't blink, so I don't know if he saw me as a threat. He focused on Lucifer again. He tightened his grip on his broadsword.

"But not before you."

Michael swept up his broadsword, a wide line of heavenfire sweeping up with it. The blast raced toward Lucifer with amazing speed. The King of Hell actually had to raise both his hands to keep it from cremating him. The angels shouted an echoing war cry then charged toward battle. Lucifer set his remaining demons and possessed humans on them, then twisted his hands and began opening portals.

The air ripped open like six knives in six different places. Fire burst out of the tears, more demons spilling out of them onto the hilltop. Reds. Shredders. Ghouls. Possessors. More Hellhounds and Wretches. A couple more Knights. Things I had never seen before. I lost count of how many there were, and they just kept coming.

The angels met them all without fear, using their weapons with ruthless efficiency. Weaker demons were cut down like weeds. Stronger demons tore the angels to pieces. They were skilled warriors, but they were human now.

But if they needed to look at someone to motivate them, all they had to do was look at Michael. He was completely fearless. Two Knights approached him and swung their scythes to cut him in half at the waist. Michael spiraled through the air, narrowly missing the hooked blades. He used his new height to cut off the head of one Knight and slashed open the chest of the second one. It staggered back even further when he pushed a wall of heavenfire at it. He finished the Knight by driving his sword straight through its chest and tearing it up and out of its shoulder.

All the demons backed away from him as fast as they could before he blasted them with heavenfire. None of them seemed to be a real challenge for the archangel. He was steadily making his way to Lucifer, probably wanting to get the portals closed. I didn't think that would be easy to do. Lucifer was perfectly capable of multi-tasking. He could keep the portals open until all the angels were destroyed.

"We have to do something," Dro and I said at the same time.

"But what?" Max asked weakly.

"Andromeda," Sephiel said, clutching her shoulders. "You can close the portals."

"I..." she whispered in a scared voice. She took a deep breath and crushed the fear. "How?"

"Con!" Max screamed.

I twisted, ducking low and kicking my foot out. I caught Mateo in the stomach, knocking him away before his machete could hit me in the back. I spun my hatchet in my hand.

"Get it done!" I shouted to the trio behind me.

Mateo charged me again, swinging his machete at my stomach. I stepped out of range then moved up and kicked for his ribs. He blocked me with his arm and tried to raise the machete again, but I kicked it out of his hand.

Before he could get another weapon, I rushed him.

I hacked and slashed wildly, constantly putting him on the defense. Mateo was faster than I remembered. His forearms clashed against mine, sending painful jolts to my hands and promising plenty of bruises later. The blades never cut him once. I stabbed for his neck with the knife. He let the blade sweep over his shoulder, then caught my arm and jabbed me in the face with his free hand. My head rocked back, filling with pain. I refocused when I heard him drawing a knife.

I flipped my hatchet into a reverse grip, brining it up and hooking his knife before it could go into my ribs. I wrenched it away, and was hit in the face again. Mateo kicked me in the chest to push me away, then spun a wide roundhouse kick. It crashed into my temple and sent me spinning onto the ground.

I nearly blacked out when I hit the grass. I thought I was rolling down a hill. I still had my hatchet. I had to get up. As I lifted my head, I could see the battle still going strong. It was an even match, demons turning to ash and angels falling in showers of blood. Someone with bright hair and a bow was running toward us.

Lucifer had given up on holding the portals open now that Michael had caught up to him. They were about twenty feet apart, flinging their hands wildly as they hurled supernatural fire at each other. Michael sent a tornado of golden fire over Lucifer's head. It bent in midair like a mouth trying to swallow him whole. Lucifer swept out his hands, creating a line of blindingly white hellfire. His flames absorbed the gold heavenfire until it was gone. Then he pushed the hellfire up and split it into a thousand, fiery darts. He flicked his wrists and sent them all at Michael. The archangel reacted quickly and raised his shield. He was protected from the darts, but the seven angels next to him weren't so lucky. I cringed at the sound of their screams and looked away before I could see them burn.

Michael and Lucifer were too busy fighting each other to see Dro standing behind them, Max holding her up while Sephiel explained what to do. My sister held out her hands and focused. I watched the portals begin to shiver and close.

A hand fisted itself in my hair and jerked me to my feet. I growled and slashed back with the hatchet. Mateo caught my wrist with his free hand, driving his knee into my ribs. I gasped, feeling him tug on my hair to make me face him. He let go of my hair, grabbing my throat instead.

"I'm not done with you yet, *babe*," he sneered.

"Yes you are."

Mateo snapped his head to the right, giving Warrick the perfect chance to smash his fist into it. Mateo stumbled, letting me go. The demon slayer kicked him in the chin, knocking him onto the grass. He was ready to advance on him before he turned and saw Drake running for him.

The bounty hunter's face was a mess of blood and anger. I brushed along Warrick's back and grabbed the fourth and final knife from inside my jacket. I hurled it at Drake, catching him in the shoulder. I couldn't tell if it was a killing blow, but the huge man dropped nonetheless.

A hand circled my arm. I jerked out of its grasp and raised my hatchet. Rorikel caught my wrist before my weapon could slam into his neck. His hard grey eyes stayed on mine.

"Peace, Constance. I do not mean you harm."

Of all the people I expected to come to our rescue, he was last on the list. I was even more surprised that he didn't look like the old Rorikel. He wasn't looking at me with the sharp, blatant hatred that he speared me with all those months ago.

I didn't trust him anymore now than I had back then. I wrenched my hand free. "Prove it."

"Gabriel sent me," he answered. He reached into his trench coat and pulled out a small gold tube. "With this."

It was another *movens caeli*, but smaller and thinner than the one Lucifer destroyed.

"It is less powerful than the one you previously possessed, but it shall take you away from this place. You must leave now."

"No, we can't," Warrick protested. "Not when Drake, Mateo and Lucifer are still alive!"

Rorikel suddenly twisted, nocking the bow with an arrow from the quiver on his hip. He drew back the string and let the arrow fly directly into the open mouth of a charging hellhound. The monster exploded into black ash in mid leap. Rorikel turned around again.

"Now is not the time for petty revenge, slayer! The hybrid has nearly closed all the portals. When she has finished doing so, Lucifer will destroy you all. If you still wish to defeat him, stay alive and close the Hell Gate!"

He shoved the *movens caeli* against my chest and started firing arrows again. Warrick wanted to keep fighting, but his eyes turned to where Dro, Max, and Sephiel were standing. The portals were slivers of flame now. Our escape window was closing fast. He frowned, but knew where his priorities were. He ran for his friends. I started following, then stopped and looked at Rorikel again.

"What about the angels?" I shouted over the roar of

combat.

He drew the bowstring back, looking at me between it. He looked tired and deflated, completely unlike the Rorikel I used to know.

"Some of us just want to go home," he called to me, though his voice was joyless. "We no longer care how."

I wanted to say something, but Rorikel was already looking away and firing another white arrow. We might have despised each other, but I wished I could get his attention to thank him. I also wished that I had time to finish off Drake and Mateo. It was going to have to wait. If we were going to get out of here, we had to get out of here now.

I turned and ran toward my sister. Just as I got there, the portals disappeared from the air. The fires of Hell were gone, but the entire battlefield was burning. It was like looking at the scorched Heaven Gate all over again.

Dro slumped, Sephiel catching her. I dropped to my knees beside her. She was awake, blinking rapidly. We all huddled close together. I put the *movens caeli* into Sephiel's hands, then looked over his shoulder.

Lucifer threw a blast of hellfire at Michael. It collided with his chest and sent him flying back about twenty feet. The King of Hell whirled on his feet, seeing what was happening. His pitch black eyes met mine. He looked at beautiful and as furious as ever.

Dro suddenly shouted words that I couldn't make out. Golden light and a massive rumbling noise surrounded us, but not before I made out the four words Lucifer mouthed to me.

I will destroy you.

The light blurred out the battle, and then we were gone...

I drove Emilio's car into the warehouse. I didn't know what time it was, or if I was being followed. My shoulder was on fire and everything was a blur. I managed to spot a small figure with white hair sitting in a corner. She stood up as soon as the car approached. I turned off the headlights so she could see me. I raised my good hand, waved weakly, then passed out.

I woke up when I felt someone sitting me back in driver's seat. I blinked my eyes open. Dro had crawled into the passenger side of Emilio's car and was pressing her pale hand against the bullet hole in my shoulder. I winced at the tingling sensation. My sister was sniffling. I looked at her, forcing myself not to look like I was in agony.

"There's so much damage inside you," Dro sobbed. "Connie, what happened?"

I hesitated. Did I really want to tell my little sister that my boyfriend had beaten the shit out of me, that his father had electrocuted me, that I'd been beaten up again, killed the most powerful drug lord in Mexico, and been shot as a result?

No. That seemed like too much information right now.

"I'll tell you later," I slurred out. "We have to get out of here. They're going to be looking for us."

Dro nodded, not meeting my eyes. Once I was healed, we got out of Emilio's Lexus and headed for the Mercedes Dro had driven. She'd hidden it in the warehouse and out of sight, like the smart girl she was. I hopped in the driver's seat, my shoulder feeling a little stiff, but at least I could use it.

I buckled up, started the car, and drove out of the warehouse. I didn't tell Dro anything as we took the back roads toward the border, and she didn't ask. The sun was high in the cloudless sky as we got into the desert. I made a stop to get some gas and make sure no Blood Thorns were on our tail, but my plan hadn't gone any further than that.

Mostly because I didn't know what to do. Emilio tortured me and I killed him. Mateo betrayed me, abused me, pulverized my heart, and shot me. He was in control of the Blood Thorns now, and he wouldn't waste any time sending them after me. He wouldn't stop until I suffered and died the way his father had.

I couldn't fight them all. Dro and I would never be safe.

My chest was caving in, like someone was reaching into it and pushing it toward my spine. My eyes started to water. I pulled the car to a stop on the road and shut it off. There was no one on this lonely stretch of desert highway. Nobody but me and an uncertain little sister watching my face.

"I'm sorry," I sobbed, unable to stop the tears from streaming down my cheeks. "I'm so sorry, little sister. I never should have said yes."

Dro unbuckled her seatbelt and turned to face me. "It's not your fault, Connie."

"Yes it is," I whimpered. "I thought it would keep us safe, and all I did was make it worse. I can't... I can't fix this. I don't know what the fuck to do."

The ache in my chest was unbearable. There was so much weight and pressure that I had to unbuckle and grab the steering wheel to support myself. I squeezed my eyes shut and felt tears splash onto my jeans.

Delicate little arms wrapped around my chest. A small head with soft hair pressed itself into my shoulder. My sobs were becoming painful now, clenching in my chest like a fist and choking their way out of my throat. My eyes were tightened together so hard that it hurt. My face was soaked.

"I'm not mad at you, Constance," Dro whispered in my ear. "I never was. I can't make you feel better about the things you had to do, but I never blamed you for them. You're my big sister, and you were keeping me safe. You helped us survive."

That should have made me feel better. Instead, I started to feel worse.

"They're going to hunt us, Andromeda," I cried. "I don't know where we can go to hide from them."

Dro hugged me tighter. I'd put us in more danger than ever before. The Blood Thorns had networks everywhere. There was nowhere for us to run.

"Then maybe we should go home," my sister said

quietly.

Home. There was nothing I wanted more. But Dro knew as well as I did that going home didn't mean we would be safe...

Chapter 18

I thought Dro would take us somewhere safe. Granted, we never had many safe places as kids. But I expected it to be anywhere but here.

At first, I didn't recognize the warehouse. The walls were still rusted from where the blood had been splattered on them. Wooden crates filled with bullet holes sat uselessly near the walls. I looked at the far end of the warehouse, staring at the support beams where the traitor had been mutilated and killed.

The smell of death was long gone, but I was having difficulty breathing. I slowly turned and found Dro. Her icy blue eyes held mine, though I could tell she was fighting the urge to look away.

"Why did you bring us here?" I asked. My voice was shaking.

Dro tried to speak a couple times, but faltered through each one. Warrick, Max, and Sephiel glanced between us, but didn't interject. They must have been completely confused about their surroundings, having never been here before, but at the moment, I didn't care.

Dro finally found the words she'd been searching for.

"We needed to escape, Con," she reasoned. "You told me years ago that you hated this place, and that the Blood Thorns wouldn't look for me here. I was safe until you came back, and I figure it will be safe again."

"No," I snapped. My body began to tremble with my voice. "No, we can't stay here. This is Blood Thorn ground. Mateo will have it guarded." I started shaking my head, as if it would wake me up and bring me back to reality.

The joke was that I was already there.

"This is the safest place we can be right now," coaxed

Dro. "Mateo will think we've gone somewhere else. This gives us time to think and plan our next move."

I knew she was right. Dro wouldn't have made the decision to come back to Júarez lightly. But I swore I'd never return here, no matter what the circumstances.

Fate. What a raging bitch.

***

It was a long walk back to the city. As much as I dreaded seeing it again, it wasn't far and I still knew the best places to hide. Fate might have been screwing me over, but at least I knew how to adapt.

I kept to myself for the entire walk. Dro and Warrick tried to make conversation, though I never said more than two words. Max and Sephiel didn't even try.

Two hours later, we saw the edges of Júarez. Thick towers of smoke chugged into the night sky. A dull orange glow shone over the horizon. Seeing the fires burning downtown was the only reason I stopped.

"Fuck," I whispered.

The group came to a halt beside me. Dro and Max stared at the city intensely.

"There are demons in the city," informed Max. "But it's not them who are lighting the fires." He narrowed his eyes, then looked at me uncomfortably. "It's everyone else."

I didn't say anything or look anywhere but the fires. Warrick asked my question instead.

"You're saying that the people who live in the city are the ones burning it down?"

"Yeah," Max answered. "It's messed up, but that's what I'm seeing."

"Lucifer's influence has stretched far," Sephiel said. "His presence over their minds must be strong. We have to be cautious."

Good luck with that, I nearly blurted. "We better take a look, then."

I started dragging myself toward the city.

"Uh, whoa," Max started. "Isn't there a place out here where we can hide? The city is on *fire*."

I whirled on him. "I can fucking see that. But chaos is great cover, so this is as good as we can ask for. Take my word or don't, Max, but don't waste my time."

I turned and started walking away before anyone could see the guilt on my face. I would apologize to Max later. Right now I just wanted to find somewhere to sleep. No one called after me, and I was both grateful and disappointed with that.

***

I thought the fires burning in Júarez would be the worst part of the city, Max's warning aside.

I should have thought harder about what he was trying to tell me.

The suburbs and housing developments of the city seemed to be inhabited by ghosts. Everywhere I looked, there had only been broken glass, knocked over trash bins, and blood smears on the pavement. Our legs were killing us from walking so far, but I didn't want to stay in the houses. For all I knew, people were hiding out in them, and somehow I doubted they would welcome us into their shelter with open arms. Even when the city wasn't caught in some kind of riot, the people living here knew better than to help strangers.

Besides, I knew the city better from its core.

Finding a car wasn't hard, once I found one that wasn't stripped, tipped over, or burned to a crisp. I chose a small Toyota with an opened door. I was suspicious of the blood stain on the pavement by the driver's side. There was a pool of it by the door, and a long smear winding around the front of the car, like the world's bloodiest comma.

After checking the car to make sure it wasn't booby-trapped or filled with dead body parts, I slipped inside and felt around for the keys. They were stuck in the ignition, which meant I didn't have to waste time cutting wires and hoping I could get the car to work.

I waited for the rest of the group to get into the car, then turned the key. The Toyota sputtered to life, sounding way louder than it should have. I winced, glancing out the rearview mirror.

My heart skipped a beat when I saw a woman in a nightgown glide out of her house. Her curly black hair was a wild mess, and blood was smeared along the front of her body. She held a bloody butcher knife in her hand. She was about three houses behind us, but I swore that she was smiling as she walked closer.

I focused on putting the car into drive, watching nervously as more front doors were opened. People stumbled out in various states of dress, all of them watching our car with hungry eyes. I wanted to say they looked like zombies, but they were too *alive*. They were conscious, completely aware of where they were and what they wanted.

The scariest part was seeing their eyes, and not finding a trace of blackness in them. None of the people stalking toward the car seemed to be possessed.

Any doubts about taking refuge in a house completely vanished.

I stomped on the gas pedal and tore down the street. I glanced in the rearview mirror when Dro gasped, and saw a man drawing a gun. He pointed at the back window of our car.

A gunshot cracked through the night, and red mist exploded from the head of the man pointing the gun at us.

Both sides of the suburban street shouted and charged one another, launching into a murderous frenzy. They meshed together, forgetting all about us as they stabbed, beat, and shot their neighbors.

Dro sobbed quietly, burying herself in Max's shoulder. He held her tightly, his shaking hand moving through her hair. Sephiel watched the chaos vigilantly, moving his hand into his jacket to grip one of his short swords. Warrick was in the passenger seat beside me, tense and angry.

I kept driving, hoping that the location I was taking us to would be marginally safer.

I had no idea what would cause so much chaos and destruction, but it couldn't be good.

***

If the suburbs were bad, the heart of Ciudad Júarez was ten times worse. Thick smoke billowed from the burning oil drums that had replaced the street lamps. Wild orange flames danced out of the apartment windows above me. Looters scurried through the street ahead, carrying as many TV's and electronics that they could, only to hurl them through the windows of the shops across the street. Blood painted the brick walls and flowed through the gutters. Motionless bodies lay broken on the sidewalk, pulped so badly they looked like raw meat instead of human beings.

We had just entered downtown, and I refused to go any further. I could see people running around the streets, some in chase and some in pursuit. It was way too dangerous to go any deeper into the city. I stopped the car and threw off my seatbelt. We were going to have to run the rest of the way. I twisted in the car seat to look at Dro.

"You remember where we're going?" I asked her.

She stared at me with wide, scared eyes before risking a glance out of the window. "Del Ray's?"

I nodded. Del Ray's was a taco shop we used to live behind. We never met the man himself, but he threw out tons of leftovers and unknowingly kept us fed for days.

"Follow me, and don't stop running," I said, referring to everyone in the car.

Taking my hatchet and a knife out, I opened the car door and stepped out into the hellhole I used to call home.

The sounds of screams and roaring fires became so much louder. I breathed in putrid smoke and rancid death. While the others hurried out of the car, I did a careful one-eighty to make sure we couldn't be seen. The city was in madness like nothing I had ever seen, and the last thing I wanted was to get into another fight.

Luckily, no one had seen us. Once everyone was outside, I turned and sprinted for the narrow alley on the left of the street. I darted into the shadows, the smell of garbage and rotting flesh wafting over to me. I coughed and glanced deeper into the darkness, seeing a bloody arm hanging out of a mostly closed dumpster.

I shimmied past it, keeping my eyes glued onto the store on the other side of the alley. I concentrated on moving forward, forcing myself not to look at the spot where I'd slept in a cardboard box with my sister, or where I had witnessed my first gang murder, or where we'd been kidnapped and taken to a man who would make me destroy my life.

It only took a couple minutes to reach the end of the alley. I pressed my back to the brick wall and glanced around the corner. Warrick stood across from me, checking the street the same way that I was. We looked at each other.

"My side's clear. Yours?"

I nodded at him, then jumped out of the street. I didn't look at anything as I ran for the faded yellow, two story building with happy, bright red carnival letters on the bottom and boarded up windows on the top. Out of the corner of my eye, I saw people running, heard more screaming, and a dark shape that looked suspiciously like a hellhound. I ran for the open front door and shouldered my way inside.

The shop looked like a bull had run through it. Chairs were tossed on the floor, clumps of food were plastered on the walls, napkins spilled from dented holders, and blood was splattered on the floor. I stood in the middle of the disgusting restaurant, waiting to see if anyone would come out of the back. No one did.

"Barricade the door," I told Warrick and Sephiel. "I'm going to check upstairs."

Warrick and Sephiel nodded and got to work. Dro and Max walked up to me.

"We're coming with you," she said.

I was about to tell them I could do it myself, but changed my mind at the last minute. Who knew what I might find up there?

"Fine. Let's go."

The stairs to the upper level were in a corridor on the left side under a sign that said *Sólo Los Empleados–* Employees Only. I walked up the creaking stairs, my eyes riveted to the top of the landing. Nobody came barreling down the stairs in a murderous rage, but I wasn't throwing caution to the wind just yet.

When I reached the top of the apartment, I looked in all four rooms. The unclean bathroom was empty. So was the tiny, unkempt living room. Two bedrooms were filled with piles of clothes and messy sheets, but just as empty. The bedroom at the far end of the hall had a large, open window that revealed a fire escape with a clothesline strung across it. I glanced out of the window. It wasn't a far jump, so we could use it in an emergency to get out. Good thing too, because I got the feeling we weren't going to stay here long.

I pulled the open window down, drew the curtains, and turned to look at Dro and Max.

"Looks like we'll be safe here," I said. My eyes went to Max. "Unless you see something different."

He shook his head, staring at the floor. "No. We should be good."

Suddenly I was guilty for the way I lashed out at him. At all of them. This was still the last place I wanted to be, but Dro chose it for what she thought were the right reasons. That was still up for debate with me, but I was too tired to argue anymore.

"You guys want this room?"

Max and Dro nodded, though their answer didn't really matter. Her eyes went over my body, seeing all of my injuries. "Do you want me to heal you?"

I waved the offer away. "It can wait until morning. Right now we just need to rest."

Dro opened her mouth to protest, but it died on her lips. She sighed and moved past me to the bed. Max let go of her hand, then moved his eyes between us.

"You know what? I need to use the bathroom. I'll be right back."

He left the room, knowing my sister and I needed to talk. I nodded at him gratefully, waiting until he closed the door and left us alone. I turned around to find Dro lying on her side under the covers. She was sighing heavily, the way she did when she was crying and didn't want anyone to notice. I crawled onto the bed and sat on the blankets beside her, like we were kids again and she wanted to talk about something that was bothering her.

My eyes drifted to the ceiling when I lay on my back and laced my hands over my stomach.

"Are you still mad at me?" she whispered.

I sighed. "I wasn't really mad," I told her. "Just unhappily surprised."

"I didn't want to bring you back here, Con. I just didn't know what else to do."

"It's fine," was the only thing I could say that was true and harmless.

We fell into silence again and stared at nothing, the only sounds coming from the restaurant downstairs as Warrick and Sephiel barricaded us in.

"I felt them all, Con," Dro finally whispered. "I felt their pain when they all fell. Their wings were torn from their backs, and it was like all their powers were dragged out with them. They all screamed in my head at once. It was horrible."

That explained part of why she'd screamed when we destroyed the Heaven Gate.

"There was no other way, right?" she asked. "We had to burn it?"

"Yeah," I answered. "Try to think of it this way. We stopped Lucifer from getting into Heaven, and now the angels won't be strong enough to get into Hell. The human race will live to fight another day," I added with a little snark.

Dro wasn't amused. I rolled onto my side and stared at her back. The pillows and sheets of the bed were white, mixing in with Dro's hair.

"We did this together, Andromeda. We can both take the blame."

Dro rolled over to face me. Her eyes were wet and red. "You weren't supposed to. It should have been me. I was the reason the Gates opened."

I shook my head. "No. That was my fault. If I hadn't let you get captured by Drake back in Texas, none of this would have happened. But if the demons and angels had just left us alone, we wouldn't be here at all. They pushed first. We just had to push back harder."

My sister frowned. "It might have helped in the long run, but things will be so much harder for us now. The demons and angels hate us, and they won't stop until they kill us."

I shrugged, as if it didn't bother or terrify me. "Then we'll make it tougher on them." I met my sister's eyes. "But Dro, I want you to make me a promise."

She shifted on the bed, looking at me expectantly. I took a deep breath.

"Don't push yourself like you did back on the hill. We don't know how much angel powers you still have, or if they're going to fade away like Michael's will.'"

Fear quivered in her eyes. She hadn't considered that using her powers too much would hurt her, or that she might lose them all together. Not that it changed her opinion.

"I can't do that, Constance. Sephiel doesn't have his powers anymore. Lucifer knows this, and he's going to take advantage of it. You promised to let me fight him."

"I'm not going to break that promise," I defended, wishing I could lie. "But you can't fight him until you know how much power you have. It's too risky, and we can't lose you." I reached out and clasped her hand. "*I* can't lose you, little sister."

Dro looked pained, her lips tight and her eyes going between frustration and compliance. I wasn't being fair. I couldn't be.

"Back at the bunker, you asked me to make an

impossible promise. And I did. Now you have to make one for me, Andromeda. Please. Promise me you won't use your powers as much, not unless we beg you to."

My sister thought it over as thoroughly as I thought about my promise to let her stand alone against Lucifer. I still wasn't sure why I agreed. Yes, she was my sister and promises mattered, but I was supposed to be her protector. No matter how terrible I was at the job sometimes, I couldn't stop myself. Dro was worth guarding. Like Max said, she never let the darkness inside her take over. If it was on the edges, she had me bring her back into the light. Now that her angel powers were weakened, Dro was going to have to use her darker abilities. She would slip more often.

But I would never let her fall.

She knew this as much as I did. Her face softened a fraction, but it was enough.

"Okay, big sister," Dro breathed. "I promise."

My heart eased. Dro kept her promises as fiercely as I kept mine. We were going to have plenty of arguments, but we were going to stick together when it mattered most. We were going to be facing angels, demons, and who knew what else, and they were going to have a hell of a time breaking us.

"Thanks, Dro. Get some sleep, okay?"

She nodded, tugging the covers up to her shoulders. She closed her eyes and sighed. It was painfully obvious that she wouldn't be able to sleep anymore than I would. Still, I got out of the bed and left her room. Hopefully she could relax enough so she got at least an hour of actual rest.

As I closed the door behind me, Max was just coming out of the bathroom. He looked exhausted.

"Hey," I said. "You all right?"

"Yeah, sure, about the same as always, I guess."

He didn't sound anywhere near convincing.

There was an awkward silence before I said, "I'm sorry I snapped at you. I didn't mean it. I hate this city and it… Well, it shows, right?" I smiled weakly, and he matched it. I counted that as a decent start.

"Thanks for looking out for Dro," I told him. "And for... you know."

Max looked a little better when he thought about my sister. But there was an apprehension in his eyes that wasn't there before.

"She's my girlfriend. I love her. You don't need to thank me for that." He ran a hand through his curly black hair. "But I'm worried about her, Constance. I felt how much she exhausted herself. She kept putting herself in pain to help us, and she didn't think I'd know." He met my eyes. "I don't know what'll happen if she keeps pushing herself like that."

I felt a twinge of panic at the thought of my little sister destroying herself to keep us alive. The worst part was knowing there wasn't anything I could do to keep her from doing it. Dro helped people. It was simply part of who she was. And she was so much stronger than me.

"We'll find out where the Hell Gate is first," I decided. "Then we can worry about Dro."

Max didn't like the sound of that anymore than I did, but he nodded all the same. "So, we get some shuteye, then start running for our lives in the morning?"

He said it with a smile, so I couldn't be mad at him. "Yeah. Something like that."

"Adventurous. See you in the morning."

He turned and took three steps before I cleared my throat. Max paused and looked over his shoulder.

"Where are you sleeping again?"

"Uh," he said. "I was gonna share with Dro. This hasn't been an easy night, and I don't want her to be alone."

Nice of him to be honest with me. "I appreciate that, Max," I said. "Really. But she needs to be alone right now."

He flinched. "Constance, I would never take advantage—"

I held up my hand. "I know. I'm not saying you would. But we didn't talk about sunshine and kittens and rainbows just now. She needs to process everything that happened." I looked at the floor. "We all do."

I folded my arms over my chest, not wanting to look as vulnerable as I felt. It grated my nerves to deny her the comfort of human contact, especially from someone she loved. But space was just as important, and that was what Dro needed right now.

"Yeah," Max agreed grudgingly. "I guess so." He shoved a hand through his hair. "I think I'll crash."

I nodded, but he didn't notice. He turned again and walked to the spare bedroom. I frowned, having wanted the space for myself, but it wasn't a big deal. There was still the living room.

The noises downstairs had stopped, so I assumed that Warrick and Sephiel had finished barricading us in. I trudged down the steps and back into the restaurant. The angel and the demon slayer stood back to check their work. The barstools and broken pieces of table formed a solid line in front of the door, looking too heavy to open from the outside. Warrick turned and looked at me.

"Well, I hope you don't plan on using this door again, 'cause we won't be getting out of it easily."

His slow smile warmed my heart. I folded my arms over my chest. "There's a fire escape in the room Dro's using. There's a living room if you want to use it."

"I shall remain here as a vanguard," Sephiel said, staring at the barricaded door as if it offended him.

"I'll take the living room," Warrick said.

So much for my sleeping arrangements. Still, it wasn't the first time I'd slept on a hard surface. It wouldn't be comfortable, but I would manage. I watched his back for a little bit as he walked away, unable to help myself. As he turned up the stairs, I pulled my face away from him and pretended I hadn't been staring at him. I hoped he didn't notice.

To get Warrick off my mind, I looked at Sephiel. He was as rigid as a statue. I actually had to remind myself that he hadn't turned to stone.

"So," I said, walking to his right side so I could have

a conversation with him. "I remember you lost your sword in the first tussle we had with Lucifer, but where'd the short swords come from?"

Sephiel gave me a tired smile. "It is not practical for any warrior to have merely one weapon. We all carry secondary arms in our coats for precautionary measures. Like you, I have a fondness for blades."

I smirked and looked at his face. He was still Sephiel, but it was clear he wasn't the being he once was. His eyes were dim, his shoulders sagging, his skin more weathered. I hadn't realized how much power his wings must have held until they'd been taken away from him.

"How's your back?" I asked.

"Empty," Sephiel admitted. "My wings were a connection to Heaven. A source of power and a reminder of what I was. Without them, I feel lost."

The smile began to fade from his face.

"There is little I can do for you now, Constance. I am completely human. I cannot heal or teleport or conjure heavenfire. I can provide knowledge, advice, and an extra sword, but beyond that I am a burden." He bowed his head. "I pray you shall not see me as such, because I do not know where else to go."

I put my hand on Sephiel's shoulder and gave him a gentle shake. His eyes rose to mine. They were still a brilliant blue, but they didn't glimmer the way they did when he was an angel.

"Don't be an idiot, Seph," I said. "You're not going anywhere."

He relaxed under my touch, but the seriousness didn't leave his eyes.

"I thank you for your generous, if crass, acceptance. But I do not have the heart to be optimistic at this time. We do not know how Lucifer has shielded the Hell Gate. It will not be shown to us as the Heaven Gate was. We cannot rely on angels, either. Rorikel may have helped us at the behest of Gabriel, but if he survived the attack on the Heaven Gate, it does not mean his position has changed. He could remain our enemy. And then there is

Michael, who shall not disregard this offence. He will seek revenge as surely as Lucifer will."

I took my hand back. "Seph, you're my friend, and I like you. But I'm not in the mood for bad news."

He flinched. "I apologize. I did not mean—"

I waved it off. "Forget it. You stay on watch for now. Warrick or me will come down and switch with you in a few hours."

"Thank you. Sleep would be useless for me, as I fear my mind is not as settled as I wished it to be."

I couldn't tell if he was thinking about his wings, Lucifer, his fallen brothers and sisters, the task ahead, Everiel, or all of the above. And I didn't ask. I turned and walked up the stairs.

My original plan was to go straight to the second bedroom where Dro was so I could sleep on the floor, but I hesitated as I passed the living room.

Despite being constantly frustrated by me, Warrick was still in our group. He'd been a mess since he saw Emma's illusion, but he still saved me from Mateo. That deserved at least a thank you.

I stood by the doorframe, watching him inspect the couch and pull it out into a sofa bed. Warrick sensed me and looked up. His hair was a bit messy, there were dark circles under his eyes, a bruise on his cheek, and a cut on his lip. His leather jacket was lying on the floor, and now I could see more dark bruises covering his arms under the edges of his black T-shirt. Warrick's cell phone started buzzing on the coffee table near the sofa bed. I glanced at it.

"Not gonna get that?" I asked.

He shrugged. "It's just the slayers. I'm torn between throwing it out the window and smashing it under a brick."

I grinned. "You can always be thorough and do both."

Warrick smiled a little, but it didn't take the sadness off his face. "I would, if I thought it would keep them from chasing us."

I stopped smiling. "You think they will?"

He nodded grimly. "Carver left a message when I was helping Sephiel. Long story short, he wants to kick me out of the circle, lock up Dro, Seph, and Max for questioning, then turn you in for that Marshal bounty so he can fund his hunts."

"Not a quitter, huh?" It wasn't a question.

"Not at all," he replied. "Carver will follow us to the end of the earth to make us pay for disrespecting him, Elle will be right at his heels, and Jackson doesn't have a choice. The last person I made this mad was Drake."

We both went silent at that. The air became uncomfortable very quickly. Coming here might have been a bad idea since Warrick was likely thinking about Drake, and the sister he'd lost to him. I debated on leaving for the bedroom, but the heavy way he sat on the sofa bed and the tiredness of his sigh changed my mind. I walked inside and slid the living room door closed behind me. I sat on the mattress next to Warrick. It was springy and hard. I wasn't sure I liked it.

"You sure you're all right?" I asked, looking at him. "I didn't see most of your fight with Drake." *Since my ex-boyfriend was trying to cut my head off.*

"Yeah, I'll be fine," Warrick said. "Nothing Drake hasn't done to me already. It isn't him that I'm upset about."

The sorrow was back in his eyes. I understood that pain. It was the same, awful ache I felt when I saw my parents in the Heaven Gate. A pain that only got worse when Dro showed me it was an illusion, and reminded me that they were still dead.

I grabbed Warrick's hand without thinking. He didn't react at first and I wondered if touching him was a mistake. Then he twined his fingers through mine. His skin was warm and callused from years of fighting, just like mine. We both had scars and pain we didn't want to carry anymore. We also had the strength to push it aside and keep fighting.

"You did the right thing," he told me gently.

"Closing the Heaven Gate with Dro."

I laughed through my teeth. "Is that why I feel like shit?" My humor didn't last. "Dro says she felt the angels' pain. I would give anything to take that from her. All I feel is numb. Sick. I don't know if I did the right thing or not, and it's too late to take it back. God might forgive, but angels don't."

Warrick looked at me for a long time. I didn't meet his eyes. "Lucifer was there, Constance. He was right behind us, about to go into Heaven and destroy it. He was going to take it over and corrupt all of humanity, after he killed all the angels. The people you saved might not see it that way for a long time, but we will. None of us will blame you or Dro for what you did."

I wanted to believe him, but the gravity of what I'd done was still sinking in. My soul was filled with darkness from the brutal way I'd lived it, yet this was different. I annihilated something that I knew should have been left alone. I felt like a hunter who just killed the last of an endangered species, and was starting to realize that there would be no more hunts after this.

Warrick gave up on looking at me. He turned his face to the floor.

"I tried to be mad at your sister, you know," he said suddenly.

That took my mind off the burden in my heart and got me looking at him. "For taking away the vision of Emma," he explained. "I wanted to be furious. I almost wanted to hate her. I really thought I had my sister again, and if she hadn't shown me it was a lie, I would have stayed there.

"But then I understood that Dro did it to protect me from myself, and I couldn't hate her for that. Not when I think about how hard it must have been for her."

"It was," I clarified. "But that's my sister for you. Always taking the hard road."

"Something tells me she got that from you," he smirked, nearly looking like himself again.

I stifled a laugh. "Yeah, I know, I'm a terrible role

model."

Warrick's smile was gentle, his eyes wonderfully bright. "No you're not. You're just a good sister."

That was all it took for me to start falling again. Sitting here with his hand in mine, it felt like we were the only two people in the world. All the problems were outside the door. In here, nothing seemed wrong. I let Warrick's presence calm my mind and fill my heart. He was relaxed and considerate when he needed to be, but tough and uncompromising when he was ready to fight. Someone this good shouldn't have been around me. I was a recipe for pain and disaster.

"I'm sorry," I blurted.

He tilted his head curiously. "For what?"

"For all of this," I said. The words started tumbling out before I could stop them. "Dragging you into this shit. Maybe you should have stayed with the demon slayers."

"No," he told me without hesitation. "I never wanted to stay with them. I made my choice to stick with you and your sister, and I would make it again."

Warrick turned on the bed so he could face me directly. His free hand came up to cup my cheek. I let his thumb slide along my skin, just under my eye. Every movement caused my stomach to flutter and my pulse to pound.

"You did what you had to do, which is exactly what you're going to keep doing, even when you know it's only going to get harder. I don't know many people who can do that, especially with this situation. But you will."

Warrick took a deep breath. "It's one of the things I love most about you."

The world stopped. I was ready for anything but that. He didn't officially say that he loved me, but he might as well have. It wasn't like his eyes were hiding what he felt.

My heart swelled, and I let all my fear fall away. Warrick wasn't Mateo. He wouldn't hurt me. He would never betray my sister or my friends. He had countless chances to turn back, but he never did. Even when I pushed him away, he came back. He never gave up. Warrick saw some spark in me that I couldn't see. He was convinced it was there, and he was going to show it to me. I was finally ready to let him.

I pushed forward and kissed him.

Warrick seemed a bit surprised at first, but then his hand slid to the back of my neck. He stayed there and let me kiss him, never pushing or asking for more.

Except that more was exactly what I wanted.

I kissed him deeper, turning so I could push him down on the bed. I slipped my tongue between Warrick's lips. His fingers left mine and trailed around my waist, gently tracing the skin of my lower back where my shirt had ridden up. He felt me shiver, and pulled away. He held me up there, torn between kissing me again and keeping me back.

"I thought I was hurting you," he whispered.

"I changed my mind," I teased.

I leaned down again, but he tilted his head so I couldn't touch his lips. He sighed.

"Constance, I don't want you to do this if I'm the one who'll get hurt."

I almost gave up right then. The last thing I ever wanted to do was hurt Warrick. I didn't know what I could offer him, but he wanted it. I couldn't take it from him. Never mind that it was time I started finding more motivation. I'd always fought for my sister. I didn't need to fight for anyone else. Now I had allies that I could actually call friends. People I was ready to die for. The more I was willing to protect, the harder I was going to fight.

I put my fingers under his chin and lifted his head to mine. Bright green eyes found me in the darkness. They were too enticing to ignore.

"I won't," I promised. "I'm going to give you at least one dream."

All the tension and grief that filled Warrick's eyes started to fade away. A new light filled them. It was strong and hopeful, and neither one of us was going to let it go out.

Warrick kissed me so hard he took my breath away. His smell was everywhere. His fingers were tangled in my hair, and then in my shirt. I pulled his off, being careful of his bruises. He was scarred and hurt like me, but he was the most amazing man I'd ever seen. He stripped my shirt from my chest, as lost in desire as I was. Each kiss was hungrier than the last. The tightrope between us was starting to loosen and fall, and it couldn't come down fast enough.

It wasn't long before the rest of our clothes were gone and we were under the sheets. Warrick's body burned with a heat that I couldn't get enough of. This was the passion I craved like a drug. He needed it just as badly.

I wrapped my arms around his back and brought him closer, loving the way he felt wrapped around me. There was nothing I needed to say to him. He knew how to touch me, where to kiss me, when to be rough, and when to be gentle.

When we were both spent, we couldn't stop smiling. He pulled me into his arms. His chest was solid and warm. I knew I would sleep well tonight, and would probably end up skipping watch duty.

Out there in the world, everything seemed to have gone wrong. I was back in the city I hated. Demons were on a rampage with Lucifer. All of the archangels and Heavenly Host were fallen. The human race was about to get a very rude awakening.

But Sephiel wasn't alone. Max and Dro were together. I was in Warrick's arms.

Obviously we couldn't stay in this one night of peace and rest. We weren't going to have many more nights like this. But I was going to hold onto this one for as long as I could.

And fight to my last breath so I could have another one.

THE END

Acknowledgments

It's a little crazy for me to think that just a few years ago, I never would have imagined that I would write a full length novel, let alone a sequel. To realize that I've managed to do just that is something I'm proud of, but I would be lying if I said it wasn't a nerve-wracking journey. After all, how many times have readers found the sequel to be weaker than the predecessor? Writing new adventures and trials for Constance and Co. was a serious challenge. They had to grow and develop, and I wanted to raise the stakes. In the end, I'm very pleased that the crew has come this far. It was worth the nail-biting and second-guessing.

None of this would have been possible if it weren't for the support and encouragement I've gotten from my family and friends. You guys really don't know how much you're helping me by asking about my writing, curious about the progress of a novel, asking what I'm working on next, or telling me about a writing prompt you heard. Hearing those things every once in a while helps me strive to write better.

To the artists and designers at Deranged Doctor Designs… Thank you. You blew my mind with the cover of *Demon's Daughter*, and I knew you would amaze me with the artwork and promo material for *Dark Divinity*. I was not disappointed.

More gigantic thanks to my editor Eden Royce. Thank you for pointing out the details and the authenticity of certain character's actions. It truly is amazing what a writer can miss or not consider, and Eden, you were a huge help in finding those flaws and advising me on how to perfect them.

Big thank you to the Beta readers who got first dibs on *Dark Divinity* to tell me what you liked and didn't like. Hopefully you enjoyed the story the second time around as much as the first.

And finally, thank you reader. You really have no idea how much it means to know that you picked up this book, read it, and enjoyed it. Hearing your feedback makes all the difference, because it's your word that helps independent authors achieve their dream. Thank you for reading *Dark Divinity*. And don't worry, the final book will be here soon!

About The Author

Amy is a Canadian urban fantasy and horror author. Her work revolves around monsters, magic, mythology, and mayhem. She started writing in her early teens, and never stopped. She loves building unique worlds filled with fun characters and intense action. She has been featured on various author blogs and publishing websites, is an active member of the Writing GIAM community, participates in NaNoWriMo, and is the recipient of April Moon Books Editor Award for "author voice, world-building and general bad-assery." When she isn't writing, she's reading, watching movies, taking photos, gaming, and struggling with chocoholism and ice cream addiction.

Website: literarybraun.blogspot.ca
Twitter: @amybraunauthor
Facebook: www.facebook.com/amybraunauthor

www.ingramcontent.com/pod-product-compliance
Lightning Source LLC
Chambersburg PA
CBHW030532270626
47155CB00024B/2800